"Tort_____ve
up to y_____w
than tho_____d
I won't!"

"There's an old trick the Indians use, Paris Frances," Nate
Brannigan threatened. "Bury a person in the sand up to his neck
so the bugs and ants can eat out his eyes. Or there's this—an old
trick of the bounty hunter."

Paris didn't like the change in Nate's deep-throated whisper or in
the sultry, smoldering glow that drifted into his eyes. Force was one
thing she could handle, seduction was entirely different. She didn't
want his kiss. Yet despite the battle inside her mind, her body answered the summons of his. Before she realized what she was doing,
her lips responded to his and she was kissing him back with an
urgency she had never felt before.

Torture. Yes. That's what he called it and how accurate the term
had been.

* * *

"A passionate tale, one sure to be treasured by those who read
it."

—Kate Cameron, author of *The Legend Makers*

"Ms. Sandifer sizzles once again with passions that ignite the
pages."

—*The Literary Times*

"This novel has it all . . . definitely one to be enjoyed again
and again."

—*Rendezvous*

"A sexy hero, a spunky heroine, an intriguing setting and a
mystery to boot. Who could ask for anything more?"

—Cheryl Biggs, author of *Across a Rebel Sea*

"Ms. Sandifer displays her tremendous talent by giving us a
book that is . . . light-hearted [with] sizzling, spicy sexual tension. . . . *Desire's Treasure* deserves a cherished place on your
bookshelf."

—*Affaire de Coeur*

LINDA SANDIFER

DESIRE'S TREASURE

ZEBRA BOOKS
KENSINGTON PUBLISHING CORP.

ZEBRA BOOKS are published by

Kensington Publishing Corp.
850 Third Avenue
New York, NY 10022

Zebra and the Z logo Reg. U.S. Pat. & TM Off. The Lovegram
logo is a trademark of Kensington Publishing Corp.

First Printing: June, 1995

Printed in the United States of America

Prologue

1767—Pimería Alta, New Spain

Father Lorenzo Castañeda paused at the base of the familiar ragged cliff. He looked behind him to gauge the progress of the twenty-five exhausted Yaqui Indian converts winding their strings of burros through creosote bush, mesquite, and cacti. Beyond the Indians, in the vast arid emptiness, from flat horizons to jagged tips of distant mountains, he saw nothing moving upon the land but shimmering mirages and shadows of rainless clouds. Satisfied that he and the Yaquis had not been followed, he led the way around the cliff to a narrow, winding trail that would take them to the very heart of the mountain.

In the scorching heat of mid-day, the trail seemed never-ending to the Jesuit priest. But at last it brought them to the top of a naked mesa. Below them, at the base of another sheer precipice, yawned a secluded green valley, and in the valley, smiling into the face of the bright, white sun, stood the stately and magnificent Misión de Santa Isabel.

It had taken two years for the padres and the Indians to construct the secret mission. But they had chosen their site well, and Father Castañeda truly believed it would never be found. It would not have been necessary, of course, if certain Catholic rulers and churchmen had not feared the Jesuits' growing power and influence in Portugal, France, Spain, and New Spain. But such was the case, so with papal consent King Charles III had been persuaded to expel the Jesuits from this new land, where they had worked so devoutly and where some had even died in order to win the conversion of the Indians. They were to be replaced by Franciscan priests whom it was believed could be more easily controlled by Roman Catholic leaders. The Jesuit priests could only hope that this change would not be permanent and that soon they would be able to return.

Father Castañeda was grateful they had not been banished immediately. The Jesuits had heard rumblings far in advance, in time for them to build hiding places for the treasures they had accumulated. They had no intention whatsoever of relinquishing those treasures to their replacements. They had also been able to destroy all the records of their wealthy holdings and the maps leading to the depositories.

Santa Isabel's wide adobe face reflected divine radiance in the searing Sonoran heat. Silent she stood, reverently waiting to take these final offerings to her great and worthy bosom.

Father Castañeda listened, head cocked to the valley. As always, no breeze touched the bells whose twin towers rose three stories on adobe walls nine feet thick. During his time there, overseeing the construction of the mission, he had heard the wind touch the bells only once. He had stood where he stood now, and even then the sound had been as distant and faint as the tinkling bell of a lost lamb. The valley was too deep, the cliffs too high, for the sound to escape. Because of this, he had left the bells suspended from the massive crossbars, believing no mission was complete without them.

Santa Isabel held the finest wealth of many missions. Priests from San Blas to Mazatlan had collected their inventories—gold icons, jewels, solid gold statues and candlesticks—and, with the aid of the Yaqui Indians, had loaded it all onto ships. Only those items made of inferior metals or too large to carry had been left behind. The priests had followed the coast northward, unloaded the treasure, dispersed into groups, and begun the long trek overland to the depositories. This mission was in an isolated country that only the padres and the Indians knew, and the Indians would not disturb the treasure. That much Father Castañeda would make sure of.

Today, he brought the last of the treasure. Too soon he would reluctantly say good-bye to Santa Isabel. And in a few weeks, he would say good-bye to New Spain.

Sadly, he turned to the Yaquis who waited patiently with indiscernible black eyes for his musings to pass. Eager now to rest his sunburned face against the cool cheek of Isabel's inner walls, he resumed the trek along the precipitous path that led into the valley.

Standing in the shaft of noonday sunlight that lit the bell tower, Father Castañeda instructed his followers to place the last of the offerings in the secret receptacles he had designed himself. He was positive no intruder would ever suspect their existence.

By evening he had put the Yaquis to their last and final task—hiding the trail that led to the mission. In the end, it took days of backbreaking work to plant cacti and scrub brush over it in such a fashion that the plants would take root and conceal the path forever. Only those who knew of Santa Isabel's presence would ever find her— those and the creatures of the desert that came to water at the many springs in the rocky valley.

When this work was completed at last, a shadow crept in from the southwest and passed over the valley. Behind the shadow advanced an awesome purple thunderhead, and rumblings came from the distant peak of Cerro Trueno, now barely visible from the valley floor. The Indians believed the rumble was the voice of a mighty god who inhabited Thunder Mountain, and their hearts grew fearful. For the first time, Father Castañeda did not try to dispel their ancient beliefs.

He lined them up, shoulder to skinny shoulder in front of the mission. They watched him with obedient eyes that occasionally lifted uncertainly to Cerro Trueno. They knew they were to hear again what they had heard before. But, this time, with the great mountain rumbling in the background, the padre's message came to them with the full extent of its meaning.

Father Castañeda's sandals scuffed the sand in front of them as he paced with his hands clasped purposefully behind his back. "This treasure we have brought here is the Lord's treasure," he said sternly in his native Spanish, which he had taught them to understand. He paused to make eye contact with each one before proceeding.

"The Lord Himself will guard this place to ensure the safety of His offerings. If any man disturbs this sacred place, or if any man discloses its location to another, he will suffer the wrath of the Lord, and sudden and immediate death will be his reward. When we leave here, we will not return, nor will we ever speak of what has taken place here. These are my final words, my friends. Do not let time weaken your memory."

The Yaquis' eyes darkened even more, until, beneath the storm-ridden sky, they appeared to be wet black pools reflecting intense fear. Castañeda was satisfied. The Yaquis would keep the mission's location a secret. They were, above all else, a very superstitious people, and few would doubt his words or the supreme power behind them. Those who did would suffer the consequences of their loose tongues, and the others would become even more careful.

He waved an arm toward the storm-shadowed desert. "Go now. Go back to your homes and your families. It is time for all of us to leave Santa Isabel to her guardianship."

The Yaquis drifted away then, fading into the saguaro forests like the other elusive creatures of the desert and carrying with them a burden far greater than the weight of golden idols and jewels. This time they carried the burden of *El Maldeción de Santa Isabel,* the curse of Santa Isabel.

One

1884—Nogales, Arizona Territory

Nothing lit the cantina but a strand of sunlight slanting through one small, filthy window. It touched the right arm of the dark-haired man sitting in the corner, looking bored with his game of solitaire.

It was siesta time; the room was deserted. Even the bartender had abandoned his post for a dark, cool corner and a sombrero over his face. But his snores were not loud enough to conceal the soft shuffling of the dark-haired man's cards, or the buzzing monotony of the flies batting themselves uselessly against the window.

Paris Frances McKenna straightened her black nun's habit and checked to make sure her red hair was tucked neatly back into the face-framing veil. She adjusted the spectacles on her nose; as usual, they had slid from their proper position. Satisfied that her attire was in order, Paris bolstered her courage and stepped through the open doorway into the dim room.

She knew the man had been aware of her presence from the first moment of her arrival. She had seen him glance up at her when her shadow had first blocked the light. Seeing it was a nun, he had dismissed her and gone back

to his game. Now, he gave her a longer, more concentrated
perusal from beneath the brim of his worn Stetson, a hat
that had more than suffered its share of Sonoran dust and
sweat. If he had any feelings concerning a nun stepping
into a cantina, Paris saw no indication of them in his
steady, unfathomable eyes.

He was the man she had come to hire: Nathaniel Brannigan, bounty hunter.

Her black, high-topped boots were soundless on the
packed dirt floor. Brannigan watched her intently, the
cards temporarily still in his motionless hands. He didn't
seem surprised that she came to him. After all, he was
the only person in the room who was awake.

Her heart pounded a fearful beat throughout her entire
body. This was foolishness. What had ever made her think
she could find anyone to help her? Maybe she should have
just stayed in Tombstone and accepted things the way they
were.

"Can I help you with something, Sister?"

She realized she'd been standing in front of his table
for several moments without speaking. He probably
thought she was crazy or lost, or both. But the speech she
had memorized had flown as suddenly as a loggerhead
shrike in a flight for prey, leaving her mind totally blank.
Quickly she tried to recover, wondering if his deep, coarse
whisper would be less abrasive if raised to a normal pitch.
And for the first time she smelled the acrid smoke of the
cigar pinned between his fingers. The smoke drifted up
her nostrils with a life of its own. She took a step back,
but to no avail. It curved doggedly and twisted its way
after her.

The sheriff of Nogales had said Nathaniel Brannigan
knew this border country better than anybody, except pos-

sibly the Indians, because he was always tracking down outlaws who were hiding out in it. But despite his rugged, dark-complected handsomeness, she couldn't help but be reminded of a scorpion dozing with one eye open. It struck her then that he was probably nothing but a self-serving adventurer, no better than the men he brought to justice. His eyes, clearly seen now in the dimness, hypnotized with a gleam more brilliant than that of a blue star sapphire. They also shone with an arrogant authority that made her wonder if even a nun's habit would keep a woman safe from the likes of him. She knew the sort, and she sensed Brannigan took what he wanted. Whether it was good or evil that lay hidden behind the steady glow in those arresting eyes, she couldn't know. She could only hope he would find her as unattractive as she had hoped to present herself. This was a dangerous country with dangerous men and she must be careful not to underestimate either.

Since she hadn't given him an answer immediately, he had gone back to playing his hand, but he was watching her from the corner of his eye. Without thinking, she reached down and laid a finger on the three of hearts. "You could put this on that four of clubs."

Instantly she realized what she'd done and jerked her hand back as if the three of hearts had stung her. Brannigan lifted his eyes to her without lifting his head. In that half-shuttered gaze she identified the shadow of curiosity.

Evading those unnerving eyes and adjusting her spectacles again, she pulled out the chair opposite him and sat down, nervously clutching her hands in her lap. "I know how to play solitaire, Mr. Brannigan," she said. "I haven't been a nun all my life."

A black eyebrow lifted, and the corner of his mouth,

hidden by a heavy, black moustache, moved into the hint of a smile. He said nothing. She had the feeling he missed nothing either. She would have to watch her step with him.

"The sheriff sent me to you, Mr. Brannigan," she continued. "You *are* Mr. Brannigan?"

He leaned back in his chair, put his cigar in his mouth, and eyed her even more thoroughly, his interest obviously piqued now that she had come to talk to him exclusively. When he didn't deny his identity, or affirm it, she hastened on.

"I know this is not your line of work, but it would be easy money for you and the sheriff said you knew this country better than anybody and that you might be interested in being my guide to the Pajaro Mountains and specifically Cerro Trueno."

She realized the words had come out in a senseless rush, not in the confident, serene way that a nun should have said them. But Brannigan's cool self-assurance was most distracting. Or possibly it wasn't Brannigan at all but rather the nature of what she was doing. Still, desperate times called for desperate measures and there was no turning back.

He took a few puffs from the cigar and blew the smoke to a low ceiling that had already been blackened by years of previous assault. He moved the three of hearts and set it on top of the four of clubs. "And why do you need a guide to the Pajaro Mountains, Sister . . . ?"

"Frances. Sister Frances," she hastily supplied.

"There's nothing I know of out there except scorpions and sidewinders," he continued. "No churches, that's for sure."

She reached into the pocket of her skirt and withdrew

a frayed piece of parchment. She handed it to Brannigan with a shaking hand. He clamped the noisome cigar between his teeth and unfolded the paper carefully. He studied it through eyes squinted against the cigar smoke.

"With all these strange symbols and a date of 1767 am I correct in assuming this is a treasure map, Sister Frances? Something to do with a mission by the name of Santa Isabel?"

Thankfully he still spoke in that gravelly whisper, and Paris wondered if he did so out of courtesy for the sleeping bartender or if it was his normal tone. Whichever, she was grateful for the confidentiality of it.

"Yes, it is," she whispered, leaning over the table and closer to him. "And I need someone to take me there so I can find it. The sheriff said you were an honest man and could be trusted."

His black brow lifted again, most of it vanishing beneath the hat pulled down on his forehead. There was definite amusement in his eyes now. "And did you trust the sheriff to be accurate in his assessment, Sister Frances?"

She shifted uneasily. Brannigan was a bounty hunter, and they were a breed with reputations about as soiled as Tombstone's scarlet women. Her heart sank. Maybe she should not have brought him, or anyone, into this but rather just set out across the Sonoran desert by herself. After all, according to the map, the mission would only be a few days' ride. But it was a big country, and when she looked out across its rugged expanse and toward sharp-tipped distant peaks, she felt greatly overwhelmed by fear and inadequacy.

"I suppose it is my nature to believe people, Mr. Brannigan," she said at last, hoping to conceal her deep distrust of him.

"Did you show the sheriff this map?" He handed it back to her, neatly folded as before.

She tucked it back into her pocket, unable to help worrying that he might have a good memory for detail. Now that he'd seen the map, could he be trusted to help her, or would he be the sort to double-cross her and go out and find the treasure for himself?

"No, I didn't show him the map. I just told him I needed a guide into the mountains."

"And he didn't question your motives?"

"He apparently felt it wasn't his business."

Brannigan picked up his cards and began to play his hand, summarily dismissing her once again.

"Then you aren't interested in being my guide?" she prompted after several moments of silence from him.

He slid three cards from the main deck and turned them over, playing the top one. "This country is rife with stories of lost gold mines, missions, and buried treasure, Sister Frances. I don't know where you got that map, but it'll just take you on a wild goose chase. And only fools venture out into the Sonoran desert in July. In case you don't know, some people call those mountains the *Sierra de Muerte.* Do I need to translate?"

She shook her head. She knew enough Spanish to know it meant the Mountains of Death. But she would not be deterred. She had committed herself to this dangerous undertaking. There was nothing in Tombstone for her to go back to—except poverty or Tully Thatcher. And she would die before taking the latter alternative.

"I'll answer a few of your questions, Mr. Brannigan," she began.

"I wasn't aware I had asked any," he cut in, his eyes lighting in that amused, derisive way again. "I'm really not interested in treasure hunting."

She ignored his sarcasm and plunged on. "This map was found among some old church records. Unfortunately, the existence of this mission cannot be confirmed by records in the Catholic archdiocese in Mexico City. I believe Santa Isabel was a mission abandoned by Jesuit priests when they were expelled from New Spain over a hundred years ago. And I believe this map is genuine. Some say that the Jesuits buried opulent treasure troves, which they had collected, so they wouldn't have to turn them over to the Franciscan priests who were being sent to assume their positions. The Jesuits fully expected to be reinstated in New Spain, at which time they intended to reclaim the treasures."

"And how do you know they didn't—reclaim them?"

"Because the Jesuits were never allowed to resume their former positions. They left the country, never to return.

"Anyway," she continued. "I tried to interest others in the church in going with me, but no one wanted to face the hardships and the danger for something they weren't sure of. I said I would go alone."

"And I'm sure they gave you their blessings?" He was distinctly mocking now.

She felt she was losing the battle with this man and was afraid that he now knew entirely too much. Still, it was a chance she had taken when she had approached him. He had been selected and confided in with considerable thought. The amusement deepened in his eyes, and she guessed it was used as a subtle way of intimidating her to back down and run from the cantina. Instead, she met his penetrating gaze and tried to fathom his thoughts. Did he believe her story? Had she made it all sound plausible enough? Or did he possibly know more about the secret of Santa Isabel than she did?

"You would be paid, Mr. Brannigan. The church did not send people, but they did send money for a guide. I am prepared to give you two hundred dollars, part of which would be used to cover the cost of supplies for the journey."

There was a flicker of expression in his eyes. Was it more money than he had expected? Or less?

"I'd have to have a percentage of whatever you find, Sister. Say twenty percent."

"The treasure belongs to the church, Mr. Brannigan," she said in a mildly insulted tone. "I don't believe I have the authority to allow that."

He went back to playing cards.

"Of course, since I'm in charge of this venture," she added, "I suppose I could consent to ten percent. I have faith that my superiors would agree with me if given the opportunity to consider the options."

He wasn't making any headway with the game of solitaire. The cards in the main deck could no longer be played. She could tell he'd lost the game, except for one move he was overlooking. She would have pointed it out to him but decided against drawing any further attention to her expertise at cards.

He let the cards rest in his hand. "What's in this for you, Sister Frances? You risk your life, you should have some reward."

"My reward will be my satisfaction in finding the items that have been lost."

He set the cards on the table. Resting his elbows on the

arms of the wooden chair, he hooked his fingers together loosely in front of him. She fidgeted under his intense scrutiny, noticing then how broad his shoulders were, how solid his chest. She also noted how the muscles bulged in his upper arms through the white cotton shirt that was amazingly clean for the dirty border town conditions. He wore a black cloth vest which allowed her to see the top of his gun belt, filled with cartridges. She was nearly suffocating in the black nun's habit, but he looked remarkably and enviably cool.

He was disturbingly handsome, the dangerous sort of handsome. And he, no doubt, knew the effect he had on women. He probably knew that right now her thoughts had strayed from lost treasure to the enticing aura of his masculinity. The nun's habit should protect her from any wayward thoughts he might harbor concerning her, but she suddenly experienced the odd sensation that she wasn't sure she wanted to be protected.

In the silence there was no sound but the snoring bartender and the buzz of the flies on the window. She glanced at the filmy window, wondering why the cantina even had it, especially if it wouldn't open. She needed a breeze. The way he was looking at her made her uncomfortably overheated. She felt cold trickles of perspiration, like tiny spiders, run alongside her face inside the coarse, black veil.

"Well, Mr. Brannigan? Are you interested?"

Nate Brannigan gave it some serious thought. He was a suspicious man by nature, but then one had to be if one wanted to stay alive in this profession. Naturally he wasn't very well liked by the outlaw crowd. He wasn't sure exactly what it was about the sister and her story, but it sounded a bit far-fetched. Not the part about the lost treasure in the abandoned mission—those stories were a dime a dozen in this country—but could she truly be heading off across the desert after treasure just for the satisfaction of it and a pat on the head from the pope? Or was she seeking something more, such as a higher position in the church for her efforts? If so, why not just admit it? And, if the church thought there could be a treasure they had a rightful claim to, they'd surely have sent someone besides a little woman who barely cleared five feet tall and was probably lucky if she weighed a hundred pounds soaking wet. They wouldn't have sent her with two hundred dollars to hire a guide either. They would have sent her out with nothing but her faith and her trust in God and mankind, and her ability to play on guilty consciences.

Along with being suspicious, Nate Brannigan was also curious. Treasure hunting wasn't exactly up his alley, but it was a form of bounty. And, like gold fever, there were few people who didn't get a tingle of excitement at the prospect of unearthing an ungodly amount of gold icons and jewels. Just the prospect of searching for a treasure could bring out the adventurer in most any red-blooded individual.

Last, but not least, Nate was bored. This town and the surrounding area had stagnated. There wasn't anybody on a wanted poster anywhere worth more than a hundred dollars. Petty stuff that was hardly worth his time to leave town, especially if he had to go into Tombstone. That place could get ugly. If a bounty hunter rode in there, he was more likely to be the prey than the predator. The Sonoran in July was safer than Tombstone.

No, Nate preferred tracking his quarry to out of the way places and catching them with their pants down—literally. He prided himself on bringing them in alive, and he didn't care for stupid heroics that forced an outlaw into a corner and resulted in bringing him in slung over the saddle, belly-down. He'd had to kill a few in self-defense—some simply refused to be taken alive—but he'd taken a few bullets himself in the process, and time and age were beginning to give him patience and wisdom.

The Pajaro Mountains were several days' ride from Nogales. He'd probably have to give the sister a few days to search for the mission, and, if by some strange stroke of luck, she actually found it, there wouldn't be a treasure anyway. It would have long ago been hauled away by a prospector, Indian, or even some other treasure hunter. Then they could come back to Nogales and he'd be two hundred dollars richer—minus supplies, of course.

He met the nun's gray eyes—pretty eyes that took up a large portion of her small face. It was hard to tell what she really looked like, though, with that garb on. What color was her hair? And it bothered him that those steady, unreadable eyes seemed familiar. They reminded him of someone he'd seen somewhere before. But they looked terribly desperate. What was it about her? Was she in trouble or something? Had she done something to be exiled out here and was going after the treasure for restitution of some sort?

He set the cards down, knowing he'd lost the game anyway. If he stayed much longer, he was going to petrify. And how much trouble could a man get into with a nun as his companion?

"I guess you know we could run into Apaches," he said.

Paris was surprised, not about the Apaches, but that Brannigan was actually considering her proposition. "I thought they were all on the reservation," she replied.

"For now. But there are always the strays who refuse

to be confined. And they're the most dangerous kind."
His gaze slid a trifle too intimately over her person, lingering on her bosom, even though it was well hidden in
the loose-fitting habit. His lips lifted in that sardonic way
again. "And I'm not sure they'd recognize a woman of
God, let alone give her proper respect."

She shifted uneasily again. There was something in
Brannigan's eyes that seemed to seek hers out, hypnotize
her, then glide right into her head and see everything she
was thinking. Would he be able to see the truth?

"Being in the line of work you're in, Mr. Brannigan, I
expect you've gone into dangerous territory before. Besides, don't the Apaches prefer the Dragoons and the San
Pedro Valley to the Sierra de Muerte? I mean, there's more
to raid over in that country."

With a faint hint of appreciation for her determination
and knowledge of the favorite Apache haunts, he conceded the argument. "They usually do."

"Then—"

"There are always the bandits to consider, too, Sister,"
he added. "They're usually worse than the Apaches, and
we have no reservations for them."

She swallowed hard, trying not to be frightened away
from her intent. "Yes, I know, and I'm willing to risk it."

"All right. One more question. Does anyone else besides your church people know about this treasure and
that you have the map?"

A new kind of fear prickled inside her. She couldn't
read anything in his steady, waiting gaze. Did he mean to
kill her and have the map and the treasure for himself?
She fingered the two-shot derringer in her pocket that she
kept for protection. She considered her options. In the
end, though, she really had no choice but to trust him.

She couldn't head out alone across the Sonoran desert, and she refused to go back to Tombstone.

"Why do you ask?" She couldn't keep the suspicion from her voice.

"Because for two hundred dollars, minus supplies, I don't want interference from outside parties."

She thought of Tully, but he probably didn't know she had the map, at least not yet. "No, Mr. Brannigan. No one."

He gathered up his worn deck of playing cards in sun-bronzed hands, the backs of which were lightly sprinkled with black hair. "Then I suppose I could take the time to help you out, Sister."

She wanted to jump for joy, to throw her arms around his neck. But Brannigan was not a man one hugged.

She rose sedately. "Thank you, Mr. Brannigan. Shall we leave tomorrow?"

"How about dawn?"

She nodded in agreement. The sooner she got on her way, the better she would feel. "Will you get the necessary supplies?"

"I'll take care of it if you want me to, but I'll have to have the money up front, Sister Frances."

She hesitated, saw a challenge in his eyes. Was he testing her intelligence, her level of gullibility? "You must understand that I can't give you the money now, Mr. Brannigan. What guarantees do I have that you would come back in the morning?"

His lips moved into the semblance of a smile. "None."

"Yes, well, that was what I . . . suspected. I'll give you half the money after we have started our journey, Mr. Brannigan, and the other half upon our return to

Nogales—with or without any treasure. I will pay the bill for the supplies before we leave town."

He came to his feet, rising over her by a good foot. He touched the brim of his black hat in a gentlemanly fashion. "Pleased to do business with you, Sister Frances. Until tomorrow."

Paris McKenna hurried across the dusty street to Nogales's only semireputable hotel. Inside her room, she collapsed against the door and breathed a tremendous sigh of relief. Brannigan had fallen for it lock, stock, and barrel. Tomorrow she would be on her way to financial independence. Tully Thatcher, owner of the Silver Slipper Saloon & Dance Hall, might have thought she couldn't survive without him, but she was going to prove him wrong. And in a big way.

She locked the door, removed the spectacles, and peeled out of the stifling nun's habit. Wearing only her chemise, she went to the bureau, poured some tepid water from the glass pitcher into the matching bowl, and, with a cloth, cooled her body off. She plucked the pins from her hair and the fiery mass tumbled from restraint. She bent forward and brushed the thick, wavy tresses until her head tingled, then she straightened and flung it all back. Looking in the mirror, she saw that it looked like a red lion's mane, but she didn't bother to smooth it. It would settle naturally back into place.

She went to the window and opened it, using a stick on the seal to prop it up. She looked across the inhospitable, rugged hills covered with scrub brush. Some rose sharply, some were lower and gentler, but almost all near town were dotted with the ramshackle dwellings of the border people, who were mostly poor Mexicans with more children than goats and chickens. But the people seemed content, taking their siestas in spots of shade while the many children who had no desire to sleep raced and played over the hills, through the washes, and down the center of Nogales's dusty street.

There was no breeze to touch her skin or to lift the edges of the white chintz curtain. At least there was fresh air. And there were food smells—tamales, enchiladas, chili—reminding her she hadn't eaten all day. She would have to get something brought to her room again, as she'd been doing for the past three days.

She closed her eyes and breathed deeply of the air, wondering for the first time how she would tolerate the confinement of the nun's habit out in the heat of the desert.

Suddenly an odd tingle rushed over her. Her eyes snapped open. Through the narrow opening where the chintz curtains did not quite meet in the center, she spotted Brannigan across the street, one shoulder pressed against the side of the cantina's adobe wall and the omnipresent cigar clamped between his teeth. Although he had a dark-haired, curvaceous border beauty clinging to him like an article of wet underwear, his eyes were not on his companion. They were lifted toward the hotel, looking straight at her!

She leaped back into the room.

He'd seen her! And in her chemise no less! Her heart thudded wildly. Damn! She hadn't wanted him to see her as anything but a black habit and a freckled face with spectacles. But maybe he wouldn't recognize her. Maybe he would just think she was somebody else.

She tried to calm herself, to slow her breathing, and to tell herself it didn't matter that he had seen her in a state of undress. There was no way for him to know the truth or even suspect it. Keeping her body concealed behind the wall, she reached over and yanked the window blind down.

In the shadowy room, she stretched out onto the bed, distastefully slapping aside a huge cockroach that was as grateful for the cool sheets as she was. She thought of Brannigan again, rethinking their meeting in the cantina. She was certainly lucky she'd stumbled onto him, and she couldn't afford to slip up and do something that would cause her to lose him. He was just the right man to have around when the bullets started flying. And if Tully Thatcher ever got wise to what she'd done, the Apaches would be, by far, the least of her worries.

Two

Nathaniel Brannigan was armed to the teeth. In addition to the Winchester in the rifle boot and the Colt revolver on his hip, he had tucked a second revolver in his gun belt behind his back. Attached to the opposite side of the saddle from the Winchester, a double-barrelled, sawed-off shotgun hung from a leather thong looped over the saddle horn. Beneath it, also looped around the saddle horn, was a wide cartridge belt filled with shotgun shells. The gun belt draped on his narrow hips, over leather chaps, was filled with cartridges for the Colt, and a third gun belt crossed his chest. Paris could only surmise the latter contained additional cartridges for the Winchester, unless the two used interchangeable .44–40s, as was often the case. And last, but not least, protruding from a scabbard on his left hip, was the hilt of a big, vicious-looking Bowie.

"Are you expecting trouble, Mr. Brannigan?"

His indifferent blue gaze slid over her face and back to the task of preparing his arsenal. "Always, Sister."

When Paris had left the hotel this morning, with her few meager belongings in hand, she had easily spotted Brannigan on the sleepy Nogales street. A number of the residents were up, tending to their vegetable gardens and their animals before the heat forced them into the shade for siestas, but Brannigan had been the only person not wearing white, not wearing a sombrero, and not wearing sandals. And, of course, he was the only one who looked like a one-man Texas Ranger force on a dangerous mission.

Sensing he wasn't any more talkative this morning than he had been the day before, Paris accepted his taciturn nature and made no further attempt at conversation. Although he hadn't tried to contact her, he had at least inquired at the livery about her horse because it was tied alongside his, saddled and ready to go. The buckskin gelding had been her daddy's and was one of the few things she had refused to sell no matter how badly she needed the money. She'd ridden it here, having joined up with the stagecoach outside of Tombstone for protection against bandits and Indians.

She tied her bedroll and saddlebags behind the cantle and secured her carpetbag just beneath the fork with a leather saddle thong. Without assistance, she swung into the saddle and straightened her skirt, pulling it over her knees and as far down as she possibly could in order to cover her black high-topped shoes and black stockings.

Sensing she was being watched, Paris glanced up to catch Brannigan eyeing her partially exposed leg from over the top of his saddle. She tugged harder at her skirt. When her eyes lifted a second time, they met his. There was something in those blue depths that suspiciously resembled a gleam of appreciation. But, whatever it was, it caused heat to leap to her face, making it feel as red as the underbelly of a black widow spider. Whether Brannigan noticed her embarrassment, she couldn't be certain. He sauntered over to a wooden bench in the shade of the livery keeper's adobe hut, picked up a sombrero that had been sitting there, and sauntered back.

Handing the hat up to her, he said, "I bought this for you when I bought the supplies yesterday. Wear it. Your skin will never hold up to border heat."

Surprised by his unexpected generosity, and wondering if she had completely misjudged his character, Paris was momentarily short of words. Finally, she managed to speak. "Why, thank you, Mr. Brannigan. How very thoughtful of you to get me a hat."

His eyes held hers a moment longer. There was nothing in their depths but bored tolerance. "Not really, Sister. I just figured I could save myself some grief later on. I don't deal well with crying women."

So, her first impression of him had been the correct one after all. He was just a ruffian who would take advantage of a woman—*any* woman—even a nun. But at least she'd ascertained one thing about him. He was brutally honest.

She placed the huge sombrero over her nun's veil, having serious second thoughts about setting out across the desert with him now that the moment had arrived. She'd never done anything so totally daring and possibly stupid in her entire life, but it was too late to back out now. And she wondered, with growing unease, if he recognized her as the woman in the window last night. Was that why he had been ogling her leg? Was that why his gaze had been so intent, as if he were trying to see inside her mind? Surely he didn't suspect the truth about her already?

She lowered her chin, effectively tilting the sombrero's brim so he couldn't see her face and the misgivings that might be explicit there. Regardless of what happened, she had already made up her mind that if he so much as touched her in an aggressive manner, she would shoot him with the derringer and suffer the consequences later.

She doubted anyone would blame her or disbelieve her. After all, bounty hunters were only one step above outlaws. Some were even a step below. She hadn't determined yet which Brannigan was.

He gathered his horse's reins. The animal wasn't striking in appearance—its dusty brown coat would probably blend in with the surroundings—but it had excellent conformation. He swung into the saddle with the ease of a man who lived there. With no further ado, he nudged his horse into a fast, swinging walk and didn't look back to see if she was following.

They had gone only two miles before the sun turned the desert into a kiln hot enough to fire pottery. A turkey vulture, seemingly heat-crazed, rode an air current in the cloudless sky just above them. Its course never deviated from theirs, and she was sure it was waiting for her to die. Nate mentioned, as if he had read her mind, that it hadn't rained on the Sonoran for eight weeks. But the rains would be coming soon, he said. Perhaps as soon as two weeks. Her only response was the derisive curling of a lip that had already cracked from air that was as dry as sand. Two weeks would be too late for much of the sunburnt vegetation, and probably too late for her, too.

By noon, shimmery waves of hot air lifted from the baked ground. She was trying to pass through every spot of shade she could find, even that of an armless saguaro. By one o'clock, she was ready to tell Nathaniel Brannigan that she wasn't a nun, never had been, and certainly never would be unless they changed their attire to something cooler than black.

It didn't matter that she'd disguised herself to protect

her virtue. At the moment she wasn't at all certain which was more important, virginity or respite from the heat. She wasn't actually afraid of Brannigan at the moment either. He hadn't said two words to her all day that hadn't been necessary, and he didn't seem to be paying any attention to her now. He kept his eyes peeled ahead and all around, watching for signs of Indians or bandits. If he wasn't exactly a gentleman, he wasn't an ignorant brute either.

The sombrero had been a lifesaver, but she would like to remove the black veil and white collar of her habit. The starched collar chafed her neck and the veil rubbed the sides of her face, making painful raw spots. There were other annoyances, too. Perspiration darkened the habit wherever it came into close contact with her skin, and she felt as if her hair had disintegrated beneath the drapery. Even with a regular application of ointment, her lips dried out as swiftly as the desert floor without rain. And the subtle but constant movement of the saddle against her fanny was doing an excellent job of abusing her body's most tender part. She could remember no time when she'd been so miserable.

Well, that wasn't exactly true. She could remember a time. It was the last six months. The entire six months. She had been in so much pain and discomfort during that period that it had led her to Brannigan and to this god-forsaken desert. How could she have forgotten so quickly Tombstone's insufferable heat, the aching legs and feet, Tully Thatcher, the smoke-clogged confines of the Silver Slipper Saloon & Dance Hall? And she was positive that over the past six months her backside and her bosom had been cradled in more palms than her daddy Blackjack McKenna's favorite deck of marked cards. No, if she never

saw Tombstone again—or another dancing man again—it
would be too soon.

She glanced askance at Brannigan and felt sudden, un-
adulterated relief. He certainly wasn't the type of man
who would want to dance. Thank God.

Despite her discomfort, Paris watched with vigilance
the country passing around her. She occasionally took her
little journal from her pocket and wrote something de-
scriptive about the scenery, making note of landmarks.
Brannigan's curiosity got the best of him and he finally
asked what she was doing.

"If something should happen to you, Mr. Brannigan, a
snake bite or something, I would like to be able to find
my way back, so I'm taking notes of our journey."

He accepted the explanation with a grunt, which she
interpreted as approval. What she didn't say was that the
journal and its descriptions of the terrain was mainly for
her protection if she was forced to shoot him for sexual
misconduct.

When the buzzard sought shade, they, too, rested beneath a mesquite and revived themselves on hardtack and
warm canteen water. She lay back beneath her own mesquite and almost longed for the Silver Slipper. She felt as
prickly as a cholla and as smelly as a creosote bush after
a spring rain. She was also upset to see her black habit
getting snagged and torn on bushes. At this rate, she'd
look like a beggar before a week's time, and she immediately eyed Brannigan's leather chaps with envy. They
were impervious to the desert's thorns, stickers, claws,
and stingers. He'd bought her a sombrero to protect her
from the sun. Why hadn't he mentioned how inappropriate
her attire was?

She tried to ease her discomfort by closing her eyes

and thinking of the desert in the spring, alive with blossoms and creatures of every kind scurrying about. But the images, like mirages, were hazy and fleeting. She opened her eyes once again to a heartless sun, an unsympathetic sky, and a creosote grasshopper sitting comfortably on her bosom, staring at her. She gave the insect a swat and sent it tumbling under a bush of its namesake.

Her energy spent, she shielded her eyes against the white hot sun and looked to the distant mountains that never seemed to get any closer. She heard the silence then, broken only by the occasional buzz of an insect. Not even a spider ventured out onto the burning ground. The desert creatures were all waiting out the heat. They'd found some shade and possibly some water.

She licked her lips, anger quickly shooting through her again at the thought of water. She had noticed early on that Brannigan hadn't given her a canteen, though he had two on his own horse and two more on each of the mules. Deciding to correct the oversight, she'd asked for water about mid-morning. She'd received it but with a frown and a lecture on how she should be conservative. "You never know when something will happen that you'll wish you'd taken one sip instead of two," he said.

"Like getting lost?"

"Yeah, like getting lost."

"But I thought you knew the way, Mr. Brannigan."

"I do, but you never know what can change your course."

"Like Indians?"

"Yes, like Indians or bandits or dust storms," he responded dryly, taking the canteen back and proceeding to ride on again. She had stopped him then and asked for her own canteen.

"We might get separated," she'd said as way of explanation.

He conceded, giving her the canteen, but obviously not trusting her to use good judgment.

"I do believe you're kin to a camel, Mr. Brannigan," she had jested.

He hadn't seemed to find much humor in her comment and hadn't bothered to respond. He had ridden on ahead, and she had decided he was nothing but a big boor. Since then she hadn't drunk water unless he had, even though her throat felt as if it was an old piece of hide left in the sun and forgotten.

On the completion of their meager meal, he moistened a bandana with water and put it to the muzzles of the horses and mules. "We'll have plenty of water by nightfall," he said. "There's a good spring at the base of those mountains where I plan to camp. And tomorrow night, I know a man who lives in the mountains and we'll stay with him."

Paris couldn't imagine anyone living out here where there seemed no possible way to make a living, unless by prospecting. But whatever his reasons for being a recluse, she was thankful they would be able to sleep beneath a roof. It was a luxury she hadn't prepared herself for.

By mid-afternoon she had a sincere argument with herself. Should she remove the habit and say to hell with pretenses? Or should she try to maintain her composure and her disguise for safety's sake? Her face felt ablaze and she was sure it had to be as red as the feathered boa that had been her trademark at the Silver Slipper.

She began to think there were only two topics that warranted consideration in the desert: life and death. And she was surely going to face the latter if she didn't get out of the heavy black habit.

An hour later, still wearing the habit, she was troubled by the mirages beginning to expand over the entire horizon before her, encompassing everything in a blurry haze. The mountains seemed to shrink and grow, fluctuating constantly right before her eyes. She was drenched with sticky perspiration, and her head was pounding. She knew Brannigan was pushing to reach the springs, but the mountains still didn't look any closer. It would have been nicer if they could have rested during the hottest part of the day and traveled during the morning and evening, but Brannigan forged onward.

She didn't feel as if she could breathe. Her heart thudded violently. The horizon undulated in a dizzying rhythm, and everything was getting extremely bright.

"Brannigan," she called to his broad, vested back. "I'm not used to this . . . heat. Do you think I—" She saw him look over his shoulder at her. "I mean, would you mind if I . . . removed part of my . . . attire? I know it . . . isn't proper . . . but . . ."

She saw him leap from his horse, a startled and irritated expression on his face. If he gave her an answer, she didn't hear it. The bright light suddenly turned black.

Paris came awake gasping. Brannigan was pouring water down her throat, and all over her face. She shoved the canteen aside and tried to get up, clutching for whatever she could find to assist her flight, which turned out to be the lapel of his unbuttoned black vest. The water bath stopped, but she was immediately pushed back down, realizing in that moment that she was not on the ground, not completely. Her lower half was, but her upper half was resting against a sturdy male thigh, and her head and shoulders were cradled in a very solid arm that felt almost like a rock beneath her head. She also realized in that moment of emerging from unconsciousness, that her nun's veil was gone and her hair was spilling out like wildfire everywhere, over his arm, over her shoulders, onto his chest. Damned unruly hair! The pins had all fallen out—or been taken out by him!

"Damn!"

She struggled upward and he effectively pressed her back down with the ends of splayed fingertips just above her bosom, which to her utter horror, was also spilling out. He had opened the garment down the front from her neck to just where the rise of her cleavage began. The upper portion of her camisole was showing. At about the same time she realized this, however, she also felt the touch of a breeze on the exposed flesh and decided modesty was not nearly as important as that cool breeze.

She relaxed. He was now wiping her overheated face with a cool, damp cloth applied in an amazingly gentle stroke.

"You should have told me you were going to faint," he growled in that voice that was as dry and gravelly as the desert itself. "I'd have stopped and found you some shade."

His tone clearly revealed irritation but his touch remained amazingly tender. It struck her then that a man had never touched her that tenderly before. Those who came to dance at the Silver Slipper were a bunch of hooligans out of the mines, rowdy cowboys just off the range, or assorted outlaws whose emotional capacity was too narrow for anything but their own selfish desires. They all danced to get their money's worth—a dollar a dance ticket—and with liquor in their bellies, a girl often found herself being flipped about like a doll with no stuffing. Even Tully treated her like so much brainless property.

For a few moments, Paris allowed herself the pleasures of Brannigan's unique contact. She felt too weak and drained to do anything else. She didn't know exactly when it happened, or if it was solely her overheated imagination, but Brannigan's touch suddenly turned sensual. Those places where his body touched hers did more than touch, they branded; the shape and feel of his hard body became impressed on her mind. The cold, wet cloth moved from her face to her neck then downward along the V of her dismantled nun's habit to her partially exposed cleavage. When she realized she was actually holding her breath, waiting for his touch to continue to that private place, her breasts, her eyes shot open and she struggled out of his arms.

She turned her back to him and rapidly began doing up buttons again. "I will be fine now, Mr. Brannigan. I will have to be more careful in the future not to get so . . . so . . ."

"Overheated?"

"Yes. Overheated. Now, are we ready to travel again?"

Nate Brannigan, still kneeling on the ground behind Paris, looked at her cloud of wavy red hair falling in disarray over the black habit. Her hair was coarse and thick and he had the peculiar urge to sink his hands in it. He'd been shocked when he'd pulled her nun's veil off and had seen the hair, realizing in that instant that she was the same curvaceous woman he'd seen yesterday standing in the window of the Nogales Hotel. Without the spectacles and the concealing veil, he was able to guess her age to be about twenty-two. That peculiar feeling he'd had earlier, that feeling that he'd seen her before, came back stronger and more defined, and yet annoyingly still elusive. Everything about her perplexed him. And she didn't quite have the demeanor one would expect of a nun.

The thing that troubled him even more, however, was the sexual urge that had sprung to his body when he'd held her, and now the thought that he really wished she wasn't a nun. Her full lips would be perfect for kissing; her body exquisite for lovemaking.

"We'll be to the spring soon." He rose to his feet, angry that he had allowed his thoughts to run so wild, and with a nun no less. "I wanted to get there tonight, and then tomorrow afternoon we'll be to Alejandro's."

He held out a hand to her. She seemed reluctant to take it, as if she knew what had been in his mind, but finally she did. Her small hand felt cool in his, but she was still wobbly on her feet and reached for his chest to steady herself. His hand went automatically around her, and he felt once again the curvaceous, tiny waist beneath the shapeless garment.

"Are you going to be all right?" he asked gruffly, feeling annoyed that he should be so attracted to her when she was so unattainable.

She nodded. "Yes, I think so."

She turned away from him and began to gather up the nun's veil and the sombrero.

"Sister Frances."

She lifted her gaze to his. Her soft gray eyes reminded him of a kitten's fur. Again, he felt the exceedingly strong pull of recognition hovering just beyond the grasp of his memory. Why couldn't he recall who she reminded him of?

"Yes, Mr. Brannigan?"

"I think it would be wise if you don't put that veil back on. Just put your hair up under the sombrero. You'll be much cooler and it's only the two of us out here."

A flash of light touched her eyes for a split second before she looked away. Was she as aware of their aloneness as he was?

"Thank you," she replied softly. "I believe that's a good idea."

"And one more thing, Sister Frances."

She avoided his eyes this time, keeping her head down while winding the mane of hair into a twist on top of her head and placing the sombrero over it.

"What is it, Mr. Brannigan?"

"Drop the mister. Brannigan will be fine."

Two miles later, Paris realized she wasn't wearing her spectacles. But if Brannigan noticed, he didn't say anything.

The springs, located at the base of a small group of mountains and surrounded by a healthy stand of saguaro and paloverde, were well worth the wait and the suffering. There were several smaller springs, but one pool was large enough that Paris immediately knew she would find a way to submerge herself in it. It was surrounded by rocks, bushes, flowers, and desert-willows, forming a natural wall of protection on three sides. The fourth side opened to a creek, slowly moving out to nourish what it could of the desert before disappearing into the ground several hundred yards farther on. Its length was colored with an abundant supply of grass and a profusion of wildflowers, alive only because of their proximity to the water.

Beyond the water, the desert crackled with dryness, harshness. Most of the plants had run their course of reproduction for the season. The ocotillo's flowers, flamered in bloom, were gone now, leaving spiny branches to catch the last rays of the setting sun. The yellow flowers and fallen seedpods of the tall paloverde had blown away or been eaten. The brittlebush was withered, the prickly pear parched. The teddy-bear cholla was as thirsty as everything else, but its fuzzy-looking clusters of spined joints at least gave the illusion of softness to the austere landscape.

It seemed the saguaro alone still offered life to the desert's birds and animals. Most, but not all, of the giant plants had lost their waxy, cream-colored flowers and bright red fruit. For many of the cacti, all that remained were empty husks on the ground, the black seeds having been picked clean. But the fading sunlight still found a noteworthy supply of ripened fruit still hugging the accordion-like limbs of a few late bloomers. Some of it was split open in star-shaped creations of crimson flesh and clusters of black seeds, resembling flowers. Paris would have removed a piece or two of the moist and delicious-looking fruit from the mighty sentinels' saluting arms if she had only known how.

Brannigan unsaddled the horses and removed the packs from the mules. He hobbled and staked the animals near the grassy creek, downstream from where he wanted to set up camp. Paris took care of her own horse, noticing that Brannigan never said anything. He was not one for conversation and never gave an indication of what was on his mind.

After he had a fire going not far from the spring and had put a pot of coffee on to boil, he picked up his shotgun and dropped a few shells in his shirt pocket. "I think I'll go out and see if I can find some fresh meat for supper. Will you be all right here alone?"

With the sun's exit over the horizon, the temperature had dropped a few degrees, but Paris eyed the spring, thinking its cool, clear water was the perfect rejuvenation for her hot, tired body. "I'll be fine. How long do you think you'll be?"

"Not any longer than it takes to find a few doves or maybe a quail."

Paris had seen so little game all day, she was sure Brannigan would be gone long enough for her to take a bath in peaceful privacy. "Take your time," she added. "Don't worry about me."

His eyes questioned the confidence of her statement, but ultimately he shouldered his shotgun and left camp.

Paris drew all the water they would need for drinking and cooking, filling all the canteens and available cooking containers. Then she hastily proceeded to discard the heavy habit. But it seemed every button was unreasonably obstinate, and the small buttons on her high-topped shoes proved even more frustrating. Finally down to her chemise, she made one last peek around the willows that protected the spring. There was no sign of Brannigan in the ruby glow of evening.

Pulling the chemise off over her head, she tossed it carelessly aside as she stepped gingerly into the spring. It wasn't deep, only about to her knees, but submerged rocks provided a place to sit near the edge. Happily she splashed herself all over, enjoying every cool, refreshing drop. When her bath was complete, she took a few minutes to soak and enjoy the desert, now that it offered no immediate threat to her life.

In the distance, saguaro stood on the horizon, an army of motionless black silhouettes against the fiery sky. She noticed one giant cloud in the west, suspended in the darkening sky, only its upper portion still catching the red-orange glow from the sunset. The cloud could be a forerunner of the rains, for they usually came in August, but it was too distant to cause much concern tonight.

She listened to the sounds of twilight, to the creatures coming out now that the sun and its searing rays were gone. In the brush nearby she heard the scurryings of small rodents, probably woodrats and mice. A coyote yipped from a canyon in the small group of mountains. Overhead, a few curve-billed thrashers had come to flutter around the saguaros and work at the last of the summer's fruit. A nighthawk in flight cried out in his neverending search for food. But beyond the animal sounds was peaceful silence. She closed her eyes and relaxed.

Suddenly two booms of the shotgun brought her out of the water, reaching for her towel. It was the warning that Brannigan had found game and would be back soon.

As she hastily dried and reached for her clothes, she saw a flaw in what had seemed the perfect disguise. In her haste to put her plan into action, she had sewn up only one habit, but that had been difficult enough to do by hand, without a pattern, and while hiding out at the Nogales Hotel. She had a nightgown but couldn't put that on yet. She had regular clothing she'd brought along, but she couldn't wear those either if she wanted to maintain her deception. She had no choice but to step back into the same soiled black garment, wondering when she would ever have the opportunity to wash it.

After dressing, she added more brush to the fire and pulled the coffee away from the heat. It had boiled, probably too long. She was braiding her wet hair when Brannigan appeared in camp carrying two rock doves. Her wet hair drew his immediate attention and a long, hard stare.

"I took a bath," she said, not sure why she felt she owed him an explanation. After all, he wasn't her keeper and he didn't own the desert or anything on it. "Is that permissible?" she added, suddenly feeling defensive. "Or is it another unnecessary use of water here on the desert?"

Brannigan didn't miss the facetious bite to her question, but he ignored it and set the gutted birds down next to her. "No, it's actually not a bad idea. I was thinking of doing the same thing myself."

He unbuckled his gun belt and let it drop. Next came the bandolier across his chest, then his chaps. He was pulling his shirt free of his pants when he seemed to remember her presence and halted in mid-action. She, at that moment, too, realized she was staring at him, but her fascination was doubly as active as her horror that he would undress right in front of her.

She dragged her eyes away from his hairy chest and grabbed for the doves that needed to be plucked. "Go right ahead. I won't look."

In her peripheral vision she caught his sardonic smile beneath the moustache, as if he didn't believe her declaration one iota. But she doubted he really cared if she looked. He probably thought his body was a shrine worthy of female adulation. Maybe it was, but she'd have her tongue cut out before she would admit it.

She busied herself preparing the doves but was still all too aware of him behind her, peeling off his clothes and stepping naked into the water. She suddenly felt overheated again and wanted to blame her hot face on her close proximity to the camp fire. The real truth was that she had never been this close to a naked man before. As a matter of fact, she had never been anywhere near a naked man. She tried to put her attention back to the plucking and cutting of the doves, but all her mind could focus on was the splash of water over Brannigan's virile body.

At last he got out. She heard him towel himself dry and pull on clothes, but when he said, "Okay, you can turn around," she saw he wore only his pants and was removing a clean shirt from his saddlebags. Instead of putting it on, he draped it on a paloverde branch and took the dirty shirt to the water's edge. Balancing on a rock, he proceeded to scrub the shirt and his socks as well.

With his back to her, Paris used the opportunity to note, in the fading light, the way the muscles in his back and arms rippled with each movement. When he stood up to hang the garments on the willow branches, she couldn't help but openly admire his taut thighs and buttocks in the snug-fitting pants.

He must have sensed her eyes because he looked at her from over his smooth, broad shoulder. "You might want to take the opportunity to wash up some of your own things."

Paris put her attention back on the meat, envisioning the intimacy of her underthings draped on the branches alongside his socks and shirts. Intuition told her to keep her underwear covered up at all costs, even if it was only displayed on a willow bush.

"Oh, I think I'll wait until we get to your friend's house. Will he mind?"

A knowing glow in Brannigan's eyes suggested he knew the real reason behind her decision, but all he said was, "No, I don't think Alejandro will mind."

He joined her shortly and offered to take over the preparation of the doves. Expertly he cut them with his Bowie, making the task look easy, and placed them in the frying pan sizzling with fat. He even proceeded to fix fried biscuits to go along with them, leaving her essentially nothing to do.

He saw her helplessness. "Why not rest, Sister Frances? Write in your journal. You've had a long day."

She had hoped he would think of some way to keep her company, to initiate a conversation perhaps, but she obeyed and settled onto her bedroll and wrote her impressions of the day's events. After that, she stretched out on her side with her back to him. It seemed she had only done so when a hand on her shoulder was gently shaking her awake.

"Supper's done," came his gravelly whisper.

Surprised, she lifted her eyes to darkness and to Brannigan on his haunches next to her, silhouetted by the fire crackling behind him. The hint of an amused smile played beneath his moustache. There was no weariness in his eyes. Didn't he feel exhausted from the day's ride? Her gaze slid to the strand of short dark hair that had fallen onto his forehead after his bath and still remained there, dry now but untouched. No, he didn't look tired. He looked as if he'd just risen from a good night's sleep. At least he had his shirt back on, which made it considerably easier to be in his presence.

They were two people with little to say. The meal was eaten in silence and cleaned up in silence, except for minimal communication to get the job done adequately. He placed his bedroll on the opposite side of the fire from hers in a clear spot just a few feet from a large paloverde. With a moan—the only indication of weariness—he stretched out on it. Staring up at the brilliant array of stars in the close desert sky, he proceeded to smoke a cigar.

Paris sat on her bedroll, feeling self-conscious and uneasy. She was too much aware of Brannigan's virility. This was their first night together. Now would be the time he would start thinking of her as a woman. Would he force himself on her? He had paid absolutely no attention to her so far. Maybe the nun's habit was doing exactly as she had hoped it would. Or maybe he simply wasn't the sort to force himself on women, a blessing indeed. On the other hand, maybe he didn't think she was pretty enough to desire her in a sexual way. Grimly she wondered if the latter might be the case. It was a ridiculous thought, of course. She should be grateful that he didn't desire her. Yet, it niggled at her to at least know whether he found her attractive.

"What did you do before you became a nun, Sister Frances?" he asked, surprising her from her tedious ponderings.

When she lifted her gaze, she saw he'd been watching her, but at the moment of eye contact he returned his attention to the fire and to his cigar.

Frantically she tried to come up with an answer. Another flaw in her plan revealed itself. She had been so busy escaping Tombstone and Tully that she had not had time to invent a past for herself. And she couldn't tell him the truth. After all, he may have heard of Blackjack McKenna. One thing would lead to another and the next thing she knew he would know she wasn't a nun and never had been.

"I . . . was raised on a ranch in New Mexico."

His brows shot up in dismay. "What a coincidence.

That's where I was raised. Was your father's ranch on the Rio Arriba or the Rio Abajo?"

Paris stared at him, appalled. Surely he couldn't be from the very place she'd pulled from off the top of her head? She knew nothing about New Mexico. As a child she'd lived in Louisiana and then come west with her parents to California when her mother had contracted tuberculosis. They had lived there until things had looked prosperous in Tombstone and then moved to the new town at her father's urging because the climate was the best in the country for her mother's illness. And of course the climate in the saloons was also the best in the country for his profession.

She summoned her limited knowledge of Spanish to tell her Brannigan had said lower river and upper river. That told her absolutely nothing. "Rio Abajo," she finally said.

"Well, I'll be damned. We're from the same area."

He actually smiled, showing white, pretty teeth. She'd never seen him so animated. He looked considerably younger with no hat and minus the arsenal strapped to every part of his body. And with that smile he didn't even look mean and ornery anymore.

"You're not serious." Her heart was sinking rapidly. He had to be playing a game with her.

"No, I am," he replied. "I'm surprised we didn't know each other. What was your father's last name?"

"Mc . . . Callister."

He frowned, looked perplexed, and finally shook his head. "I haven't heard the name."

"Well, it was a small ranch. We were poor. Now, you know I'm really quite tired. I think I'd like to go to sleep. Maybe we could discuss this later."

She rolled over and pulled the blanket up over her shoulder, praying he wouldn't want to talk anymore. Minutes ticked by in silence. She felt his hard eyes penetrating her back. Was he angry that she'd cut the conversation off so abruptly and so rudely? Would it make him suspicious? She would like to know about him, but in order to learn about his life she would have to tell him about hers. And she had to have time to think of something.

She closed her eyes, somehow believing that by doing so she could block out everything, including his presence. But immediately images of him sprang to mind: his broad chest, his blue eyes boldly scrutinizing her bosom, his gentle touch.

"You know, Sister Frances," came his dreaded continuation of the conversation, "I have to hand it to you. I mean a little bitty thing like you heading out across the desert with a man you don't know. . . . Well, you took a lot of chances. You could have tied up with a real low-life."

She tensed. Wariness suddenly pulsed through her. So he was very much aware of her femininity after all. Was he thinking of overpowering her, taking advantage of her now that they were miles and miles from anything or anybody? It was little consolation that he didn't consider himself a renegade. Most of them didn't.

She turned just enough to look over her shoulder at him. With bravado she didn't feel, she said, "I wasn't worried, Brannigan. You see, if you so much as lay a hand on me, you'll never get back to Nogales alive."

Across the firelight, she thought she saw an amused gleam in those startling blue eyes of his. His moustache lifted beneath a mocking smile. "You're small but not helpless?"

"Yes, and God protects His children."

His mood changed so suddenly it was as if he'd slammed a door in her face. A black scowl obliterated the smile, and his eyes hardened in an angry sort of way. "Tell that to the Apaches, Sister." He grabbed his hat and placed it over his face. "Good-night."

Paris stared at his prone figure, lean and hard and very unyielding. What had gotten into him? Why the comment about the Apaches?

She began to have serious thoughts about just who this man was she had entrusted with her life and the secret of lost treasure. The longer she was with him, the more dimensional he became. That was only natural, she knew, but instead of questions being answered, he was becoming more of an enigma.

She forced her eyes from his perfectly masculine form and curled back into her favorite sleeping position. It wouldn't be wise to wonder too much about a man like him or to develop a strong compassion for him. Compassion led to indecisiveness and poor judgment. And something inside her heart told her that a woman with those particular weaknesses would be much too easily hurt by a man like Brannigan.

Three

It was not Alejandro Escalante's small adobe house that first drew Paris's attention but Alejandro himself, shaded beneath a huge sombrero and dressed in white flowing trousers and shirt. Painstakingly he was watering a small garden that had been fenced with netting wire to keep the rodents out. Despite the loose clothing, she recognized the confident posture of a man who demanded respect and attention, even while doing a menial chore. She didn't know why but his stance told her that Alejandro Escalante might be dressed as a peasant, but he certainly wasn't one.

The sun had just barely slipped beyond the horizon, casting a fuchsia glow into the cobalt sky and dimming the intense heat and white brightness of the desert. Alejandro's adobe house was the same color as the mountains that enclosed it like the great bosom of a loving grandmother. It had been built in the center of cacti and nestled back in a deep thicket of mesquite, all of which provided a natural camouflage. Not far from it were enclosures for chickens and goats, whose clucking and bleating apparently kept the owner from hearing their approach.

A cream-colored chihuahua ran up to the garden fence and began an obnoxious yapping, finally drawing Alejandro's attention to his visitors. In Spanish he told the dog to shut up and it obeyed. Even from a distance, Paris saw

the slow, fluid way Brannigan's friend moved. There was
no hurry to him, but she recognized wariness when he
reached out to a spot near a post and came back with a
shotgun cradled in his sun-bronzed grip.

Brannigan said then that Escalante was a *mestizo,* half
Yaqui Indian, half Spaniard. She was surprised when he
also mentioned, in an off-handed way, that the Escalantes
had adopted him as a child and that he and Alejandro had
been raised as brothers. She would have inquired further
about his past, but a hard set to his jaw didn't seem to
open doors to further questioning, such as why hadn't he
mentioned it earlier? And if they had been raised on a
ranch in New Mexico, why was one now a bounty hunter
and the other living like a hermit in the desert? She sensed
it was something Brannigan preferred not to talk about,
at least not to her.

As they drew closer to Escalante, she felt rather than
saw the piercing intensity of his dark eyes. Like Brannigan,
she knew he was a man who missed nothing. He must have
recognized Brannigan then, for something about his stance
relaxed. He left the garden enclosure through a mesh wire
gate and walked out to greet them. His gaze drifted over
Paris in what seemed to be an ambiguous combination of
intense scrutiny and utter disinterest, but in just the few
short seconds he'd looked at her, she sensed he had memorized everything about her. His attention shifted to Brannigan. A smile creased his handsome face, probably one
of the most handsome faces Paris had ever seen. Where
Brannigan's features had been chiseled and left rough, Escalante's seemed to have been polished, refined to aristocratic perfection.

Brannigan swung to the ground. Paris watched the two
give each other a brief, rough male hug then spend a few

seconds slapping each other on the back, laughing, and talking in a rapid flow of Spanish. The exchange suddenly made Paris realize that Brannigan wasn't as old as she had perceived him to be. When he smiled, she saw that he must be only thirty, if that. In the cantina there had been a hardness about him that had left the impression of age she had not since dispelled. She guessed that Alejandro was older than Brannigan by a few years.

"So what brings my long-lost brother out this way?" Alejandro's smile was a mile wide, his white teeth gleaming in a deeply bronzed face. Upon asking the question, his gaze lifted to Paris. His smile remained, but hooded caution entered his eyes as his gaze once again slid over her in a few seconds of scrutiny. "Don't tell me you have brought someone to save my soul, Nathaniel?"

Brannigan's gaze, too, lifted to Paris. With the two of them eyeing her, she shifted nervously in the saddle, suddenly wishing she had thought to put her veil back on beneath the sombrero. What would this Spaniard, who was surely Catholic, think of her impropriety? Would he guess immediately that she was an impostor?

"No, Alejandro," Brannigan said at last, speaking now with the hint of a Spanish accent himself, as if it was an old habit easily fallen back into. "I'm taking Sister Frances on a treasure hunt. I was wondering if we could stay here for the night?"

Alejandro Escalante sifted the information through his brain in silence, all the while smiling at Paris. He didn't ask about the treasure hunt, but she saw many questions behind those piercing black eyes. She knew he would ask them later when he and Brannigan were alone.

"Of course you may spend the night, Nathaniel. When would one brother ever close his door to another brother?"

He motioned toward Paris. "Please, help your companion down. I'm sure she is weary of the saddle."

Paris realized Alejandro's dark, probing eyes never left her now. Was he only attentive, or suspicious?

Brannigan's hand—a hard, calloused vise—swallowed hers as he lifted it in assistance. Shocking heat bolted from his coarse flesh through her fingertips and clear to her toes. Her eyes snapped to his. Had he felt the heat? But all she saw in the brilliant blue depths was a twinkle of amusement, and all she could discern from that was that he must know the effect he had on her and found it most entertaining.

Irritated with herself for finding such a scoundrel even remotely attractive, she swung to the ground. Brannigan stood in front of her, unmoving, and with the horse behind her, she was forced to step to the side to put distance between her and her abrasive traveling companion. He surely seemed to enjoy making her uncomfortable, even to the point of not releasing her hand in a timely fashion.

She forced her gaze from his rugged features and extended her hand to Alejandro. To her amazement he bowed and lifted her fingers to his lips. "It is not often I get such a lovely woman as a visitor," he said. "This is indeed a pleasure."

"Thank you, Señor Escalante," she said, feeling embarrassed but flattered by his chivalry. "You are most kind." Then she rushed on, feeling she needed to explain her appearance, for once again she sensed Alejandro was no peasant, but a man of aristocratic background. She touched the floppy brim of the sombrero. "I nearly fainted from the heat, and Mr. Brannigan suggested I wear only the hat. I know it isn't customary. . . ."

He gave her a charming smile. "Do not worry, Sister

Frances. Nathaniel was right to look out after your health."
He gave her hand a slight squeeze before releasing it.
"Now, will you come inside where it is cool? I will fix
you something to eat. After such a long, hot ride you will
be tired and hungry and will want to bathe and sleep as
soon as possible."

"I'll take care of the horses," Brannigan said. "I'll join
you in a few minutes."

Paris followed Alejandro along a stone path, bordered
by an array of bright flowers. But it wasn't the flowers
that held her interest. Rather, she found herself considering the hundreds of stones so neatly intertwined to form
the path and the patience required to search for them all,
to cut them to shape, and then to stay on one's knees for
days, possibly weeks, laying them. All in the suffocating
border heat. And why? For company that seldom came?

The path was the work of someone who had nothing
else to do except eat, sleep, and think. It was the work of
a man who welcomed manual labor and the ramblings of
the mind that went with it, the philosophies of life and
death, the memories of the past. The man who had per-
spired over this path had no apparent images for the future
nor a purpose beyond the day. So he had carved out a
purpose in the rocks. And yet, Paris thought, he must not
want too much purpose, for if he did, then he would have
to leave his sheltered adobe dwelling in the wilderness
and face the larger world beyond.

She eyed the broad-shouldered, gracious Spaniard leading the way down the intricate rock path. Like him, she
had questions to ask. But like him, she would seek her
answers later when she had Brannigan alone.

Closer to the house they passed a fire in an open pit.
A large black pot dangled over the low-burning flames

on a metal tripod, giving the desert evening the tantalizing aroma of chili and reminding Paris it had been hours since her last meal of hardtack and jerky.

As they approached the garden fence, as neatly constructed as the rock path, the little chihuahua set up a tirade of yapping then dove under the fence and came up barking at her heels.

"Shut up, you stupid dog," Alejandro reprimanded, swiping at the dog with his sandaled foot. But the chihuahua tucked his butt under, and Alejandro made contact with nothing but air.

"One day I will give that dog to the mountain lion that roams these hills," Alejandro scowled at the bug-eyed dog. "Please forgive his rude behavior, Sister Frances, but we seldom have visitors. And to my recollection he has never seen a skirt before."

Paris's curiosity about the handsome Alejandro Escalante increased tenfold. What was he doing out here by himself? Had he no woman, no lover? How could a relatively young man like himself be content to live alone so far from civilization? Did he have the law after him and Brannigan protecting him?

Paris was thankful for the cool respite of the house's interior buff-colored walls. Because Alejandro was a bachelor, she had expected the house to look like a hovel, but she realized right away that it was furnished in such a spartan manner that it would be impossible for it to be anything but orderly. A cot, neatly made with clean bedding, lined the lower wall of one of the room's corners. An open fireplace, appearing to have seen little use, was centered on the end wall of the large room, while a homemade table and four chairs claimed their place of existence in the middle of the room in front of the fireplace.

Paris saw the necessities of life: an ample supply of food, pots, pans, clothing, firewood, a broom. There was nothing on the walls, nothing in the house that did not have to be there. For all appearances, Alejandro Escalante did not live here; he merely rested his tired body on the cot and ate his lonely meals at the table. And possibly, on infrequent nights that chilled, he stared into the hypnotizing flames that blackened the sand-colored walls of the fireplace.

She did not like being alone with Escalante because, unlike Brannigan, she knew he would try to be the perfect host and attempt to engage her in polite conversation. He would ask questions. And he did, even before the thought could completely cross her mind.

How had she found Brannigan? How had she convinced him to leave his duties as a bounty hunter? What church did she serve? She must be very brave to come out here and face the hardships of the desert. Most women wouldn't, even for treasure. And what treasure was it that she had come to find?

She hadn't been able to answer that last question when Brannigan himself stepped through the door, looking even taller and slimmer without the leather chaps, which he had left outside. She was never so relieved in her life to see his hard, unsmiling face. It wasn't that she didn't like Alejandro, but she sensed a sagacious air about him, despite his living as a hermit. She feared keen insight might allow him to see that she was not who she pretended to be. Yet, seemingly the perfect gentleman, she also suspected he would do nothing to cause her embarrassment.

The little dog did not like Brannigan any better than he liked Paris, and upon the bounty hunter's entrance into the house, he began to yap again with extreme purpose.

Before Alejandro could respond, the chihuahua lunged at Brannigan and attached itself to his ankle with its small, sharp teeth. Of course Brannigan couldn't feel anything through the thick leather of his boots, but he began cussing the dog and trying to shake it off nonetheless. The dog clung tenaciously even though Brannigan gave it a tooth-jarring ride back and forth through the air at the end of his foot.

"Pedro," Alejandro reprimanded again in a voice that had gone weary. "If you don't let go of Nathaniel's leg, he will not come to visit us again."

Pedro didn't seem to care; he held on that much tighter, growling deep in his throat.

"Get him off, Alejandro," Brannigan said in a deadly serious tone. "He's putting holes in my pants. Don't force me to resort to drastic measures."

Escalante cussed the dog again but to no avail. Finally, he shrugged his shoulders. "Do what you must do, Nathaniel. That dog has never liked me much either. He has no respect for me."

"He ought to mind you. You feed him."

Alejandro stared at the dog dispassionately. "No more than I have to. He and I have what might be called mutual contempt."

Brannigan pulled out his Colt.

Paris was appalled at Brannigan's "drastic measures" and even more appalled that Alejandro seemed so indifferent to whether his dog lived or died. She had no idea if it was some perverse joke they played, but seeing an immediate need for intervention, Paris stepped forward and lowered herself to one knee. "Come here, Pedro. Leave Mr. Brannigan alone. Come here, Pedro. *Now.*"

Her tone held authority but not harshness. The dog did

not release Brannigan's pant leg, but he did relax his frantic attempt to gnaw through it. He eyed Paris curiously. She coaxed again, cajoled, smiled, until finally he released Brannigan's leg. He was confused but interested in this strange new person in the black flowing garment. She continued to speak to him, and at last he took a cautious step toward her, then two, then three. Finally, he allowed her to touch his nose. She patted his head, then gathered him up in her arms, stroking his back. He tried to lick her face and she laughed and told him no. He perked up his ears and cocked his head at the sound of her laughter.

"Why don't you get rid of that dog, Alejandro?" Brannigan asked, returning his gun to its holster and looking down irritably at the damage the tiny dog had done to his pant leg.

Alejandro went to a basin and poured a small amount of water into it. "Oh, I suppose because he kills mice and snakes."

"So will a trap or a shotgun."

Alejandro just chuckled and reached for a towel to dry his hands, then he emptied the contents of the basin outside. "You may both wash and I'll make tortillas to go with the chili." To Paris he said, "Send Pedro outside, Sister Frances. He is not allowed in the house when I eat. I do not like him begging. It is a bad habit for anyone to get into, and especially a dog. He must learn pride and manners, if he is to expect respect."

Paris wasn't at all certain that she agreed with Alejandro's philosophy for the upbringing of dogs, but she did as she was told. Outside the door, she pressed Pedro's hind quarters to the ground. "Now, sit. We will feed you later."

He stared up at her with doleful eyes much too large for his small head, but he seemed to understand the routine and finally collapsed to his stomach with his head on his paws so he could watch them eat in front of him through the open door. Apparently it was something that didn't bother Alejandro or Brannigan. Paris decided they were both extremely insensitive.

After both she and Brannigan had washed and Paris had discreetly put her nun's veil back on, they were seated at the table. Alejandro dished up the chili and fresh flour tortillas. He placed a bottle of tequila next to Brannigan's plate and a pitcher of fresh water from the spring at Paris's plate.

The chili had to be the best Paris had ever tasted—hot enough to put blisters on cowhide but excellent nevertheless. The only thing that kept her from gulping it in an unladylike manner was the necessity to cool her mouth off with the water after every bite. She did, however, manage to lose her lusty appetite when Alejandro began with his questions again.

"There are many tales of lost treasure in this desert, Sister Frances. Which one are you hoping to find?"

Paris preferred the lost treasure to remain as lost as possible in the minds of her present company. She didn't really know her tablemates and it had been hard enough to trust Brannigan. She was thinking of a polite way to evade the question when Brannigan spoke up.

"It's the lost mission of Santa Isabel she's after, Alejandro. According to her map it's supposed to be somewhere over by Cerro Trueno. Ever heard of it?"

Paris was struck with the almost uncontrollable urge to lay a boot toe to Brannigan's shin from under the table. Instead, she encircled her spoon handle in a death grip and pretended it was his neck.

She wasn't prepared for the sudden stiffening of Alejandro's shoulders or the tightening of his expression. He stopped eating, leaned back in his chair, and dropped his spoon back into his chili. A muscle jumped in his jaw, and a combination of fear and anger enlarged his black eyes. He came to his feet, turning to the fireplace and running a hand through his thick black hair in an agitated movement. Then, in a precise about-face, he turned to them again, gripping the back of the chair he had just vacated so tightly that his dark knuckles lost color.

His voice was low and stricken. "You cannot do this thing, Nathaniel. Return to Nogales and go no further on this journey. Cerro Trueno is a treacherous place, shunned even by the Yaquis."

Brannigan stared at him, confused, then tried a smile to lighten the sudden tenseness. "Come on, Alejandro. It's just lost treasure."

"No, *mi hermano*. It is not just lost treasure. And if you try to take the gold of Santa Isabel, you will die."

Nate Brannigan lowered his spoon to his bowl of chili. A peculiar chill entered the candlelit room. Darkness had found the isolated dwelling sequestered in the barren hills, but the chill that crept down Nate's spine did not come from the night. How odd that sinister shadows had crept into the room, consuming those who had been friendly and warm only moments before.

"What are you talking about, Alejandro?" He had seen Alejandro so visibly upset only a few times in his life, and in those times he had learned not to take his adopted brother too lightly.

Alejandro paced back and forth in front of the fireplace. When he faced them a second time, none of the fear had left his eyes. It had only been joined by grave concern.

"There was once a Yaqui, Nathaniel. He was from my

grandmother's people. He was a very young man. Younger than you or I. He was in the wilderness one day, hunting, and he stumbled upon this mission you speak of, the Mission of Santa Isabel. He sensed it was a sacred place, so he did not enter the hidden valley where it was but returned to his village instead. That night while around the camp fire with his companions, he was bursting with the news of his discovery, and he could not refrain from telling them what he had found. He told them in elaborate detail of the greatness of the mission. But he had no sooner finished his story when he was stricken with a great pain. And, clutching his throat, he was dead in less than thirty seconds."

Alejandro suddenly stalked from the room, stepping over Pedro, who still blocked the doorway, and vanishing into the night.

Nate felt the hair at the nape of his neck prickle. The night beyond the open door was silent. Inside, only their breathing could be heard. He stared at his bowl of chili.

"Surely you don't believe that nonsense?" Sister Frances asked, leaning across the table closer to him so her whispered words could be heard by him but not Alejandro. "It's just an Indian superstition, for Pete's sake."

Nate met her gray eyes. How was he going to tell her that he very much believed what Alejandro had said? He didn't know why, and he didn't understand it, but he had to trust in Alejandro's beliefs, or superstitions, if that's what one chose to call them.

"Did you know there was a curse placed on the treasure of Santa Isabel?" he asked in a low accusatory voice.

Paris stared at him in utter dismay. "Of course not, and even if I had, I wouldn't have paid any attention to it."

"Maybe you should."

Having had enough of spooky stories, Paris shot to her feet and paced the floor in front of the fireplace the way Alejandro had done, forgetting that her behavior wasn't that of a nun at all. "Listen, Brannigan, if you don't want to go with me that's fine. I suppose any excuse is better than none, even this cockamamie story about dying Yaquis. But if the truth be known, you and your friend are probably just trying to scare me off so you can go after the treasure yourself. I knew I should never have shown anyone that map. Well, I'll tell you one thing. You're not going to scare me away. I'm going after that treasure if I have to go alone."

She started to stalk past him on her way out the door, but he caught her wrist. In the same second he was on his feet, towering over her ominously, his blue eyes snapping.

"Let go of me," she demanded, trying to wrench free of his iron grip.

"We are not going after that treasure, Sister Frances. And neither are *you.* Tomorrow we'll head back to Nogales."

She tried harder to get away from him but found herself pulled up so close to his chest she could feel his vest lapels brushing her bosom. For a moment, she almost forgot the point of their argument. Her gaze drifted from his angry eyes to his lips, but the hard line she encountered there immediately banished the wayward notion of kissing him and merely confirmed that he was totally inflexible to compromise of any kind.

"Then I will pay you nothing," she said belligerently, realizing even as she said it that the threat sounded weak and without conviction.

"You already have, Sister."

"Then you will give it back. It . . . belongs to the Church."

"Sure, I'll give it back. Minus four days' travel time from Nogales and back."

"I can't believe this. Of all the stupid things! I had to go and hire a superstitious bounty hunter!"

She felt the grip on her wrist loosen. She could have escaped him then, but for some unknown reason she didn't.

"I've known Alejandro all my life, Sister Frances," Brannigan said. "I've learned to respect his opinions and heed his advice. We will not go. That's final. And if you're still determined, you'll have to find someone else."

"I'll go by myself."

Movement in the doorway drew their attention. Alejandro had returned. "Perhaps because you are sent by the church then God will protect you, Sister Frances," he said dryly. "But the story I told you is only one of many. There are scores of people who have lost their lives trying to remove the treasure of Santa Isabel. I can tell you more if it would be enough to convince you."

Paris looked from one to the other with total disgust. Finally, she wrenched her arm free of Brannigan. "More stories you have made up, Señor Escalante? No, thank you. I'm not interested in your stories. And you're right. God will protect me. I'm the one who has been sent to retrieve the treasure."

She tried to move past him, but he took a step and blocked her way, sandwiching her between the two of them. If they would kill a small dog, or threaten to, then how could she trust them to behave as gentlemen toward a nun? Slowly she slipped her hand into her pocket. The derringer was still there. Two shots. One for each of them if necessary.

Then Alejandro stepped aside. "You will sleep in the house, Sister Frances. Nathaniel and I will go outside and let the stars be our roof. And tomorrow, you both will stay and visit with me, and then you will go back to Nogales. I am sorry you are disappointed about the treasure, but I do not want to lose an old friend. Or a new one."

Paris did not like being ordered about. *You will do this, you will do that.* Paris Frances McKenna had always done what she damned well pleased—unless her daddy had told her otherwise—and this time would be no exception. She would sleep in the house, but that was as far as she would go in obeying Alejandro Escalante's imperial orders.

The stub of Nate's cigar burned a red spot in the darkness. He lay on his bedroll, one hand behind his head, the other navigating the cigar in and out of his mouth while he and Alejandro talked.

They had been through much together. In all of their childhood years they had seldom been apart. They were more than brothers, they were friends. But of course they were only brothers in heart. At a young age, Nate had asked his parents why he looked different from the rest of the family and why he had a different name. They told him they had awoken one morning years ago to the sound of a baby crying. They had followed the sound to the barn and had found a child wrapped in a dirty, tattered blanket. A note had been pinned to the baby that said, "I have named him Nathaniel Brannigan. Please make a good home for him."

They could have turned him away to an orphanage, but

Don Diego Escalante had been easily persuaded by his wife, Doña LaReina, that they must keep the child. She sincerely believed that he had been a gift left by God since she had never been able to carry a child to term after the birth of Alejandro. And, as far as Nate knew, they had never regretted the decision to keep him, for they had always treated him as one of their own. Nate had tried unsuccessfully to find out who his real parents had been. In the end, he had decided it didn't matter. The people who had called him their son had been, and always would be, Don Diego and Doña LaReina.

Theirs had been a grand hacienda encompassing some of the best land in New Mexico. Unfortunately, the Rio Abajo was also the prime target of the Apaches. One time while Alejandro, Nate, and Don Diego had been away driving cattle to a buyer in northern New Mexico, the ranch had been raided by Apaches. Doña LaReina had been killed as well as Alejandro's wife, Paloma, and their young son. Many of the vaqueros had also died trying to protect them.

Alejandro had walked away from the hacienda then and come to this desolate place, where he had stayed ever since. Don Diego had suffered his losses alone at the hacienda. He wanted his sons to return. He had told this to Nate every time he had gone to visit, but he accepted their departures and waited and hoped for a change. Nate didn't truly understand his own departure from the hacienda. Paloma and little Alejandro had not been his wife and child, but he had felt the terrible wrenching grief just the same. And he had been unable to ease Alejandro's pain because he had suffered too greatly his own. Even now he remembered how beautiful Paloma had been.

Even though Nate had always been treated like a son

by Don Diego, Alejandro was the heir. With him away from the ranch, Nate had felt displaced and inexplicably wrong to ever try to fill the void meant for Don Diego's own flesh and blood. So he had taken up the gun, along with Rafe Cutrell, a good friend of his and Alejandro's and one of the hacienda's top hands. The two of them had gone looking for the renegade band of Apaches, found them, and had given them no quarter—just as they had given Doña LaReina, Doña Paloma, and little Alejandro no quarter. Then he and Rafe had given the bodies over to the buzzards, who had been eternally grateful.

After the revenge had been complete, he and Rafe had separated, each to sort things out in his own way. Nate had experienced a great emptiness. He had realized that his youth had been taken and would never return. His faith and trust in humanity had been decimated, and neither could be healed without even greater risk to the heart. He sensed that his two friends had experienced similar feelings, though they never spoke of that tragic day again. And he sensed he would never love again. He had buried all desire when they had buried Paloma.

"I don't suppose you've seen Rafe?" he asked suddenly, but regretted the question immediately. It brought the memories back not only to him but to Alejandro as well. And he hadn't wanted to open Alejandro's wounds.

The Spaniard responded in a voice more animated than Nate had expected. "Like you, he comes by here once in a while. The last time he was here, he said he saw you in Albuquerque."

Nate nodded. "Yeah, he had a job on a ranch breaking horses. He was always good with horses."

"*Sí*. Rafe works. He drifts. And like us, he looks for something he cannot find."

The memories were a mixture of joy and sorrow and the disturbing truth of what the three of them had become. For a few moments each man silently remembered and wondered how different things would have been.

"She is very pretty," Alejandro said quietly, closing the door to the past as easily as Nate had opened it.

"She is a nun." Nate knew his friend spoke of Sister Frances. What other woman could he be speaking of?

"No, Nathaniel, I think not. She did not bless the food."

"Neither did we."

"But that is different. What can be expected of men like us?"

Nate considered Alejandro's keen observation. Even though he, too, had had his suspicions about Sister Frances right from the beginning, he had tried to give her the benefit of the doubt.

"Maybe she just recognized that we were heathens, Alejandro, and maybe she didn't want to make us unduly uncomfortable."

"No. She would have at least said a silent prayer and then crossed herself. She would have tried to make us pray or include us in her prayer. She became a sister to help the poor, the orphaned, the sick, the imprisoned. You and I each fall into at least one of those categories. I know these people who are dedicated to God, Nathaniel. They do not pass up an opportunity to rescue a lost soul."

"Maybe she isn't like the others."

"No, I do not believe she is. For one thing, she said her church was the Sister Mary of the Sacred Heart in Santa Fe. I have never heard of such a church there."

"You've been gone a long time, Alejandro. Maybe it's there now."

"Maybe, but there is still something very wrong about your Sister Frances."

Nate puffed on his cigar. There was a lot about Sister Frances that niggled at his mind, too. Last night while trying to sleep he had thought of her. She was so close, her womanly curves so enticing. Her gray eyes, her red hair, even the smell of the rose soap seemed to jar something from a distant yesterday, reminding him of something that hovered on the edge of his memory that refused to be identified. But it wasn't another woman she reminded him of. No, it was something more elusive.

There was much more about her that didn't seem quite right. She'd said she'd been raised on a ranch, which accounted for her having such a fine horse and for being such a good horsewoman. It probably accounted, too, for her muttering the expletive after regaining consciousness when she'd passed out from the heat. Living on a ranch she would have been exposed to such language and had probably used it herself when her father wasn't listening. It was an easy enough slip. But she'd also gone to sleep without a prayer, without opening the Bible. And as Alejandro said, she had not blessed her food, not once on the entire journey.

There was more. Her writing their journey down in her journal and looking about nervously all day had bothered him. It was almost as if she was expecting to see someone. Possibly Apaches, but he didn't think so. She didn't seem overly concerned about Indians because she had convinced herself they were all on the reservation far away from the Sonoran desert.

And last but not least, she had left her spectacles on the ground when she had fainted and she had not seemed to miss them at all. He had deduced that she could see perfectly well without them.

He had been raised in the Catholic faith in the house of Don Diego, and even though he'd stayed on the periphery of the religion, he knew enough to know that two and two did not add up to four where Sister Frances was concerned.

"She is trouble, Nathaniel," Alejandro said, ending his private musings. "She is very determined to get that treasure. I did not see defeat in her eyes, regardless of death awaiting her if she proceeds with her foolishness."

"Maybe we should force the truth out of her tomorrow," Nate responded, thoughtfully blowing smoke to the stars.

"*Sí,* maybe we should."

In the distance the crystal-clear hoot of an owl filled the gap of silence.

"Do you want this treasure, Nathaniel?"

"Maybe."

"But why, Nathaniel? It will not buy you happiness."

"No, but maybe I'd like it just for the hell of it."

"Ah, for the same reason you want everything. For the same reason you do everything. Your motivation has always perplexed me, *mi hermano,* but then maybe your idea is the right one after all."

Nate glanced at Alejandro, who had both hands under his head and was also contemplating the stars. "Haven't you just ever wanted something for the hell of it, Alejandro?"

"I think I always have reasons, Nathaniel. Our mother always said I thought too deeply, and I suppose she was right. How can we change that which we are?"

"You ought to leave here, Alejandro. You've been here too long."

"How long is too long? I will leave when I am ready. But I am not ready yet." He pulled his arms from beneath his head and rolled to his side. "Let's get some rest. We will talk again tomorrow before you return to Nogales."

"I think tomorrow we should make Sister Frances answer some pointed questions."

"*Sí.* Maybe. You know, I hope she is not a nun, though I don't understand why she would pretend to be one. It has been a long time since I kissed a woman, and I think I would like to kiss her before you take her away. She makes me remember what it was like. This will be a hard night to endure, for I will be thinking of how good it would feel and how very close she is."

Nate felt a peculiar rise of jealousy tightening in his gut like a noose around an outlaw's neck. If Sister Frances wasn't a nun, and would admit to it, then he wanted first dibs on her. But wasn't it just like Alejandro to step in and steal the girl? He didn't do it intentionally. He just had a gravity that captured the female gender, and Nate had never been able to hold that against him.

"What makes you think she'd want to kiss you?" he asked lightly, trying to conceal his true feelings.

Alejandro's perfect white teeth gleamed in the starlight. "She will see my desperation, maybe? And find charity in her heart?"

Their deep-throated chuckles disturbed Pedro and made him spring to his tiny legs in concern. But realizing the sound was not a threat, he dropped back to his stomach.

"She doesn't act like one who would take pity on anyone," Nate added, remembering the heated words he'd had with her, and wondering why he would even want to kiss her. But he did. Very much so.

"All the more reason to believe she is an impostor," Alejandro replied.

"Then we will end all our conjecturing and find out the truth tomorrow. Agreed?"

"Yes, *mañana*. I would like to touch that hair the color of fire and gold. I wonder if it would burn in a man's hands the way it looks that it would."

The conversation ended and in seconds Alejandro had drifted off to the privacy of his dreams. Nate continued to stare at the desert sky. The stars were thick and big and close enough to touch. And so was that redheaded woman. Nothing had ever come between him and Alejandro. After all these years, he hoped it wouldn't be her.

The only light in the adobe house was starlight filtering through the open windows. Paris clumsily removed her nightgown in the darkness and put her habit back on. It had given her safe passage so far, and for as much as she would have liked to don her trousers and blouse, common sense told her to stay with the nun's habit, at least for a while longer.

She still had a lot of questions about the men that hadn't been asked or answered, and she felt a pang of regret knowing she'd never see the bounty hunter again. She didn't know what it was about him that intrigued her—maybe it was the way he'd touched her when she'd fainted. She wouldn't mind feeling that touch again, but a woman had to do what a woman had to do, even if it meant walking away from the two most handsome men she'd ever met. Such was life. And if she didn't get her hands on that treasure, her life wouldn't be worth two cents.

She gathered up her belongings and crept to the door.

She opened it successfully without one squeak. Thank God Alejandro kept his hinges oiled. But suddenly Pedro let out a tirade of yapping. Her heart leaped to her throat then dropped to her toes. She should have let Brannigan shoot the pesky little creature. He was going to wake up the world. He ran up to her, still yapping, so she scooped him up and hurried inside with him, closing the door as quietly as she had opened it. By talking and patting his head, he was quickly pacified. He even tried to lick her face again, and this time she let him. Anything to shut him up.

He was complicating her escape. Fearing he would start his obnoxious yapping if she tried to leave again, Paris decided she had no alternative but to take him with her. Besides, he might be good company for her, and Alejandro would probably be grateful to be rid of him. So, tying the four corners of one of Alejandro's towels together, she made a pouch and put the dog in it. He could poke his head out but couldn't get out as long as she kept the pouch off the ground.

Silently she crept back out into the night, loaded down with her bedroll, her saddlebags, Pedro, and her carpetbag. She loaded some supplies on one of the pack mules and led him from the corral as quietly as possible. The sun was not far from lifting the curtain of darkness when, with Pedro's pouch hooked over the saddle horn, she headed west toward the golden riches of Santa Isabel.

Four

Paris had absolutely no idea where she was going. By the time the blazing sun had turned the desert into eye-blinding whiteness, she was wishing she would have stayed back at Alejandro's. It had seemed easy when Brannigan was in charge of the direction. But now, no matter to what direction she turned, the desolate mountains lining the horizon appeared to be replicas of each other. And the ground, even though it supported some vegetation, shimmered with white, monotonous, unending heat. She saw a rattlesnake side-winding across a flat spot, and she stayed clear of his path. As the hours passed, she pushed her horse slower. Her heart grew heavier. If she could have seen them, the furrows in her brow deepened.

She could gauge west only by the position of the sun, and as it crept toward noonday even that became difficult. It merely looked like a round fireball that could go to any horizon in a forbidding dome. For the first time she began to hope there were no renegade Apaches or bandits out and about.

Quiet fear grew inside her. She searched the horizon more intensely, nervously hoping to see Brannigan galloping after her. But why should he come after her? He was a hardboiled man who would probably figure that it served her right to die out in the desert from her own foolishness. He would just head back to Nogales and play some more cards at the cantina until another job came along. Besides, he was superstitious. That alone was enough to keep him back at Alejandro Escalante's adobe hut.

She hadn't bothered to wear her nun's veil this morning. She had simply dressed quickly in the habit and wound her hair on top of her head then covered it with the sombrero. Once again she silently thanked Brannigan for the hat. Even with it, she felt the sun burning her fair, freckled complexion. At least her arms and body were completely covered by the habit and were subjected to none of the sun's vicious rays. She wore her leather gloves. They were hot, but they kept the delicate skin on her hands from burning.

She didn't know what time it was when she stopped and decided to wait out the heat of the day beneath a tangle of mesquite and cacti. She knew her fear was only increasing with the mid-day mirages. The brush offered some shade for her and little Pedro. She had tried to send him back home once, but he had chosen to follow her. It could have been that by the time she'd set him to the ground and tried to get him to go back, he had discovered he didn't know the way any better than she did. Dogs were supposed to be able to sense things like that, but Pedro seemed as frightened of the vast, empty land as she was.

In the sweltering heat beneath the mesquite bushes, Paris realized that in her haste to leave she had brought only one canteen of water and had forgotten to even fill that one. She had no idea where more springs were. She looked behind her, or what she thought was behind her. Maybe she should just return to Alejandro's, follow the footprints she had made, and give up the idea of plundering the mission of Santa Isabel. She could go back to Tully and become his mistress, let him support her.

Anger surged inside her along with a stubbornness that revived her flagging spirit. She would rather die right there in the Sonoran desert than to give that smooth-talking, manipulative saloon owner control over her life and her body. She had not given herself to a man yet and Tully would not be the first. She'd seen too many young girls hand their bodies over so they could survive or could simply have more money. It had done nothing but hurt them in the long run. She had seen some even commit suicide after becoming prostitutes. She had saved her own virtue only by adamantly refusing to do anything but dance. Tully had tried to get her to be "more receptive" to the men, but she would have died dancing before resorting to entertaining in one of the upstairs bedrooms.

She removed her horse's saddle and staked him securely on a long rope, hoping he could find enough to eat to satisfy him. She sank down to the sand in the shade of the mesquite. She would just rest for a little while, and when it cooled off she would be better able to determine the direction the sun was taking.

She pulled out her map and studied it again. She searched the horizon for a big mountain, for Cerro Trueno, and figured it should be about another day or two away. She could not see it now, but she was positive she would see it soon, very soon, just over the next horizon.

Nate Brannigan stared at the pole corral that was now minus one packhorse and Sister Frances's saddle horse. "You know, Alejandro, that woman is causing me a lot of grief. So much, in fact, that I've got half a notion to let her get by out there by her own devices."

Alejandro wore his typical calm expression, apparently not considering it a situation to get upset about. "That must have been what Pedro was barking about early this morning. He is gone, too, I see. It's no wonder I have never liked that dog, but I guess I didn't realize why until now."

"And why is that Alejandro?" Nate asked absently, his mind on the unpleasant task ahead of him. When he caught up with that woman he ought to turn her over his knee, nun or no nun. She had absolutely no business setting out across that desert alone. He was beginning to think she was suicidal.

"Because he was not loyal," Alejandro said rather sadly. "A man does not need a dog that is not loyal."

"Maybe you should have fed him better and spoken more kindly to him."

Alejandro nodded and continued in his dry, cynical way. *"Sí,* maybe. But he had a good life here. What more could he have asked for?"

"A female dog?"

A faint smile moved Alejandro's lips. "He has never had one. How could he miss what he has never had?"

Preoccupied, Nate didn't hear the question. "You know I've got to go after her."

"Sí. What else can you do?"

"I could go back to Nogales. It would serve her right for pulling such a harebrained stunt."

They both considered that alternative for a silent moment. Finally, the Spaniard said, "No, I don't think you could live with yourself, Nathaniel. She is a pretty woman alone out there. You must go after her."

"She's a stupid woman," Nate said gruffly.

"Maybe. Maybe not. I think she is a desperate woman. I saw much fear and uncertainty in her eyes. She is hiding something. I am certain of it."

Nate conceded that point with a bleak expression. "Yes, I'm afraid you could be right. But one way or the other, I'd better get going. She can't be too far ahead of me."

"Bring her back tonight and I will have something good fixed for you to eat. Then maybe we will hog-tie her so she can't get away again. Tomorrow you can go back to Nogales and forget this nonsense about Santa Isabel. And she can go back to the church and learn how to pray."

"I'm all for that."

Alejandro patted Nate on the shoulder and headed back to the house but stopped halfway there. When he turned around Nate was in the corral catching his horse and the other pack mule.

"Nathaniel."

Nate looked up.

Amigo, no matter what you do, don't let her talk you into going after the treasure. *Por favor.* I do not have a good feeling about it."

Nate led his horse and the mule from the corral. "Don't worry. Sister Frances won't talk me into anything except going back to Nogales."

Sister Frances was so far off course it was alarming. It was amazing how, with even a map, she could get so turned around. It was easy enough for him to find her. Her tracks were as blatant as if she'd nailed signs to the saguaro. And she wasn't too far ahead of him. From time to time he could even see her. He held back intentionally, though, because, for some perverse reason, he decided it would do her good to wander around for a while. Maybe she would learn her lesson and not try it again.

He waited until she had settled down for a siesta in the mesquite bushes with her sombrero over her face before he allowed himself to catch up to her. He saw Pedro vanish over a little rise, probably searching for a mouse to eat. So with the yapping little creature temporarily out of the way, Nate decided to do some investigating of Sister Frances's belongings.

Not wanting her or the dog to hear the horse and mules, he left them some distance away in a low spot behind another clump of mesquite. He moved quietly from years of practice sneaking up on sleeping outlaws. The shapely form of a sleeping woman, however, was considerably more distracting than that of a ratty renegade. Nate found it a most difficult task to force his eyes from the lovely feminine curves and back to the matter at hand.

The sister's carpetbag was the first item he ransacked. Along with the standard lingerie, he was surprised to find a pair of men's brown trousers, two bodice-fitting blouses, and a black, flat-brimmed, Spanish-style riding hat.

He also found a bottle labeled "Tonic Water." He thought it might be whiskey, but after smelling it, determined that it must be medicinal, probably something for female problems. Recorking it, he dug deeper beneath the clothes and found a well-worn Bible. At least here was the tool of her trade, though he had never seen her use it. He opened it and on the inside page saw the inscription:

Presented to Paris Frances this twenty-first day of September, 1874. May God watch over you when I am gone.
                              Your loving mother, Margaret

A smirk twisted Nate's lips. Sister Frances needed more than God watching over her. She needed a brigade of guardian angels to keep her out of trouble.

Finding nothing else of interest in the carpetbag, he moved to the saddlebags. He wasn't sure what he was hoping to find that would incriminate her, but he finally found it. As a matter of fact, he found several things: a short-barrelled Peacemaker .45, a deck of dog-eared cards, some bright red rouge—the kind actresses and whores used—and an envelope with a letter in it.

Having little or no conscience when investigating a case—and Sister Frances had become one—he immediately opened the envelope. Inside, he found the map she'd shown him in the cantina, and on closer inspection, he noticed there was something written on the back of it in fading ink:

I sign this map over to John "Blackjack" McKenna for money I owe him from this damn-blasted card game. Wish I'd never set eyes on the Silver Slipper and just stayed out on the old Sonora. Anyway, here is the game of your life, Blackjack—if you're fool enough to ante in.

                              (Signed) Beacher Cogan

Blackjack McKenna. The name was synonymous with gambling. Nobody could be in this part of the country long without hearing of McKenna. Why Nate himself had lost over a hundred dollars to the man one time in a card game in Tombstone. Blackjack had been shot in an alley of that infamous town not even a year ago. Rumor had it, a disgruntled card player had believed McKenna had cheated him, which he probably had.

Nate folded the map carefully and replaced it in its envelope.

He studied the sleeping Sister Frances again, unable to keep from noticing her lovely bosom rising and falling in gentle rhythm. What did she have to do with Blackjack McKenna?

He picked up the Peacemaker again, automatically testing the feel of it in his hand. It was a beautiful piece, ivory-handled and scroll-engraved. Even the holster that protected it was fine embossed leather. The short barrel was preferred by gunfighters because it was easier and quicker to clear leather. He searched his memory and found only vague images, but he remembered the ivory handle of McKenna's gun poking from his embossed gun belt that day in Tombstone—it was hard not to notice a fancy rig like that. He sensed that this gun belonged to McKenna, and probably the cards, too.

Last, he found the journal Sister Frances had incessantly written in on the journey here. The first entry was on the day they had left Nogales. All he found were descriptions of the terrain they'd traveled over and about how long it had taken to get from one place to the other, where water holes were, etc. It was just what she had said it was. There was nothing unusual about it; she had a right

to know where she was going. But one entry troubled him.
It read:

*I'm sure I'll be able to find my way back home
now with no difficulty, in the event that Brannigan
should meet with an untimely end.*

He looked again at the gun, the cards, the journal, the
envelope with the tattered map. Then he looked at the
prone figure of the fine-boned, shapely woman still
breathing heavily in the groggy throes of mid-day sleep.

Who was the woman with hair the color of a fox? What
had she said that first day in the cantina when she'd
pointed out the card move to him?

I haven't been a nun all my life.

No, and he'd bet his bottom dollar that she wasn't one
now either.

He didn't know how the daughter of a rancher from
New Mexico had ended up with the possessions of gambler Blackjack McKenna, but some other things made
sense. Paris Frances, if that was her Bible and her name,
must have been McKenna's mistress. After he was killed,
she was on her own and destitute. She found the map and
wanted the treasure so she hired a stranger to take her
there, planning all along to kill him when she had what
she wanted—probably so she wouldn't have to share it
with him or pay the remainder of the promised fee. Then,
with her journal and her map, she would find her way
back alone.

He had to get the truth out of the little impostor. But
how?

Tucking the Peacemaker into his gun belt behind his
back, he took silent steps toward her until he was close

enough to touch her. He lowered himself to his haunches next to her. He picked up a wayward tendril of hair that had tumbled out onto the sandy desert soil. The heat of it radiated into his palm. Alejandro was right, it did feel like fire.

He felt a tightening in his loins. The black habit concealed her body but did nothing to block his memory. He saw her once again standing nearly naked, small and shapely, in the window of the Nogales Hotel. He saw, too, from memory, the creamy softness of her bosom the day he'd had to revive her from the heat.

Perhaps there was a way to get the truth from her. A way that would serve curiosity and satisfaction both in the process.

For as careful as he was, stretching out on the bedroll with her and easing his body the length of hers made as much noise as a military reveille. Or at least to his ears it did. His gun belt squeaked; his boots scraped across the sand. Even the rustle of his clothes seemed loud enough to bring the snakes from their mid-day slumbers. And yet, she stirred only slightly, seeming to have difficulty pulling herself from that drugging day-time sleep. He hated the feeling. It was why he never took siestas.

He removed his hat and set it on the ground, then gently slid an arm across her and pressed his length closer to hers. He lowered his head until his lips touched the fiery tresses. Easing down more, his lips found her ear, her neck, touching her soft skin in feather-like caresses. She stirred, moving her head, groping for consciousness. He envisioned her mind struggling to escape the gluey net of afternoon sleep. His lips moved to her lips and closed over them.

She came awake and into immediate combat. She managed one swat to the side of his head before he caught both of her arms and propelled himself completely over her, pinning her to the ground with his weight. She tried bucking him off but quickly realized that that action was only stirring bodily sensations better left unstirred. She halted the action and froze beneath him, her gray eyes shooting flames of anger and, he thought, fear. All she tried to do now was to wrest her wrists free of his grip, with no success, of course.

"How dare you accost me, Brannigan! I took you for a low-life bastard right from the first moment I set eyes on you, and I see I wasn't wrong."

For a moment he was hard-pressed to remember what had originally driven him to his present prone position. It took some doing to drag his mind away from the soft, luscious curves beneath him and back to his intentions. When a man was in this position with a woman, the only natural thing to do was to make love to her.

"I know what you thought of me, *Sister* Frances, and I didn't want to disappoint you. Now, you and I have something to discuss."

"You can't blame me for leaving Alejandro's place. I don't believe in that silly curse. It's just a ploy for the two of you to get me out of the way so you can go after the treasure yourselves."

Nate was finding it increasingly difficult to concentrate on what she was saying. His loins nestled against hers perfectly, creating a heat that was hard to ignore. The erratic rise and fall of her soft, full bosom pressed into his chest. He felt the tightening in his loins increase to an urgency that would eventually require fulfillment unless curbed right away. Her lips were full but slightly dry from the desert sun. The remedy would be to put some moisture to them, in the form of a kiss. And the red hair beckoned him, weakened him. He wanted to gather it in his hands like a bundle of flames, but if he let go of her wrists he knew his face would carry the scars of a lioness in attack.

"It was no ploy, Sister. The Yaqui Indians believe the curse of Santa Isabel, mainly because they've seen too many people die who told its secrets. Some things in this world can't be explained, but sometimes we must believe the unbelievable. However, I'm not here to talk to you about running away. I'm here to talk to you about who you really are. And this time I want the truth. In case nobody told you, you have to do more than wear the proper clothes if you're going to pretend to be a nun. And you shouldn't say things like damn and bastard."

He was quick to observe the spark of wariness lighting her cloud-gray eyes. "What do you mean? I am Sister Frances."

"And I'm the pope, whoever he is. Pardon me for not knowing. I'm afraid I don't keep up much on things of that nature. What is his name anyway?"

Panic joined the caution; her eyes darted nervously, evading his. "Pope John."

"Ah, Pope John. I wonder why I don't believe that, Sister? Maybe because you really don't know either? And maybe because I did a little investigating and found some odd things for a nun to have in her possession." He paused, watching the expression on her pretty face change from wariness to fury.

"How dare you go through my personal belongings!"

He continued, ignoring her tirade. "How would you like to explain a short-barrel .45, a deck of cards, a pair of men's trousers, a hat, a map that belongs to one Blackjack McKenna, and a journal that makes me wonder if you didn't plan to kill me after we reached our destination. I have a sneaking suspicion the gun and cards belong to Blackjack as well. Did you kill him, too? Was he your lover?"

"My lover! How twisted your mind is!"

She attempted to wrestle free of him again. He easily subdued her and continued. "Naturally, I'd like to know why all these questionable items are in the possession of a good, pure woman whose hair is as red as a whore's. Is the hair color fake, too, Paris?"

Her lips compressed tightly, and she gave all indications of stubbornly refusing to speak at all now.

"Am I going to have to pressure you into talking? You know, we're out here all alone, and I have all the time in the world."

Her eyes danced fire. She struggled beneath him again. He knew her wrists were going to be burned from twisting them in his hands and he wished she would stop. It wasn't his objective to hurt her, but still she persisted.

"Torture me all you want, Brannigan. You can even leave me out here to die. Live up to your reputation—a vile bounty hunter who's more outlaw than the outlaws he tracks down! Pick on a woman half your size! I don't have to tell you anything, and I won't!"

"There's an old trick the Indians use, Paris Frances. They bury a person in the sand up to his neck and then, after a while, the bugs and the ants find him and they start by eating out his eyes."

Her glare deepened.

"Or there's this—an old trick of the vile bounty hunter. I've used it many times on women. Most of them have been so tortured they answered any question I asked. If not before, then after."

Paris McKenna didn't like the change in Nate Brannigan's deep-throated whisper, or in the sultry, smoldering glow that drifted into his eyes. Force was one thing she could handle, but seduction was entirely different. She had to admit she was not immune to his hard body pressed against hers or his hips moving in a near-undetectable motion. She also found that his shock of dark brown hair, free of the Stetson, was much too touchable.

She saw his hard, demanding lips descending, and she did the only thing she could do. She turned her head. But he seemed prepared for her evasive action, and his mouth covered hers anyway. She found, to her chagrin, that his lips were not as hard as they looked but rather firm, masculine, and very sensual. They were also possessive and intoxicating and easily forced her to turn her head back to more fully meet his.

She fought desperately to remain motionless beneath the barbaric assault. She didn't want his kiss. She only wanted him to leave her alone. He was a rough renegade who had no respect for women. He made his living by preying off others. And yet, despite the battle inside her mind, her body answered the summons of his. Her resolve crumbled. A fascinating heat spread throughout her, and she wanted nothing more than to put her arms around him. Before she realized what she was doing, her lips responded to his and she was kissing him back with an urgency she had never felt before. No man had kissed her the way Brannigan was kissing her. When she responded to him, she felt an immediate change in his body. Satisfaction.

He lifted his head slowly from hers. "Do you want more, Paris? Or will you tell me now?"

Torture. Yes, that's what he had called it, and how accurate the term had been. The smoldering heat ignited, and a slow burn began deep inside her.

"Release my hands."

"So you can claw my eyes out? Not on your life, honey."

"Don't 'honey' me. I'll tell you nothing, Brannigan."

"As you wish."

His lips descended again, taking hers in another masterful kiss that drew her response quicker and easier this time. She felt her arms being pulled up tighter over her head until they came together. One big hand easily held both of her wrists, freeing his other hand. She felt his fingertips toying with her hair, then sinking into it. His fiery touch sent scorching heat to her ear, her cheek, then trailed downward slowly to her neck. She inhaled sharply when his lips abandoned hers to follow the trail of his lean, experienced fingers. Her pulse pounded wildly wherever his lips made contact with her flesh. She felt it and knew he did, too. She didn't want him to know the effect he was having on her, but she could not help it. She wanted to tell him to stop because he was doing something to her that frightened her in a shamefully titillating way. He was making love to her, something no man had ever done.

His lips found points in her neck that by mere feather-light touches made the rest of her body come alive. Breathlessly she waited for his next move. With a prowess born of experience, his hand moved to the swell of her breast, scorching her even through the cloth of the habit. His lips followed in that trail of fire, moving ever downward. When they found the point of her breasts, she gasped a breathless retort.

"You despicable bastard, Brannigan. All right, I'm not a nun."

"I thought not." He lifted his head from her bosom only long enough to say the words, then his lips returned to their intimate quest.

"Brannigan, stop."

"Do you want me to?"

"Of course."

"That's a safe, noncommittal answer. Are you really Paris Frances, like it says in that Bible? Or did you kill her and assume her identity?"

"Stop it!"

He lifted his head. She was breathing so hard she could barely speak.

"My name is Paris Frances."

"So the Bible is yours. But who would name a child such a name? And what's your last name?"

"My mother named me. I was . . . conceived . . . in Paris while my parents were on their . . . honeymoon."

"M-m-m-m . . . I see. In a moment similar to this one, I presume."

She felt the buttons down the front of the habit being unbuttoned by his deft fingers.

"You're McKenna's wife?"

The cloth came open. She felt the coolness of the air then the heat of his mouth.

"No, I'm his daughter," she confessed softly.

His gaze shot to her eyes. The memory that had been nagging at his mind snapped into focus. She had McKenna's eyes. The gambler's had been steady and un-fathomable. Hers were, too, to a degree. But hers contained uncertainty, an emotion that had kept him from identifying the memory.

"So old Blackjack had a daughter. Knowing him, he probably had a lot of them, scattered all over the country. Sons, too."

"Speak for yourself, Brannigan," she snapped. "You didn't know my daddy so don't you be saying mean things about him. He was faithful to my mother. Now, let me up. I'll tell you what you want to know."

"I like you where I have you."

His lips burrowed deeper into the V he'd made of her garment. He spoke against her flesh. "I knew McKenna. He beat me out of a hundred dollars. Maybe I should take payment from his daughter."

"Damn you. . . ."

The hand left her bosom and slid down past her thigh. He shifted his weight and soon she felt her skirt going up, his hand beneath it.

"I'll kill you for this, Brannigan."

"I figured that was what you had in mind anyway."

"Not in the beginning, but don't bet that I haven't changed my mind."

"That doesn't explain the journal, and if you're McKenna's daughter then the ranch in New Mexico must have also been a lie."

She tried to concentrate on something besides his mouth moving toward her nipple and his hand moving toward her inner thigh. "Yes, the ranch was a lie. And the journal . . . well . . . I . . . thought that if something happened, I . . . I would want to be able to get back . . . in case something happened to you. I told you that already."

His lips lifted momentarily from her bosom, but he didn't look at her. Instead he nudged the cloth out of his way with his chin. "Like a fatal bullet from your daddy's revolver?"

"I'm not a murderess, Brannigan."

"You're not a nun either."

His lips were driving her mad. The slow heat in her body had turned to a consuming flame. His hand was inching higher. She felt the odd necessity to let him continue with his quest. She felt a gnawing need for his body to fulfill her. She'd heard enough about men and women coupling to know what it was about. She had always expected she would wait until she found a man who loved her. A man who would marry her. But Lord, that could be years away. How could it be possible that this rogue could kiss her and make her want to forget marriage? She was coming very close to allowing him to finish what he had begun.

She began to talk very fast before her resolve crumbled entirely and she lost her virginity to a handsome but worthless bounty hunter who would more than likely leave her high and dry and pregnant.

"I found the map in my daddy's things," she said frantically, her bosom heaving against his lips. "I had to go after it. I need the treasure, Brannigan. Tully wasn't going to let me keep my job unless—"

He lifted his head. This time his steely blue eyes did meet hers. "Unless what?"

She tried to pull her hands free of his but his grip was like a pair of manacles and merely tightened down more. "Unless I did the same thing with him that you're doing to me! And I would rather die first than to let that slime touch me!"

His hand left her thigh. He rose over her and stared down at her. "Who's Tully?"

"The bastard I used to work for. He owned the Silver

Slipper Saloon & Dance Hall in Tombstone. But he didn't own me, and he never will. I'll see him in his grave first."

Brannigan's eyes narrowed. He fingered her hair again, winding a finger around one wavy strand. "Dance hall girl, huh? Then why are you fighting me, honey? Let's just finish what we started. Have a little fun here in the desert?"

She swallowed hard, suddenly realizing that his love-making threats had been only that, threats. Until now.

"Get off me," she warned in the deadliest tone she could muster. "I may have danced for that beady-eyed little snake, but I wasn't one of his girls."

Brannigan was amused. "And I suppose the next thing you're going to tell me is that you're a virgin?"

"And I'm sure you never were."

He pulled her up against him even tighter, putting a hand on her backside and pulling her hips tightly to his. His smile was excruciatingly arrogant. "Let's get you out of that nun's habit, honey. It's totally inappropriate for a scarlet woman."

Five

Neither Nate nor Paris saw his return, but Pedro was suddenly there, attaching himself to Nate's pant leg again, growling viciously and tearing cloth. This time his sharp little teeth even made contact with flesh. Nate forgot about his romantic intentions and rolled off Paris, swatting at Pedro with his hat and cursing the dog profusely.

"Call him off, Paris!"

Paris found Brannigan's dilemma rather entertaining. He was getting his due for being so cocksure of his sexual prowess. He didn't need to know his tactics had been working much too well.

Finally, she grabbed Pedro and tried to pull him away from Nate, but the little dog's teeth remained hooked in the cloth. His growls seemed to be as much a warning for her not to interfere with his mission as they were for Nate to leave her alone. After some coaxing, the dog released his hold and Paris scooped him up in her arms.

Nate stuck his hat back on his head and examined the tear in his pant leg. "I'm going to kill that skin-headed, little—"

"He was only protecting me," Paris interjected with a smile. She gave the dog a peck on the head. He in turn licked her face. "Good little dog, aren't you?"

Nate came to his feet, unimpressed by their affection

for each other. "If he wasn't Alejandro's dog, he'd be some coyote's supper right now. Why'd you steal him anyway?"

"I didn't steal him!" She was clearly insulted. "He refused to be quiet so I had no choice but to bring him along. I have every intention of returning him to Alejandro."

Nate glared at both her and the dog, sincerely believing they were equal accomplices in his misery. "We're not finished, Paris."

Her smile grew wider, the twinkle in her eyes deeper. "Oh, I think we are. I will remove my clothes now, but only because I'm tired of sweltering in this habit. And I will do so only if you turn around. I'll tell you what I tell all the men, Brannigan. I dance for a living, nothing more. And now, I don't even dance."

"You're going to get rich off the treasure of Santa Isabel, I presume?"

"Yes, and you're going to turn around."

He silently debated whether to obey her order as his gaze, burning with irritation, slid over the open throat of the habit. "I'll only turn around if you tie up that dog."

"Oh, don't worry. He won't attack . . . if you don't."

Cursing under his breath, he finally stalked back to his horse. "Let me know when you're decent."

With Nate gone, Paris's heart finally resumed its normal speed. But with his absence came a peculiar emptiness. She took a steadying breath, reminding herself of her purpose. It certainly wasn't to be sexually manipulated by a renegade, no matter how persuasive his kisses might be.

She went behind a mesquite tree to give herself further protection from his prying eyes. But upon looking in her bags and saddlebags, she found her Peacemaker missing.

"Damn you, Brannigan!" she cursed from behind the tree. "You've taken my daddy's gun."

"You don't take me for an idiot, do you, Paris?" came his gravelly response some distance away.

She remembered seeing the flash of a gun protruding from the back of his gun belt. She had thought it was part of his arsenal. Now she realized it had been the Peacemaker.

"I want it back," she demanded.

"You'll have it back when we reach Nogales."

Paris was furious but decided there was no point in arguing over it. She'd get it back one way or another. He couldn't guard his saddlebags constantly. She still had the derringer, but it was hardly sufficient for anything but close range. She might have even used it on him earlier if he hadn't caught her so completely off guard.

She resumed pulling her riding clothes from her bag. It was with extreme relief that she removed the hot, sticky habit. Her struggle with Brannigan had caused extra exertion and she felt a trickle of perspiration slither like a snake down the center of her back. But it had a cooling effect, and she enjoyed it for a moment before wiping it off with a corner of the habit. Seeing that her flat-brimmed hat was smashed, she reverted to the sombrero once again, which was better protection against the sun anyway. She stuffed the carpetbag with the habit and, for lack of space, had no choice but to hang her hat from the saddle horn.

Feeling wonderfully cool in the lightweight clothing, she summoned Brannigan to rejoin her. He sauntered back, pausing in front of her to light another of his odoriferous cigars and eye her new attire through the smoke. She sensed the garb was much more to his liking than the shapeless nun's habit. She was self-conscious, however, about how little the trousers did to conceal the curve of her hips, something he also seemed to be noting with a degree of appreciation. But she had bought them for practicality and because they had taken up less space than a riding skirt.

"Tell me, Paris," he finally said. "Why the nun disguise? What did you hope to gain?"

She wound her long hair on top of her head and covered it with the sombrero. "It was not what I hoped to gain, Brannigan. It was what I hoped to preserve. Not many men would accost a nun nor steal what belonged to her."

"Oh, we're back to the subject of virginity."

"Yes, virginity and gold."

Brannigan's eyes roamed her boldly again. He took a drag on the cigar, blowing the smoke out in a slow, lazy stream past eyes that held their own smoldering glow. The smoke blew right into her face again. Gagging, she tried to wave it away. He didn't seem to notice.

"Virginity and gold," he said in a contemplative way. "I think I'm beginning to like the combination more and more all the time, Paris."

"Don't get to liking it too much, Brannigan. Since you're determined to go back to Alejandro's, you'll never have the chance to have either."

Going back to Alejandro's was a fact that seemed to have slipped his mind but not one that was going to change it. "Then perhaps another time and another place, Paris. Maybe when you're back in Tombstone at the Silver Slipper."

"I'm not going back to Tombstone."

"Suit yourself. But you are going with me to find a spring and make camp for the night. Does that suit you?"

"Do I have a choice?"

"No."

"Then I suppose it suits me."

But, if Nathaniel Brannigan thought he was going to put

Paris Frances McKenna under his thumb, he was sadly mistaken. She was still the employer and he the employee, even if he'd temporarily gotten the roles reversed. Brute force might work in some battles, but wits worked wonders in others. Little did he know the battle had only begun. She had several plans to bring him around to her way of thinking, and one of them was in her saddlebags in a little glass bottle. By morning the presumptuous bounty hunter would have things back in the proper perspective.

Brannigan found the spring with no difficulty. While he built a fire, Paris watched a tarantula take a detour around their camp. She wondered how many of the hairy creatures had crawled over her while she'd taken her afternoon siesta. At the thought, a chill raced down her spine uncontrollably.

"Shoot that damn thing, Brannigan," she said suddenly. "Or give me back my gun so I can." She would have used the derringer, but it was her ace in the hole and she didn't want him to take it, too.

He looked up from his tinder, following the direction of her interest. He finally spotted the hairy spider lumbering around a cacti. "I'm not going to waste a bullet on a spider. Besides, it's not hurting anything."

"I won't be able to sleep with it around."

Brannigan went back to feeding tinder to the fire. "There's more where that one came from. This time of year the males are in search of females. I wouldn't want to deprive him of one of the few pleasures he might find on this godforsaken desert. But if you want protection, you can share my bedroll."

Her gaze shifted from the spider to him. "I'd rather sleep with a scorpion."

"Well, you might get your wish on that, too, before the

night's over. Now, how about shouldering your share of the load and fix us something to eat."

Paris gripped her temper. He'd been much nicer to her when he'd thought she was a nun. But verbal sparring with him was going to accomplish nothing; she could see that already. If she wanted to get him to change his mind about going to Cerro Trueno, she would have to work from a different angle, play on his compassion—*if* he had any and *if* she could cool her temper long enough. Maybe cooking was just the thing to accomplish that. She enjoyed cooking, had done it for years, and was quite good at it.

Toward the end when the tuberculosis had left her mother too weak to do anything, Paris had taken over all the household responsibilities. She had abandoned her own life to care for her mother and father. Her father, she'd found, was quite helpless without a woman. He couldn't iron a shirt, mend anything, or fix a meal. He could tell wonderful stories, and he was a good teacher and listener. He'd taught her how to use a gun as efficiently as he did himself. He'd taught her the ins and outs of poker and faro. He'd taught her how to ride. But when her mother had died, Paris had seen him become like a lost child, wandering aimlessly. His purpose seemed to have vanished. He had even accumulated quite a gambling bill because, as he had put it, he no longer had his "lucky lady" standing at his shoulder. It didn't matter that his wife had never actually stood at the gaming tables with him. She had been waiting for him at home, and to Blackjack McKenna it had been the same thing.

The gambling bill was what had left Paris in financial straits after his death. She'd had to sell everything to pay it and then take the job as a dance hall girl to support herself.

But she didn't blame him. She knew his luck would have changed in time, if his time hadn't run out first.

The map hadn't been found in her daddy's belongings. She had gone to Tully's office safe to take her wages and run. She had seen the map in the safe with her father's name on it. Figuring Tully had probably stolen it from Blackjack or cheated him out of it in a card game, she had decided to keep it for herself.

She had risked everything to search for a lost treasure, but if she found it, she would have enough money to live comfortably and like a lady. She'd have enough money to open a business of her own in a nice little town somewhere. To quit the search now would mean to return to Tombstone and Tully, and, more than likely, those upstairs bedrooms.

Despite all the financial problems her father had left her with, she would not hesitate to sacrifice those years again for either him or her mother.

She and Brannigan didn't have much to say over supper. They ate canned corned beef, fried soda biscuits that Paris had made, and dried fruit. Afterward, Paris washed the tin plates and cups in the spring while Brannigan staked the horses and mules on fresh grass for the night.

The sun dropped behind the jagged line of mountains that ran roughly northwest by southeast. Their shadows spread out into the valleys, filling them with dusk and creating cooler pockets of air and lonely silence. The saguaro, thinly scattered along the ridges, seemed to be lifting their rubbery arms from the darkness in a good-bye salute to the last rays of sunlight.

Sitting a few feet from the campfire, Paris pulled her daddy's deck of worn cards from the saddlebags to begin her first plan of action. It was time to get into Brannigan's brain and see if he had any compassion in there or if he was just a big bundle of machismo behind a handsome face. She started a game of solitaire, spreading the cards out on her blankets.

He settled onto his bedroll, smoking another cigar and watching her hands expertly shuffling the cards. He seemed content to just watch and didn't suggest they play a game together.

"Tell me, Brannigan," she began, silently wishing he would find something to smoke that didn't smell so nasty. "What do you think of a woman opening up a boarding house?" She didn't raise her eyes from her game, trying to make the comment sound innocently conversational.

His scowl suggested that he didn't want to discuss the subject of her financial demise, understandably so since his insistence on returning to Nogales was going to make it worse. It was a moment before he responded, and then his gravelly tone was laced with suspicion, probably suspecting an ulterior motive behind the question. "I suppose you mean for yourself?"

"Well, since Mama and Daddy are gone, I need a way to support myself, and if I can't get my hands on that treasure, then I'm forced to think of alternatives. While I was cooking, I realized I could probably run a boarding house—that is, if I could get financial backing. But it's so hard, you know. I mean for a woman. Banks just don't want to loan money to women unless you're an older woman and have had business ventures before, or unless you have a male co-signer."

"I can't see you running a boarding house, Paris."

She looked up sharply from her card game. "And why not?"

"Considering your background, maybe you'd be more comfortable as the owner of a gambling house."

She didn't miss the sarcasm in his voice. Her first reaction was to take out her derringer, force him to drop his gun, tie him up, and ride off and leave him. He certainly thought she was nothing but a trollop. She was sure she would never be able to convince him otherwise, unless she gave him her virginity to prove it. However, that would be a rather counterproductive means to an end. So, rather than be hasty, she forced herself to have patience, like a spider weaving a web.

"Oh, what an excellent idea!" she exclaimed with enthusiasm, deciding it wasn't such a bad idea after all. If she found the treasure, she might very well invest the money in such an enterprise. Ah, but first things first.

She forced a shadow over her mood again and returned to her game. "I can't start a business in Tombstone, Nate," she said sadly. "Not with Tully there. He'd see a way to run me out of business, maybe even out of town. No, I would have to go to a new place, where gold has just been found. Do you know of any place?"

He listened to her with a mocking half-smile, as if he was only humoring her and didn't believe for a minute that she would follow through with any of her plans. Did he think she would just give in and go back to Tully? Succumb to a life of prostitution?

"I hear they've found gold up in Idaho Territory," he finally said. "But it's awfully cold up there, Paris. Maybe you ought to stick around these parts."

She considered that while continuing to play her cards. Then she said, "You know, Nate, Idaho may be a long way from here, but it might be a good place for a girl like me to make a fresh start. I wonder if bankers loan women money up there."

Nate couldn't put a finger on it, but he had the feeling he was being taken for a ride, and on a high gallop no less. Paris was being terribly congenial, too agreeable for a woman who had wanted the treasure so badly that she had set out across the Sonoran by herself. Maybe it was time to see what kind of stuff the little redhead was really made of. If she could put on a show, so could he. It wouldn't be the first time he'd sweet-talked a woman right out of her lacy underthings. And ever since he'd found out she was a dance hall girl, that had been the predominant thought on his mind. He'd been a little disappointed that she was, but it was a disappointment he had gotten over quickly enough.

"I don't know, Paris," he replied. "Some bankers would probably do just about anything for a pretty woman."

He gauged her reaction to his compliance and saw a twitch around her lips. She was getting impatient and irritated. He curbed a smile.

She continued. "You know, Nate, I liked Alejandro, but does he honestly believe that thing about the curse? I mean, he seems such an educated man and all."

Nate tossed his cigar aside. She was indeed being much too sweet and agreeable, too conversational. "I saw the fear in Alejandro's eyes, Paris, and there isn't too much in life that frightens him."

"And you believe in it, too, just because he does?"

"Not necessarily, but like I said before, I can't turn my back on the possibility that he knows there's a power out there stronger than us."

She played her hand for a few minutes, pretending to be engrossed in it, but Nate saw her miss two plays. This time he couldn't contain his smile; he doubted the daughter of Blackjack McKenna ever missed a play.

"Couldn't you see your way clear to just take me to Cerro Trueno and then leave," she said, innocently continuing with the game and not looking at him. "You don't have to be a part of anything. I'll be able to get back with the help of the journal."

"The desert is a deceptive thing, Paris."

She took a deep breath, pausing with the cards in her hands. She had a faraway look in her eyes. "Yes, I know. I'm afraid I found that out."

"You won't want to try it again."

"And you won't take me to Cerro Trueno?"

"No."

Suddenly she tossed the cards down and curled up on her bedroll, putting her back to him. He heard some sniffling and saw her wipe at her eyes. "Why did I have to go and hire a superstitious bounty hunter?" she said in a pouty voice.

Nate studied the curve of her back, the hollow of her waist, the swell of her hip, and the way the men's trousers hugged her hips and backside. He realized there was one more profession she could go into: acting.

He smiled and stood up. "I don't know, Paris. I guess you just got unlucky."

"I took a gamble on you, Brannigan. Damn you for letting me down."

Trying to wipe the smile from his face, he stepped over the fire and paused at the edge of her bedroll. Even though he was going along with her act, he felt the tell-tale thump of excitement in his heart as he lowered himself to his haunches and then his knees. For as small as she was, she had the strange capability of setting a terribly big fire inside him.

He touched her shoulder, turning her toward him. "I'm sorry, Paris," he said, continuing with the act. "But I just can't take you out there in good faith. I mean . . . you might die, and then I'd have to live with a guilty conscience."

She sat up and flung herself into his embrace, burying her face in his neck. "Oh, Nate! I need this treasure more than you can imagine. I'm destitute. I'm afraid I'll be reduced to becoming a prostitute or Tully's mistress if I go back to Tombstone. And I don't have enough money to go anywhere else. You've got to help me. You're the only chance I have."

From what he'd seen of Paris so far, she was neither weak nor helpless. Desperate maybe. Helpless, no.

He held her tightly, stroking the long flaming hair while laying kisses on the top of her head. "It'll be okay, Paris, honey. Things always work out."

"Oh, Nate. I'm all alone. My nearest relatives are in Louisiana and I can't go back there."

"Why not, honey?" he asked with his most sympathetic voice, but wondered if she was telling the truth. She did have sort of a soft southern drawl blending with the western accent.

"My daddy was a riverboat gambler on the Mississippi in his early days, and when my mama fell in love with him, her daddy refused to let her marry him. So she ran off. They disowned her and told her never to come back. I'm sure they wouldn't want to see me. You've got to help me, Nate."

Brannigan eased her back to the bedroll and stretched out next to her. He smoothed her hair from her face, kissing away her salty tears, and lavishing more over her entire face and her closed eyes. He felt the tremble of her lips beneath his. "Don't cry, Paris," he murmured against her soft, yielding mouth. "Everything will be okay. I'll take care of you."

He felt her relax, felt her hand on his back loosen, then tighten again. It was a subtle change, but if he wasn't mistaken she wasn't holding onto him out of need anymore but out of desire. He pressed closer, slipping a leg between hers, wondering how grateful she'd be for his offer of help. Things may not have been going according to her plan, but they were going according to his.

Her lips tasted soft and velvety, like the petal of a wild rose. A slow burn started in his loins. Her breasts, young and firm against his chest, were just two more reasons to make him lose sight of his deception. It was hard to remember he was seducing her merely because she was seducing him, and he wondered who would be the victor in this game.

"Nate, I couldn't ask you to do that," she insisted adamantly. "Just take me to the treasure. I'll make my own way."

Her hands caressed his back and made him weak. He opened her lips with the expertise of his own and tasted the sweetness of her tongue against his. But only for a split second before she pulled back and stiffened beneath him in an action he interpreted as one of surprise. He lifted his head.

"What is it, Paris? What's wrong?"

"Do you always kiss that way?"

"Don't you like it?"

"I . . . don't know. I've never done it before."

He squelched an inner moan. Surely she didn't expect him to believe that? Was she still trying to convince him that she had only danced for a living?

He kissed her again in the same fashion. This time her hands slipped into the hair at the back of his neck. She pulled back again, pressing tentative kisses to his cheek. "Please, Nate, take me to Cerro Trueno."

"How bad do you want to go?"

"Bad. Real bad."

His lips found her neck, his hands the buttons on her shirtwaist. In seconds he had it open, scalding her bosom with his kisses, treating his lips to the softness of her flesh. Meanwhile, his hands found the front buttons on her trousers, opening the placket that held them snug to her flat stomach.

"Wha-what are you doing, Nate?" she managed from beneath his kiss. For the first time he heard apprehension in her voice. Had she honestly thought she could stoke him up hotter than the Sonoran and then throw cold water on him?

"I'll take you to Cerro Trueno, Paris, but it'll cost you more than the original price. And this is my price."

Before he knew what had happened, she lifted a knee to his mid-section and gave him a mighty shove that sent him sprawling almost into the camp fire. Pedro was jarred out of his sleep and camp up snarling.

Paris stood up, called the dog down, and put her clothing back in order. "Always looking out after your best interests, aren't you?" she snapped, her gray eyes flashing. Gone was the innocent, pleading woman, begging for his help.

"You're one to talk, honey," he said wryly, picking up his hat that had fallen dangerously close to the flames. "You should have been an actress. You might have been able to fool somebody with that little act, but if you thought you could get me to say yes with a little kissing and hugging, you were wrong. We're going back tomorrow and that's final."

He stepped over the fire and settled back onto his bedroll with his back to her. She'd left him in a miserable condition, but he wouldn't let her know it.

Paris contemplated his broad back and narrow hips with a feminine eye for appreciation. Little did he know that she hadn't feigned everything. His touch, his masculine scent, and especially his bold and intimate mating of her mouth had found her inner weakness and touched off an insane wildfire of desire that still seemed to be running rampant through her body. A man had never made her feel that way before, as if she wanted to forget their argument and go back and finish what they had started. Now, standing there alone, she felt more lonely than she could ever remember feeling. It was a different type of loneliness from what she had felt at losing her parents. It was something that made her feel very incomplete as a person and as a woman.

She crawled beneath her wool blanket. Brannigan couldn't understand what she faced back in Tombstone. His offer to take care of her was tempting—she would much prefer his bed over Tully's—but she wouldn't be a bought woman. He probably hadn't been serious about it anyway since he'd guessed that she had staged the entire scene to win him over to her desires. Well, she shouldn't have been surprised that he'd seen through it all. From the first moment she'd met him she'd known he didn't miss much.

No, she had only one choice, and she would have to use her last plan of attack to accomplish it. She was going to Cerro Trueno even if she had to go alone. Before breakfast was over, Nate Brannigan was not going to be in any condition to stop her.

Six

Paris had hoped to wake up first and get the coffee brewing. But when she sat up, pushing the sleep from her eyes, Brannigan was already sitting on a nearby rock, coffee cup in hand, basking in the morning sun like a snake that has just slithered from its hole. Paris did have to admit that, although Brannigan might harbor the deception of the devil, he looked so fresh and so disturbingly handsome that for a moment, just a fleeting moment, she actually considered foregoing her final plan and returning to Nogales with him, if his offer to take care of her still stood.

Gauging by what she knew of him so far, the offer had probably been as much to coerce her into giving up her treasure hunt as her pleas had been to manipulate him into continuing. She was positive their feelings for each other were mutual and about as shallow as a dust-filled well. Physical attraction for each other seemed to be their only common ground. After a few nights together, even that would be gone. Then Brannigan would be in search of a new *señorita* and she would be out looking for another treasure.

"Mornin', Paris," he said, sipping the hot coffee. "I was beginning to think I'd have to give you a good morning kiss to wake you up."

She glanced at his lips touching the rim of the cup,

remembering too vividly how they'd felt against her own last night. She'd even dreamed of their hot arousal until she'd tossed and turned restlessly, waking numerous times to find her arms empty.

She forced her mind from the tantalizing memory and flung her blanket aside. "Don't press your luck, Brannigan. We were using each other last night. Now, we're back in the real world."

"Are we?" His lurking smile was most annoying.

"Yes, we are."

She reached for the coffee pot and poured herself a cup. Brannigan eyed her over the rim of his cup, steam wafting up into his face. "You ought to reconsider, Paris. You and I would make a good pair. A dance hall girl and a bounty hunter would be a perfect fit."

"And how do you figure?"

"Because we're both without scruples."

"Speak for yourself," she replied indignantly.

"Now, Paris, be honest with yourself if not with me. What woman with scruples would take a treasure belonging to the church and then do it in the name of the church?"

"It's not a lack of scruples, Brannigan. It was desperation and self-preservation."

"Just a matter of survival, eh?"

"You could say that."

He set his cup aside and stood up. "Fix us something to eat. I'll get the animals saddled and packed."

"Remember who's paying your feed bill, Brannigan. It might serve you to say 'please.' "

Amusement deepened the faint crow's feet around his eyes. "Please."

"That's better."

He chuckled and walked off. His attitude toward her

had changed considerably when the nun's disguise had fallen by the wayside. From over the top of her coffee cup, she watched the way his body moved in a provocatively male swagger, reminding her how masterfully he had taunted her with his prowess last night. But all thoughts of his physical attributes aside, it was time to put her last plan into action. She really hated to do it, but his stubbornness had left her no alternative.

Making sure he wasn't watching her, she removed the bottle of tonic from her saddlebags and poured a few drops into the coffee pot. By the time he returned, the bacon was cooked. She dutifully placed his portion, along with some flapjacks, on a tin platter. He tossed out his cold coffee, as she'd seen him do before, and refilled his cup with fresh.

She watched him closely. By the time he was to the bottom of his cup, his food was gone. He stood up and patted his stomach with satisfaction. "Well, Paris, it's time we headed back. Let's get things cleaned up and packed."

A puzzled frown creased his forehead then and he reached for his head.

"Is something wrong, Nate?" she asked innocently. "You look terribly pale."

He shook his head but sat back down. "No, I just feel a little . . . dizzy . . . and . . ."

"Sleepy?"

He didn't answer. In that instant, his eyes rolled back and he fell flat on his face on his bedroll, out as cold as yesterday's fire.

Paris stood up and emptied the rest of the coffee onto the ground. She found her daddy's Peacemaker in Brannigan's saddlebags, hastily rolled up her bedroll, rinsed the coffee pot out, bundled up the last of the items onto the mules, and latched Pedro over the saddle horn in his

traveling pouch. She kicked the fire out and went over to
Brannigan, feeling confident he would be unconscious for
a few hours.

She gathered up his hat from the ground and covered
his head with it. She didn't want his neck to get sunburned.
Patting his shoulder, she said, "I really hated to do that
to you, Nate, old buddy, but you left me no choice. Don't
feel picked on. You're not the first man I've left in such
a condition. I doubt Tully's happy with me either—I did
the same thing to him. But, well . . . a girl has to do what
a girl has to do."

She removed his hat again just long enough to give him
a kiss on the cheek. She did like the way his skin felt
beneath her lips, and his particular scent was undeniably
erotic. But she supposed a relationship between them just
wasn't meant to be. She allowed her gaze to slide over
the enticing lines of his back and buttocks one last time.
She felt something akin to regret tumble inside her, making her question her decision. But there was no turning
back now. Brannigan would be madder than a wet hen
when he woke up. The only thing she could do was to be
long gone when that moment came.

She swung onto the back of the buckskin and took her
bearings the best she could from the morning sun and the
surrounding mountains, this time trying to brand them on
her mind. Not feeling comfortable with her memory, she
took her journal out of her saddlebags and made some
quick notations and crude drawings.

Leading the mules and Brannigan's horse, she headed
northwest toward a gauzy band of clouds floating just
above the mountains. A mile from camp she tied Brannigan's horse to a mesquite tree and transferred enough of

the water and supplies to the ground next to it to support him until he got back to Alejandro's.

As for herself, she didn't relish venturing into the Sierra de Muerte alone, but she was going to have the treasure of Santa Isabel, curse or no curse.

Nate had a dream that he was being roasted alive over a bed of hot coals by some mean-spirited Apaches. When he finally pried his eyes open, he felt the rough texture of his bedroll. Slowly and painfully, he rolled to his back. His head was splitting, and he couldn't seem to pry his eyes open against the blinding light. He held his hand up to shield his eyes, but a sharp stab of pain, piercing clear to the center of his brain, forced him to close them again.

He felt the desert, heard it, smelled it, baked in its unrelenting heat. Gradually his memory came back, and he remembered drinking the coffee, remembered the way Paris had been watching him intently.

Paris!

He sat up suddenly, grabbed his head, and swore as a tremendous tidal wave of pain nearly drowned him. He sank back to the ground, groaning. When the pain finally subsided, he tried to get up again, slower this time. He struggled to his knees, holding his head. He forced his eyes open to mere slits and saw a gecko lizard watching him from a few feet away, its eyelids opening and closing to the same throbbing pulse of the pain in Nate's head.

Irritated that his misery was being observed, even by a blinky-eyed reptile, he swung a hand at the lizard and it shot behind a rock. Shading his eyes, he looked toward the sun suspended in the afternoon sky, as motionless as everything subjected to its perpetual, hellish torment.

"My God," he moaned. "I've been out cold for hours."

He groped around on the bedroll and found his hat. Staggering to his feet, he weaved, fighting the hammering pain and trying to gain his balance. The little impostor had left him there to die. She'd taken his horse, the mules, the supplies. All she'd left was his revolver, his knife, a canteen of water, and the blanket he'd fallen on.

"How wide of her," he mumbled, rolling up his bedroll and tossing it over his shoulder. Well, there was no doubt where she was going, and when he caught up with her, she'd have hell to pay. For this he could even temporarily overlook the curse. It would mean breaking his promise to Alejandro, but surely his brother would understand.

He found her tracks easily enough and followed them despite occasional blurred vision and the pain in his head that had settled into a dull and steady throbbing. With his feet burning inside his boots, making each step a fiery agony, he contemplated ways he would get even with that little redhead if it was the last thing he did. When he caught up with her, she'd regret that she had ever fooled with Nathaniel Brannigan.

Sometime later, he came to a sudden stop. He peered into the distance and wondered if he was seeing a mirage instead of a horse, his horse, tied to a mesquite. Forgetting his burning feet and his aching head, he started off with renewed vigor—and anger. But he quickly saw that Paris wasn't with the horse.

He searched the horizon, seeing her tracks heading northwest. "That crazy little fool," he muttered. "She's determined to get herself killed."

He did have to grant her one thing though. She had left him a few supplies on the ground and a piece of paper,

torn from her journal, anchored down by a rock. On it
were the words,

> *Please understand, Nate, but I simply can't go
> back without the treasure. Tell Alejandro I'll bring
> Pedro back when I return. Paris.*

He sat down, right there on the ground in the shade of
his horse, and looked at the beautifully flowing script.
"The woman should have been a school teacher instead
of a dance hall girl," he muttered. "Maybe she would have
been able to stay out of trouble."

Amazingly, some of his anger had dissipated. She hadn't
been completely heartless. He could see she'd only meant
to slow him down, not leave him to die. He knew he should
be thankful for small favors. He folded the note up and
stuck it in his vest pocket. What in the world was he going
to do about her? She would more than likely die out there
by herself. She couldn't possibly know where she was going. She wouldn't know how or where to find water.

As for the treasure, he supposed he could just take her
out to a tall mountain, tell her it was Cerro Trueno, lead
her around in circles until she got tired, and then bring
her back. One way or the other, no matter what a source
of aggravation she was, he simply couldn't leave her for
the buzzards to feast on. No, if anybody was going to
feast on her luscious young body, it shouldn't be a damned
ugly bird.

And then he felt it. The caress of a hot wind. It drew
his head up and he looked toward the sun, sinking now
toward the horizon. It was enveloped in an all-too-familiar
grayish-yellow haze.

He flew into action, tying the few supplies Paris had

left him behind his horse. He swung into the saddle and followed her tracks. He had to find her before dark. And before the dust storm.

Paris had seen the odd grayish-yellow cloud that was closer to land than sky moving steadily toward her. The breeze was not strong yet, but she felt it lift the sandy soil into her face and eyes. She had to cinch the sombrero's string down tight beneath her chin to keep it on, but still the wind rippled the big brim and threatened to tear it off her head. She pulled her bandana up over her nose and moved on toward a healthy stand of mesquite. It would be a good place to seek shelter against the increasing wind. As late as it was, she'd have to set up camp, too. She didn't want to do that with no water, but the oncoming storm was giving her no choice. Through the binoculars she'd been looking for spots of green, indicating springs or a creek, but she had seen nothing since she'd left Nate.

She had not gone a quarter of a mile when the dust storm hit with all its ferocity, frightening both her and the animals. The gelding fought the reins and the mules fought the lead ropes. It seemed every animal wanted to flee in a different direction, except Pedro, who just buried his head in his sack.

Paris was barely able to see the clump of mesquite a hundred feet away. Only an occasional break in the storm allowed her to keep her course. Upon reaching the mesquite, she had difficulty bringing the jittery animals under control. Finally, they obeyed and accepted the shelter as their only reprieve from the biting wind and stinging sand.

Paris could barely see anything as she dismounted, all the while keeping a solid grip on the ropes and reins to prevent any of the animals from running away. The wind howled and ripped at her cotton shirtwaist and pulled at the animals' manes and tails. The bandana she had placed over her nose was nearly useless. The sand blew under it and through it, sifting up her nose and into her mouth, making it difficult to breathe.

She pulled the animals toward the mesquite and tied them so their fannies were to the wind. They huddled with their heads down and together, their eyes shut against the biting grains of dirt and sand.

A strange yellow darkness had fallen over the land. The dust obliterated what was left of the sun before it dropped behind the mountainous horizon. Paris pulled the gear from the animals and shoved it beneath the mesquite, using the pack ropes to wind around it and tie it down. There were times when she had to cling to a branch herself or be picked up by the mighty force of the wind. Before she could stop him, Pedro had deserted her, dashing off into the storm to look for protection better than what she had provided.

She hunkered down in the mesquite, wrapping herself in her blankets. She cursed her foolishness again and wished Nate was with her. She wondered if he'd found his horse by now, hoping he had or the animal might break loose, leaving him stranded. The wind howled around her and over her. Sand filled her eyes, scraping them raw until they stung. There seemed no respite from it. Wondering how long the storm would rage, she huddled into a smaller and tighter ball, feeling very alone and very lost . . . again.

After a time, her mind settled into the droning, hypnotic howl of the storm. She focused on the sound, trying to find a soothing factor in it. If she could accept it as nature and as something that wouldn't last, then she could deal with it and not panic. She forced herself to think of to-

morrow and the sun bright and stifling hot again, the sky
as clear as crystal, and in the distance the rising bulk of
Cerro Trueno. And there, hidden in a green valley, the lost
mission of Santa Isabel!

Something closed around her arm and she screamed.
She fought her way out of the blankets only to find herself
embroiled in the cloth and tangled beyond escape. Then
she was down and the thing was on top of her. The body.
The man's body.

"Nobody double-crosses Nathaniel Brannigan and gets
away with it, Paris."

She couldn't have imagined how wonderful that gravelly voice sounded. Her arms were the only thing she had
out of the blankets and she threw them around his neck.
"Oh, Nate, I'm so glad to see you!"

He just as quickly grabbed her arms and pulled them
free of his neck. Through eyes squinted against the whip-
ping dust and sand, she saw his face covered with a bandana up to his nose and a layer of gray dust over all. Even
his black lashes were white. His eyes weren't just blue
and white anymore; they were the color of the American
flag. And she could tell by the sharp daggers shooting out
of them that he was not to be appeased in any way by her
gratitude at seeing him.

"I can explain, Nate."

"No need to, Paris. I saw your little love letter. I've got
it right here next to my heart." He patted his chest, then
lifted his weight from her, grabbed the edges of the blankets, and literally rolled her out of them. He grabbed her
wrist and hauled her up to a sitting position. "We're sleeping together, honey. Whether you like it or not."

Before she realized what had happened he had them
bound up in the blankets again as tight as ground meat in

a tamale. But they didn't sleep. They didn't even lie down—at first. They just sat there for what seemed hours, hunched together shoulder to shoulder, eyes pinched tightly shut while the wind and dust sliced through the blankets as if they were mosquito netting instead of tightly woven wool.

While Nate seemed to think his presence was an irritant to her, it was all Paris could do to keep from snuggling against him even closer than she was. He was very warm, and now that the sun had gone down, the wind turned as cold as a knife blade that had been pulled from a frozen lake. Her teeth began to chatter uncontrollably and a chill settled into her bones.

To top it off, she felt Brannigan stirring around like a restless five year old, causing cold drafts to curl around her. She was about to ask him if a scorpion had crawled up his pant leg when she found a glass bottle thrust into her cold hand.

"Drink some of this, Paris. You're shivering so hard, you're even making me cold."

She couldn't see the bottle, but it was a pocket flask of some sort. She was obviously skeptical. "What is it? Snake poison?"

"Don't worry," he replied dryly. "It isn't knock-out drops. Just whiskey."

Ignoring his sarcasm, she lifted the flask to her sand-coated lips. On the job at the Silver Slipper, the girls had only been allowed to drink weak tea, disguised as expensive liquor in fancy bottles. The men paid a lot to buy the girls drinks, the girls didn't get drunk, and the house got rich. Paris had, however, as a curious child, occasionally pilfered whiskey from her daddy's cabinet at home, so she was ready for the burn that trickled down her throat and fanned out into her stomach like a radiating wave of welcome heat. After a second swallow, she handed it back to Brannigan.

"A virgin, huh?" he said, peering at her face only inches from his. "And I suppose you've never had the taste of whiskey on your lips either."

"Did you expect me to choke?"

"Yeah, as a matter of fact." He lifted the flask to his own lips and downed a good belt before recorking it. He returned it to his vest pocket and hunkered down next to her again.

"I'm sorry to disappoint you," she said. "My daddy taught me a lot of things, Brannigan, and one of them was how to take a shot of whiskey."

"Something every young girl should be able to do, I'm sure."

She didn't feel like telling him that Blackjack McKenna may have taught her a lot, but he had absolutely forbidden her to drink anything alcoholic. Not only did he think it was unladylike, but, unlike riding, shooting, and winning at poker, it was also unnecessary in his estimation. He had needed a level head to make his living at the gaming tables and so would drink only on occasion.

She didn't know exactly when exhaustion took over, but a long time later, she woke up to silence and to the suffocating heat of Brannigan's body perfectly molded to hers. She was on her side, and he was behind her, her buttocks tight against his loins, her back and his chest like two pieces of paper glued together. He was asleep, and little puffs of his breath hit the top of her head at regular intervals, ruffling her hair and tickling her to near insanity. His arms were around her like manacles, and she deduced that he was probably holding onto her so tightly because he was afraid she would get away again. But why should he care? Unless, of course, he intended to make her pay for drugging him. In that case, this would be a good time to put some distance between them.

Carefully she tried extricating herself from him, but they were wound as tightly in the blankets as two worms in a cocoon. She tried again. Suddenly his arms tightened.

"Going somewhere, Paris honey?"

"Yes. I . . . uh . . . I need to . . . go out to the bushes."

"Likely excuse."

"It's not an excuse."

In one easy roll, she found herself on the bottom again and him on the top. She couldn't move and it wasn't entirely due to his weight and confining embrace. The blankets were still hopelessly tangled around them, or at least around her.

She lifted her eyes to his. His bronzed face was still covered with the thick layer of gray-white dust that also coated his black lashes like flour. His blue eyes sparkled at her like sapphires in that bed of flour, as if he knew exactly why she was suddenly so amused. And she might have laughed, but she had the sobering realization that she looked exactly the same way.

"You don't play fair, Paris," he said in a low whisper. "Not fair at all. And now it's time to even the score."

Her adrenalin began to pump. How exactly did he plan to achieve his objective? She tried to moisten her lips with a dry tongue but only got more grit in her mouth for the attempt. "You wouldn't go with me," she bounded into an explanation. "You said you'd hog-tie me and make me go back to Nogales. I'm sorry, Nate, but you backed me into a corner. If you'll recall, I tried persuading you through other, gentler methods, but you simply refused to cooperate. Maybe you'll realize now how desperately I need to find that treasure. I never would have resorted to such drastic measures otherwise."

Nate found himself not really listening to her explanation. His focus was on the softness of her breasts and the curve of her hips. She had been so close all night, the way a lover would be.

"What are you going to do?"

Her question jarred his pleasant thoughts, nudging him to make a decision. Since he'd never been good at making decisions before morning coffee—and he definitely didn't want another shot at her particular brew!—he just stared into her hypnotic, hopeful gray eyes. And then he kissed her.

A delicious feeling sank and rose inside him, spreading warmth throughout him more effectively than the whiskey had, and stimulating even more than morning coffee. It wound around inside him, hitting tender spots that left him weak and senseless and protective of her. Even after all she'd done, he just wanted to cradle her and lavish more kisses on her.

He lifted his lips from hers, wondering exactly what the peculiar feeling was that seemed to be wrapping itself around his emotions as tightly as a lariat settling over a wild horse's freedom.

"I won't do it again," she whispered, her mouth just a fraction of an inch from his. "I promise."

"Don't make promises you can't keep," he whispered back.

The tightening increased uncomfortably in his loins, and his thoughts of making love to her became foremost in his mind. But there was sand everywhere, probably even where one definitely wouldn't want it. He suddenly and insanely forgave her for drugging him and running off with his horse and the mules. She hadn't intended to kill him, just to get away from him. Now, how could he honestly hold that against her? He supposed if he was in her shoes, he'd have done the same thing. She was just a resourceful woman in a situation she considered desperate; a man couldn't fault her for that.

He felt her hands on his back, caressing. Felt her lips open beneath his and her tongue meet his. Lioness. Seductress.

Suddenly he dragged his lips from hers and silently cursed his foolishness. He couldn't stay in this position for long and still think clearly. He couldn't become a prisoner to her wiles. Just being near her was blinding him.

"What are you going to do, Nate?"

He untangled himself from the blankets and stood up, helping her to her feet. "We're going to find a spring and wash this grit off. Then we're going back to Alejandro's."

"Alejandro's!" She leaned toward him in an angry stance. "Oh, you're nothing but a stubborn jackass! After all I've tried to tell you—well, all right. We'll just go. Then I'll find someone else to bring me out here. Someone who isn't superstitious!"

Suddenly he swore, yanked his hat off, and threw it on the ground. For a moment Paris actually thought he was going to stomp on it, too.

"For heaven's sake," she snapped. "What's wrong with you now?"

"What's wrong?" He snatched his hat back up and plunked it down on his head. "Oh, nothing much, Paris, my love. The horses and mules are just gone. That's all."

Seven

Paris whirled around, and then around again. The horses and mules were definitely nowhere in sight. There was not even a sign of a hoofprint, thanks to last night's wind. The only animal still present was Pedro, who appeared from wherever he'd hidden during the storm. His bug eyes were watering, leaving dirty streaks down his white face. He didn't look happy.

Paris sank to the ground in despair.

"Your daddy taught you a lot of things, Paris," Brannigan said. "Why in the name of God didn't he teach you how to tie a knot?"

"I tied those animals good," she replied defensively. "And if my knots were so poor and yours so strong, why is your horse gone, too?"

Nate's jaw hardened belligerently. "It seems he broke a branch off the mesquite to go with the others."

Paris saw the branch, dangling by a thread. "Maybe you should have picked a bigger branch."

His glare burned with a threatening quality. "They could be hours ahead of us and traveling a sight faster. We may never catch up to them. I suggest we quit squabbling and get moving."

"And which way would that be?" she asked sardonically. "The dust has covered the tracks."

Brannigan's keen eyes took in the unending miles of cacti and brush and the ragged mountains upthrust from the desert floor. "They would have drifted with the wind," he said. "They wouldn't have gone into it. That way." He pointed and set off on a fast, angry walk.

Paris struggled to her feet, thinking that if he had been a gentleman he would have helped her up. She brushed at the seat of her trousers to dislodge some of the grit. "Aren't you going to take along some supplies? Maybe a little water?"

He stopped in mid-stride, obviously having been so angry he had actually forgotten the most important thing for survival. He stalked back. "We can't carry much, Paris. Hopefully, we'll have the horses by nightfall and can return here for the rest of the gear. As for the water, the canteens are only half-full and there's no water anywhere near here."

With quick determination, he sorted through the supplies, shoving some into their saddlebags, leaving others. Paris went behind him and took what she thought she would need and what she didn't want to leave behind. He rolled up a blanket for each of them and tied them into a thin bundle attached to a rope strap that would aid in carrying them over their shoulders. Then he gathered up his Winchester, slung one of his bandoliers over his shoulder, and set off.

Feeling numb and tired, her body aching all over from sleeping on the ground, Paris gathered up her saddlebags and blanket and followed, finding it difficult to keep up with Brannigan's long strides. Pedro stared after them, seemingly confused that he was being expected to walk. But apparently after deciding it was either that or abandonment, he followed.

"Aren't we even going to eat breakfast?" Paris asked.

"Sure, get yourself some jerky and dried fruit out of that pack," Nate replied from over his shoulder, never slowing his pace. "We don't have time to stop if we ever want to catch those horses."

Paris dug into the saddlebags while trying to keep up with him. The least he could do was stop for one minute. And it was already getting hot enough to bake bread. First you freeze out here and then you broil, she thought.

"Are we going to a fire or something, Brannigan?" she called after him. "Why wear out the soles of our boots in the first hour?"

He stopped long enough to give her a deep scowl from under the brim of his hat, but at least he waited for her to find some jerky in the saddlebags. When she had it, he also took a piece, then they were off again.

For all the discomfort of walking, Paris didn't want to think of what she would have done if she'd woken up alone and found the animals gone. She never thought she'd be so happy to see Brannigan, even if he was being extremely cranky at the moment. The only thing that bothered her more than walking in that heat was the terrible feeling they were heading northeast instead of northwest, which was taking them farther from Cerro Trueno. But that was the way the wind had been blowing the night before, Nate said, and that was the way the horses would have gone.

Dolefully, she bit into the jerky and began to chew. Her teeth ground over something crunchy. With a disappointed sigh, she realized that even the food had suffered from the dust storm. She ate anyway, after trying to brush off the jerky as much as possible. Her stomach convinced her to do so and her brain convinced her she would need the strength if she was going to make it through. Besides, maybe the more she suffered, the more beautiful the treasure would be when she found it. She focused on that thought, envisioning gold coins, ingots, jewels, solid gold statues, candlesticks. Yes, even gritty jerky would be worth such a splendid reward.

They wandered for hours. Perhaps it wasn't actually wandering; Brannigan seemed to have a course. But by late afternoon they were no closer to any sign of the horses and mules and much farther from Cerro Trueno. The heat was so intense Paris could no longer think straight. She could only numbly endure, follow in Brannigan's tracks, and watch his back to make sure it didn't get too far away. Pedro began to whine and lift his feet one at a time; the ground temperature was so hot it was burning the pads of his feet. But Paris didn't have the strength to carry him.

The only sign that Brannigan wasn't immune to the heat was when he removed his vest and tied it to his blanket. It was then she noticed the perspiration matting his shirt to his body. A while later, when he turned to survey the countryside, she noticed the shirt was unbuttoned down to the band of his pants, gaping open and revealing a matt of heavy black hair on his chest coiled in wet curls. While he searched the terrain with the binoculars, her eyes strayed to that matt of hair. Although her brain felt fried, there was enough still functioning for her to give feminine approval to what she saw.

But sometime during the course of her observation, she felt Nate's eyes on her, too. It only took a minute for her sluggish brain to realize that her own shirtwaist was clinging to her bosom the same way his shirt clung to his muscular torso. His heat-crazed perusal suddenly made her seek a diversion.

"Do you see anything yet?" she asked. "When the wind

stopped, the horses' tracks should have become noticeable."

"Yes, unless we're going in the wrong direction."

"I think you're lost," she said, mustering a spark of irritation. "Here I thought I hired a man who knew this country. I swear, Brannigan, I have half a notion not to pay you when—no *if*—we ever get back to Nogales."

"Don't do something foolish, Paris honey." His eyes pierced her, revealing his weariness and irritation at the situation. "I've been known to take my payment out of people's hides when they thought they could double-cross me. You've double-crossed me twice. You'd be wise not to do it a third time."

Those piercing eyes slid to her bosom again, and she wondered how he would make her pay. She already knew he wouldn't do something drastic like stake her in the sand or kill her. She was positive he wouldn't even physically abuse her in any way. So what was there left for him to do?

She licked her lips, remembering the musky, male taste of him. An anticipatory tingle rushed through her at the thought of facing that particular form of "punishment." As a matter of fact, she was tempted to initiate it if it meant finding a spot of shade to lie down on. Unfortunately, their course had taken them out on a flat and arid plain where nothing grew taller than a jackrabbit.

"You don't scare me, Brannigan." She looked across the plain, wondering how many miles it was to those distant mountains where there might be a spring and a scrubby tree. "As for making me pay, I think you already are. I can't believe you're dragging me all over this desert and not even going in the right direction. Maybe we just ought to go back to Alejandro's—that is, if you know where it is."

Nate opened his canteen and took a sip. Paris noticed his canteen was nearly empty, too, and they hadn't seen a sign of another water hole all day. It had been so long since rain that there wasn't even any hope of moisture in nature's *tinajas,* the cisternlike holes that often formed in rocks and collected rainwater.

"I've been trying to pick up the horses' tracks," he said, looking through his binoculars for the thousandth time. "And yes, I know where we are . . . approximately."

"Approximately?" She staggered back a step or two in shock, feeling the terrible heat in her face rise a degree or two. She was positive her skin was as red as her hair by now, for it surely felt aflame.

He retaliated to her anger. "Well, following you yesterday got me so far off course to start with, and then I had to stumble through that dust storm like a blind man down on my hands and knees, looking for a track that hadn't been filled in completely with sand, while fighting a splitting headache caused from *your* knock-out drops! Can you fault me for waking up and seeing mountains where I didn't remember seeing them yesterday! You can take some blame for this situation, too, Paris. No, on second thought, I think you can take *all* the blame. I'm seeing damned mirages. My feet feel like they're in a furnace; my boots have rubbed blisters through my soaking-wet socks. I'm sick of hardtack and jerky. And I don't like walking!" It was his turn to become livid.

Paris let his tirade run off like tepid water. "You know, Brannigan, if you would take me to Cerro Trueno, I'd give you half of the treasure."

His eyes suddenly looked as if they might explode from his face. She lifted a hand protectively to her throat, having the peculiar feeling he was going to strangle her.

"Are you suffering from heatstroke, Paris?"

"No, I'm fine. Half. What do you say?"

"Half is a sizable amount of nothing." He removed his hat and wiped at the sweat running profusely down the sides of his face.

"It's there. I feel it."

He shook his head disbelievingly and continued to mop at the sweat with his shirtsleeve. "How can you even think about lost treasure right now? What do you propose we do? *Walk* to Cerro Trueno?"

"No, of course not. We go there right after we find the horses. *If* you can find them, that is."

"If *we* can find them, you mean. Just get it out of your head, Paris. I don't even want to hear the word 'treasure' again. Do you understand?"

Seeing he was in no mood for negotiation, Paris dropped the subject and remained silent until later in the afternoon when she fell down and couldn't seem to get up no matter how she tried. "Let's rest, Brannigan," she pleaded, sprawled on her back with the sombrero over her face. "We need to. *I* need to."

"We can't afford to, Paris." He hauled her to her feet and put his shoulder under her arm, lifting her nearly off the ground, she was so short, but at least it kept her on her feet. "The horses will shade up in this heat," he continued, half dragging her now. But she finally asked him to let her go. Their body contact was only creating more heat and exerting more energy from both of them. He released her reluctantly, making sure she could stand. He made her drink more water. She noticed there were only a couple more swallows in the canteen.

"If we stop now, we'll never get any closer to them," he was saying. "We've got to move when they rest."

She nodded, too exhausted to argue. "Then lead on. Do you know where you're going yet?"

"I'm following the horses' tracks."

"Tracks?" The slump went out of her back. "Why didn't you tell me you'd found them?"

"I thought I did."

"No, you didn't."

"Well, I'm sorry. I found tracks a while back. Are you happy now?"

She nodded.

They followed the tracks until it got too dark. By then they had reached another group of mountains. The foliage was thicker, taller, and they collapsed beneath a paloverde and ignored the brittlebush jabbing them in the face. Paris longed for nothing more than a downpour of rain, but the darkening sky contained only a lone hawk, drifting on an undetectable air current and uttering a single raspy cry to the silence below him.

Nate wanted to continue when the moon came up, but gauging from the time it had come up the previous nights, it would be hours. In the end, he decided it would be foolish. They were both exhausted and needed to rest. They had only a little water left and he hoped the horses would lead them to a spring the next day.

"God, that feels good," Paris said, lying next to him.

"Are you hallucinating?"

"No. The sand feels good. I didn't know I was so tired. The pain in my back is a glorious sort of pain."

He turned his head to look at her. She was sprawled on her back ungracefully again, as dirty as he knew he was. But she was still beautiful. Even in his present condition he felt a stirring of desire at the sight of her breasts thrusting up through the thin cotton shirtwaist clinging to her.

Her trousers were filthy from all the times she'd fallen, but they still molded too perfectly to her small, curvaceous hips.

"You're hallucinating."

"No, don't you know how your body hurts in a good sort of way when it's so tired you don't think you can go another minute and you finally, *finally*, get to lie down?"

He licked dry, cracked lips. "Yeah, I guess I know what you mean. We'll find the horses tomorrow, Paris."

"We'd better, or else we'd better find Alejandro's."

It was a moment before he spoke. "About Alejandro's . . ."

She turned her head on the sand and stared at him. He wanted to hide from her knowing scrutiny. Suddenly she was up and pummeling his chest. He grabbed her wrists to fend her off, surprised she had that much strength left in her. He surely didn't.

"You miserable bastard!" she cried. "You *are* lost, aren't you?"

He was as weak as a kitten, but he found one last reserve of strength and managed to topple her. He laid on her with his full weight because he was too exhausted to hold himself up. His forehead rested just above her shoulder in the sand, his cheek lay hot against hers. "Just a little."

He thought she was going to cry, but no tears came, and he decided there was probably not enough moisture or energy left in her body to produce them. She relaxed beneath him and put an arm around him, patting him on the back in a manner that almost felt affectionate.

"Well, don't worry, Nate," she mumbled against his stubbled cheek. "We'll get straightened out here just as soon as we get some water and sleep."

A few minutes later, when there was no more movement

from her, Nate lifted his head and saw that she'd fallen asleep. He rolled off her and onto his back on the ground. At least it had cooled off. It would be much better to travel at night, if only they could get enough starlight and moonlight to find the tracks in the dark. Maybe he'd let her sleep for a while and then when the moon came up, they'd head off again. Yes, that's what he would do. He'd just get a little sleep first . . .

The sun, poised just under the horizon, cast a golden haze across the desert, making it look temporarily rejuvenated from the scorching heat of the day before. A raven winged its jet black body down to a giant saguaro and watched the two strange interlopers to his land. They were a curious sight but did not appear to be threatening. After a time he lost interest in their motionless forms. Lifting his head, he cawed raucously to the desert, waking its creatures, one and all.

Nate sat up with a start. "Damn," he said. He'd slept the whole night. Casting an angry eye at the noisy raven perched just overhead, he scooped his hat up from the ground and plunked it onto his head. He glanced over at Paris and was surprised she could sleep through the bird's racket. But as tired as she was, he'd let her sleep while he got his bearings. Morning was the best time for that, when the sun's position could be accurately gauged.

With binoculars in hand, he hurried up the side of a mesa to a position high enough that he could see what was around him. The first rays of the sun hit him full in the face when he reached the top, and he finally knew which direction was which. He mapped it all in his mind, recognized landmarks that had looked alien the day before, and repositioned things with a clear head and a new perspective. They were far north of where they should've been. He had hoped the horses would lead them back to Alejandro's, but they hadn't. Cerro Trueno was nowhere in sight, still hidden behind the mountains serrating the western horizon. It was farther away than ever.

Lifting the binoculars, he took in every inch of the country. It was then that he saw, and recognized, the green band of mesquite that hid water. If he had his bearings straight, it had to be Angel Springs, a place he had camped often when on the trail of outlaws. It was about a mile distant, and he couldn't see the horses but was sure they were there or grazing nearby.

He hurried back to Paris and gently shook her awake. Sleepy-eyed but looking incredibly sexy, she sat up, pushing her wild mass of hair away from her face.

"Paris, get up," he said with encouragement in his voice. "There's water about a mile from here."

"Water! Oh!"

He took her by the arm and helped her to her feet. Quickly, without wasted words, they gathered their belongings and started around the mesa toward the springs. Because they were so anxious to get there, it seemed farther than a mile. Upon topping the last small hill before reaching their destination, Nate suddenly signaled Paris to be quiet. Almost simultaneously he yanked her to the ground next to him, wedging them between two teddy-bear cholla and a cluster of prickly pear.

"What?" she whispered, moving closer to avoid the barb of a cholla in her back. "What's wrong?"

"Sh-h-h." Nate inched backward down the hill on his belly, pulling Paris with him.

"What is going—"

His hand clamped over her mouth; his blue eyes held a warning she knew she'd better heed. "Indians," he whispered. "Probably Apaches, and they've got our horses and mules."

Paris's heart began to pound viciously. She, too, looked for something to hide in or under. There was nothing, not even a big cactus. "What are we going to do now?"

"I don't know, but get Pedro before he smells them. And keep him quiet."

Paris quickly obeyed, scooping the dog up and holding his mouth gently closed. He did not seem aware of the Indians or the horses. Maybe he was simply too tired of the whole ordeal to care. Or maybe his nose was too clogged with dust and his throat too dry to make a squeak.

"We could try to steal the horses back," Nate was saying, "but we'd have to wait until dark. And I don't think, from the time of day it is, that they'll be staying here that long. My guess is they camped here last night and will be moving on."

"How many of them are there?"

"I only caught a glimpse but four, maybe five. Renegades, probably, and that's the worst kind."

They remained stretched out on the sand, side by side, behind the hill, each trying to think of a way to get the horses and mules back without having to engage in battle. The very least they could do was wait until the Indians left and hope they went in the opposite direction. They would walk away alive, but how long could they stay alive? Without the horses, they would be able to go only a few more days. Nate was at least confident that he could figure out where they were and get back to Alejandro's. He also knew there was no more water before then. What they could carry wouldn't be enough, traveling on foot the way they were. But both silently knew that death by thirst was preferable than death at the hands of the Apaches.

"How well can you handle that Peacemaker?" Nate whispered while quietly slipping additional cartridges into his Winchester until it was full.

"Pretty good," Paris replied confidently.

"Ever killed anybody?"

"No."

"Well, get ready. You may have to. And Paris . . ." He hesitated, looking deeply and seriously into her eyes. "If they find us, we'll fight our damndest, but if it looks like we're going to be taken captive . . . you won't want them to take you alive."

She stared at him with frightened eyes. Even though she'd heard of women who'd committed suicide in the face of captivity, she had never dreamed she would be faced with it herself. "And what about you?" The words came out as a defensive croak. "I've heard what Apaches do to men. Am I the only one who's supposed to shoot myself? That hardly sounds fair."

"They'll try to kill me first when they realize it's just the two of us. They'll want to keep you alive."

She tried to swallow but her dry, swollen tongue stuck to the roof of her mouth. She'd give nothing more than to have a drink of that water those renegades were hogging. She could hear them, laughing and carrying on in a language she didn't understand. It wasn't right that they could bully people the way they did and force women to shoot themselves. This desert was big enough for everyone who was foolish enough to be out on it.

"Aren't Indians superstitious, Nate?" she asked, an idea forming in her mind.

"I think so. At least that's what I've heard," he replied absently, stuffing bullets into his Colt.

"And they're particularly afraid of crazy people, aren't they? Afraid the evil spirits will somehow harm them?"

Sudden wariness darkened his eyes. "That's what I've heard. But who knows about Apaches? You're not getting some stupid idea, are you?"

"Yes . . . no. Well, maybe."

"Damn it, Paris."

"It might work, Nate," she rushed on. "If they start coming at us, how fast could you shoot all five of them?"

"As fast as I can pump bullets into the firing chamber and pull the trigger."

"Yes, if none of them fires back. How fast could you shoot them if they did?"

"The same, only I'd be less likely to kill them all."

"All right, then. I'll be the decoy and you come to my rescue."

"Christ. You're not serious?"

Paris released Pedro and commanded him in a stern whisper to sit. He did better, he stretched out on his stomach and acted as if all he wanted was sleep and water. She then rolled to her back and pulled her shirtwaist out of her trousers. First, she rolled up the long sleeves, then unbuttoned it and rebuttoned it, mismatching the buttons and holes so they were out of alignment. She tucked her daddy's Peacemaker into her trousers beneath the tails of the blouse. "Just in case I have to shoot myself," she explained as Nate watched her with an expression of confusion and disbelief. She removed her sombrero and let the flaming red tresses of her hair cascade around her small freckled face like a lion's ruff. She rummaged to the bottom of her saddlebags and found the tin of rouge. Sparing none, she spread it lavishly over her hands, arms, and face.

Finally, she turned to Nate with a satisfied grin on her face. "Do I look crazy?"

"I think you are."

"I'm serious."

"So am I. Listen, Paris, I don't like what you've got in your pretty little head."

She flashed a concerned look. "Pretty? I don't want to look pretty, Nate. I want to look ugly and insane."

"You're not going to do this. I won't let you. We'll just wait and see if they go the other direction."

"And if they don't?"

"Then when they see us we'll open fire. Between the two of us we ought to be able to kill all five before they can kill us."

Considering the matter settled, Nate scooted on his stomach back to the top of the hill, removing his hat and carefully peeking over the top to see what the Apaches were doing. "We'll just sit tight and—"

From around the hill came Paris, staggering, gesticulating, and speaking to the sky in what sounded like some of the mumbo-jumbo from Shakespeare he'd had to read when he was in school. All he could do was stare—he and the Indians both. Then, behind her came Pedro, not seeing the Indians at first. When he did, he acted as if he'd seen ghosts and started yapping to the top of his lungs. Paris walked on, as if she didn't even hear him, or know he was with her for that matter.

Swearing under his breath, Nate pumped a bullet into the Winchester's firing chamber and put the Indians in his sights. Paris's voice rang out crystal clear through the calm morning with true conviction as if she were an actress speaking to an audience.

"Out, damned spot! out, I say! One: two: why, then 'tis time to do't. Hell is murky! Yet who would have thought the old man to have had so much blood in him?"

She seemed not to see the Indians and walked away from them, right through the water and toward the distant hills, trudging along, all the while talking and waving her arms in accordance to the expression of her words.

The Apache braves slowly came to their feet, dumbfounded by her presence and her apparent insanity. They didn't seem to know what to do, save stare at her, while she tried to rub the blood-red rouge from her hands and face.

"What, will these hands ne'er be clean? . . . . All the perfumes of Arabia will not sweeten this little hand. Oh! oh! oh!"

The braves began backing toward their ponies, fear enlarging their black eyes to the size of a sidewinder's horned head. They began exchanging words, but Paris seemed to not even see them or hear them. She continued, moving ever northward, giving her soliloquy to the sky.

"Wash your hands, put on your nightgown, look not so pale. . . . To bed, to bed: there's knocking at the gate: come, come, come, come, give me your hand: what's done cannot be undone: to bed, to bed, to bed."

Suddenly they ran. They leaped on their ponies and fled to the east, never looking back. As good fortune would have it, they didn't bother with the stolen animals they had tethered on a long lead line a distance from the water. Their obvious objective was to get as far away as possible from the crazy white woman in trousers.

When all that was left of them was a cloud of gray dust, Nate scrambled from cover. Paris had already hurried to the horses, grabbing the tether line to ensure that they wouldn't try breaking it and running after the Indian ponies.

Nate stalked over to her and yanked her around. "That was the stupidest damn thing I've ever seen, Paris McKenna! You could have gotten an arrow or a bullet in your back, and there was no guarantee they wouldn't have taken the horses! And what if they'd decided to come after you and see if you were really crazy?"

She clung to him, visibly shaking now that it was over. Her face was as white as a ghost's in the spots that weren't streaked with rouge. "They wouldn't have come after me because they greatly fear crazy people. From what I've heard, they won't go near them."

"From what you've heard? You staked your life on rumors?"

"I took a chance, Nate, but I had confidence that you were there to back me up." She looked up at him for approval and understanding, even forgiveness. "I believed you would open fire and come to my rescue. Like a knight in shining armor."

His jaw clenched and he released her so abruptly that she almost lost her balance. "Well, I'm not a damn knight, Paris," he ground out in his most gravelly voice. "Don't do something stupid like that again. I won't have another woman's death on my conscience."

He stalked off and Paris didn't try to catch up. Something told her not to question that statement. But whoever the woman had been, Paris knew she must have meant a lot to the bounty hunter.

Eight

Tully Thatcher strode up to the cherry wood bar of the noisy Bird Cage Theatre and demanded whiskey. The slick-haired, red-coated bartender poured him the house's best and stood patiently until he had flung it down his throat. The bartender refilled the shot glass three times before he spoke.

"You must have come to see Miss Crabtree's performance tonight, Mr. Thatcher. From the looks of this place, I daresay every man in town is here."

Tully, feeling more in control now that he'd had his whiskey, turned to the stage at the end of the long, rectangular gambling casino and dance hall. Across scores of gaming tables, over a hundred heads, and through a curtain of smoke, he watched the nightly production of the French can-can girls. They performed their dance to the lively music of the grand piano nestled in the orchestra pit at the base of the stage.

Feeling the whiskey mellow him out, Tully finally replied, "Yeah, I wouldn't want to miss her performance." He dug into the pocket of his brocade vest, found some coins, and tossed a few on the bar. "I'll keep the bottle."

The bartender nodded and went on to another customer. Tully wound his way through the crowd to the narrow set of stairs against the far wall. Passing beneath the bullet-marred painting of Fatima, he took the stairs to the "bird cage" he'd rented for the evening. The cage, or crib compartment, like thirteen others on both sides of the room, looked out over the casino below. Lined with red velvet draperies, they offered an excellent view of the gaming, but particularly the stage, and they came equipped with a girl to bring drinks and to make sure the male occupant's every need and request was fulfilled. The curtains could be pulled for privacy if the need became of a nature too intimate for the eyes in the cages across the room. Normally the cages rented for twenty-five dollars a night, but because Lotta Crabtree was going to perform, Tully had had to pay twice that.

Tully's girl for the night was a pretty dark-haired child, who couldn't have been more than seventeen. But he'd had her before and she was an expert at pleasing the customer.

"Tully, love," she smiled as she entered the cage. "You haven't been here for a long time. I was beginning to think you didn't like me anymore." She immediately began massaging his shoulders, easing the tension she inherently knew was there.

He watched the can-can girls with only minimal interest, except the short one with the red hair, who reminded him too much of Paris. "Well, Vevila," he said, "a man would be foolish to give all his money to the competition, wouldn't he? I've given more than my share just to see Miss Crabtree tonight."

Vevila found a particularly tight muscle along his neck and pressed her magic fingers deeply around it. "Of course, but you could always come by my house for a visit."

The invitation barely piqued Tully's interest. He could

have any woman in this place as his mistress, or his wife—he knew he had the looks that turned a woman's head—but the one woman he wanted had side-stepped him like she would a plague-ridden rat from the sewers of London. He'd offered her a life of luxury as his mistress and she'd preferred dancing with rowdy cowboys and miners. He'd thought he could pressure her into his bed by threatening her job security, but all she had done was run out on him, leaving him looking like a fool in front of the whole of Tombstone. And he hadn't even been able to trace where she'd gone because she hadn't bought a stage ticket. She'd apparently left on Blackjack's horse, vanishing from the face of the earth.

Vevila began to nuzzle Tully's neck. He let her experienced hands and lips do their work, and, after a time, she drew the red velvet curtains and dropped to her knees in front of him, releasing his extended organ from his trousers. He closed his eyes and let her do her work. She was so efficient that he was finished in plenty of time for Miss Crabtree's performance.

Three hours later, Tully stepped out of the Bird Cage Theatre into the coolness of the desert night and made his way back to the Silver Slipper. He knew he wouldn't be able to sleep, and he wasn't even going to try. He'd met an old friend who'd talked him into joining the house poker game at the Bird Cage, but he needed a thousand dollars to ante in.

In his office, he went to his safe, twirled through the combination, and swung back the heavy metal door. It wasn't until he'd counted out the thousand, closed the safe, and started for the door, that his liquored mind realized something was missing in the safe.

The map.

He had last placed it on top of everything because it was so old he hadn't wanted any damage to come to it until he had the opportunity to make use of it. Hurrying back to the safe, he opened it a second time. His search started slowly and carefully. But soon, in a growing rage, he had everything in the safe torn out and scattered on the hardwood floor. The map was gone. But how? Nobody knew the combination but him.

He sat back on his heels and glanced over at the brocade settee, remembering. He had had Paris in the palm of his hand that last night he'd seen her. He had been sure she would come to his bed because he had given her no other choice. Actually she'd had three choices: she could keep her job and start seeing the male customers upstairs like all his girls eventually did; she could live the life of luxury as his mistress; or, if she didn't want to do either of those, she could be out on the street looking for another job. The Silver Slipper was the only dance hall in town that would hire girls just to dance. Even then it was done under the assumption that sooner or later the girls would "come around" and start bringing some real money to the establishment by giving the men some real entertainment in the upstairs rooms.

He ran an angry hand through his jet black hair. He had been sitting on the settee, waiting for her to fix him a drink. The last thing he remembered from that night was gazing into her smiling face as she handed him the drink. As was his fashion, he'd tossed the entire contents of the glass down his throat, realizing too late that she'd drugged it. When he'd opened his eyes again, Paris was gone, and his head had felt like there was someone hammering inside it.

Having a hunch now, he dropped to his knees in the center of the papers strewn on the floor. He sought and found the envelope that had contained her wages for a month. He'd withheld her wages, even dangling them in front of her that night as added incentive because he knew she was about to lose her room at Belfair's Boarding House for back rent. Old Lady Belfair hadn't wanted to make Paris leave. She had taken pity on her from the very beginning because she'd known Paris wasn't a bad girl, even if she had been forced to go to work at the Silver Slipper. But sooner or later, as Tully had expected, Mrs. Belfair had looked to paying customers.

Tully had done it all in an effort to force Paris to come to him. But she had somehow found out the safe's combination and taken her money and the map that had belonged to her father. Where she'd gotten the sleeping potion he didn't know, but anything could be had in this town. And now he knew where she'd gone.

A slow smiled crossed Tully's face, and he meticulously replaced his valuables in the safe. He was no longer interested in the poker game at the Bird Cage. He had unexpectedly found the incentive to take a few weeks off work; his manager could keep the Silver Slipper running. He had a map to find. And a redheaded woman who was going to pay dearly for what she'd done.

Nate filled the canteens as soon as the water had cleared again, all the while keeping his eyes to the horizon in case the Apaches should return to steal back the horses and mules. Afraid they might circle around the hill where he and Paris had hidden, he tied Pedro to a bush to stand guard. The little pest wasn't happy about it and snapped and growled at him, but with Paris's crooning voice and soft hands on his nearly hairless body, he had given in to his fate, collapsing at last beneath a creosote bush and panting from the heat. Nate designated one of the tin cups for him and filled it with fresh spring water. The dog settled down grudgingly to his task, casting longing eyes toward the rest of the camp near the spring. But the dog would alert them to danger.

They were both reluctant to leave the spring after the ordeal they'd been through, so they agreed to spend one day resting and taking the time to cook a decent meal. The latter came about in the form of a sidewinder crawling through camp. Paris wasn't sure she wanted to eat snake meat but Nate assured her it was quite tasty. She finally relented because the way her stomach was twisting and rumbling she was sure her large intestines had resorted to eating her smaller ones.

While Nate cooked the snake over a campfire, Paris bathed in the spring and tried to scrub the rouge off her face and hands. Try as she might, though, her skin remained tinged, giving her the appearance of a sunburn. During it all, Nate dutifully kept his back turned, or at least it was turned whenever she happened to look in his direction.

She finally stepped from the spring feeling refreshed from their ordeal. She had no towel to dry with but brushed the water off with her hands; the sun was quick to dry the remainder. In order for her to wash her trousers, as well as her shirtwaist and underthings, Nate had offered her the use of his spare shirt. Even though she had brought along her extra shirtwaist, it was hardly sufficient to cover her decently, while Nate's shirt dropped nearly to her knees. So she buttoned it up, rolled up the sleeves, draped her clothes on bushes to dry, then settled on a rock to brush out her damp hair. She was conscious of her lower legs being exposed and considered covering them with a blanket, but in the end she decided it was much too hot for modesty.

After a time, she felt Nate's enigmatic eyes following the movement of the brush, and occasionally lowering to her bare legs. Oddly enough, instead of feeling embarrassed, she simply wondered if he found them attractive. And she wondered if he was still angry with her. Emotions tangled inside her; weariness, relief, mellowness. She wanted to be held and comforted by him, but her last escapade had tossed another row of bricks on the rapidly growing wall between them. It troubled her for some obscure reason, and she would have liked nothing better than for that barrier to be gone.

"I can watch the . . . snake," she offered, deciding it was time to break the spell of his unreadable eyes and to try and make amends. "That is, if you want to take your turn in the spring."

He slowly unwound his tall, lean body and stepped over the fire, handing her the fork. "I'd like nothing better. Just keep turning it so it won't burn."

She decided he must not have felt the same way she had at all, nor thought the same thoughts, for he merely turned toward the spring, paying her no more mind than he would have Pedro.

She watched him strip from his shirt, enjoying the play of the sunlight over his broad shoulders and back. When he started to remove his pants she forced herself to look to the pan of frying snake fillets. All the while he bathed she grew more angry. He hadn't said anything more than necessary to her since she'd run the Indians off. Annoyance surged inside her. If it hadn't been for her bravery they would more than likely still be afoot.

He returned fifteen minutes later, bare-chested but with clean pants. His wet hair was slicked back from his face. Without a hat, his rugged handsomeness was clearly defined by the bright white light of the sun, by the plane and angles of his face, by the stern set to his jaw.

They ate in silence and Paris decided the meat wasn't bad if she tried not to think too seriously about what it was. She gave some of it to Pedro, after removing the bones. When she returned to camp, Nate was on his blanket, his back to the sun and to her. He heard her, and without turning over, said, "Let's take a nap. It'll do us both good."

She went to her own blanket, having no desire to sleep. It was an odd thing for Nate to want to do, too, since he always claimed to detest siestas. His actions seemed to make it quite clear now that he was doing his utmost to avoid her, and suddenly she'd had enough of his cold shoulder.

"If something is bothering you, Brannigan, I wish you'd just say what it is. You're being an unpleasant pain in the derriere."

Yanking aside a paloverde branch that draped itself between them, he came up off his blanket so swiftly it startled her. On his knees, he faced her. By the sparks in his eyes, she realized he'd been on a fuse as short as hers.

"And you're not a pain in the butt, I suppose?" he snapped. "You could have gotten killed today. It was a stupid thing you did."

She sat up, too, wanting to step over the fire and tell

him to put up his fists if he had an inclination to fight, but she knew she'd lose a battle of that nature before it even began. Her only recourse then was her tongue, which at this time seemed inadequate to express the anger she felt.

"If it hadn't been for me, we would have sat there and watched those Indians ride off with our horses. Besides, what do you care if I would have gotten myself killed anyway? I've caused you nothing but trouble, to listen to you talk. I should think you would have been more than relieved to have me out of the way so you could go back to Nogales and rot in that stinking cantina."

"There's just one minor thing you're forgetting, Paris honey. With you dead, I wouldn't be able to collect the two hundred dollars you owe me. I need to get something out of this stupid wild goose chase you've had me on."

"You've forgotten one minor little thing, too," she immediately countered. "I don't intend on paying you the full two hundred since you haven't completed the job. But I might have known your first and only concern would be money. After all, that's why you're a bounty hunter."

"That's right, and don't forget it. Why else would I have come out here? Not for the scenery, or the company, that's for sure." He plopped himself back down on his bedroll, giving her his back. "And you'd better cover up your legs. You'll wake up with insect bites all over them."

She stared at his back. He'd dismissed her as easily as that. But at the memory of his hurtful words—that he hadn't come out here for the company—something inside Paris twisted painfully, as if he'd put a knife in her heart and turned it. Why did it hurt so much that he didn't like her? Did he just want to get back to those dark-haired border beauties in Nogales?

She returned to her bedroll, closed her eyes, and tried to sleep, but even though her blankets were in the shade, the heat of the sun and the undulating heat of her temper blocked all hope of relaxation. When she heard Nate's steady breathing, indicating he had easily fallen to sleep, it made her just that much more angry. She actually had to fight the unexpected urge to cry. She was beginning to think it wasn't the curse at all that was making him so determined to get back to Nogales, but rather his dislike for her.

She sat up again and stared at his motionless body. Suddenly, in a need to vent her anger, she picked up a pebble the size of a pea and threw it across the fire, hitting him square between the shoulder blades. His only reaction was a minor twitch and a temporary disruption in his breathing pattern. He was so content she suspected he would start snoring any second.

"Some protection you are," she mumbled. "Those Apaches could sneak in here and have your scalp and you'd wake up in the morning and wonder why the top of your head was cold."

She curled up on her side again, pulling her Peacemaker closer. Maybe it wasn't as pleasant as muscle, but it was a lot more reliable.

Nate wasn't sure what brought him awake. It wasn't a noise; it was more a feeling that he was being watched from behind. His senses leaped to alertness and all traces of sleep vanished. He knew it wasn't Paris because he could hear her breathing heavily a few feet away, deep in sleep. But neither could he hear the faintest footstep of man or beast. Yet, something was there. Had the Apaches returned? And, if they had, why hadn't Pedro given a warning?

In one swift, sure, and calculated movement, he rolled to his back, his gun leaping from its holster and into his hand in that same instant as if by magic, ready to fire. But at the end of the barrel stood, not an Apache, but a tall man in a long black, flowing robe, calmly staring at him. A priest.

"There is no reason to be alarmed, my son," the priest said in a low voice, heavy with a Spanish accent. "I am Father Castañeda, and I was only passing by on my way to my mission."

Nate, temporarily frozen in his half-prone, half-sitting position, finally curled his body to a full sitting position and then came to his feet. He hated to be suspicious, but it was the nature of his profession. The priest was standing with his arms folded, hands out of sight inside the immense, loose sleeves of his black robe. Nate had no way of knowing if the priest was really a priest or if he was an impostor with a concealed weapon. How was Nate to know this handsome, distinguished fellow of sixty-five or so wasn't one of Paris's friends? Maybe he was that Tully guy she'd mentioned, although she had made Tully sound as if he resembled a rat snake and this man was considerably better looking.

"You can put your gun away," the priest said. "I do not have a weapon." He removed his hands from the robe and held them up for Nate to see, then returned them to their former position.

Feeling as if he'd just had his mind read, Nate reluctantly put his gun back in its holster. Just because the priest wasn't carrying a gun didn't mean he might not have some accomplices somewhere, waiting in ambush.

Nate glanced over at Pedro to gauge his reaction to their afternoon visitor. The stupid little dog was taking a siesta, too, curled into a tight ball with his head tucked nearly beneath his back leg.

Father Castañeda followed the direction of Nate's interest. Smiling congenially, he said, "He is not a very good watch dog, is he? But then I think he is a good companion for the woman."

Nate shifted uneasily, wondering how the priest inherently knew that the dog was Paris's friend, not his. He stepped around the fire which was nothing but coals now. He placed a hand on Paris's shoulder, shaking her slightly and speaking her name until she came awake slowly, groggily. But when she saw the priest her sleep cleared quickly and she, too, was on her feet in an instant, grabbing up the blanket with which to cover her legs.

"We have a visitor, Paris," Nate said unnecessarily. "Father Castañeda."

Paris's first thought was that by some strange stroke of ill luck she'd been caught impersonating a nun and the church had sent an official seeking the proper reparation for her heinous misdeed. But the man smiled warmly at her, saying, "I am sorry to wake you, *señorita*. One never likes to have a siesta interrupted. I debated whether to go on when I saw you both here, but it is hot and the water at this spring is always cool."

Paris was suddenly struck with a chord of hope. "You mean you have a mission nearby?"

"Sí," he replied. "It is not far. Just through those mountains to the north. It is small and old but serves the Yaqui and Papago Indians of this region."

Excitement filled Paris. "And what is the name of your mission, Father?"

"Sister Mary of the Sacred Heart, Sister."

Paris blanched. Her eyes locked with his. Had he known what she'd done? Known she'd used that very name as the fictitious church she herself had come from? Or was this just a terrible coincidence? And why had he called her Sister? She was no longer wearing the habit. She searched his face and eyes for answers. To her relief, there was nothing in the deep blue pools to indicate that he had knowledge of her treachery. Unless he was simply very good at concealing everything on his mind.

"What brings the two of you so far from the comforts of civilization? A journey, perhaps, to Mexico or California?" The padre's smile remained forever constant, forever tranquil.

Paris wished Nate would give the response, but when she glanced up at him, she realized he was waiting for her to speak. "We were looking for something we'd heard was out here," she replied evasively.

The priest's smile deepened and understanding warmed his eyes even more. "I suspected as much. It is about the only reason I see white people on this desert. They come looking for lost gold mines or even silver mines. Some even come looking for lost treasure or the elusive mission of Santa Isabel that has been rumored to be here."

He looked dreamily out across the mountains as if he would truly like to see it himself. Then he turned his eyes back to them. There was disappointment in them, but there was also indisputable wisdom. "But Santa Isabel does not exist nor has it ever. It is only an old tale that has grown very large in size. I hope you have not come here hoping to find it."

His perceptive eyes shifted from Nate to Paris as he waited for their response. When neither said anything, he acknowledged their silence as a positive response. Sadness darkened the tranquility in his eyes. He shook his head slightly, as if deeply regretful. "Searching for it will only bring you death, as it has many others before you. Go home, my children, go home. And now, I must heed my own advice. God be with you. *Adios.*"

"But won't you stay for . . . for something to eat?" Paris quickly asked, hoping to detain him longer so she could get more information from him.

He smiled, seeming to know her intentions. "No, *señorita.* I am not hungry, but *gracias.* You are most kind."

Paris and Nate stared after him as he worked his way patiently and steadily toward the north. They were both perplexed by his strange visit.

"His mission must not be too far away," Paris said. "He didn't even get a drink of water."

"No, and he wasn't carrying any canteens or water flasks either. He must have a stomach like a camel."

"I wonder why Pedro didn't bark at him."

Both Paris and Nate turned their attention from the priest to the dog. He was sitting up now, watching them. When he saw he had their attention he began to whine and paw at the thin cord around his neck.

"Look at him," Nate said disgustedly. "He always acts like he wants to eat me alive whenever he sets eyes on me, and those Apaches scared five years off his life. Yet he doesn't even act as if he can see that padre."

"Maybe he recognizes a man of the cloth," Paris teased. But the dog couldn't hold her attention. Her curiosity was too great about their afternoon visitor, and she had too many questions still popping into her head about the padre and his mission. She hated to say it of a man of God, but for some reason she didn't feel as if he'd been completely honest. She had the feeling he was trying to get them to go back, to not look for the mission. Did that mean they were getting close?

She turned again to study his departure, only to find to her amazement that he was gone. The sun streaked white hot over the desert floor, leaving no shadows on the land that one could hide in. There was no sign of the black-robed priest.

"That's odd," she said. "He was there just a second ago."

Nate turned to the north again, too, but neither did he see any sign of the man. The mountains were too distant for the padre to have reached them so quickly. But the desert was always deceptive and could have temporarily swallowed him in a low spot. They waited and watched for him to reappear. Minutes ticked by but there was no further sign of him. It was as if he had been part of a mirage or a dream they'd shared, vanishing back into their imaginations.

Nate finally turned to the fire to add more sticks to the coals and began to make coffee.

"Would Alejandro know if there was a mission out here?" Paris asked, still keeping an eye out for any sign of the mysterious priest.

Nate shrugged as he filled the coffee pot with fresh, cool water from the spring. "Probably, but I doubt he'd come this far to attend services."

"The Indians around here must. You've been here before. Have you ever seen anything?"

"Yes, I've been here, but not in every nook and cranny of every group of mountains. It's a big country, Paris. I don't think one man could see it all if he did nothing but spend his entire life exploring it."

Paris felt a growing concern inside her, a temptation if you will, a nagging thought that began to speak louder and louder.

"I think he's hiding something."

Nate had felt the same thing but hadn't wanted to accuse a priest of deception. "Why should he?"

"It's obvious," Paris continued. "He knows where Santa Isabel is and he's hoarding the treasure for himself. He doesn't want us to find it. I'll bet you if we followed his tracks, they'd take us right to the mission."

The fire was going well now and Nate placed the coffee pot on a rock next to the flames. "Maybe so, Paris, but I already told you I'm going back to Alejandro's, and unless you want to start off across that desert again by yourself, so are you. I would hope that by now you've learned your lesson."

"You're still afraid of that stupid curse, aren't you?"

He turned his back to her. "I've dealt with some deadly things, Paris, but they were always things I've understood. If Alejandro says we should leave it alone, then I think we should. I saw the fear in his eyes, and he isn't afraid of much of anything."

"Yes, he is," she said defiantly. "He's afraid of life or he wouldn't be living out in this desert alone."

Nate gave her a hard look. "He has some things he has to sort out, Paris. He lost our mother, his wife, and a son a few years back by Apaches. He just isn't ready to pick up where he left off."

Paris's thoughts were for a moment of the handsome Alejandro, and she regretted her judgmental comment. "There's so much I don't know about him . . . or you." She paused giving him the opportunity to explain further because she truly would have liked to know about their pasts and what they had done before embarking on the unorthodox lives they now led. She wanted to know if Nate had had a wife, a child. Had they, too, been killed?

But Nate looked away, seeming to know what she was waiting for, and he clearly declined to discuss his personal life. It was just one more brick going up between them. He was the one who had put it there this time. He would have to be the one to take it down.

"I'll bet that priest knew something about Santa Isabel and was probably afraid of the curse like everybody else around here," she continued, dropping to her knees next to him. "I think we're getting close to something here and we need to follow him. Just give me a couple more days, and then if we come up against a dead end, I won't ask you to help me look any longer."

Nate met her hopeful, gray eyes, then his gaze strayed to her slender bare legs, and suddenly he didn't care about anything but pulling her into his arms and kissing her senseless. Maybe he could make her forget her precious treasure and think of him as someone besides an unsavory traveling companion with whom she had to contend.

"What will you do? Look by yourself?"

"Of course not. I wouldn't come out here alone again."

"Don't give me that, Paris. You won't quit as long as you have any hope that the mission's out here."

She lifted her chin defiantly. "You don't seem to understand how badly I need that treasure to set my life straight, to get set up so I can support myself. Men don't understand the plight of women. You can find work. You can go out and kill somebody and collect reward money."

He rose to his feet, her words obviously not sitting well with him. "I don't kill anybody if I don't have to, Paris. I'm not a damned murderer."

She rose slowly, tears forming in her eyes. "Well, I have my daddy's gun. I guess I could become a bounty hunter, too."

He grabbed her wrist and pulled her to him. This time her breasts touched his chest, making his heart ache and throb with a growing need. "Don't even think it."

"Why not!"

"Because it's too dangerous. Jesus, Paris, you barely clear five foot. How do you think you could apprehend a criminal as big as me? He'd just laugh in your face and do this."

He crushed her against his chest, taking her lips in a hot, passionate kiss that did little to appease the growing hunger he had for her. But he released her as suddenly as he'd taken her, turning away from her, angry with himself for the peculiar feelings he was having toward her. He'd never held a woman in his arms who had felt so right, who had charged the primitive need to possess and protect and to fight all men who might try to win her. He was beginning to believe her claim to virginity. He was beginning to fear that a woman like her could never love a man like him, a man who had no family of his own, who didn't even know whose blood ran in his veins, who had seen too much and done too much and who could barely remember innocence, his own or anyone else's. He didn't want to tell her about himself for fear her reaction would be what he had experienced from women before. It didn't matter that he'd been raised by the powerful and respected Escalantes; he could not claim their blood or their name. And women wanted the name.

He remembered well all the young girls who had flocked around Alejandro, wanting to be his bride. They had wanted it not only because Alejandro had been very handsome but because they had sought his status, wanting it to be theirs. They had all virtually ignored Nate, beyond a few lively romps in the loft, because he had no bloodline that would make them rich and respected. He had not been jealous of Alejandro, but he had come to have the same cavalier opinion of himself as the young girls had. And he had lived the life of a man they would bed but not wed. Time never changed some things, though, and he didn't like that role any better now than he ever had.

"What would you do then, Paris?" he asked, turning back to her. "Tell me."

He saw the desperate thoughts wheeling through her head like thrushes caught in a wind storm. She was probably thinking she'd have to go back to Tombstone and Tully Thatcher again. He didn't know if she was lying about being a virgin, but he didn't want her to have to go to another man for survival. No woman should be forced into prostitution just to eat and have a roof over her head.

She made no comment.

"We would need the supplies and the gear we had to leave behind after the dust storm. It would delay us a couple of days." God, what was he saying? He couldn't believe he'd opened his mouth.

Suddenly, she squealed and threw her arms around his neck and her small body against his. "Then you'll do it! You'll go!"

He scooped her up in his arms. She felt small and fragile and vulnerable. A man could forget his intentions, good or bad, with the softness of her breasts pressed against his chest, her cheek touching his, her bare, silky legs brushing his loins. A couple more days wouldn't hurt anything, and he had no desire to return to the border whores. Paris had a sweet wholesomeness that refreshed his dreary life and made him forget the cynicism, emptiness, and loneliness that had become his these past years. She had made him feel different. Younger, more hopeful.

True, she had caused him nothing but trouble, but while his common sense said go back to Nogales, another voice, one that liked the innocent feel of her in his arms, said stay. Besides, it would be an excuse to be with her a little longer.

It was all he could do to set her away from him when he wanted nothing more than to set her back on her bedroll and make slow, passionate love to her. But, finally, he followed the direction of his better judgment. Looking into her happy eyes, his own heart lifted, but he concealed it with a stern note of caution. "Just a couple of days, Paris. That's all."

She was about to throw herself in his arms again, but he knew if she did it a second time, he would have to engage in another battle with his conscience, and he was sure the latter would lose this time. If she really was a virgin, then he had no business trying to seduce her.

He turned to the boiling coffee. "We'll head out for our gear first thing in the morning. Then we'll come back here and try to pick up Father Castañeda's tracks. If we're lucky, they won't have vanished as quickly as he did."

Nine

Their tracks were easy to follow back to where they'd left their supplies and gear after the dust storm. On horseback with plenty of water, they made the trip quickly and without incident. They then returned to Angel Springs, renewed their water supplies, ate a meal, and headed north, this time searching for the tracks of Father Castañeda. But while they had easily followed their own tracks back to retrieve their gear, they were unable to pick up any evidence that the padre had ever been there.

"I know he went right through here," Paris said, getting down from her horse and searching the ground. "Maybe the wind covered them."

Through eyes squinted against the sun and the heat, Nate searched, too. "There hasn't been any wind, Paris, not since we saw him."

"There has to be an explanation for this. The ground isn't so hard it wouldn't have shown footprints. And he was a big man." Paris was deeply disturbed by it, but Nate could offer nothing, although the absence of tracks left him with a very uneasy feeling.

Finally, they remounted and followed the course they'd seen him take until he had vanished from sight.

Climbing steadily, they wound their way some five miles into the front range of the new cordillera that folded and twisted west by northwest. They found a trail winding through rocks and organ pipe cactus that took them down the center of a green valley. Blue-gray rock walls rose nearly perpendicular on either side, and at the base of the walls were heavy thickets of mesquite, paloverde, iron-wood, and brittlebush. The grass was abundant there, an indication of water. They saw many recent tracks of peccaries, jackrabbits, and deer. Hope rose that they had stumbled onto the padre's mission, for the trail was surely well traveled at this point.

When they came to the end of the trail, there was another natural spring but no mission. In the canyon there was only an old shack, thrown together with a sorry assortment of wood and tin. The place was as silent as death, giving the impression it was no longer inhabited. Still, Nate led the way cautiously, whispering that it might be an outlaw hideout.

Suddenly, a horrible noise startled them, frightened the horses, and set Pedro into a tirade of high-pitched yapping from his sack. The noise seemed to be coming from a mine entrance at the far end of the canyon. They recognized it now as the braying of a mule interspersed with the raucous shouts of a rough male voice.

"You no good worthless mule!" came the human voice. "I should have taken you back to that stupid border-liner who sold you so you could have laid around with him, drinking mescal and getting drunk. You shore ain't no good to me. I need a mule that will work when I say *work!*"

The mule charged through the mine opening straight down the canyon toward them, dragging harness, reins, and a small cart filled with ore. Just before the mule reached them, it made a sharp turn toward a dilapidated corral, and when it did, the ore cart tipped over, scattering the ore all the way to the corral. Bursting from the mine behind the departing mule came an old miner, running a few steps, then hopping a few, running a few, hopping a few. He was obviously trying to make time on a leg that for some reason wasn't functioning as it ought to. The mule made a beeline into the corral and stopped. The old man was nearly there before he looked up and saw he had visitors. He came to a halt as sudden as the mule's and looked around him as if he'd been caught with his pants down.

"Hello!" Nate called, hurrying to allay the old man's confusion at their unexpected appearance. "Mind if we water our animals at your spring?"

The startled expression left the old man's face and he began laughing, a tee-heeing sort of sound that was as obnoxious as his mule's braying. Hobbling, he hurried toward them, all the while rattling in a voice loud enough to carry well beyond them to the end of the valley. "Sure, sure, strangers. You can have all the water you need. It ain't goin' dry. No, sirree, that's the best dang spring around. I call it my fountain of youth." He was only a few feet away but still hadn't lowered the volume of his voice. He was either hard of hearing or he simply knew no other level. "It's about suppertime. You're welcome to join me. I got plenty in the pots over there. I been working my mine and that damn old mule just told me it was quittin' time. I ain't got no watch but that bugger always knows when it's six o'clock. He used to work with me in the mines in Tombstone. Don't know why I bought him from the company and came out here. Biggest mistake I ever made. Oh, not coming out here, but bringing that damn mule. He never was any good. Damn reformed alcoholic.

Some Mex had turned him into a drunk then had to sell him. But he's ruint. Can't get that lazy streak out of him."

Neither Nate nor Paris knew what to say in regard to the prospector's explanation, so finally Nate introduced himself and Paris and said, "We'd be happy to join you for supper."

The old man offered Nate a dirty hand to shake. "Name's Wiley Winslow, but everybody just calls me W.W."

W.W. squinted up at them through spectacles which sported several days' worth of mine dust and one cracked lens. His cheery smile puckered the white stubble on his face and revealed a nearly toothless grin. He wasn't tall and stood stoop-shouldered. His head appeared to come out of his upper back instead of his neck and shoulders, a deformity probably brought on by a lifetime of stooping in mines. White hair poked out from beneath his mangled hat, and the rank smell of creosote and greasewood drifted up from his tattered britches, held in place by a pair of red suspenders that matched his red plaid shirt.

"Spend the night," he was saying. "This is the only spring around for another day's ride. Course, don't know how you found the dern thing, lessen you knew it was here already."

Even though he wore a smile, Nate and Paris were still able to detect his curiosity simply from the way he watched them through his dirty spectacles. Nate knew his kind; he would have considered it impolite to ask too many personal questions. It was an understood law out here, where criminals sought sanctuary, that you didn't get nosey if you didn't want your head blown off.

"No, we didn't know the spring was here," Nate replied.

"We came on it accidentally. We were looking for something else."

That comment piqued W.W.'s curiosity even more, and he hobbled rapidly to keep up with them as they led their horses to the spring. His problem was apparent now. He had one leg that was considerably shorter than the other.

He ran his tongue over lips caked with dust and, trying to sound casual, said, "What would you be lookin' for? Maybe I can he'p you find it."

Paris was beginning to think that in no time at all the entire world would know what she was after, but if she didn't ask questions, she'd never find it by herself. "We were just looking for an old mission," she replied. "We were told by a padre yesterday that he had one out here, and we wanted to . . . visit it."

W.W. looked as if he'd been startled from sleep. "This padre you seen wouldn't have been a Spanish feller about six feet tall, would he?"

Paris's heart leaped with hope and began hammering wildly. "Why, yes! Do you know him?"

W.W. hooted in delight, slapped his knee, and began dancing about on his uneven legs like a crazy leprechaun. He began his horrible tee-hee again, this time so loud it spooked the horses and sent Pedro into another yapping tirade. But W.W. didn't seem aware of the commotion. He laughed so hard tears came to his eyes and he had to remove his grimy spectacles and wipe them away with a shirtsleeve that was equally grimy. If he wasn't crazy, he was certainly doing a good impression. Finally, he got control of himself and looked up at them, still wiping tears from his eyes and face. The moisture had streaked the dirt and made his face look dirtier than before.

"Well, now, Miss McKenna," he managed between

breaths. "I don't know the feller personally, but I've seen him wandering about. Ain't never spoke to him. Don't know of *anybody* that's ever spoke to him."

"Well," Paris pressed. "Who is he? Where's his mission?"

"Oh, he ain't got no mission. Leastwise not anymore. He's been dead for over a hundred years. It was his damnblasted ghost you seen!"

He slapped his knee again in sheer delight, disturbing a cloud of dust from his pants that encircled Nate and Paris, nearly choking them. He sent up another round of laughter. Paris and Nate stared at him in disbelief. Surely the old buzzard was incurably insane.

"You don't understand," Paris tried again. "We spoke to him."

"Yup, but did you touch him?" He squinted at her. His stooped shoulders and concave chest still shook with repressed laughter.

"Well . . . no, we didn't, but—"

W.W. started laughing again so hard Paris wondered if he was going to start rolling in the dirt and holding his stomach. But suddenly Nate had had enough. With slow deliberation he pulled his gun from the holster and, with gentle but firm pressure, planted the muzzle on the end of the old man's nose. Although W.W. calmed down a bit, his eyes still twinkled with glee. He seemed to find almost as much humor in the gun flattening his nose, as he had in relaying his story about the padre's ghost.

"You know, old man," Nate said, his tone serious and his eyes deadly. "I'm tired, real tired, and so is the lady. We're not in the mood for your pranks. Just cut the crap and tell us the truth or that jackass over there will never pull another ore cart because you won't be around to hook up his harness."

W.W.'s smile slowly faded. He recognized the edge of danger, and he was standing on it. He wiped all but a twitch from his lips. He gently placed a dirty finger to the Colt sharing his face and warily nudged it aside, all the while keeping his eyes locked on Nate's just to make sure the big man wasn't going to mind if it was removed. When the gun didn't pose an immediate threat any longer, the twinkle returned to his eyes.

"I'm as serious as I can be," he said. "The old Sonoran has more ghost stories than you could ever believe. But the story about the padre is true. I've seen him with my own eyes. I tried catching up to him a couple of times just to chit-chat, you know, carry on a little tête-à-tête. But he'd always disappear like those dern mirages, leaving me grasping nothin' but heat waves. Then a Yaqui Indian told me the real story and told me to leave that priest alone 'cause he was likely to put a curse on me and I'd die. I guess the padre just wanders around, looking for his mission, or protecting it. The Yaqui didn't know which, but the Indians around here are scared to death of his ghost."

"What do you mean, *protecting* his mission?" Paris queried, her heartbeat quickening.

"Well, pretty little redhead," W.W. said, "I'll tell you. The story goes that there was a big fancy mission built out here by some priests so's they could hoard a bunch of gold statues and things of that nature. Went so far as to cover their trail by planting cactus on it before they left."

"Yes," Paris cut in. "I've heard the story. The priests were banished back to Spain."

W.W. looked at her closer. He was keen, and it became clear from his expression that he was beginning to put two and two together. They weren't here just looking for a mission, they were looking for *the* mission.

"Sure enough," he replied, nodding his grizzled head. "But one of them there priests didn't go back. He just up and vanished, didn't get on no ship. Rumor was that he came back here to his mission. He died here, too, and now his ghost roams the desert, following the old trails he followed when he was alive, trails that took him to the Indians that needed convertin'. Did you see him at a spring not far from here?"

Paris and Nate exchanged a glance, then nodded.

"The whites call that Angel Springs, but the Indians around here call it Place of the Spirit."

Paris shifted uneasily, realizing she couldn't solely take the credit for frightening the Apaches away. They probably hadn't thought she was crazy at all but a ghost or someone who had been cursed by the ghost. She supposed it didn't matter one way or the other, but she had had more than mere luck on her side when she'd played Lady Macbeth.

Still, she wasn't completely ready to swallow W.W.'s story about the padre. Surely the old man was merely having a fine time trying to frighten them. She was determined to get to the bottom of things.

"Do you know what the priest's name was?" she asked, losing her patience. "And the name of his mission?"

"Sure do." W.W.'s grin rivaled the span of a pick ax. "It's Father Castañeda and the Mission of Santa Isabel."

Paris had been expecting two different names so she could smugly tell the old man that the padre they met had not been his so-called ghost, but suddenly she felt as if she'd been rolled in a wet, steamy blanket and left to smother in the Sonoran sun. She glanced at Nate; his tanned face was looking unusually pale.

"The padre we met told us his name was Castañeda," she admitted, "but he could have been a descendant. Or the same name could have simply been a coincidence. He wasn't a ghost, for heaven's sake." Even as she spoke, she doubted her own words. The man had, after all, seemed to vanish into thin air, leaving no tracks. Pedro had not even seemed aware of his presence. It was as if the man had been there only for her and Nate's eyes.

The old man sent up another round of laughter that doubled him over this time, forcing him to finally grip his stomach. "That's him, all right! I told you so!"

"But he said his mission was the Sacred Heart," Paris snapped, holding to the one piece of the puzzle that didn't fit.

W.W. leaned toward her, nearly pressing his dirty nose against hers. "You don't think he'd tell you about Santa Isabel, do you? For all he knew you might go pilfer his treasure."

Paris glanced at Nate, and the wizened old man didn't miss the look. He slapped his knee again, sending another cloud of dust into the air to engulf them. "By golly! That's exactly why you're here, ain't it? And old Castañeda knew it."

W.W. headed off to the house, cackling, and bobbing from one side to the other on his uneven legs and calling over his shoulder, "Come on out of the heat. Put yore horses in the corral there with old Frank. That fat old jackass will enjoy the company for a change. I'll dish us up some supper and we'll talk some more."

Nate watched the old man depart. There was no concealing the annoyed set to his mouth. "Let's fill up our canteens and get the hell out of here," he said. "How do we even know that old bastard isn't a ghost, too?"

Paris watched the old man hobble into the dilapidated shack. He was certainly annoying, but he knew things. "You can leave if you like, Nate, but I'm not through picking his brains."

"I hope you're not expecting to glean too much," he added sarcastically. "I think the buzzards have been there before you."

"You're not going to let his stories get to you, are you?"

"I don't like this whole thing, Paris. First curses and now ghosts. I think I should have listened to Alejandro."

Paris flashed him a look of impatience. "You don't believe that, do you? The old coot's just making it all up, trying to scare us out of here. He's probably in cahoots with that padre—who probably *isn't* a padre—and they either know where the mission is or they're protecting this mine by trying to scare everybody away with ghost stories."

Nate handed her the horses' reins and walked to the spot where the careening ore cart had lost its load. He gathered up a couple of samples and brought them back to her. "If he's got something in there worth protecting, it isn't in this cart. These ore samples are worthless."

"Then he must be hiding something else," Paris said confidently. "I'm going to join him for supper and see if I can find out what it is. Are you coming?"

She didn't wait for his response but headed off toward the shack. Nate watched the swing of her curvaceous hips as she headed to the house. Shaking his head in disgust over the entire situation, he followed, leading the horses. "I think everybody on this friggin' desert is crazy," he mumbled. "Including me."

The interior of W.W.'s shack made it clear immediately

that he was a man who threw nothing away. Scraps of wallpaper lined the walls. Tacked to it were odds and ends ranging from calendar pictures to yellowed recipes from off the backs of food cans. There were clothes, both clean and dirty, and a clock that no longer worked. Several sets of deer antlers, mounted on pieces of wood, had been used to drape towels and hats on. The tawny hide of a mountain lion covered one wall. What wouldn't fit on the walls was piled up in the corners. There was a disarray of items too numerous to segregate with the human eye alone. Only a pair of gloved hands could have actually sorted out the mess. Curtains that looked as old as W.W. himself hung at grease-filmed windows, and Paris was sure that the cloth's thick coat of dust was the only thing that held its rotten fibers together.

Like Alejandro, he cooked outside. His technique was slightly different, however. He cooked in Dutch ovens placed in a hole in the ground over red hot coals then covered with dirt. The heat from the coals allowed the food to cook slowly in the ovens all day. He removed them and carried them inside to the wooden table, talking nonstop the entire time, telling them about his mine, his mule, how he'd found the place, and just about anything else that happened to cross his mind. He was a man who didn't get company very often but loved company when he got it.

Before he put the food on the table, he washed his hands. And the tin plates he removed from the wooden shelves on the wall didn't look as if they'd ever been used. They were dulled by a thin layer of dust, which he asked Paris to wipe off with a towel. He placed a big spoon in the beans and told them to help themselves. But he served himself first. Then he started talking again between spoonfuls of mesquite beans and gulps of corrosive coffee.

"I came out here looking for the fabled *planchas de plata*," he said, "but all I ever found were some gold nuggets. They were in a little valley. I knew they didn't get there by themselves. Just had the feeling somebody had salted the place. The *planchas de plata* were found only once over near Guanajuato, but I figure that if they was found once, there's sure to be more. Sometimes I think I see those sheets of silver just sparkling in the sun on some mountain ledge, but when I get there, it's nothing but a mirage. Sometimes I wonder if this whole dern country ain't a mirage."

At last he stopped to ponder the possibility of illusions, and Paris grabbed her chance to speak. "What about the mission of Santa Isabel? Have you ever searched for it?"

"Sure. Ain't we all? I looked for it for years while I was searchin' for the silver, but I never seen hide ner hair of anything remotely resembling a mission."

"There must have been a mission at one time," Paris added, "or this 'ghost' of Father Castañeda wouldn't be out roaming the countryside. Did you ever look over on Cerro Trueno?"

"Paris—" Nate flashed her a look of warning.

W.W. released another roar of laughter and the twinkle deepened in his eyes. "Don't worry, sonny. I ain't goin' to go take it from you. I been to Cerro Trueno lots of times. There ain't no mission there. Ain't nothin' there. Nope, ain't nothing there but death. You may not even find water, depending on how dry the year is. You two ought to go back where you came from and forget about the treasure of Santa Isabel."

A conspiratorial look came to his eyes, and he hunched

over the table, closer to them. His voice lowered as if he was afraid someone lurking outside would overhear what he had to say. "I had me a couple of friends, you see. They were prospectors out in these parts. Then one day they found a guy dead at the bottom of a wash. It appeared he'd been killed in a flash flood. Anyhow, they found a map in his pocket and it was a map for that lost mission, Santa Isabel.

"Well, the oldest brother, Four Finger Fred—"

"Four Finger?" Paris cut in.

W.W. shifted impatiently, not liking to be side-tracked by explanations. "Yep. Four Finger. You see, Fred only had three fingers on his right hand—born that way, apparently. With his thumb that made four, technically. He'd grown up being called Four Finger Fred. His own brother called him that, so everybody else did, too. Fred didn't mind. He called his younger brother Shark cause he hated his real name so bad.

"Anyhow," he continued, taking a long breath. "They set out looking for this lost mission. They started hearing rumors from the Indians about a curse placed on the treasure that was supposed to be hidden in it. Shark started getting scared and decided he wasn't going to look anymore. Four Finger Fred just laughed and said he was getting close. He could smell it. So he headed out alone and told Shark to bring him supplies—they had a designated meeting place over near Trueno. Shark had the map 'cause Fred had made a duplicate. He didn't want the original getting ruined.

"Now Shark came back from one of those trips and said Fred had found the mission. He'd gone to see it, too. Said it was the prettiest thing you ever saw. I asked him where it was, but he said it would be better if I didn't know. They hadn't found no treasure, but he believed that curse stuff, you know.

"Anyhow, he headed into Tombstone to get Fred some more supplies. He came back a while later but he didn't feel good. There was nothing wrong with him that I could see. He started mumbling something about the curse. Said he'd gotten drunk and lost that map in a poker game. Said he shouldn't have done that. It was the same as telling where the treasure was and now he was going to die. And by golly, he did, just a few minutes later right here in this house.

"I searched for the map, thinking I'd better get out there and find Fred and tell him the news about Shark, but I couldn't find the map. I figured Fred would come in when he got hungry and I'd tell him then. Well, sir, he never did. Nobody ever saw Fred again and that was prob'ly five years ago. I buried Shark about a mile from here in a spot he liked."

"Did you ever go out to look for the mission on your own?" Paris's heart was thumping wildly. If Four Finger Fred had found it, she could, too.

"Sure," W.W. nodded. "I scoured old Cerro Trueno. Didn't find nothing. Course, maybe I gave up too quick, too."

"Where is Trueno from here?" she asked.

W.W. slurped his beans and wiped his mouth on his shirt-sleeve. "Just over to the west, a couple days' ride from here. But it's some pretty rough country back in those mountains. Easy to get lost. You got to keep your eye on Trueno to keep your bearings. But I tell you, there's a lot of country to cover and it could take months, maybe years, to get into every cubbyhole where that mission is likely to be hid. Course now, if you had the map, it might narrow things down some. If you don't, and you just go out there wandering, you'll find you can't stick with it, mainly because yer food and water will give out before you do.

"It's a rugged range of mountains. Trueno has a twin, too, called Cerro Risa, Laughing Mountain, and sometimes and from some angles she looks as big as him. When I go into town I don't tell people I believe in ghosts and curses—they'd lock me up—but after what happened to the Cogan brothers, well . . . if you've got a mind to go out there, you be dern careful."

A cold chill settled over Paris. Her appetite vanished. She glanced sharply at Nate, who also recognized the name W.W. had spoken. "What did you say their name was?" She had to be sure.

"Cogan. Fred and Beacher Cogan. That Fred was crazy, but old Shark—Beacher was his given name—he was a good man and I sure do miss not having him around. Things ain't been the same since he left the old Sonoran."

Nate suddenly stood up, excused himself and left the table. W.W. stared after him. "What's gotten into him? My beans make him sick or something?"

Paris, too, came to her feet, watching Nate's long strides take him from the house. "No, I don't believe so, W.W., but if you'll excuse me, I'd better go see."

Ten

Nate was down on his knees in the middle of creosote bushes and cholla, pillaging Paris's saddlebags when she found him. Infuriated, she grabbed his arm and tried to pull him away. "This is the second time you've gone through my belongings, Brannigan, and I'm getting darn tired of it."

He shrugged her off and continued his search, this time dumping everything out onto the ground. She shoved her way farther into the bushes and dropped to her knees next to him, picking things up as rapidly as he was tossing them.

"What do you think you're doing?" she demanded. "I'm beginning to think you've lost your mind."

"I'm getting rid of that damn map before it gets us killed the same way it did Cogan and your father."

At that moment he saw the envelope Paris kept it in. He grabbed for it, but Paris was quicker. Whirling away from him, she stuffed it down her shirtwaist and scrambled to her feet. "It's mine, Nate Brannigan, and you're not taking it. Besides, this map had nothing to do with my father's death."

Nate came to his feet, towering ominously over her. She was able to recognize his moods by now, and from the hard, unwavering look in his eyes, she realized his present one had turned dangerous at best. He began taking slow, purposeful steps toward her. With each of his she took two quick ones back, stumbling her way over cholla and wincing at it jabbing her through her trouser leg.

"How do you know that map wasn't what killed your father?" he asked, his eyes narrowing to resemble glittering blue shards of glass. "Maybe somebody killed him thinking he had it on him. You're lucky they didn't come looking for you to get it." He held out his hand. "Now, hand it over, Paris. This treasure hunt of yours is going to end right here."

How could she tell him that she was positive her father hadn't been killed for the map? If she told him that she hadn't even found it in his possessions, then she'd have to tell him she'd stolen it from Tully, and she didn't want to do that. It would give him one more reason to head back to Nogales. He would say Tully was probably after them this very minute to get it back. And she couldn't be sure he wasn't. She didn't know how Tully had gotten the map, but since Cogan had gambled it off to her father, she suspected her father had in turn gambled it to Tully. Unless Tully had killed her father for it. But she refused to believe that. Tully was a low-life snake, indeed, but she would hardly credit him for having blood cold enough to murder someone.

It didn't surprise her that her father hadn't come looking for the treasure. He wouldn't have wanted to leave the comfort of Tombstone's gaming rooms to gamble his life against treasure in a lost mission. He would have preferred better odds.

As a matter of fact, she seriously doubted Tully would face the heat, the scorpions, and the sidewinders either for something so elusive, unless there was added incentive. Tully had made good money as the owner of the Silver Slipper. He hated the sun and he loved his French whores, silk sheets, and imported liquor. The only thing that could possibly bring Tully out to the desert was if he thought he was going to lose the treasure to someone else—namely her—and wanted to make her pay for drugging him. Tully was a petty man and dealt in the trivialities of life. He wouldn't be happy about being tricked, especially by a woman.

"Nate, listen to reason," she said, finding herself still in retreat from his long, slowly advancing steps and that determined look in his eyes. "I know you don't want to go any farther on this job and I've really forced you when I shouldn't have. I'll tell you what. Why don't you go on back to Nogales, and I'll see if W.W. will take me to Trueno. He doesn't seem to be afraid of the curse."

Nate stopped, his blue eyes piercing her like bolts of lightning. "Laugh if you want about me being superstitious, Paris, but something's not right here. Now, you'd better give me the map or I'll take it."

His gaze slid threateningly to her bosom. Only the shirt-waist and her chemise formed the barrier between him and what he wanted. Protectively, she put her hand over the hidden map. "It's mine, Nate. If you don't want to be involved, then just get on your horse and ride."

"I'm already involved. I've seen the map. And if I ever tell anybody about it, I'll probably die of that stupid curse."

"But you saw all the strange symbols on it," Paris argued. "You can't really tell where the mission is supposed to be anyway. All the map shows is the approximate area." But suddenly suspicion entered her eyes. "Unless you know what all those symbols mean. Do you?"

"Some of them," he admitted.

"Then tell me what they mean so I can find it by myself, unless you still plan on getting me out of the way so you and Alejandro can go after it yourselves."

"We never did plan that, Paris."

"No? Well, then tell me what the symbols mean."

"I won't tell you."

"All right, you don't have to go any farther," she continued. "I won't ask it of you again. Feeling the way you do about the curse, you probably will die because you've convinced yourself you're going to."

"Don't make fun of me, Paris. I think you'd better start taking this whole thing seriously."

"I have. I'm convinced the mission exists and all these people who have died. . . . Well, it's just a coincidence, that's all."

"And what about Father Castañeda?"

She shrugged. "I don't know. Probably just somebody playing tricks."

"People have better things to do than wander around the desert pretending to be priests that died over a hundred years ago, Paris. Besides, he couldn't have known we'd be there and that we were looking for Santa Isabel. And Pedro didn't even act like he saw him. I'm beginning to think I know why he didn't see him—because he *was* a damn-blasted ghost! And for some reason dogs can't see ghosts!"

"But they can sense them, I'm sure of it," she said, trying to convince herself. "He just didn't see Father Castañeda as a threat."

"Paris, face it. Something's not right about this."

"Don't be naive, Nate. This is all a big joke. As I said before, W.W. and the man we saw at the spring are in on this together. They're just trying to scare us off."

"No, I don't think so, unless they knew we were coming and that you had that map with Beacher Cogan's name on it. And I guess only you know if that's possible."

"No, it isn't possible. Nobody knew I was coming out here before I spoke to you in Nogales." Again, thoughts of Tully leaped to mind, but again, she kept quiet.

"Then give me the map, Paris. We're dealing with something here that I can't explain, but I feel like that map is going to lead us right to our graves."

Paris knew from the determined look in Nate's eyes and the stubborn set to his jaw that he wasn't going to give up, give in, or take no for an answer this time. The only thing left for her to do was hide it so he couldn't find it. She bolted for the mesquite thicket on the other side of the spring. Dropping to her hands and knees, she dove under the thick growth, dodging pincushion and fishhook cactus. Rapidly she made her way to a brushy part where she hoped he couldn't follow because of his size. But suddenly she felt his hand curl around her ankle and her progress came to a halt. She kicked at him but couldn't get away. Lying nearly on his stomach, trying to get under the low-growing branches, he began pulling her back toward him by her ankle. She grabbed a mesquite branch and held on.

"Stop it, Paris," he growled. "Just give me the map. You might as well. I'll get it one way or the other."

"No. Never!"

She closed her eyes, concentrating on holding onto the branch. Its rough bark bit into her hands, but she refused to give into him. He released her ankle and she was sure he'd given up. She was about to breathe a sigh of relief and open her eyes when she felt him crawling on top of her. Her eyes shot open and she tried squirming out from under him, but the quarters were too tight and a pincushion cactus was stabbing her in the shoulder. He reached for her buttons and began undoing them.

She grabbed his hands. "Stop it, Nate! Right now. You have no right to . . . to go to such measures."

"I said I'd get that map however I had to, Paris. And I will, with or without your cooperation."

His hot hands slid down into her chemise and onto the swell of her bare bosom. She gripped his hands. He halted his search momentarily as their eyes met, revealing the awareness of the sensual contact. His scorching touch on her tender flesh made her virtually forget the map. Strange new sensations streaked to every part of her body like bolts of lightning emanating from the ends of his fingertips. For a moment the battle with the buttons ceased, but his hands remained on her, gentle and hot. Warily, she wondered why he was no longer groping for the map.

In the course of the struggle he'd lost his hat to the branch of a mesquite. Even though his eyes were no longer shaded by the brim, they were made unfathomable by the shadows in the thicket. All Paris really knew was that Nate was watching her as sharply as a hawk watches an open meadow for a mouse.

He moved his body more fully over hers, sliding up her length in slow, torturous eroticism, all the while never removing his eyes from hers. She shifted, relieving her shoulder of the pincushion. Something warned her that he'd forgotten his search for the map and had now engaged in a search of a more dangerous nature. Yet, when he continued to unbutton the shirtwaist, pulling its ends from her waistband and spreading it wide to reveal her chemise, she found herself unable to protest. He untied the ribbons on the chemise next, and she finally managed to tell him to stop. But he must have known from the tone of her voice, or possibly the look in her eyes, that there was no true conviction behind the command.

Gently, slowly, he moved his hands over her breasts and up to her shoulders, searing her senses. His lips brushed her collarbone, sending shivers of delight storming through her. She forgot the map entirely, even forgot to hold the chemise closed. She could only focus on the delicious jolts of pleasure surging through her from every intimate place he touched. She turned her head to his, seeking his lips. He sensed her need and his mouth closed over hers. Her lips parted, readily accepting the play of his tongue with hers, giving back as she received. She felt his response, felt his excitement grow as her own did. She slid her arms over his shoulders, exploring by fingertip his strong, sinewed back. She touched the dark hair curling soft and silky at his nape.

She didn't understand the exciting feeling pervading her. She only knew she wouldn't mind if it continued forever. Never had she wanted to know a man so intimately, to explore and touch, to taste, to be a part of him. How could his touch and his kisses drive her to mindless ecstasy when the rest of the time he merely drove her to utter distraction?

His lips left hers to drift down her neck and to follow in the wake of his fingertips upon the sensitive skin of her bosom. She held her breath while he kissed her so intimately, all the while fighting inner voices that couldn't seem to agree on what was best for her. One voice warned her that she was stepping into extremely dangerous territory; another begged her not to deny herself the wondrous touch of his lovemaking; a third was stronger than the previous two and the most successful in finally convincing her that she may never experience such an exquisite assault again in her life and that she really should allow herself the pleasure. The final voice was her own, coming from a niggling suspicion that seemed the weakest of all but was still valid enough to listen to. She was thinking that since he hadn't gotten the map by force, he was now trying to get it by seduction. Well, it wouldn't work. It simply wouldn't. And any second now she would tell him so.

He cupped her breasts in warm palms, lifting them gently. She stifled a gasp of pleasure when his lips closed, hot and moist, over first one nipple and then the other. A deeper desire shot through her to the very core of her womanhood, making her lift her hips involuntarily to his manhood, seeking a fulfillment that primitive instinct told her was there.

Yes, any second now, she would tell him to stop, just as soon as she'd had enough of his seductive torture.

It was Nate, however, who finally lifted his head, swore softly, and drew her chemise back over her naked breasts. He rolled away from her and onto his back where he stared straight up at the lacy patterns just a foot overhead as if his eyes were glazed. Paris saw the rise and fall of his chest and heard his ragged breathing. Her body still burned from his touch and her breasts ached for a continuation of the glorious manipulation of her senses.

"It won't work, Paris," he whispered gruffly.

"What won't work?" Suddenly feeling embarrassed by the intimate exchange and wondering now how she'd let it get so far out of hand, she hastily tried to get her clothes back in order.

"Seducing me won't work any better than trying to play on my sympathies like you did the last time."

"Seducing you!" She sat up so suddenly she hit her head on the mesquite branch and was forced to her back.

She continued buttoning her shirtwaist, but her hands had begun to shake with the anger boiling inside her. "You have certainly got a skewed idea of things, Nate Brannigan! If anything, you were seducing me so I'd give up the map and then the path would be clear for you and Alejandro to take my treasure!"

He turned his head to her. "Are you still stuck on the ridiculous notion that Alejandro and I want the treasure? Besides, just because you have the map doesn't make it your treasure."

Mention of the map brought them both struggling up from their prone positions until they were once again on hands and knees, frantically searching the dim shadows of the underbrush. They both saw the envelope and grabbed for it simultaneously. It came apart with a distinct ripping sound, leaving them staring in horror at the two ancient pieces of the map, one in Paris's hand and one in Nate's.

"My God!" Paris was the first to react. "You've ruined it!"

"I've ruined it! How can you blame me? You're just as much at fault." But satisfaction seeped into his eyes, and he tucked his half of the map into his front pants pocket.

With a sinking heart, Paris watched it disappear, wondering how in the world she'd ever get it back. There was no way she would ever get her hands into that particular pocket without him knowing it.

"That settles it," he said. "We're heading back tomorrow."

He started out of the thicket. Scrambling on hands and knees, Paris inserted herself in front of him and grabbed his shoulders. "It doesn't settle it, Nate. I'll go without the map if I have to. I remember what the other half looks like. I'll just draw up a copy. I'll get W.W. to take me."

Nate couldn't believe her unrelenting determination. For a moment his heart went out to her and he felt a suffocating wave of guilt flood over him. There was the impulse to give into the desperation in her eyes, but the memory of Alejandro's fear haunted him, too. She would certainly be stubborn enough to do exactly as she said, and then she'd get herself killed. And he couldn't trust W.W., or anybody else for that matter, to protect her adequately. The Sonoran was a dangerous place and not everybody knew how to deal with it. No, he wanted to be the one to protect her, to have her safe in his arms, happy and content like a cream-fed kitten. He even had a strong visual image of her making love to him like she would have done a few moments ago if he hadn't brought it to a halt.

Not knowing which set of feelings he should listen to, he gave her one last look and crawled from the thicket. He headed off toward another thicket farther down the grassy canyon. He needed time away from her to clear the confusion from his brain. He was glad she didn't follow.

But Paris did watch his departure. Then she lay back down in the thicket's shadows, resting her head on her arms. She had boastfully said she would go alone or ask W.W., but could she? Did she even want to ask the old prospector? How did she know he wouldn't double-cross her, knock her in the head and take the treasure himself? How did she know he wasn't in cahoots with the man at the spring who claimed to be Father Castañeda? But how could he be? They could never have known she was on her way unless Tully had gotten there first and paid them to stop her.

Or unless Castañeda really was a ghost.

But, no, she didn't believe in that nonsense.

Tully, however, was a different matter. He was a tangible threat and worthy of her concern.

The shadows in the thicket deepened. She began to hear sounds of insects and small scurrying creatures. Fearing scorpions and snakes, she finally crawled out and began looking for Nate. He was nowhere in sight.

Worried about the indecision of her next move, she returned to her saddlebags and repacked the scattered contents. It would be tomorrow before she wanted it to be. And what would she do then?

Alejandro missed Pedro. Mainly because he always started to yap if anything or anyone came around, and in so doing he would alert Alejandro to danger. This time the visitors surprised Alejandro. He didn't hear their approach over the clucking chickens, the bleating goats, the grunting pigs. When he finally saw them, he straightened from his work of watering the corn. There were six of them, and they came from the east. Casually he set his bucket by the wire fence and moved to where the shotgun was propped against a gnarled mesquite post. When they stopped their horses in front of the wire mesh fence, the gun was in place, cradled loosely in his arms.

Alejandro had ridden many trails, some of them with his brother, some alone, but instinct and experience told him these strangers could not be trusted. If he had been Pedro, he was sure he would have smelled trouble. His senses picked up other things, such as the dangerous apathy in the eyes of the man who rode in the lead and the curl to his top lip that could only be described as malicious. He was a big man with small eyes set close together, and he was dressed too fine for a man on the trail. Women might have considered him handsome in his way, despite the close-set eyes, but Alejandro recognized evil. And, in his opinion, the man was ripe for killing.

Alejandro feigned a friendly smile, but even in the shadow of the sombrero he was sure a wise man would be able to detect the wariness in his eyes. "What can I help you with, *señores?* Would you like some water for yourselves and your horses? There is all you can drink there in the spring." He inclined his head in that direction.

The men nodded, went to the spring, filled their canteens, then allowed their horses to drink. When they were finished they sauntered back to a spot in front of the wire fence where Alejandro had remained, shotgun in hand.

"Mind if we spend the night here, *amigo?"* the leader said, amicably. "It'll be dark soon."

Alejandro's words belied his gracious smile. "I am not your *amigo, señor,* and yes, I mind if you spend the night. You see, I came here to the desert to live alone and I do not want company. If I had wanted company, I would have opened a hotel or a cantina."

Their pretense at friendliness vanished, and the leader moved his hand toward the revolver on his hip. Alejandro's smile never faltered, but the wariness in his dark eyes shifted to a gleaming, deadly challenge. "Go for your gun, *señor,"* he encouraged. "You remind me of someone I knew one time. I killed him. And I would like nothing better than to kill you, too."

The leader took a harder look at Alejandro and the shotgun aimed at his heart. "But you don't even know me. Why would you want to do that?"

Alejandro's shoulders lifted in a slight shrug, and possibly for the first time in his life, he said, "Oh, *señor,* maybe just for the hell of it."

The man slowly moved his hand back to his side, away from his gun. "All right, Mex, we won't intrude on your privacy. Just give us some information."

"And what is it you would like to know?" Alejandro's finger still rested on the trigger of the twelve-gauge, double-barrelled shotgun. He liked the gun. It would blow a hole in a man that could never be repaired. Because of that, most men didn't want to risk foolishness or a false move.

"I'm looking for a woman."

Alejandro chuckled. "Ah, but aren't we all? If I had seen a woman out here, *señor,* I would have gladly opened a hotel for her and me."

"Don't get smart with me, Mex," the black-haired visitor snapped. The coldness in his eyes became more pronounced. "She's a short, redheaded woman who came into these mountains with a bounty hunter by the name of Brannigan. I believe she was dressed like a nun, from what information I've been able to piece together from people in Nogales."

Alejandro's smile faded at the man's rudeness, and it was all he could do to keep from satisfying the itch in his trigger finger. He had to be careful that they didn't read the truth in his eyes. He had been looking for Nathaniel and Sister Frances to return and was concerned that they hadn't. Because of that, he had planned to ride out in the morning to see if he could find them, for he feared they had lost their direction in the dust storm and could be in trouble. But whatever these strangers wanted with Nathaniel and Sister Frances, it couldn't be good.

Never batting an eyelash, he feigned total ignorance. "I am afraid I have seen no woman, *señor.*"

The leader's eyes locked with his, probing his mind to see if he could see a lie. Alejandro held his gaze steady.

"Listen, Mex," the leader said, trying to curb a mounting temper. "We've been following tracks that lead in this direction. Two horses and two more that are carrying supplies. We lost them after that dust storm, but they were headed here."

"Maybe like their tracks, they were lost in the dust storm," Alejandro replied. "I have seen no one."

Finally, the man yanked back on the reins, jerking his horse to attention. "All right, boys, let's find a place to camp. We're not going to get any answers from this greaser." He gave Alejandro one last look before wheeling his animal away.

Alejandro picked up his bucket and went back to apportioning water to his plants until the men were gone. Then he went into the house and quickly prepared his arsenal. It would be dark soon, and when it was, they would return. Whatever they wanted with Sister Frances was apparently serious and the leader hadn't believed him.

He waited for hours. When the moon was high, enabling them to see, they made their move, just as Alejandro knew they would. He barred the front door and securely latched the wooden shutters over all the window openings, except the front one where he took up a defensive position. He had built the house strong and with few windows so it would withstand a siege. But he had always figured that if a siege came it would be from renegade Apaches, not white men.

He saw them ride quietly back up the canyon and dismount from their horses a short distance from the house. They scattered, vanishing like ghosts into the shadows and behind the saguaros. No doubt their plans were to come through a back door or window and catch him by surprise. But when one of them tried the front door, he found it was barred from the inside. He looked toward the open window just in time to see the steely flash of Alejandro's knife flipping silently through the moonlit darkness toward him. It caught him in the throat before he could warn the others. Clutching the quivering blade, he fell to his death on Alejandro's immaculate stone walkway.

Alejandro could hear them whispering now as they circled around the house, trying to find an entrance. He could hear the muffled scraping of boots over the sandy soil, like the scurrying of midnight mice over a dirt floor. The second one stumbled on the body of the first man and fell silently near his partner, uttering no more than a startled gasp when another of Alejandro's knives sank deep into his back. The third, however, had rounded the corner just as the second had fallen, and he quickly opened fire at the open window. Alejandro hated to alert the remainder of the men with gunfire, but he had no choice but to kill the third man with his revolver.

The black-eyed leader and the two remaining men, seeing their numbers diminishing rapidly, finally looked seriously at the odds. They decided to take cover, opening full fire on the house when they considered themselves protected. The bullets bit into the adobe and the wooden window frame, sending pieces of mortar showering down into the house and onto Alejandro's head. He ducked down behind the thick adobe walls until the barrage ceased.

"Tell us where the redheaded woman is," came the leader's voice from the dark.

"I told you, *señor*," Alejandro called back, "I have seen no woman. Am I to be killed for my ignorance?"

"If that's the way you want it, Mex!" came the answer from the dark.

"Then at least let me know the name of the man who plans to kill me."

"I'm Tully Thatcher," came the proud response. "And don't you ever forget it."

"Ah, *señor*," Alejandro countered. "I do not think I will. I will take it with me when I go so I can tell the Lord and He can put a black mark against your name in His big record book."

"You sonofabitch!"

The firing started again, and Alejandro smiled as pieces of adobe flew over the top of the window sill, some falling into his black hair. He reloaded his guns, thinking he had not had so much excitement since he had left the hacienda on Rio Abajo. It was a welcome relief from watering the corn, which had to be practically begged to grow. He didn't realize until this moment how much he had come to hate watering the corn. He wondered if he might have been more tolerant of the strangers and their questions if he hadn't been at that particular task when they had arrived. But maybe he had just needed a good fight to vent all the years of frustration, to somehow make up for not being at the hacienda when the Apaches had come.

As soon as the bullet barrage ended, he leaped up and fired toward his assailants, knowing now where they had taken cover. Alejandro's targets began to move. His greatest fear was that they would find the weakness in the house—the roof—and set it on fire. But even then he had a means of escape. He had built a trap door that led to a cellar beneath the house, and from there a tunnel led out to the corn field. If only Paloma had had such an escape, she and his son and his mother might be alive, and he would not be fighting this stupid Tully Thatcher.

What Alejandro had not been expecting though was the bullet that came through the window, ricochetted off the metal pot on the table, and penetrated his chest. At first it was just a dull thud. Then he felt the wetness on his hands, and in the moonlight he saw the black spot he recognized as blood.

He had not expected to die this day. He had been too prepared for that. He had expected to kill them all, or at least enough of them that they would leave. Then he had planned to find Sister Frances and Nathaniel. Now his plans were changed.

With bullets flying in through the open window, he crawled across the floor and found some towels with which to make compresses and soak up the blood. It was not a big stream that would kill him right away, but it was steady and it would weaken him. It was very close to his heart, too. He'd been lucky it had not been an inch or two lower or he would have died instantly.

"Hey, greaser!" came Thatcher's voice. "You could save yourself if you'd just tell us what we want to know. If you don't, we'll cut you to ribbons."

Alejandro ignored the threat while he tied bandages around his chest, using his teeth to help pull the strips of cloth into knots. He gathered up some canteens and made ready to vacate through the cellar. The outlaws were running out of options, and he knew soon enough they would think of burning him out.

He gave them no answer and received no responding bullets. He knew they were wondering what he was up to.

"Answer me, you bastard!"

"But I do not know what you want to know, *señor,*" he called back. "If you wish to kill me you will have to come and get me. I do not care to come out."

"You're out of ammunition, aren't you?"

Alejandro answered with two more shots from his rifle. "No, *señor,* the gun still seems to be working fine!"

There was silence for a long time. Then he saw one of the men run, head down, toward his garden. He could do nothing while the man proceeded to rip the corn and other vegetables from their roots, laughing as he did. Alejandro could have fired on the man, but he could not get a clear shot in that direction from any of the windows and there was no point in wasting his ammunition. The garden was not large and very soon the man had finished the desecration.

Done with that, the outlaw began shooting the goats and chickens and pigs. It put Alejandro in such a rage that he battled the urge to burst from the house with guns blazing, which was exactly what they wanted him to do so they could cut him down. And he couldn't die yet. He had to warn Nathaniel and Sister Frances first.

"What'll it be next, Mex?" Thatcher called.

"I'm sorry, *señor,*" Alejandro replied, feeling the pain intensely now in his chest. "I have so little."

"Tell us where they went."

"If I had seen these people, I surely would tell you. I am not a fool."

"You've got a nice little place here, Mex. A nice house. And that roof will make a good blaze. What's that woman to you anyway that you want to protect her? She's nothing but a dance hall girl."

Alejandro pondered that bit of information. He had not believed that Sister Frances was a nun, but she had seemed too pure and innocent to be a dance hall girl. "If that is so, *señor,* then why do you want her so badly? You could just go get yourself another, couldn't you?"

"Because she stole something from me."

"Ah . . . then I see now why you want her, but I cannot tell you where she has gone, *señor,* if I have not seen her. Three of your men have died because of this woman. Do the rest of you want to die, too? There is no point in continuing this war. I have no answers for you."

"I don't believe you. And we're not leaving until you tell us something."

"Okay, *señor,* I will tell you something. I will tell you that she was here with the bounty hunter and they filled up their canteens and they told me that they were going to Tajitos. By the way, what is this bounty hunter to the woman? Is he her lover or something?"

He heard Thatcher cussing. "Don't lie to me, greaser! If you won't tell me where the woman is, then tell me where Cerro Trueno is from here."

"Cerro Trueno? I do not know, *señor.* I have lived here many years and there are many mountains out there, as you can see, but I have heard of no mountain by that name. Maybe it is far to the west of here, or the south. Or maybe even the north. Forgive me for not knowing, *por favor.*"

The house was hit with another barrage of bullets, but when something landed on the roof and Alejandro saw smoke curling down through the timbers, he knew it was time to make his exit.

He dropped a full belt of ammunition over his shoulder. Carrying his revolver, Winchester, and an unlit lantern, he left the smoky house through the cellar. He lit the lantern when he was in the cool dampness of the tunnel. He

Wish You Were Here?

You can be, every month, with Zebra Historical Romance Novels.

AND TO GET YOU STARTED, ALLOW US TO SEND YOU

4 Historical Romances Free

A $19.96 VALUE!

With absolutely no obligation to buy anything.

ZEBRA HOME SUBSCRIPTION SERVICE, INC.

120 BRIGHTON ROAD

P.O. BOX 5214

CLIFTON, NEW JERSEY 07015-5214

AFFIX
STAMP
HERE

quickly realized he could not crawl on hands and knees and carry everything. He had no choice but to leave the Winchester behind.

At the end of the tunnel he carefully lifted the hatch door which faced the house. He saw only one man watching the roof of his house burn. The other two had probably gone to guard the other exits, expecting his attempted escape. Only the roof would burn; the adobe bricks would be blackened but they would still be there when he returned. If he returned. Now, he must get to Nogales and quickly. If he could live until he got there, maybe he could find the law or someone who would be willing to find Nathaniel and Sister Frances and warn them of the danger they were in. But he could go nowhere until they left. And while he waited, the blood spread deeper into the bandages.

"You'd better come out pretty soon, Mex," yelled Thatcher. "Or you're going to be part of the bonfire."

Many minutes ticked by but the door didn't open. One of the men crept from around the house, keeping a cautious eye on the flames should any of the thatch come down on him. "Looks like you're wrong, boss. The windows are still barred tight. He ain't coming out."

"I think maybe we hit him and he's already dead."

It wasn't until the roof caved in that Thatcher angrily swung into the saddle, followed by his men. Staring at the flames surging toward the desert stars, he said, "It serves the greaser right to die. I know he was lying. He's seen them and he knows where Cerro Trueno is, too. If she's following the map, that's where she's gone."

"But where is it, boss?" came one of the men's voices. "Like he said, there's a lot of mountains out here."

"How in the hell should I know, you fool? I can't remember every detail on that map. I wouldn't have wasted my time interrogating that sonofabitch if I'd known how to get there."

"And what if she didn't even come this way? Maybe she just hired that guy in Nogales and lit out for California or Texas. Maybe that guy really is her lover, as the Mex said."

"Shut up!" Tully snapped. "All I know is that the hotel keeper rented a room to a redheaded woman who came out dressed like a nun. Then the nun was seen leaving with the bounty hunter, headed this way. They could be heading to California, sure, but she's after that treasure first. I know she is. She'll pay for stealing my map and leaving me for another man after everything I've done for her."

Finally, they were gone and Alejandro knew they wouldn't come back. They had no reason to. He crawled from the tunnel into the flattened corn field. He put his fingers to his lips and gave a whistle. It sounded loud and clear in the still night and soon his horse came from the canyon where it grazed. With pain and a clumsiness that frustrated him, he bridled it. He didn't even attempt to heft the heavy saddle onto the horse's back. Using the chopping block as a stool, he managed to half-crawl, half-swing onto the horse bareback. Holding his throbbing chest, he headed east, alternating the horse's gait, but never exceeding a lope because of the pain it forced him to endure.

He didn't know how long he rode, clinging to the horse as he weakened, but the night passed and the desert sun came up to blaze down on him. The towels he'd used to staunch the blood were filled now and the blood oozed out and down the front of him into his pants. He dared not get off the horse for fear he would not be able to get back on. He had not wanted to think of how far away Nogales was, but now he could not dispute the fact that he might not have enough blood in his body to sustain him until he reached it.

As his thinking blurred, he began to think of Sister Frances. Until he'd seen her, he had lulled himself into contentment. He had made himself happy tending his little garden, his house and yard, caring for his animals, making his cheese and bread, and taking long rides in the desert on his horse. To think. Just to think. But when she had gone, with Nathaniel riding after her, she had taken more than just Pedro. She had taken Alejandro's contentment, and now all he saw was emptiness swimming before him like a huge gray sea.

Through his pain, and possibly because of it, he realized that even if he lived until he got to Nogales, he would never again be happy in the little adobe house in the desert. He wanted what he had seen in Nathaniel's eyes when he had looked at Sister Frances. Nathaniel may not have recognized his own feelings, but Alejandro had. For the first time in years, Alejandro wanted to live. He wanted life and another woman who could comfort him and love him. It was all so simple now . . . and so very far away.

Eleven

From his position in the thicket, Nate watched the mountains change from deep purple silhouettes to what looked like a line of giant black arrowheads against the night's first spattering of stars. The darkness came in degrees, adding to itself, until he could barely see W.W.'s shack, still without a light of any kind. At least it was cooling off, although the air was still so dry it felt brittle. He wondered absently when the rains would come and bring some relief to the water-starved Sonoran.

Perhaps it was just his mood, but the twilight seemed to have taken on a gloomy silence. The only creature stirring besides himself was a black-tailed gnatcatcher, darting from place to place in search of insects.

He wondered if Paris was asleep yet. He didn't want to return until she was. Being around her left him constantly fighting a multitude of emotions ranging from anger to mesmerizing desire. She was no bigger than a minute and as contrary as a mule. She was innocently sweet, as clever as a wizard, and fearless to a fault. But she was too naive to know she needed protection, and he knew as surely as he knew his own name that if he left her to find the treasure on her own, he'd be sending her to her death.

He tossed his cigar to the sandy soil and ground it out with the toe of his boot. He looked toward the west. Another couple of days could easily find them at Cerro Trueno, but this entire situation of ghosts and curses didn't bode well with him. Damned if Paris wasn't going to get him in more trouble than following an outlaw trail. But what choice did he have? He couldn't let her go out there alone.

He returned to W.W.'s shack but didn't go inside when he heard the old man snoring. He looked around the darkened yard and saw Paris curled up on her bedroll on a bare piece of ground not far from the corral. She had a blanket over her but only up to her knees because of the heat that still hung stagnant in the air. He noticed she'd given up her trousers and shirtwaist for the comfort of a white, cotton nightgown. It was not yet so dark that he couldn't make a mental note of the way her hip curved gracefully and sensuously into her small waist beneath the fragile material and the way her red hair, subdued to a dark mass by the night, fell out behind her in a thick, wavy mass onto the blanket.

Rocks crunched beneath his feet. Startled, she lifted her head. He silently cursed, having hoped she was asleep. He remembered too well the way her body had so perfectly and pliantly molded to his. His senses still reeled from the sweet scent of her skin that had threatened to drive him beyond control. She was nothing but trouble, so what special magic did she possess that kept him giving into her every whim?

She returned to her side, apparently finding no good reason to talk to him.

"I didn't mean to wake you." His voice, even though low, carried easily across the distance in the evening's stillness. He stood there like a fool, finding it difficult to pull his eyes from her curves and to go about the business of preparing his own bedroll for the night. All he really wanted to do was share hers again. The only way he'd probably ever get her into his arms again, though, would be if there was another dust storm.

"I wasn't asleep," she said after a moment or two.

He found his bedroll and laid it out a few feet from hers. "Want me to build a fire?"

"I suppose we might need one before morning." She ignored him beyond that, closing her eyes as if trying to go back to sleep.

Nate easily found some dry mesquite and brittlebush and soon had the fire blazing in the space between them. For some reason he felt he needed that barrier. It was getting harder and harder to stay away from her.

He glanced at her, the flames dancing over her perfectly oval face, touching on the smattering of freckles across her nose. Even though her eyes remained closed, he knew she wasn't asleep, and he sensed she wanted to avoid him the same way he wanted to avoid her.

He stretched out on his back, pulling his hat down over his face and folding his arms over his chest. His conscience kept badgering him about what he was going to do come morning, but he finally drifted off to sleep, convincing himself that it was best to let W.W. go with her after all. He would just go back to Nogales, get on with his life, and get her out of it. This growing attraction for her was getting dangerously out of hand, too close to controlling his better judgment. Maybe he'd just been out on the Sonoran too long and needed to get back to Nogales, where women neither wanted his heart nor could win it.

Besides, the man who had a woman on his mind was dangerous to himself. Those thoughts, feelings, and desires eroded caution and destroyed his sense of danger. A man had to have a clear head to survive in this country and in this profession. Tomorrow he'd head back to Nogales, and Paris Frances McKenna would just have to get by the best she could.

Paris listened intently to the crackling fire, the night noises of insects and small animals, of a nighthawk crying somewhere in the dark, and the horses snorting, stamping, and moving about in the nearby corral. But most of all, she listened to Nate's breathing. She waited until he had settled into what appeared to be a deep sleep, then slowly, quietly, she rose from her blankets, stepped around the fire, and lowered herself to her knees. Holding her breath, she questioned her sanity. Her gaze traveled over his strong, muscular body, pausing on points of particular interest. His hat had slid off his face for the most part, exposing everything below his nose. The firelight played across his firm lips, not hard as they sometimes could be, but sensuous and warm and inviting. His hands rested on his chest, begging her to pick one up and place a kiss to the light sprinkle of black hair on the back of it. They were attractive hands; lean, with long fingers, calloused, capable of just about anything from handling a gun to handling a woman.

She wasn't sure why she was having such a hard time doing what she was about to do. Maybe it was because she'd like to feel those lips and hands again on her too-willing flesh, and she knew that she never would again if she carried out her plan. But she had to face reality; dreams didn't put food on the table or a roof over one's head. She could return with him tomorrow and face a reality too unpleasing to even think about, let alone to live. And, after feeling Nate's lips that so easily summoned a wicked and delicious desire she had not even known existed, she was sure she could never cope with Tully Thatcher ever touching her again. If it could be Nate's lips and arms that offered her sanctuary, she would be tempted indeed, but she knew his offer had been made only as a way to convince her to give up. He would want nothing of her after they reached Nogales, when he could warm his bed with that dark-eyed, voluptuous beauty she'd seen him with.

He was a thoroughly infuriating man, and superstitious no less. But he was strong and immeasurably exciting to be around. He made her feel secure and yet vulnerable. There were times he'd even felt like a friend. Most of the time he had her in a turmoil. So doing what she was about to do was probably for the best.

With her heart pounding, she took a deep breath and eased her hand onto his hip just above the pocket where he'd stashed his half of the map. He didn't move. She eased her fingers past the edge of the pocket and cursed him silently for wearing such snug-fitting trousers. Her hands were small, but seemingly not small enough.

He moved. She didn't. Her heart stopped. After what seemed forever, he finally settled back to sleep. She pushed her hand deeper into his pocket and there at the end of her fingers she felt the map.

Twisting her hand slightly, she was able to get two fingers around the edge of the paper. Ever-so-slowly she drew the map out a fraction of an inch at a time.

Then, like a bolt of lightning, his hand came down over her wrist. She shrieked and tried to get away, but he held her fast. He shoved his hat the rest of the way off, and she saw his eyes glittering in the moonlight with smug satisfaction.

"Now, Paris, *love,* you really didn't think I wouldn't notice, did you? Even asleep, there are some parts of a man that can't help but respond to a woman's touch."

Mortification washed over her in a suffocating sheet; she was sure her face was as red as her hair. "I wasn't . . . I mean . . . I didn't mean to . . . I didn't know I . . . touched you . . . *there.* All I wanted was the map. Honestly." Her eyes pleaded for his mercy, but something about the way he was looking at her suggested she wasn't going to get it.

He sat up slowly, using nothing but the iron bands of his stomach muscles to do so. At the same time he pulled her hand from his pocket, and she had no choice but to release the map in the process.

He drew her into his arms and propelled her helplessly to the blanket that was still warm from his body, tucking her more securely in his embrace. The glow in his eyes reminded her of a hot, dark coal whose interior is still red and ready to burst into flames if only it could be fanned.

"Tell me something, Paris," he whispered so seductively she shivered. And he must have thought she had shivered from the cold because he held her tighter. "Is it all you care about, finding the map and the mission? What about other things?"

With alert senses, she watched him. She felt the hard length of his manhood pressed against her thigh and she knew then that the bulk of his interest was not in the map. Nervously, wondering if she'd pushed him beyond his limit, she moistened dry lips and spoke cautiously. "I'm not sure what you mean, Nate. What sort of other things?"

"Things like this."

His lips moved over hers, intoxicating her with their warm, sweet liquor. He repositioned his hips, sliding them more fully over hers. She knew all too well now what he wanted and knew how very easy it would be for her to succumb to a passion and a need that was equally hers. Oh, but what a fool she would be to give into that desire! Brannigan was a man who would use her and toss her aside. He wasn't a man to keep promises.

His lips halted their drugging assault and moved to the corner of her mouth, hovering just beyond her reach unless she were to grow bold enough to seek their caress.

"Tell me, Paris," he continued softly. "Is the map and the treasure all you care about?"

"It's all I can afford to care about."

"I see."

His lips moved along her neck, stirring feelings she hadn't known before she'd met him but was beginning to crave more and more. A faint moan of rapturous delight escaped her lips, despite her efforts to stifle it.

"I've been thinking," he whispered between kisses. "I might be persuaded to go with you."

His words filtered through the thick haze of desire consuming her. "How? What do you want?"

His lips tickled her ear. "You offered me half once. Does that offer still stand? I couldn't risk my life for anything less."

She had offered him that, hadn't she? But maybe she'd been delirious from the heat at the time. "Half? Well, I . . . don't know . . ."

"It's either me or W.W."

Paris couldn't think. She tried to clear her head, but his lips were driving her to distraction. Her main thought was a selfish one. If he came along, she might have the opportunity to experience more of his kisses and the feel of his strong arms around her. But shouldn't she really be making the treasure her priority?

"Why did you change your mind?" she managed.

"I haven't . . . yet. What will it be, love? Half of everything?"

His lips burned through the thin cotton cloth of her nightgown, caressing the curve of her breasts. Half of everything? Such a price to pay. And if she gave him half, what would he give her? A broken heart?

She would never know unless she said . . .

"Yes."

He lifted his head. Coolness filtered over her where his lips had been. "What did you say, love?"

"I said . . . yes . . . I think. Half of . . . everything. Or nothing. Depending on what we find."

His lips took hers again possessively. His tongue did an erotic dance with hers. The coolness of the night was pushed away by the heat of his body and the fire in her soul. Then, much to her disappointment, he rolled to his side. Even though he kept her in his embrace she knew he planned on sleeping, not making love. He touched her forehead with a kiss. "Sleep well, love, and say your prayers. Tomorrow we search for Santa Isabel."

Paris came awake by slow degrees, feeling first the ruffling of a warm desert breeze across her face, then the heat of the body behind her, conforming to every inch of hers. Nate. She snuggled closer to him, and the arm draped over her tightened in a gesture that might have been loving or protective, or both. She preferred to think of it as both and decided almost instantly that there was no point in making her eyes open before they were ready. So she allowed herself to drift back into sleep and pleasant dreams.

It was, however, an annoying and vaguely familiar tee-hee that cleared the night from her mind once and for all. She pried one eye open and saw W.W. bent over from the waist, hands on his knees, peering at her and Nate through his cracked spectacles. But she did notice they had been cleaned. His expression was one of unfettered amusement. Staring at his snaggle-toothed grin, Paris was suddenly very relieved that she hadn't been forced to ask him to accompany her to Cerro Trueno. She was sure she couldn't have woken up every morning to that face, even if it was only from across a campfire. She had agreed on entirely too much last night in order to get Nate's consent, but she was confident she would ride away from the Mission of Santa Isabel a rich woman nonetheless.

"Here now," W.W. said, still tee-heeing. "Sun's up, breakfast's on. You two get up and come in the house and eat. I got work to do, and if I don't get old Frank into the mines on time, he'll think it's his day off and he won't go at all."

Nate stirred and finally came awake, mumbling and wondering what in the hell was going on.

"Didn't know it got cold last night," W.W. said knowingly as he gave their separating bodies a thorough scrutiny.

Nate's morning scowl deepened at the sight and the sound of the old prospector. He sat up, rubbing the arm both he and Paris had been laying on. He lifted his shoulder as if it pained him, rolling it to get the movement and circulation going. "How would you know," he growled in response to W.W. "You weren't on the ground, you old geezer."

"My, my, ain't we kin to a diamondback this mornin'? You ought to be all cheerful after sleepin' with that pretty little redhead."

The old man gave Paris a hungry sort of look, and Nate's dark brows shot together over blue eyes that sparked a warning. "Get on back to your breakfast, W.W.," he said. "I think something's burning."

W.W. laughed in that imbecilic way of his again, then hopped back to the house on his uneven legs, calling over his shoulder. "Something's burning all right, sonny, but I don't think it's the food."

Nate came to his full height, reaching for a sore spot in his lower back. "I swear this ground gets harder every night. Next time let me pick where to throw the bedrolls," he complained.

Paris was stiff, too, but she couldn't help but laugh at his grumpiness. "Nobody told you to sleep there."

"Well, nobody told me to leave either."

His eyes lifted and locked with hers. In them she saw the recollection of what had transpired between them last night. She wondered if he'd kissed her just to get her to consent to half of the treasure. But female intuition told her that Nate Brannigan had kissed her for another reason that had had no ulterior motive, simply because he'd wanted to. And maybe she'd given into him because she'd needed a guide in the most desperate of ways. But maybe she'd given into him, too, because she'd wanted to.

They could hear W.W. cursing. It seemed he never spoke in a voice quieter than a roar.

"Sounds as if he burned the bacon," Paris said.

"Yeah. We'd better go see if there's anything left fit to eat."

Paris went to the outhouse to change clothes. She joined Nate again and they started for the shack. Pedro, seeing them leave, roused himself from his bed of sand, shook out his short hair, and followed them. Paris felt very conscious of Nate walking next to her, aware of his every movement, his presence, and the memory of their bodies so warmly and naturally intertwined. Something had changed because they'd willingly spent the night in each other's arms. There was an easy space between them this morning. Her heart picked up speed in a frightening yet exciting way, and suddenly she wondered if there might be a future with Nathaniel Brannigan beyond Cerro Trueno.

The Pajaro Mountains stretched thirty miles along the border. The desert fell away from the range's gabled peaks in either direction. The mountains were blessed with scores of springs and natural rock water tanks, cropping up in narrow valleys and deep canyons, springs whose water flowed a short distance then disappeared into subterranean channels that eventually emptied into the gulf or into the Colorado River.

The mountains were named for the many birds that nested there, flocking around the springs for water. It was true, the Pajaro Mountains were treacherous and were shunned by Indians and outlaws alike. Nate knew this, but he didn't draw attention to the fact, mainly because he recognized how ecstatic Paris was when, after two days from W.W.'s, the range came clearly into view and she feasted her eyes on Cerro Trueno for the first time.

But as the creeping shadows of dusk moved over the cordillera, Nate felt something invisible yet tangible to the senses clinging to Thunder Mountain and the smaller ragged peaks that brushed its massive shoulders. It was as if the big mountain had a life of its own and stood guard over its domain to ward off all unwanted interlopers. Even though it was a hot day, that invisible something made Nate shiver.

He had come this far before, looking for outlaws, but he had never had to follow anyone into the Pajaros. The lawless seemed content to stay on the mountains' less forbidding fringes. There was a disturbing silence despite the birds filling the sky, a silence that went deep into a person's soul and threatened to send him running to a safer place. Nate wondered if it was because of the curse of Santa Isabel. Was the mission truly somewhere in the Pajaros? Was death awaiting all of those who ventured in?

They stopped to look at the big mountain, which they would not reach until tomorrow. A game trail indicated a spring somewhere ahead. Nate nudged his horse, following the trail, and hoped to reach water before it became too dark to see. The trail wound upward over rocks, through mesquite and an abundance of cacti. Saguaro were predominant, covering the mountains in thick patches. As the trail dimmed in the purple shadows of nightfall, it took them into a narrow canyon whose rock walls rose close on either side.

It was a box canyon, a place that a man in Nate's profession spurned at all costs. He was after no outlaws, and they were well beyond the area of the Apaches, but as he moved their horses deeper into the canyon, he felt more and more like a cornered animal whose instinct is to run before it is too late.

They reached the water, a natural granite tank secluded by rock walls. Shelf-like granite protrusions graduated down to the water's edge like stepping stones. Fresh water, from a source higher up on the mountain, trickled down over shelves and into the tank, keeping it filled and overflowing and preventing stagnation. The smooth surface of the granite shelves indicated that the waterfall did at times roar with heavy run-off from winter and monsoon rains.

From outcroppings of rock grew twisted ironwood, brittlebush, scrub paloverde, and a tangled assortment of cacti. Flowers were still in colorful bloom next to the water—orange globe mallow, desert lavender, late-blooming red hummingbird trumpet, and yellow beggar's tick.

Their approach sent hundreds of birds flocking to the sky in a black mass. Smaller animals and reptiles, too, scurried to the security of the undergrowth. A female coyote fled with her five pups up a rocky incline and out of sight.

Nate, wishing they'd been able to set up camp before it had become so dark, stepped down reluctantly from his horse. He preferred seeing a place in daylight so he could better gauge the direction from which an attack might come. With the walls of the canyon rising up so close around them, he took the best visual note of the terrain that he could. Paris, too, was quiet, perhaps perceptive to his concerns. Or maybe she was just tired. He didn't know, but he didn't want to frighten her by the strange uneasiness he felt.

He stepped to the ground and gave her a hand to help her from her horse. "Tomorrow you'll be on Cerro Trueno," he said, giving her a wry smile, hoping to ease the eeriness of the canyon. "And who knows, by tomorrow night you may be a rich woman. Word gets out, and you'll have every bachelor on the border looking to make you his wife."

She accepted his help to the ground, giving him a speculative glance. "Is that all men care about is money?"

He chuckled. "No, that's second on their list."

She innocently met his teasing blue eyes, liking this lighter side of him that he seldom revealed. "And what is the first thing on their list?"

His grin deepened. The word that came to mind was not exactly what he knew most women would want to hear, so he said, "Why love, of course, Paris. Haven't you ever been in love?"

She gave him a coquettish toss of her head and turned to look at their surroundings. "Have you?"

"Just like a woman to evade the question."

She laughed and turned back to him. "No, Nate Brannigan. I have never been in love. Your turn."

Something coiled tightly inside Nate as he looked down at her lovely, smiling face. She was very pretty when she smiled. He had the impulse to pull her into his arms and see if what he was feeling for her was love. He also had the nonsensical need to be the man she finally gave her heart to. But what about that other love for Paloma? The one so deeply etched in his heart and his memory that it still hurt almost too much to even think about it. Surely that was true love and could never be replaced. What he felt for Paris was probably just a reaction from being out on the desert too long with her. Once this was over they'd both go their separate ways.

Odd how that idea seemed to take the spark out of him.

He turned back to his horse, trying to laugh it off. "No, I never have been," he lied. "Why love one woman when you can love them all? Now, if we don't get camp set up, we'll be fumbling around in the dark."

They shared in the preparation of the meal, fixing it by the light of the fire. Nate found his thoughts focused equally on Paris's nearness, aware of every move she made, aware of when she brushed a hand against him, or a shoulder. They ate quietly, talking only of trivial matters such as the trip, W.W., and why Pedro hadn't been hungry for two days.

"Maybe he's homesick," Paris suggested.

"Maybe he regrets running away with you."

"I borrowed him. Remember?"

"Ah, yes, but you stole his heart first, so it was easy to borrow his body."

"I think he's getting to like you more," Paris said.

Nate looked at the dog, who looked back at him indifferently, as if he knew he was the topic of conversation. "No, he only accepts me because I'm with you. He likes you."

"You need to be nicer to him. Talk to him."

Nate shrugged. "Tell him to be nicer to me. He's bit me twice."

And so the conversation went until it faded off into nothingness.

Paris didn't mention tomorrow and the search for the mission, but Nate caught her looking toward the big mountain looming above the canyon.

"Are you afraid you won't find it?" he asked quietly. "The treasure?"

Her gaze lifted to the stars as if in them she might see the dreams she'd come there to find. "Yes," she admitted. "I haven't wanted to think of that, but now that I'm here, I'm beginning to think how foolish I was to come. Sometimes I think, 'Good heavens, Paris, there's nothing out there but scorpions and cactus. There's no treasure, no Santa Isabel. If there was, someone would have already found it.' "

"Maybe not," he replied, sipping his second cup of coffee.

"I'm not the first to have the map," she said, her voice showing uncharacteristic discouragement. "How many others had it before Cogan, before my father, before me?"

Nate had tried to discourage her, dissuade her, force her back to Nogales, anything to make her give up her crazy search. But now that she was beginning to show some doubt on her own, his first inclination was to buoy her spirits. He realized how it hurt him to see her ready to give up, to see that sad look of defeat in her eyes. He couldn't believe the words that came out of his mouth.

"Sure others have seen it, Paris, but who could find anything from it? There's all those strange symbols and lines. No X to mark the spot. And just look at these mountains. There's thirty miles of them. That map just shows a series of humps indicating peaks. The only one marked is Cerro Trueno. That treasure could be any place in this range, and these desert mountains tend to be as sneaky as a snake, winding, twisting, filled with hundreds of hidden canyons and valleys."

"Yes, I know. It could take years to explore them all. Even then a person could miss half of them."

He reached over and took her hand in his. "You're just tired. Things will look better by the light of day. I'll clean up if you want to take a dip in the pond."

Her eyes lit up. "Are you sure?"

He nodded.

She rose with new enthusiasm, but stopped and looked

over her shoulder at him. "Are you still sure you want to go through with this, Nate?"

He chuckled. "If Father Castañeda doesn't show up again."

Laughing, she left him, gathered her things, and went to the water tank. Its granite walls secluded her from his eyes. He contemplated this place, this situation he was in, and the lightness he'd forced on himself for Paris's benefit slipped away as his thoughts once again focused on his surroundings, prickling with that omnipotent sense of danger he couldn't quite pinpoint. Yet he knew it was out there . . . somewhere.

Maybe it was just his mind working overtime, or the vivid memory of the look on Alejandro's face when he'd begged him not to go. He couldn't believe he'd lost his mind and consented. It was madness, pure and simple. Where it would end he didn't know, except that he was like a rangy old longhorn bull driven by instinct to stay with the female until she no longer needed or wanted him. And right now he needed her, badly.

He proceeded to lay out the bedrolls and found himself putting Paris's next to his. She'd been a warm, sensual woman in his arms last night, and if he played his cards right, he might get her there again. Maybe the little spitfire would be looking for protection and warmth, and such things always led to other things. He still hardly believed her claim to virginity, although she did possess a refreshingly innocent quality, but few saloon girls were virgins. Even if they hadn't gone into prostitution, they'd taken a lover or two. The way she'd kissed him that night at W.W.'s, the way her hands had roamed his back, her fingers curling into his hair, all made him think she was more experienced than she would have him believe. He might have taken her then if it hadn't been for the old prospector so close by.

He could hear her splashing around in the pond now and occasionally caught a glimpse of her white skin through the narrow rock doorway leading to it. The blood seemed to flood from every part of his body to his loins, driving him to moonlight madness once again.

With little thought to the outcome of his actions, he pulled his boots off, tossed his hat on his bedroll and peeled out of his shirt. Wearing only his pants he made his way to the tank, once again following nothing more tangible than male instinct and inexplicable desire.

The desert night sky was brilliant with stars that lent sufficient light to the vision in the water. She was submerged to her waist, splashing her face and shoulders, tilting her head back so the cool stream ran down her neck and over her breasts in rivulets. His gaze held to the lovely sight of her breasts for a moment, high and firm and enticing. Her hair spread out over the surface of the water like lengths of silk.

She was making so much noise splashing that she didn't hear him quietly remove his pants and underwear and step into the tank from behind her. He lowered himself to his knees. The shallow water barely came up past his thighs. He wound the length of her hair around his hand. She felt the slight tug and started up out of the water with a fright, but he caught her and pulled her to her knees, facing him.

"It's just me, Paris," he whispered.

But her eyes still ovaled with shock as flesh met flesh. She tried to protest, but he covered her lips with his. As he had hoped, she weakened to the stimulating assault. Her clenched fists resting against his chest relaxed and splayed out over his shoulders. Her mouth relaxed beneath his, too, and opened, allowing entry of his tongue. His manhood leaped with the renewed stimulus of her response and he lifted her upward, allowing his shaft to glide between her legs.

Her immediate response was a muffled, "No," but she soon submitted to the pleasure he knew she was feeling. He wanted to open her up, to slip deep inside her. But not yet. She must want him as badly as he wanted her.

"I won't hurt you, Paris," he said against the corner of her mouth. "Just come to me. Take the pleasure I can give you."

"I shouldn't, Nate. It would be a mistake."

"Don't worry," he softly persuaded. "Everything will be all right."

She moved closer and opened her mouth eagerly to his kiss. He took her breasts in his hands, arousing the nipples with his thumbs. A moan of pleasure rose from her throat and she tilted her head back, sinking into the sensations. His lips traveled down her neck, leaving a wake of kisses, until his mouth closed over the hardened nipples, suckling each in turn. Her head fell back wantonly as she gripped his shoulders tighter, her movement against his manhood increasing in fervency. He joined in with the movement, going mad with his need to plunge deep inside her.

He felt the sweet moisture coming from inside her now, gliding the length of his shaft. How easy it would be to lift her up, slide inside her, and take what he wanted. But he had decided he much preferred winning her trust and waiting for her to come to him with no qualms about intercourse. So he maintained the position, as she moved rhythmically over his extended organ until suddenly she arched her back and cried out with ecstasy. As she did, he shuddered with his own pleasure and released his seed to the water. She clung to his naked shoulders as the sensations continued to lurch through them both, gradually receding like ebb tide from the shore.

Nate studied her expression, soft with rapture. She opened her eyes slowly, drifting out of the sensations the way darkness eases into dawn. As her gaze met his, he recognized a sudden flash of embarrassment cross her face just before she looked away. He wondered again if she might indeed be a virgin, as she claimed. Otherwise, wouldn't she have taken him inside her of her own free will?

She made a motion to rise, but he held her snugly. "Don't run away, Paris."

She avoided his eyes. "Let me go, Nate. We shouldn't have done that."

"Why? Didn't you enjoy it?"

"Yes, but . . . just let me go."

"Paris." He pulled her down and kissed her cheek, her neck. "Nothing's going to happen. You won't get pregnant."

"We . . . shouldn't be talking about . . . this. It's . . ."

He chuckled and finally released her. Floundering, she managed to get to her feet. He stood up next to her and pulled her close again. "There's nothing wrong with lovemaking, Paris. It's a natural thing for men and women to do."

"When they're in love," she clarified. Again she tried to get away.

"And when they just think they're in love," he demurred.

Her eyes locked with his. "What do you mean?"

"I mean, sometimes men and women just need each other, Paris. Don't worry, you'll still be able to find some fine, young upstanding gentleman who will marry you. He'll never need to know about your moonlit escapade on the old Sonoran with a renegade bounty hunter. Of course, I can't guarantee it won't happen again."

His eyes were warm with that seductive glow Paris was learning to recognize. Heat rose again to her face and she wondered if he meant to do it again right now. The feelings started all over and she fought her conscience, which seemed to be a terribly weak opponent to this new physical desire. She broke away from him, sloshed to the granite-edged bank, and pulled her towel around her.

She heard him behind her, also stepping out of the water onto one of the rock shelves. He was unashamed of his nakedness and walked without modesty. She watched the play of the starlight over the strong muscles in his back, buttocks, and thighs. The throbbing inside her began anew. She wanted him again. Only this time she wanted him fully.

She left the tank's rocky alcove and hurried back to camp and her bedroll. She'd brought her derringer to protect herself from his advances, but she hadn't thought of bringing something that would protect her from her own desires.

"Damn," she muttered as she dried and put on her nightgown.

He sauntered back to camp wearing only his pants. He looked rakishly handsome, with one strand of dark, wet hair falling onto his forehead. His body still glistened with moisture. What would she do if he joined her on her bedroll? She didn't know if she could turn him away again and deny herself the exquisite pleasures he offered her body.

She curled up in a ball, drawing her blanket over her,

even though it was too hot for it. She heard him go to his bedroll, heard him shift around on the blankets, trying to get comfortable. Finally, after what seemed an eternity, she heard him breathing deeply in the throes of full sleep. She rolled to her back and tossed back the cover, feeling restless and vaguely disappointed that he hadn't come to her bed.

She had bargained for a lot of things when she'd hired Nathaniel Brannigan and set out after lost treasure. But she had never bargained for love.

Twelve

Paris lay quietly watching a flicker hopping around on the ground, licking up a breakfast of ants with its long tongue. The morning sun hid just out of sight behind the eastern mountains, and as yet the heat had not risen to scorching levels. The desert creatures were out and about, gathering their food, drinking their fill at the springs and *tinajas,* before they would be forced to retreat to shade for the afternoon.

Paris suspected she should take a lesson from them, but she was enjoying just watching them in their morning routines. Woodpeckers were busily making new holes in the giant saguaro, many of which were already riddled from the extensive excavation of the sharp-beaked birds. The holes that had been abandoned by the woodpeckers had been taken over by the tiny elf owls, now at rest from their nightly excursions. Occasionally, the shadow of a hawk, swooping down to rest on the crooked arms of the cacti, sent all the smaller creatures scurrying for cover.

Her gaze lifted to Cerro Trueno, cast in amethyst and gray morning shadows. It seemed to be a live entity, watching her, waiting. For what, she had no clue. But if a mountain could have eyes, Trueno surely did. Or perhaps it was not the mountain at all, but someone who knew she was there and what she wanted. Father Castañeda perhaps?

She shivered involuntarily, telling herself she didn't believe in ghosts and curses. She sat up, drawing her knees to her chest and encircling them with her arms. Now that she was fully awake, her thoughts drifted, then darted from one thing to the next. From Trueno to a roadrunner gulping a scorpion, to a tortoise painstakingly digging a burrow in the sandy soil, to the melancholy *coo-ah, coo, coo* of a distant mourning dove, and finally to the night before in the pond with Nate.

The latter she quickly tried to block from her mind. She had even refused to glance over at him this morning. How would she ever face him when he finally woke up? She was thoroughly humiliated over her behavior. She had acted like one of Tombstone's most notorious whores. He would never believe she was a virgin now. What had stopped him from going further with her last night was beyond her. She had surely offered everything. But possibly her greatest fear was of herself and of a passion she hadn't known existed. She still had weeks in his company. How would she ever be able to tell him no again, when last night all she had wanted to say was yes.

"The desert's a pretty place in the morning, isn't it?" Nate's voice startled her. She turned and saw him standing, fully clothed with the barrel of his shotgun resting on his shoulder, and two doves dangling in his hand. She scrambled to her feet, self-conscious in her nightgown.

"I didn't know you were up." She glanced at the doves. "I didn't hear a shot. I just woke up."

He set the birds on the ground and began building up the fire for breakfast. "You were sleeping so soundly I didn't want to wake you. And I didn't have to fire a shot.

Ground doves aren't easily frightened and I walked right up to them. I killed them with a couple of well-aimed rocks."

Paris watched him, wondering if his thoughts, too, were on the night before, although they didn't seem to be. All he seemed concerned about was preparing the doves for the frying pan. Hadn't it meant anything to him at all but a physical interlude that served to quench his lusty passions? She supposed that for Nate Brannigan seducing women in the shadows of the moonlight was simply second nature, like eating. She would be foolish to think she meant anything special to him. She wasn't sure why she was beginning to feel a disturbing attachment to him. He would never feel a responsibility toward her.

She no longer looked upon him as a low-life bounty hunter a mere step above the outlaws he tracked down for money. No, whoever and whatever Brannigan was, he was a man of morals, respectability, education, intelligence. But he was still a man who wouldn't be interested in staying with a woman for love, or for any other reason. Somehow, in the course of his life, he had detached himself from emotional feelings that ran too deeply. She didn't know how she knew this. She merely sensed a reluctance in Brannigan's nature to become too close to anyone, except maybe his brother Alejandro. It was as if he feared getting hurt or tricked by extending too much trust. She wondered if that was the nature of his personality or if something had happened in his life to leave a scar.

Angry at herself for even thinking of Brannigan devoting any kind of attention to her, she gathered her clothes and announced that she was going behind the bushes to change. Nate's only response was a long and steady scrutiny that encompassed her nightgown-clad body from head to foot. Knowing he was remembering how she had looked the night before, she scurried off like a little desert mole hiding from a hawk, wishing she had a hole in which to hide until the shadow of danger had passed. From the look in his eyes, she was sure he harbored thoughts of repeating their moonlit escapade.

When she emerged, fully dressed, that look was still in his eyes. But she couldn't afford to succumb to his seduction again. She couldn't let his magic touch allow her to lose sight of the fact that she was there to find the lost mission of Santa Isabel. And the sooner the better.

With the two pieces of the map held together, Paris drew a copy onto one of the pages of her journal, which she would use rather than the original. Right after breakfast she and Nate had once again loaded their belongings on the mules and set out toward higher ground and a better perspective of the Pajaro cordillera. From a distance it had seemed to be nothing but a solid wall of rock, but all mountains were elusive in that way, hiding from the eye their secrets within.

Paris saw all too well why the location of the Mission of Santa Isabel was still a mystery. The mountains twisted and curved over miles, and even though their breadth was considerably narrower than their length, the composite before her was filled with canyons and valleys, large and small, visible and invisible. Trueno stood above it all, keeping guard, while the smaller mountain—its seemingly feminine counterpart which W.W. had called Cerro Risa, Laughing Mountain—stood in Trueno's shadow, light moving over her shoulders and breasts as the sun passed behind a few billowy, rainless clouds. The lady did indeed seem to be laughing, or at least she didn't have the dark ominous quality of Trueno.

Frustration and defeat nearly overwhelmed Paris for the second time. Finding Santa Isabel in the maze before her was going to be about as impossible as finding the proverbial needle in a haystack. But she had come this far. She wouldn't give up. She couldn't! There must be some rhyme and reason to where the priests would have finally built the secret mission. Seclusion, first and foremost, would be important. But there would have had to have been water, too, not only for use in the molding of the adobe bricks but to sustain the Indian converts who had spent years in the construction of the sacred building.

She opened her journal and agonized over the map's strange symbols, hoping that now she was here they would start to make some sense. There were a series of humps that indicated the mountain range. Only Cerro Trueno was labeled. Other symbols included a square; numerous circles within circles; three letters of the alphabet combined with numbers, T1R2X3; a rising sun; some U-shaped characters; lines that looked like snakes; and a wavy line cutting across one of the mountain peaks.

Nate sat astride his brown horse, arms folded over the saddle horn, waiting patiently for her to make a decision on where she wanted to go next. He'd been terribly agreeable all morning, telling her that she was in charge and he'd go wherever she wanted to go. It had raised her suspicions and also made her wonder if he really cared at all about the treasure, even though he was now in for half of it. She felt like he was placating her, humoring her until she grew weary of wandering in the desert and decided to go back home. The trouble was he seemed to fail to remember that she didn't have a home and that the treasure was her only chance for any kind of future.

She glanced at him irritably, wishing for a little help or guidance. His horse had even taken on his rider's attitude of absolute and complete boredom; it stood with its head drooping, occasionally kicking at flies and bees that lit on its tender underbelly.

Nate lifted his hat and wiped the sweat from his brow with his shirtsleeve. "Well, Paris, love. Where do we start?"

Paris squinted over at Risa, still silently laughing at her, and at Trueno, still frowning on her and hoping she would go away. How unnerving that the mountains seemed to have taken on personalities, and yet in Paris's eyes they surely had.

"I don't know," she finally admitted. "Nothing on this map seems to coincide with anything on land. If I knew what all these symbols meant, maybe it would make sense to me. Whoever made this map certainly didn't mean to make anyone's search easy."

"No, I don't suppose he did." A smile flirted beneath Nate's moustache and he held out his hand. "Let me take a look."

With complete exasperation on her face, Paris handed him the journal. He studied her drawing intently, turning it this way and that, looking up occasionally as if to line it up with the terrain. Finally, he turned the journal upside down and said, "I think this is how it's supposed to go, but I couldn't be sure." He leaned from his saddle toward her, and, using his index finger, began to explain the symbols. "The rising sun is usually indicative of treasure. However, in this case, since it's right on the mountains, it could also be indicative of the direction east. The snaky

lines are either streams of water or trails. I suspect that
the circles within circles are springs or water sources. At
least one coincides with where we camped last night.
These U-shaped characters suggest horse or mule tracks."

"But what could that possibly have to do with the treasure?"

"I don't know, unless it means you would probably have
to travel three days by horseback to get there, or three
miles by horseback, but you would need to know the start-
ing point. As for the square off to the side here and the
letters and numbers, I have no idea."

She looked across the mountain ridges again, how they
stretched to the east and west, all shaped nearly the same
like the gabled roof of a long house. And beneath that
roof, somewhere, was Santa Isabel. Maybe. Unless the
map was all just someone's idea of a joke. W.W. said people believed the mission could be anywhere from here to
the California coast. It was feasible that numerous missions had been built to conceal the hoards of treasure coming from the Mexican missions.

She released a sigh. "It's nothing but a riddle."

"Do you want my suggestion, Paris?" he asked, crossing his forearms over the saddle horn again.

"No," she said bluntly and defiantly. "You'd just tell
me to go back."

She was met with silence but felt his eyes boring into
her until she had no choice but to lift her gaze to his. She
saw he was indeed studying her intently, but for the first
time she saw compassion in his eyes. Had he finally come
to realize what this treasure meant to her?

"I wasn't going to say that, Paris," he replied. "We're
here. We've only got a couple more weeks of supplies in
our packs, so if you don't want to live off snakes and

birds, I'd suggest we head toward Cerro Trueno, search what valleys and canyons we can before we have to go back. If those symbols are correct, there should be more springs up ahead, but we'll have to search for them." He glanced to the sky and the hundreds of birds circling against its blue canopy. "The animals and birds should show us where the water is."

"Will you lead the way?" she asked, feeling lost and wondering if he saw it in her eyes.

In a slow, purposeful movement, he reached over and put his hand on the back of her neck. With gentle pressure his hot fingers pulled her slightly toward him while he leaned out from his saddle. Turning his head and dipping his hat brim beneath the wide brim of her sombrero, he touched her lips with his in a brief kiss that felt strangely gentle and yet possessive, as if he had a special right to her lips. When he straightened he said nothing, but his eyes were thoughtful for a moment before he finally gathered his reins, straightened in the saddle, and moved out toward Cerro Trueno.

Alejandro dreamed of Paloma. It was not unusual for him to do so. He had dreamed of her lovely face nearly every night since he had lost her. In those dreams she was always making love to him. At times the dreams had seemed so real that he could taste the sweetness of her lips and her body, only to awake to the cold emptiness of his adobe hut. This time the dream was different. Paloma was not making love to him. She was standing very far away. He would move toward her and she would move farther away. Love was in her eyes; he felt it rather than saw it, but worry was there, too. And sadness.

"Go back," she seemed to say. "Go back. You have much to do. You must help Nathaniel. And . . . and there is someone else you must wait for. I love you, but it must be this way."

"No," he mumbled through fevered lips and eyes that saw the desert before him now as only a glittering, heat-intense blur. There had been rain in the distance behind him but nothing now, only a few wispy clouds.

"Ayudeme, por favor," he continued to talk to Paloma's vision. "I need your cool hand upon my brow."

She walked away into the desert and vanished. He opened his eyes, seeing nothing but the bright sun glaring down on him where he had fallen. The dark form of his horse stood nearby, cropping blades of grass and brush. He couldn't get back on the horse. He knew this. He was too weak. He closed his eyes. All he wanted to do was dream of Paloma. Beautiful Paloma. But she wouldn't come back. Oh, why did she have to be so stubborn? Were all women like that?

He struggled to his elbows but fell back to the sand, out of breath. His horse nudged him, then backed away, not liking the smell of the blood. He reached for the reins and caught them. It shouldn't be far to Nogales. If only he could remember the way.

For five days they searched, and nothing seemed to change except the weather. It got hotter. The days were spent searching every canyon and valley for the hidden mission; the nights were spent with Paris doing her best to evade Nate's watchful eyes. She was very careful to bathe in the springs only while Nate was hunting. She knew, though, instinctively that if he had wanted her, he wouldn't have let that stop him. Only a tiny fire separated them at night. It was no barrier to the determined man.

She began to feel miserable, on several accounts. Not only did finding Santa Isabel look hopeless but she was beginning to think that Nate had regretted the night in the pond. She had regretted it, too, at times. But at other times, when the heat got too unbearable and the mirages too annoying, and the hope began to wane, her mind would wander and she would envision them doing the same thing again. She had many times longed to feel that wonderful explosion of feeling that he had pulled so expertly from deep within her. But she kept reminding herself that a man like Nate, a bounty hunter, a man without roots, would never become seriously involved with a woman to the point of commitment. And Paris had no intention of getting romantically involved with a man who would not give her a commitment. Not the sort Tully offered either. It was all very explicit in her mind. She didn't want a lover if she couldn't have his love.

It seemed no man in her twenty-two years of life had wanted her for anything but a one night stand. She supposed she was far from gorgeous, even though her father had told her plenty of times how pretty she was. But fathers always did that. No, she supposed the red hair and freckles, the breasts that weren't exactly ample, the small frame all combined to make a man look elsewhere for the woman who could finally turn his insides out and make him think of marriage. All she had was the hope of treasure to sustain her through her life. With that thought, she smiled ruefully. Maybe she could buy a man's love.

On the seventh day, with supplies running low, Paris sat beneath a mesquite in the heat of the noonday sun while Nate did the same a few yards away. It had become too hot to do much searching during this time of day, and for as badly as Nate said he hated siestas, he'd started taking them simply because there was nothing else to do until things cooled off and they could search again in the evening before setting up camp.

She removed her sombrero, tilted her head back, and closed her eyes against the sun bearing down on her. A small breeze touched her. It felt so good she promptly removed her shirtwaist, too, leaving only her chemise to cover her. Perspiration trickling down her back and between her breasts had become a constant annoyance and she looked forward to each night when they could find water and she could feel the cooling effect of it. More and more frequently she thought that perhaps when she found the treasure she would go someplace where she would never have to be this hot again.

She glanced over at Nate. He was the same as he had been every day. On his back, an arm beneath his head, his hat over his face, his long legs crossed at the ankle, his shirt tails pulled from his pants and then unbuttoned to let the air touch his hairy chest. Her eyes touched his body intimately, making her remember how it had felt against hers. She hungered for him. How odd. When she'd first met him she had thought she would have to use her derringer to fight him off; she had thought him the sort who would spare no woman his desires. Now, she was beginning to wonder if she would have to use the derringer to encourage him to make love to her. But she supposed that technically that would be considered unlawful, and if anybody knew the law, it would be Brannigan.

She forced her eyes from the narrow hips, the bulge of his experienced manhood, the rise and fall of his brawny chest. She closed her eyes, feeling the sun beat unbearably

on her face despite the spot of shade. Hopeless. She felt
so utterly hopeless. And she had come with such high
expectations. In a short time their supplies would be gone
and they would have to go back to Nogales. She knew
she would never get Brannigan to return, even if she could
afford more supplies and could pay him more, which she
couldn't. No, she would probably have to stay right in
Nogales and become the town's first redheaded whore.
That was a prospect that made her think it might just be
better to stay out on the desert and shrivel up like the
ocotillo after spring rains. Or maybe she could con W.W.
into letting her stay with him and cook or something.
Knowing that old geezer, he'd probably want more than
a cook. Her options certainly were not good.

"A pretty sight," came Nate's gravelly whisper from
behind her. "But even in the shade, skin as fair as yours
will burn."

Paris opened her eyes, finding it hard to do, as if the
heat had melted the upper lids to the lower. She knew she
should grab up the shirtwaist and cover herself, but she
couldn't make her arms obey the mind's weak command
of conscience. She didn't move, just shifted her gaze upward to him in a way that felt very somnolent. "You've
got yours off, or partially."

"But I don't burn. I must be part Indian or Mexican.
The sun hits me and I just get darker."

"Well, I'm so hot I don't care if I burn."

"You will when you blister."

"I thought you were asleep." She switched the subject
and saw his gaze move to the lace decorating the top of
her chemise and the ribbons that kept it closed in the front.

"I hate siestas," he reiterated. "I decided I'd feel like
hell if I took one. And I hate feeling like hell. But the rains

will come soon. They call it the monsoon around here. Can you feel the hint of humidity? The faint alkaline taste in the air? There's the smell of creosote in the wind, too, which means it's rained farther south. And look at the clouds building, coming up from the Gulf of California."

Paris glanced disinterestedly at the distant gray-white mass of cumulus clouds. If they were moving, it was imperceptible. They seemed to have been suspended over the same part of the desert all morning. "I can't feel any humidity. And the air tastes as dry as a month-old crust of bread."

He only smiled a knowing smile and closed his eyes. "It's coming."

Nate's bare chest was more interesting to Paris than the possibility of rain, and her eyes strayed to its broad expanse. He was indeed dark-skinned, bronzed as if he always went without a shirt. All of his body had that tanned appearance, though not as dark as his face and hands, which were most exposed to the elements. Maybe he was a half-breed. While that might not appeal to some women, it didn't bother Paris.

"You said you were raised on the Rio Abajo, Nate. Adopted by the Escalantes. Tell me about your life there."

Nate debated whether to tell her the whole truth. Paris already had the preconceived notion, as did most people, that because he had taken up the profession of a bounty hunter he was a man of no moral code. What would she think when he told her he was a bastard as well?

Back on the Rio Abajo, there had been those fine-blooded women from neighboring haciendas who had been interested in him until they'd discovered that Alejandro was the oldest and therefore the heir. He'd watched them run from him to Alejandro like greedy horses from one pile of hay to another which they had considered better. He'd soon gotten a perverse pleasure in telling them he was a bastard, just to see their reaction.

Paris was different from all those women, fluttering their fans and waving their dainty handkerchiefs in their attempts to snare a wealthy husband. The redhead's only goal seemed to be to make it on her own without the help of any man. Her life had not been lived in high society circles. She was not coquettish and simpering, and if she looked down on him at all, it was because of that notion she had about his current profession.

Deciding to chance the truth, he joined her on the blanket beneath the mesquite. "I can tell you nothing about my real parents," he began, looking out across the Pajaro Mountains. "I was taken to the Escalante ranch by someone, probably my mother, and left there in the barn when I was barely a week old. Doña LaReina took pity on me, adopted me, and raised me as her own. Until I was about eight years old, I didn't realize I'd made my illustrious entrance into the world as an unwanted child, probably a bastard."

The light in Paris's gray eyes was soft and understanding, not harsh or condemning. "The Escalantes must have been very warm and generous people," she said. "Alejandro certainly cares a great deal for you even if you're not blood brothers."

He said nothing, just nodded.

It was she who continued. "I envy you having a brother. I was an only child. My mother couldn't carry any more babies to term after she had me. Then she contracted tuberculosis and we moved to Tombstone, for the dry climate. I did have a very good friend, but she married at the age of sixteen and moved away. We lost touch. Now, it's just me."

Even though she forced a bright smile, Nate saw the loneliness in her eyes and the distant look that searched the horizons as if she were searching for much more than lost treasure. Just like he and Alejandro and their friend Rafe Cutrell, she searched for that elusive "something" to fill her heart, that something she would recognize only when she saw it.

He sat back down, glad that she had so readily accepted his unwanted entrance into the world. He suddenly felt a kinship with her and took her hand in his. They stayed that way, side by side, able to do little else but breathe in the intense heat and watch creosote grasshoppers bounding about, the only creatures out this time of day.

"Tell me more about your life with the Escalantes," she said.

If Nate wasn't mistaken, she seemed genuinely interested, so he continued. "It was a grand hacienda that my father, Don Diego, had built on the river. It had been handed down to him from many generations before him and he was very proud of it. He instilled that pride in Alejandro and me. We were wealthy, by most standards, but our parents refused to allow us to get spoiled. Alejandro and I had to work for what we got. We worked with the cattle, right along with the other vaqueros. We were not put into positions of authority until we were older and genuinely deserved the promotion and the responsibility. It was a place of fun times and good memories." He smiled, thinking of it. "It was a place that made a person feel safe."

"And loved?"

He glanced at her. "Yes. My mother, Doña LaReina,

was the sort who held her arms open to everybody. She had more love than she knew what to do with."

"I would have liked to have known her."

Nate's gaze locked with hers. What he wanted to say was, *And I would have liked her to meet you. She would have liked you, Paris McKenna. She would have approved of you. She would have understood your wild, impulsive streak and she wouldn't have tried to bridle it. She would have said, "Let her run, Nathaniel. She'll come back to the corral when she tires of the wind in her face."*

Instead he merely said, "She would have liked you."

"Why did you leave there?" Paris asked quietly.

Nate picked up a pebble and nervously turned it over and over in his fingers. As briefly and as unemotionally as he could he told her about the Apache raid that had taken his mother, Paloma, and little Alejandro.

There was a long silence when he had finished. Then Paris said, "But your father is still there. You and Alejandro should go back for his sake. He probably needs his sons."

Nate stood up suddenly and began pacing. "Yes, he does need Alejandro. But I'm not his son, Paris. I can't go back and try to claim what isn't mine. The ranch belongs to Alejandro. Not me."

"Has Alejandro made you feel this way?"

"No, of course not."

"Then your father?"

"No." Her questions were getting too personal and were making him uncomfortable. Yet he answered them, not knowing why he felt it was all right to share his innermost feelings with her when he never had with any other woman. "I guess I've just made myself feel that way. My father has offered me a piece of land from his vast holdings, but if I took it, I would be taking it from Alejandro. The land has always been passed down from generation to generation to the oldest son. It's for me to make my own way, Paris. That's just the nature of things. It's Alejandro's place to go back and claim what is rightfully his. Our father is old and alone and needs him to help run things. Alejandro needs to pull himself together and go back."

"Don't you think Don Diego might need you, too?"

"I don't know," he admitted. "We were close. He was always good to me. He was and is my father. As I said, I never knew differently until I was older. But I can't step into the place that was intended for Alejandro."

"Then you've pulled away from your father because you felt you didn't have a right to him the same way Alejandro did?"

"Maybe."

Gauging from the clipped response, Paris wondered if she'd overstepped her bounds in being so personal with him. It really wasn't any of her business after all, but she was finding herself caring very much for him, hurting when he hurt, being upset when he was angry with her, wanting to comfort him when he looked young and lost and alone, the way he looked right now.

"I'm sure he considers you his son and would be as happy to see you as he would be to see Alejandro. When we go back, maybe you should see if Alejandro will return there with you, for a visit if nothing else."

"Alejandro will go when he's ready, Paris. I can't make him do anything. He loved Paloma deeply. There are simply too many memories at the ranch. For both of us . . ."

A shadow passed between them. Paris didn't actually see it; she felt it. Alejandro had had Paloma and that was why he couldn't go back. But who had Nate had? What memories were stopping him from returning? Should she ask? Did she even want to know if there had been a woman in his past whom he had deeply loved? Surely it hadn't been Paloma? But she had seen the light in his eyes fade when he had mentioned the woman's name.

He tossed the rock away, as if with the action he was also tossing away the memories of the past. He dropped down next to her again. "We may not find anything out here, Paris. Where will you go when we return? Have you made any decisions?"

She looked away at the austere beauty of the desert, feeling her own burdens press down onto her once again and wishing he wouldn't have broached the topic. He may not have been comfortable talking about his past, but she wasn't comfortable thinking about her future.

She stood up and tried to button her shirtwaist with fumbling fingers that revealed her sudden distress. "We've discussed this before and nothing's changed." She tried to walk away but he caught her arm.

"Are you going back to Thatcher?"

Did he care if she did? Would he prefer it if she didn't? She couldn't read his mind because once again indiscernibility fell like a cloak over his eyes.

She pulled her arm free and moved a distance away. "What do you care, Nate? Once we're away from here, what I do shouldn't concern you at all."

He came to his feet. Fires of anger suddenly burned hotly in his eyes. "No, I guess it doesn't," he replied with a sarcasm that matched hers. "And I guess you don't give a damn what I do either just as long as I wander around in these mountains for a few more days so you can look for something that doesn't exist. Maybe you ought to go back to Thatcher. Maybe he can put more sense into your head than I can."

She felt like slapping his face. Instead she turned on her heel and ran for her horse, shouting over her shoulder. "Just get the hell out of here, Nate Brannigan! I'll find the mission on my own. You just go back to Nogales and your whores and your cards and your outlaws. I don't care anymore, and I'm not going to ask you or beg you to help me ever again! You can keep the damn money, too!"

Paris didn't know where she was going. She just rode. She was so angry, she didn't care if she wandered around on the desert until she died. There was nothing to go back to anyway. Except Tully. Nate knew it, and he actually seemed to be encouraging her in that direction. Why had she thought, for even a minute, that he might care about her and her well-being? They had sat together and held hands, like friends, like lovers. Then he'd as much as told her to let Tully take care of her. Why hadn't he offered? She might have even given up the idea of the treasure if he had. There had been times over the past week when she thought she would give up the treasure hunt just to spend her life in his comforting arms where she felt secure. But it was all an illusion, like desert mirages. He didn't give a hoot about her. He just wanted to get shed of her.

Paris didn't know how many hours had passed before she finally became concerned about the ominous thunderhead building in the distance beneath the sunset and the eerie silence descending over Cerro Trueno. Nate had been right about the subtle change in the air. A storm was coming, and this time it wasn't a dust storm. It was rain.

She could feel it. Smell it. See it. The rains were already pelting the land in the distance, extending in gray-black slanting lines from the black cloud mass and streaking in front of the red-orange glow of the sunset. The wind flared on occasions, riffling the brim of her sombrero, lifting the branches of the paloverdes and mesquite so that they rubbed against other branches, creating haunting whines and squeaks.

She looked behind her, in the direction from which she'd come. The wind touched the sandy soil and swirled it, made it sound as if it was whispering. Risa laughed and Trueno rumbled. Was that only the distant thunder echoing off the mountain's bulk? Or was it, as the Yaquis believed, a brooding power that somehow knew the interloper was lost?

Thirteen

Nate Brannigan knew he was a fool, as surely as he knew Paris was going to be in danger if she got caught out in that storm.

She never ceased to be trouble, and she kept him in a constant state of turmoil. She had him wanting to make love to her one minute and strangle her the next. Now she'd run off and probably gotten herself lost again. He didn't know what had gotten into him to tell her she should go back to Tully. That was the last thing he wanted her to do. And he shouldn't have expected, or even hoped, that she would throw herself at him, declare her love, and ask him to take care of her instead. She had too much stubborn pride to be kept by any man.

The storm was moving swiftly toward them. Did she realize the devastation that desert storms could leave behind? If the rainfall was significant at all, flash floods were sure to follow. Would she know not to take refuge in a low-lying area?

With a tight rein on his nervous horse, he cupped his hand around his mouth. "Paris!"

His voice fell flat, pressed downward into the canyons by the weight of the great black clouds lumbering across the sky at an alarming speed. Their shadows swirled in and around Trueno and Risa, darkening their peaks. Thunder rumbled through their dark masses and resounded on the great mountain with such intensity that it seemed to shake the very ground beneath him. The sheet of rain slanting from their dark bulk looked to be just beyond the ridge where he was positioned. He was already feeling the smattering of its first drops.

"Paris! Paris, answer me!"

He continued moving, calling her name, but at the same time wincing every time a flash of lightning rippled across the black shoulders of the clouds. He was too easy a target on the ridge. He saw the skeletal ribs of several ancient saguaros stretched out on the ground, and he wondered if they'd merely died of old age or if they had been the victims of previous storms, previous bolts of lightning.

Finally, he heard it, the distant sound of her voice between rolls of thunder. "Nate! Nate, I'm over here!"

The sound was elusive. As it came, so did the rains, hammering the ground, pounding his ears. The water collected rapidly, running over the dry slopes and gathering in streams that took old paths and cut new ones through rocks and brush. He had to call to her several more times and then listen intently for her answering call before he could discern where she was. When he did, he moved his horse as swiftly as he dared down the rocky incline. She was exactly where she shouldn't be, in a major wash from the big mountain.

He leaned into the blinding onslaught of rain. It poured off the brim of his hat, nearly blocking his vision as he wound his horse down the slick slope. He pushed the horse as swiftly as he felt the animal could safely take the descent. But the horse's instincts told it not to take lower ground, and Nate had to fight it to get it to go onward against its will.

It seemed he would never reach Paris. He saw her huddled near a mesquite, her sombrero brim having collapsed down around her shoulders and her clothing plastered to her body. It was a warm rain, but she looked chilled to the bone.

He forced his horse up alongside her and extended a hand, shouting above the torrential downpour. "Get up behind me! We've got to get out of this wash before we're caught in a flood."

She removed the sombrero, holding it in her right hand and giving him her left. She could barely open her eyes against the rain as he pulled her up behind him. She wrapped her free arm around him and clung to him. He grabbed the reins of her nervous buckskin and headed up the side of the muddy ravine to higher ground. For each mighty lunge the horses took, it seemed they slid back six feet.

Beneath an angry sky, the massive downpour raced into low spots and collected in roiling torrents that mounted in size by the second. At first Paris thought the wind had come up, for she heard a low, persistent rumble. But suddenly the rumble was louder and right behind them, like a freight train about to overtake them. In alarm, she looked over her shoulder to watch with horror and awe, a giant wall of reddish-brown water capped with foam, sweep across the spot where she had taken shelter. Like a bursting dam, it brought with it giant boulders, brush, cacti, even small animals. It spread across the ravine to a depth of at least six feet and a width of forty.

Paris reflexively tightened her hold on Nate's stomach and felt his hand come over hers in a protective gesture, as if he, too, realized they had escaped the middle of the maelstrom by only a few minutes.

Nate finally brought the horses to a halt on the downside of an outcropping of rocks and brush on the side of the mountain. Once both he and Paris were on the ground, he tied the horses to some scrub mesquite and they sought shelter beneath the branches. These offered little protection from the rain, but at least they diffused its onslaught.

"I'm beginning to think you're trying to get not only yourself killed but me, too!" Nate snapped. "Don't you know better than to go down in a gully in a storm like this? If I hadn't found you when I had, you'd be rolling along right now with the boulders and the brush."

Paris was so frightened by the lightning and thunder and the tremendous force of the surging waters, so miserable from the rain, and so humiliated by her own stupidity that she tried to pull away from him and scramble out from under the brush on hands and knees. But he tackled her and dragged her back through the mud, his arms locked around her middle like iron clamps.

"Just let me go!" she cried. "If I get myself killed, it's my business and not yours! I didn't ask you to come looking for me!"

"Yes, and I'm beginning to be damn sorry I did! I had the tent all set up back at camp. We could have been in it and at least halfway dry. But no. . . . You had to come out here and get lost."

"I wasn't lost!"

"Paris, you're always lost."

She could barely refrain from lighting into him with claws open. How insensitive of him to say such a thing. "How do you know? Maybe I just wanted to get as damn far away from you as I could!"

"You were calling my name."

"Only because you were calling mine," she quickly countered.

"And I was only calling yours because I thought you were lost and needed help."

"I don't need help."

"Then why did you hire me and then offer me half of that damn-blasted, cursed treasure to bring you out here? I'm sure you didn't do it because you feel any fondness for me."

"Well, you can bet your life that's true. Now, just let me go. Now!"

He did, and she fell flat on her face in the mud.

Her cursing joined with uncontrollable tears as she struggled to get up. Finally, she did, and with her came two big handfuls of mud which, with perfect precision, she lopped on either side of his face.

He roared like a bull moose and came at her, knocking her back into the mud, this time on her back with him on top of her. He grabbed her arms and pulled them up over her head. They'd nearly rolled out from under the mesquite, and the rain was not only hitting her full in the face but running off Nate's hat brim into her nose, threatening to drown her.

She turned her head to the side to get away from the downpour. The thunder rumbled across Trueno, shaking the earth beneath them. In the distance it echoed off Risa, softer, like a woman's amused laughter. Mingled with the rain were Paris's tears. Feeling totally exhausted and defeated, she let them flow, burning hot against her cheeks in contrast to the cooler touch of the rain.

She realized then that when she had surrendered to Nate's superior power, he had grown quiet. Still she refused to open her eyes. She didn't want to look at him.

She hoped he was feeling like an ass for making her cry. It would serve him right. But a man like Brannigan probably never felt a twinge of guilt.

She didn't know when the roar of the flood softened. Perhaps it came when the tender touch of his lips on hers seemed to block all the noise from her head until she couldn't hear, only feel. She began to sob and she lifted her arms to his shoulders, clinging to him as if her life depended on him.

"It's all right, Paris," he murmured against her mouth. "Don't cry now. You know I'm no good with crying women."

It was all sweet softness, gentleness, tenderness. His lips took the scalding tears from her face until all she felt was the cool breath of the rain washing over her face and the little mud that it washed from his onto hers.

The delineation of his lips seemed extremely pronounced as she felt their firmness, their moistness, their strength, their provocative movement opening her lips to the hot and precise entrance of his tongue. She felt the heat of his hand slide from her waist upward to her breast, molding over it caressingly, her drenched clothing offering little barrier to either his touch or what he was feeling in his palm. He lifted her slightly, putting his arms beneath her and around her, drawing her snugly to his chest. His kiss deepened until she felt as if it was his goal to become a part of her through a kiss alone. She felt his male length harden against her leg, seeking once again ultimate satisfaction.

Suddenly, though, he ended the kiss and buried his face against her neck. He held her so tightly she could scarcely breathe. In another moment he had risen from her and had pulled her with him back into the brush. She found herself sitting next to him with his arms still around her. His lips no longer sought hers but he continued to hold her.

They sat like that until the storm rumbled away and until the water had ceased its torrential run through the canyons. At last they crawled from beneath the brush, two sorry-looking creatures covered with mud from head to toe but too exhausted from the storm overhead, and the storm inside, to muster either anger or laughter. Grimly, they returned to base camp to see what they could salvage from the storm.

"That little redhead sure must mean a god-awful lot to you, Tully," Enoch Lennox said, shivering beneath his drenched blanket. "Or else that treasure map does. Personally, when I said I'd come out here on the Sonoran with you to find her, I didn't figure we'd get caught in the worst rainstorm this country has probably ever seen in its entire history."

"Yeah, and to make matters worse, we don't know where the hell we are or where that damn mountain is," added Halford Smith.

"I wasn't expectin' no shoot-out at the OK Corral either. Why that damn Mexican came close to killing us all!" Lennox added, stabbing Tully with an accusatory eye.

Tully Thatcher lifted cold, indifferent eyes to Lennox and Smith. Without getting too specific he'd told them about the map leading to a big treasure. He had also told them he would give them part of whatever was found, although he had absolutely no intention of doing so. He figured that if they were fortunate enough to find the treasure, he would have them help him excavate it and load it on the pack mules, then he'd kill them.

Thinking of the other three fools who'd gotten themselves killed so early in the game added to his irritation.
It was certainly getting difficult for a man to find reliable
help these days. All those bums in Tombstone wanted to
do was drink, gamble, whore, and shoot each other over
whores. Most of them couldn't aim straight enough to
shoot off their own cocks.

As for the rain, they had set up camp and constructed
a tent and now sat huddled in it for what good it did. The
rain had been deflected only for a few minutes then it had
begun pouring through the untreated canvas like a waterfall. What wasn't coming in from the top was coming in
underneath, leaving them several inches deep in mud. He
wondered if they wouldn't be better off outside. It was
bad enough being soaked to the bone, but the men's whin-
ing was turning an uncomfortable situation into one that
brought him to the brink of murder.

He reached for his revolver, drawing it from his holster
without Lennox and Smith even noticing until the gun's
muzzle was staring them in the eyes. Lennox's eyes enlarged to the size of Cactus Kate's nipples, and Smith
acted as if he might wet his pants. They both gripped the
edges of their soggy blankets until their fingers turned
white. With the rain dripping down onto the gun from the
canvas roof overhead, the long, black barrel quickly became a gleaming, wet silencer.

Tully cocked the hammer with decisively slow clicks.
"If you boys don't want to be here with me, then you can
just get out right now. Of course, don't expect to get past
the flap on this tent because I'll kill you. You see, you
know too much about that treasure, and I couldn't possibly
let you leave here with that knowledge."

Smith swallowed so hard his Adam's apple traveled the

full length of his throat and back up. "That ain't much choice, Tully," he whined.

"No, and it won't get any better. I told you I'd pay you good for coming with me. Taking you into my confidence was a big risk, so you'd better either hate this rain bad enough to want to die or else you'd better decide you like it real well."

Lennox and Smith stared down the barrel of Tully's .45. But even that didn't hold the threat of their boss's narrowed, black eyes. Lennox shifted nervously in the mud and Smith managed to force a weak smile to his lips. "Oh, I think it'll quit real soon," he said, sounding much more optimistic. "Then the sun'll come out and the old Sonoran will be like it's always been . . . maybe just a little more steamy for a while."

Tully released the hammer and put the revolver back in its wet holster. A thin smile moved his lips but didn't reach his eyes. Lennox and Smith breathed a sigh of relief. They'd forestalled the devil . . . at least for a while.

Paris's discouragement was almost more than she could bear. The camp hadn't been washed away by a torrent of water; it had thankfully been spared that. But the downpour had been so hard that it had soaked through the packs and ruined many of the supplies, such as the flour and cornmeal. The salt could be dried, as well as the sugar, even though the latter would probably end up so hard it would have to be broken with a hammer.

She had only herself to blame. If she hadn't gone off, Nate wouldn't have come after her and they might have been able to secure the supplies before the storm had hit. Now they'd probably have to return sooner than ever to

Nogales unless she could convince Nate—and herself—that it would be just fine to eat rattlesnakes for a few days. But Paris had the feeling Nate wouldn't want to sacrifice unnecessarily for treasure in which he really wasn't interested. Not only did he believe it didn't exist, but if it did exist, he believed it was cursed. Because he was so superstitious he might even be leading her astray so she wouldn't find it.

She glanced at him and saw the grim set to his lips as he surveyed the camp. He hadn't started another tirade on her though. Maybe, like her, the rain had washed all the fight from him. Nevertheless, she felt she should apologize for this unfortunate piece of bad luck.

Pedro came out from beneath a creosote bush, drenched to the bone and looking very miserable. He came to her feet and she picked him up, absently stroking his small back.

"I'm sorry," she said to Nate. "I guess I'm to blame for this."

Nate's eyes lifted to hers; they were filled with cynicism. She saw a muscle jump along his clenched jaw. "You surely do seem to have the unique ability to step in all the cow pies, Paris honey. But aren't you giving yourself a bit too much credit where this is concerned?"

His scowl had a threatening quality, but she caught the tiniest spark of amusement in those blue eyes. She picked up a frying pan filled with sandy mud. "I suppose you're right. I'm good at causing trouble, but only a master could have done this."

Nate's laughter was soon joined by hers. With the tension suddenly gone between them, they changed into dry clothes. All Paris had was her nun's habit, so she was forced to don it once again. The soil and the sun quickly soaked up the rain and dried the clothing hung on bushes. After the spring had bubbled itself clear of the muddy water, Paris cleaned all the pots and pans, and Nate reshaped her wet sombrero, adding a little sugar water for starch to help it hold the shape.

The sun was nearing the western horizon when Paris finished washing the dishes after the meal. Nate settled himself on a rock and lit up a cigar that had managed to come out of the storm without a drop of water on it. It was one of few, and he had stressed his greatest concern as running out of cigars before they ran out of food. He had carefully set the other wet cigars out to dry, along with everything else.

"I guess you know this means we'll have to go back sooner," he said, from his position on the rock.

The pain of it hurt so deeply that Paris couldn't bring herself to look at him. "I know," was all she could say, but inside a stubbornness swelled to bursting point and she set her mind in defiant determination. She would simply have to work that much harder to figure out the map and find the mission. She was obviously not going to get any help from Nate. Damn him for being so superstitious, she thought, and damn Alejandro for scaring the pants off him.

Taking her journal, she gave Nate one glance then dashed up to the ridge to be alone. He must have known she wouldn't go far this time because he didn't follow or tell her to come back.

With only thirty minutes of sunlight left, she opened the journal and studied it, comparing it against the lay of the mountains. After about ten minutes, seeing no new revelations, she sat down on a rock, feeling discouragement grow to threatening proportions inside her. She an-

grily flung the journal onto the ground at her feet and
stared out across Trueno's peak, which was very close
now. She watched the sunlight play across the mountain,
dancing in and out through a few strands of clouds that
lingered from the storm, leaving shadows shifting across
its massive surface.

But then, suddenly, she stood up. She peered not at
Trueno this time, but at Risa. If she wasn't mistaken, there
were bits and pieces of a thin, white line, a scar, curving
across the lady's face.

The clouds shifted, blocking the sun, and the line vanished.

But she'd seen it. She knew she had!

She grabbed the journal. Opening it to the map, she
found the wavy line that cut across one of the unmarked
mountain peaks near Trueno. In that instant, she knew
without a shadow of a doubt that the scar on Risa's face
was a trail.

With heart hammering, she lifted the hem of the nun's
habit up to her knees and raced down the hill toward Nate.

He came to his feet when he saw her, concern jetting
across his face. He grabbed her arms, pulling her up to
him. "What is it, Paris? What's wrong?"

"Nothing!" Her face lit as brightly as the sun itself.
"I've found a trail, Nate, and I just know it's got to be
the one that leads to the mission." She shoved the journal
into his hand and pointed at the wavy line cutting across
the unnamed peak. "That line is the trail. It's got to be.
The peak isn't named on the map but it's near Trueno."
She grabbed his hand and dragged him along behind her
back up the ridge. "Hurry, you can see it before the sun
goes down."

On the ridge, though, the smile on her face wilted. The

clouds had moved on, changed shapes, and the sun was touching the rim of yet another distant cordillera.

"It was there. I saw it," she insisted.

Nate looked at Risa, feeling a sudden relief. He didn't want Paris to be finding any trail. He didn't want her to be finding any mission that harbored cursed treasure. "It was probably just a trick of the light, Paris. Forget it."

She continued to search Risa's lovely, calm face. "I *won't* forget it. It was there. It must have had something to do with the position of the sun and the clouds and that's why I was able to see it a few moments ago but not now. But it was there, Nate. I wasn't dreaming."

He placed his hands on her shoulders. He had to discourage her from this nonsense. He still couldn't shake the feeling that something wasn't right and that whatever it was, they, as interlopers, should leave.

"Paris, I understand why you wanted to see that trail, but it was probably just a trick of the light and nothing more."

"I wasn't imagining it or making it up! Tomorrow I'm riding over there and see if I can find it." She pulled free of his hands. "You can come if you want. I'm close, Nate. I feel it. And Risa is over there laughing at me for being too foolish to figure it out before now."

Nate watched her march back to camp. There was certainly a stubborn set to her shoulders. He sighed, glancing over at Cerro Risa. He really hoped there was no such thing as curses.

For three days Paris and Nate forged their way up rocky slopes and down, through quiet canyons and over the crinkles and creases on the face of the Pajaros. The saguaro thickened, the mesquite thickened, the flies thickened, and so did the heat. The rain storm was only a distant memory, something possibly imagined like so many things in the desert.

Nate wore chaps again to protect his legs from the brush, but Paris's trousers were getting tattered and torn. She tried numerous times to mend them with the small sewing kit she'd brought along, but the efforts were wasted. Nate even offered his chaps, but they couldn't be adjusted down enough to fit her small frame.

The unmarked paths they chose to take led to unbreachable cliffs and dead-end canyons. Steps had to be retraced. At times it seemed that Cerro Risa receded in the distance, getting even farther away. Even after they reached the hem of her rolling foothills, they were frequently led astray. Finally, they climbed to her breast, and Paris surveyed the illusion of her bulk, knowing much lay hidden in the folds of her raiment. The trail Paris had seen was not visible, and finding it could prove to be as difficult as getting to the mountain itself had been. She would simply have to start somewhere, scouring every square inch. There was nothing else to be done. But time was running out. And so were the supplies.

Fourteen

Camped in view of the ominous cliffs of Cerro Trueno, Paris could barely sleep for nervous excitement and fear. She was sure she'd seen the faint scar that could be none other than the wavy line on the map, indicating a trail—*the* trail—to Santa Isabel. And yet the fear lengthened over her, like advancing black clouds of a storm, slowly shadowing her, swallowing her up. What if she'd seen only a mirage, an illusion? Or what if it was a trail used only by mule deer and pumas? What if the gold did lay at the end of that trail and Alejandro was right about the curse and W.W. about the ghost of Father Castañeda?

She tossed her cover back and sat up, reaching for her boots. She turned them upside down to shake out any scorpions that might have taken a liking to the darkness inside. Nothing dropped out that she could see or hear and she finally felt confident enough to pull them on over her stockings. She wasn't going anywhere, only pacing the perimeter of the camp by the glow of the fire, but one didn't step out onto the desert floor without the protection of leather up to his or her knees.

She looked around for Pedro, wishing for a little company, but as usual he'd gone off to find his own place to sleep.

She glanced at Nate, lying on his back in his favorite

position with his hat over his face. He had been quiet since they'd started the search for the trail. She couldn't discern his thoughts, and he hadn't been as vocal about his opinions as he normally was. She was positive he didn't want her to find the trail, let alone the mission. He was still worried about the curse. But it was just one of hundreds of tall tales that grew out on the desert. She thought that perhaps the heat drove people to illusions and desperation when nothing could be seen but miles of cacti and nothing found but mirages. Those poor souls unfortunate enough to hook their dreams to desert stars had to invent hope in any shape and form that they could, even if it meant wild tales that were but figments of their imaginations.

She wanted to believe that gold would be at the end of her rainbow. Never had she wanted anything so badly. Maybe it was just hope and desperation that drove her, but she had to cling to something. At least she had a map where others hadn't. She had direction, and if the mission was there, she would find it.

"We'll get started again at daylight," came Nate's muffled voice from beneath his dusty, sweat-stained hat. "No sense in wearing yourself out tonight."

Paris stopped her pacing and stared at him. "How long have you been awake?"

"Long enough to know you're going to wear your own trail around that bedroll if you don't stop."

"Am I keeping you awake?"

"No more than a fly buzzing in my ear."

For an inexplicable reason, his testiness made her testy. Why couldn't he try to understand how she was feeling? Why couldn't he see she needed someone to talk to? Someone to hold her and tell her that everything was going to be all right.

"I don't think you know what you want," she snapped irritably. "Except to saddle up and go back to that . . . that woman in Nogales."

He lifted his head and shoved his hat off his face, giving her a sharp look.

She stiffened defensively. "Don't look at me like that. I saw her hanging all over you in front of the cantina."

Her words seemed to bring the memory into sharp focus in his mind. "Oh yeah, I remember her, and you, standing in front of that window watching us. You remind me of her."

She was appalled. "How could I possibly remind you of her? I don't look a thing like her. And she was a whore."

He sat up, curling his arms loosely around his raised knees. Something in his eyes told her that, regardless of his saying she was keeping him awake, sleep was actually the furthest thing from his mind. "No, you don't look like her, Paris," he said. "And you don't act like her. But you have one thing in common."

She was almost amused now, wondering how he would ever find a similarity between her and that exotically beautiful, border town woman. "And what's that?" she said, unconsciously tossing her flaming red hair back over her shoulder.

His eyes burned intently, locking with hers. A subtle shift of light in their depths, from glowing to smoldering, made her leery of the thoughts that had sprang to his mind. "You're both female," he said in his gravelly, sensual whisper. "But I wonder . . . can you satisfy a man the way she can?"

He came to his feet and stepped over the fire. His leonine movements alerted her defenses but at the same time seemed to have a hypnotic effect. She remembered all too well the night in the granite water tank. Her heart skipped a beat and took off running. She knew her feet should, too, but they seemed to have taken root in the desert floor. Suddenly, she felt very silly in her riding boots and cotton gown. How could he compare her to that beautiful Mexican seductress and not burst out laughing? Yet the heat in his eyes burned with anything but amusement. She was reminded of the lion, stalking its prey.

He stopped just inches from her and circled her waist with his hands. "I'm beginning to believe you really are a virgin, Paris."

The touch of his whisper sent a chill racing down her spine. "Wh-why?"

"Because an experienced woman would know better than to keep a man awake . . . unless she planned to pleasure him. Is that what you planned to do?"

"No. I . . . I . . . just couldn't sleep. I . . . didn't mean to disturb you."

His hands slid up to her rib cage, coming to a halt just beneath her breasts, disturbing her with slow, erotic heat. "But you did," he said. "Don't tell me you haven't thought of the night in the pond?"

She felt hypnotized by the intense blue gleam in his eyes. She couldn't look away. She was sure he knew that if she said no, he would know she was lying. He was a clever man who missed next to nothing. So she didn't say anything, not realizing that her silence alone was her answer.

His hands moved up over her breasts, gently cupping them. The rush of fire through her body blocked her mind of any further response, other than the one she knew he was eliciting. What an odd thought it was that came creeping like sunset shadows, but she wanted to prove to him that she was every bit as desirable as that black-eyed seductress in Nogales. But was she? And if she wasn't, could she pretend to be? Could she possibly impersonate one of the ladies of the night and win his heart? She had gotten him to go her way once before by pretending to be something she wasn't.

How odd that her intent could change so dramatically. She had come wanting only to find lost treasure and to keep the sagacious bounty hunter at bay. Now, she wanted it all, both the treasure and the man, and she wasn't sure in which order.

She could muster no argument when she felt her gown being deftly unbuttoned and lifted from her, leaving her to stand in vulnerable apprehension wearing only her skimpy underthings and her boots. The desert had cooled but wasn't cold yet, and her skin burned from his touch and his nearness. She needed no other source of warmth.

With eyes closed, she allowed herself to slip into the dreamland of sensation created by the gentle exploration of his hands and lips over her body, all the while clutching his waist to steady herself. He must have sensed the increasing and overwhelming weakness threatening to debilitate her because he lifted her into his arms and laid her back on her blankets, covering her with the length of his hard body.

His lips ignited the fires he had quenched once before, but Paris sensed that the fires she entertained for Nathaniel Brannigan would never die completely. They would lay forever as dormant coals until a look, a touch, a word would be the breeze that would fan them back to raging flames.

She lost touch with reality. She found herself shifting one way or the other in order to aid him in the removal of the remainder of her attire and footgear. It hardly seemed fitting that her flesh should face the desert night alone in its nakedness, and she put her fingers to work removing his shirt. When it had fallen to the ground next to her gown, her hands glided up his taut stomach then around to his brawny back and shoulders. Her lips were just as eager as her fingers to touch him, to know him. She scattered kisses across the dark mat of hair on his chest, making him the first man with whom she had ever shared such intimacies. There was a point when he left her side to strip from his pants and boots. She watched with shy admiration, the firelight flickering over his bronzed body. Then he was back in her arms, spreading her legs with his, and settling into the intimate place of her womanhood. She felt his shaft hot and hard against her. As his lips teased every inch of her, she felt the growing need for complete satisfaction rise again.

She forgot to behave like she thought a seductress should. She found her body gave its own commands and left her obeying wantonly of her own desire, completely shameless.

His lips moved down the center of her stomach to the golden core of her womanhood, shocking her with pleasure, working a magic she could not deny. The burgeoning crescendo inside her grew until she thought she might explode. It was a sweet pain that ambivalently sought an end and yet yearned to go on forever.

He rose over her again; his hot hardness tried to make an entry into her womanhood. She instinctively lifted her legs to better accommodate him, gripping his narrow hips. But suddenly he stopped and in a tortured, ragged breath whispered, "My God, you really are a virgin."

"Yes." Her response was just as tortured as she held tightly to him, needing him, wanting him to continue this thing he had begun. But she wouldn't beg him. It wouldn't be proper, unless she truly was a whore.

He swore again, with more force this time, and pushed himself away from her in a movement so swift it left her confused. While he grabbed up his pants and began yanking them on, she reached for the blanket to cover herself, feeling extremely humiliated and angry. Tears leaped into her eyes.

"For heaven's sake, Nate, I'm a virgin, not a leper."

By now he was down on his backside pulling on a sock with movements that indicated he couldn't possibly move fast enough to suit himself. "Paris honey, you're extremely naive. You'd be wise to stay away from men like me."

"I know about sex, Nate Brannigan, even if I haven't done it myself. I've listened enough to the whores at the Silver Slipper. Why, even the dance hall girls—or most of them—have taken a lover or two. I never did because I never met a man I wanted to share those intimacies with. But now I have."

He couldn't find his second sock, which seemed to have been swallowed by a saguaro, or possibly the wandering ghost of a padre. "Virgins are for men with marriage on their minds," he growled like an angry dog, refusing to look at her. "And . . . there are consequences to pay. You'd better do some serious thinking about them before you decide I'm the man you've been saving yourself for."

"I know I could get pregnant, but why should you care? You'll just head off into the wild blue and forget about me anyway."

"My point exactly. So you ought to be damn thankful I do care or you'd have lost your precious virginity three weeks ago! And you'd better drop the subject or I just might change my mind."

He finally had both boots and both socks on. He stood up, stomping his feet down into his boots. Giving her one last final glare, he stalked off into the darkness, scooping up his shirt from the ground as he went.

Paris stared after him, mad enough to shoot him and humiliated enough to crawl under her blanket and never emerge. She hoped a sidewinder would bite him so she would never have to set eyes on him again.

She began to cry, thinking, Damn him! What's the matter with me? What's the matter with me that he doesn't want me?

Through blurry eyes, and with shaking hands, she groped for her underwear and gown. After she was dressed again, she curled up and pulled the blanket protectively over her. Facing the fire, she continued to sob quietly and uncontrollably. She knew she should be thankful he had cared enough to leave her alone, but somehow that was small consolation to the bitter pain of rejection piercing her heart.

Nate paced. He paced around rocks, over rocks, through cacti and mesquite. When he stopped pacing, his attention was always caught by the glow of the fire below and the woman he knew was there in the darkness.

"A virgin," he muttered. "She really wasn't lying, for once."

He ran a frustrated hand through his hair and realized he was being watched. A few feet away, next to an organ pipe cactus, was Pedro, curiously following his erratic movements. He expected the dog to come at him, attacking him for the sheer delight of it. Instead, the animal lowered himself to his stomach near the cactus and rested his head on his paws, watching Nate with doleful eyes.

Deciding he was in no immediate danger of an attack from the pesky little creature, Nate resumed his pacing.

"Virgins expect marriage, commitment," he found himself talking to the dog who seemed to be a good listener. "What if she was to get pregnant and had to give it away because she couldn't support it? I know for a fact she wouldn't come to me and let me know. She's too proud.

"No. I can just visualize her sneaking into somebody's barn the way my mother did and leaving the child, my child. She might even pin a note to the kid's blanket with the name she wanted him to be called. I don't want that to happen to a child of mine. For one thing, he might not be so fortunate as to be loved the way I was by the Escalantes."

The dog emitted a little whine, which to Nate sounded mildly argumentative, or maybe it was just his own guilty conscience at work.

"All right," he said. "I know I've never worried about getting a woman pregnant before. That's because all the women I've fooled around with were experienced and knew how to prevent that sort of thing. Even the highbrows had their connections, their ways. I was never the first for any of them. But Paris is a naive virgin. She needs to save that for the man she's going to marry. She's been saving it too long to give it over to a renegade like me."

He sat down on a rock and stared disconsolately at the ground. "She's just trouble, Pedro. She's been a trial right from the beginning. If anybody knows that, you should. Look at the hell she's put you through. I'll bet you wish you'd stayed with Alejandro."

The dog shifted and whined, as if recognizing the mestizo's name.

"You miss him, don't you? Well, Alejandro never figured you for having a conscience. People don't figure me for having one either. But I was raised with morals and a conscience both. It's just that they sort of fell by the wayside in Nogales. Border towns will do that to a man who doesn't have anybody to think about but himself."

Nate noticed that Pedro's eyes had closed. But, after a minute when Nate said no more, he opened them again and looked up at Nate expectantly, as if waiting for the story to continue. Nate obliged.

"I guess I should have never gotten up from my bedroll, you know. She just looked too enticing standing there in her nightgown. A man would really be a fool to get hitched up with her permanently. It would mean a life of turmoil and aggravation. After all, she's a petty thief, an accomplished liar," he started counting on his fingers, "a grand trickster, a convincing impersonator, an irresistible seductress. But on the other hand," he switched to the other hand, "she's determined, spirited, brave, strong, fair."

Pedro lifted an ear as if he questioned that final assessment.

Having run out of fingers, Nate stood up and started pacing again. "I don't know why she's throwing herself at me. She's making my life damn miserable. I don't know how long I can stay away from her. I'm only a man, not a saint."

Pedro released a sharp, brief yip, as if agreeing wholeheartedly to that statement. Nate's lip curled into a sneer, and he suddenly felt like throttling the dog again, wishing he hadn't confided all his secrets to him. There were times when the animal acted as if he actually understood. Even if he could—and some strange things were happening out on that desert that would make one believe such an oddity was possible—the stupid dog would never be able to tell anybody.

There was one thing Nate couldn't tell the dog. He couldn't tell the little varmint he was scared, that he had a hollow, frightened feeling that if Paris found that mission and its riches she would take her half and walk out of his life forever.

The treasure was all she wanted, and she had already proven that she would risk everything to get it. Although he wondered if she wanted it badly enough to risk her virginity after holding onto it for as long as she had. She hadn't wanted to give herself to Tully for the sake of survival, but maybe the stakes hadn't been high enough. Could her willingness then to make love to him mean that she actually had genuine feelings for him that surpassed all ulterior motives to get the treasure?

He was tremendously confused over his feelings for Paris Frances McKenna. And he was confused over her feelings for him. One minute she called him a vile bounty hunter; the next minute she was offering him her body in the moonlight.

But it would all end soon. She'd go somewhere, maybe back to Tombstone. Soon they would head back to Nogales, and he would get back to his life finding thieves and murderers and bringing them to justice. He would grow old in Nogales where nothing changed and where emotions were as consistent as the cheap tequila and the flies.

He wasn't sure why, but that thought was not as comforting as it once had been. And he would have told Pedro so, except the stupid dog had fallen asleep.

* * *

Lennox grabbed Tully by the arm, nearly yanking him from his horse. "Holy cow, boss! Did you hear that?"

Tully yanked his arm away from Lennox and glared at the man with disgust. "Of course I heard it, you fool. I'm not deaf."

"What do you s'ppose it was?"

"Dynamite. Somebody's blasting."

"Sounds like it's right up that canyon. Do you think it's that woman you're after?"

Tully shook his head thoughtfully. "No. It's probably just an old prospector, looking for the mother lode. But he might know something, or he might have seen something." With his eyes on the canyon ahead and the coil of dust rising above it, he nudged his horse forward with his knees. "It won't hurt to go see if he knows more than that stupid Mexican did. We might just find he's as agreeable as hell."

Paris awoke to the clattering of pots and pans, a sun that had risen long ago, the vicious growls of a dog, and a man's uninhibited cussing.

"Give it back, you little, bug-eyed bastard, or I'll cook you for breakfast."

Paris sat up, the haze of sleep rapidly vanishing. Nate was a few feet away and Pedro was another two feet from him. Strung tautly between Pedro's bared teeth and Nate's clutching fingers was the bag that held the last of the salt pork W.W. had sent with them. They'd been able to keep it fresh by submerging it in waterproofed canvas at night in the cool spring, then insulating it by day with layers of muslin and blankets. The coolness was thus held in and the heat kept out. Pedro had somehow pulled the bag, which was bigger than him, from the spring and had made up his small mind that its contents were going to be his.

Paris came to her feet, scolding the dog and pulling him away. He didn't want to release the sack but finally had no choice if he wanted to keep his teeth. When it was safely in Nate's possession again, Paris received a clipped thanks and nothing more. Not even a glance.

She gathered Pedro in her arms and watched Nate cut slices off the meat in angry movements with his big Bowie knife. She readily determined that he was as testy this morning as a sidewinder trying to make time over a patch of pincushion cacti. She was sure it had something to do with the previous night. Maybe he hadn't gotten any sleep. She hadn't heard him return to camp, and a glance at his bedroll suggested it hadn't been used. He looked like hell, he hadn't shaved, and there were dark circles under his eyes.

"Damn!" he grabbed his thumb. Blood sprang to the surface and began to drip on the ground.

Paris set Pedro down, warning him to stay back lest he take a notion to steal the meat again. She hurried to Nate, dropping to her knees in front of him.

"Let me see."

"It's nothing," he snapped. "Just a nick. It'll be okay."

Paris eyed the wound and the blood dripping out at a steady pace. A good-sized piece of skin was dangling from the main portion of his thumb. Her stomach turned at the sight of it, but she forced herself to be strong.

"Don't be heroic," she said sternly. "It's more than a nick and it needs to be bandaged."

He reluctantly gave a gruff consent, and Paris swiftly found the pack that held the few medical supplies they'd brought. He kept his eyes averted from hers the entire time she dressed the wound. He watched her hands but refused to meet her gaze. When she had it wrapped, she stood up. "The way it's bleeding I may have to change the dressing again shortly, but it's snug enough that I think it'll help stop the flow."

"It'll be okay," he insisted, turning back to cutting the meat.

She stood over him, watching him and trying to irritate him enough to look at her. His stubbornness was more enduring than hers, however, and finally she clicked her tongue in disgust and returned the medical supplies to the pack. Paris didn't understand his attitude toward her. The right to be irritated should go to her. After all, she was the one who had been spurned last night.

The tension clung to them like the rank smell of creosote bush right after a rain. They saddled up and silently set out looking for the trail again. Paris suggested several times that he stay behind and let her look alone because she knew he didn't want to go.

"The treasure's half mine, remember?" he said. "I want to be there if you find it."

But his tone of voice suggested that he didn't believe for a minute there would be a mission or a treasure and that they were wasting their time roaming in the desert like crazy old prospectors who had succumbed to gold fever.

It wasn't until late afternoon found them weary and at the base of a tall granite cliff that the sharp edge of testiness Nate had been on all day finally eroded into obtuseness. They stepped from their horses to take a break from the saddle.

"How's your finger?" Paris asked, seeing the bandage was blood-soaked, although the blood was dry.

"It's fine." He dropped to his haunches, studying the ground, searching for a sign of the elusive trail.

"Maybe you should let me change the bandage."

"You can do it tonight when we camp."

Paris's patience with him had run out hours before; finally, it snapped. "Listen, Nate, we need to talk."

He stood up, a strange look crossing his face. There was a new light shining in his eyes, a peculiar excitement that made her forget what she was about to say. He was looking around the base of the cliff to either side with an interest that he hadn't expressed during the entire search.

"What is it, Nate?"

He grabbed her hand and pulled her over next to him. Pointing in an angle that went around the base of the cliff, he said, "Look there. You can hardly see it except in just places where it hasn't grown over, but it looks like a trail."

Paris's heart began to thump wildly. Nate secured the horses to the limbs of a stunted ironwood tree. Taking Paris's hand again, he started around the base of the cliff. Pedro was tired of their escapades and disinterested in going another step farther. He collapsed in the shade of the horses and promptly fell to his side, deciding it was as good a time as any to take a siesta.

Keeping a watchful eye peeled for the ubiquitous snake or scorpion, Paris and Nate wound single-file through the undergrowth, following what appeared to be remnants of an old trail.

"Why haven't the animals continued to use the trail?" Paris asked.

Nate stopped, allowing her to catch up to him. "I don't know, but maybe it wasn't a natural trail for them. Or maybe it used to lead to a water source that has since gone dry. One way or the other, it's been abandoned and the cactus and bushes have slowly begun to take over."

"Then it's just like W.W. said," Paris replied, vaguely awestruck. "The Yaqui converts planted the path to hide the trail. My God, Nate. This is it. I feel it."

Nate suddenly grabbed her hand and started off again. "It'll be dark in a few hours. Let's keep moving."

Paris was surprised to see him so enthusiastic. She wondered if he had finally put aside his fear of curses and ghosts.

Both of them kept their eyes focused on the ground. They lost the trail at one point and searched back and forth, around in circles, lifted brush out of the way, even got down on their hands and knees, and finally had to admit that it had vanished.

Paris's heart took a tumble, a bad one all the way to her toes. They were too close to lose it! Disheartened, she sat down on a rock, removed her sombrero, and wiped the sweat off her brow with the hanky she carried in her pocket. Nate offered her a drink from his canteen. It was warm, something she'd grown accustomed to, but a few drops on the ends of her fingers transferred to her face seemed cool enough to ease the fiery flush that perpetually stained her freckled cheeks.

Nate brushed a few drops of the water over his own face while visually scouring the side of the mountain for a sign of the trail farther up.

It was then that Paris heard it. Music. A sound that was almost like the wind touching chimes. It was so distant she had to focus all her concentration on it. Then it was gone.

"Bells," she mumbled.

"What?"

With her head still cocked to the faraway sound, Paris held up a hand, motioning for Nate to listen. "I heard something," she whispered, her heart pounding with renewed excitement. "You're not going to believe this, but it sounded like bells."

Nate, too, listened, but the sound didn't come again. "It was probably just the wind, Paris."

"No." She stood up. "I heard it. It was far away, but I heard it. I know I did."

She looked up the side of the mountain. It was steep, but going straight up was the shortest way to find out what was at the top. They could find an easier way in the morning, but she had to know what was up there and darkness would be coming sooner than it was welcomed.

She started scaling the mountain, grabbing brush and rocks to help her ascent. She looked back only once and saw that Nate was following her.

With heart hammering from exertion and expectation, Paris finally reached the top and stepped out onto a mesa. It stretched before her, void of anything taller than brittlebush and ocotillo. When Nate joined her, she set off again, skirting the edge of the mesa, determined that she had not been led on a false chase this time.

Then, far below, something white stood out from the taupe-colored canyon walls. She grabbed the binoculars dangling from a cord around her neck and lifted them to her eyes.

Suddenly, she could scarcely breathe. Her hands began to shake. "Nate, come here."

He heard the urgency in her voice, saw her excitement. He rushed to her side. "Paris, what is it?"

"There," she whispered, her voice in quiet awe. "It's the mission. The lost mission of Santa Isabel."

Fifteen

Nate stared at the distant adobe building nestled in thick brush. From his position on the mesa, and to the naked eye, it appeared as small as a doll house. It wasn't until he tried to lift the canteen to his lips again, to ease the sudden dryness threatening to close off his throat, that he realized his hands were shaking. Like echoes in the canyon, Alejandro's words began reverberating in his mind, then W.W.'s. Uneasily, he glanced about, thinking of Father Casteñada.

He wiped his lips with the back of his hand and recorked the canteen. His stomach churned nauseously, but he knew it wasn't due from drinking too much water. Surely the curse of Santa Isabel wasn't working so soon?

"We've got to find a way down there," Paris said, interrupting his thoughts. "The trail has to be around here somewhere."

"Do we have to do it now?"

She gave him a sharp look.

"The sun'll be down soon," he pointed out, hoping she wouldn't realize that he didn't want to go down there. He especially didn't want to go down at night. "Maybe morning would be a better time."

She had gone back to looking at the mission through the binoculars, unconcerned with his opinions. "If we can find the trail we'll go back and get the horses and camp down there. It would be closer than going back to last night's campsite. In the morning I can go right to work on finding the treasure. Just look at all those springs behind the mission, Nate. There must be half a dozen." She handed him the binoculars. "They're just at the base of the rear canyon wall."

Nate took the binoculars and focused on the springs. Their source was in the perpendicular canyon walls that rose high behind the mission. Apparently, seepage formed the pools, which in turn ran through the narrow valley and then disappeared into the ground.

He couldn't dispute her logic about staying down there, but getting there would be the problem. Steep canyon walls rose all around the mission, high and towering, probably four hundred to seven hundred feet high. There had to be a way into the canyon or the mission could never have been built, but scanning the area from their vantage point revealed no such route.

Nevertheless, Paris set off, searching for a way to the canyon floor. Reluctantly, Nate followed. Even though the sun still warmed the mesa, evening shadows had begun to creep into the canyon, lengthening the silence to an unearthly quality that settled deeply and disturbingly into Nate's soul. The sun still illuminated the upper portion of the canyon, casting a reddish glow to rocks whose colors seemed to change like the skin of a chameleon, depending on the sun and shadow.

He didn't like the place, but he wouldn't tell Paris so. She had already niggled him enough about being superstitious.

"Nate!" she called excitedly from a few feet ahead. "Come here, quick. I think I've found a way down."

He dragged his feet but inevitably arrived at Paris's side. She grabbed his hand and pulled him down on his knees next to her, pointing to a thin trail that zig-zagged off the mesa between cactus, brush, and rocks, following the only slope remotely feasible for man or beast to descend.

"It's been traveled heavily," Paris said. "The animals must be using it to get down into the canyon for water."

"Yeah," he responded dryly. "Or else Father Castañeda keeps it packed down going back and forth on his hauntings."

She gave him another look, a thoroughly disgusted one this time. "Nate, I wish you wouldn't make so much of that. It was probably just W.W. having a good time with us. Come on, let's go back and get the horses."

She held his hand, pulling him along like a rowdy boy, reprimanded and being forced into the toolshed for the switch on his behind. Still, her hand felt good in his so he let it remain there until they had to separate and make their way back down the mountain to the horses and Pedro.

By the time they had scaled the mountain a second time, leading the lunging horses and pack mules up the steep incline, dusk had settled into the canyon, making the trail hard to see. Without the sun warming the soft, almost feminine face of Santa Isabel, the mission was barely visible against the cliffs.

After a time it became evident that the trail's circuitous course had been laid out on a landslide that must have occurred thousands of years ago. Occasionally it was lost completely to giant slabs of rock that proved to be treacherous for the horses, or it narrowed precariously, falling off hundreds of feet into nothingness. Nate led the way, testing the ground for weaknesses that could send one of them to their death.

In the dim light, the progress was nerve-wracking and slow. By the time they reached the security of the canyon floor, they had to strain their eyes to see through dusk's murky covering. And Santa Isabel was lost to them behind a jut in one of the canyon walls.

It seemed a sacrilege to break the silence of the canyon. The only sounds were the distant hum of flies and crickets and a few croaking frogs. Paris and Nate said nothing as they set off again, this time side by side. Even Paris moved with slower steps as they advanced through the canyon on the unsure footing that evening brings. An eerie reverence in the solitude of the place made her feel very much like an anxious intruder, although she would never admit it to Nate. Or maybe it was just the mysterious quality that belonged to the advancing darkness and had nothing to do with the place itself.

They splashed across the dark ribbon of a shallow stream whose seasonally higher waters had left behind a sandy bar on either side, almost like beaches. Blue-flowered smokethorn, mesquite, paloverde, desert willow, and hummingbird bush were just a few of the desert plants crowding the area for a place close to the stream. The canyon's floor seemed a rich carpet of plants and cacti of every kind, growing so thick it was difficult to find a way through it all. Rocky ridges and outcroppings also supported an abundance of life.

Saguaro stood tall and abundant on the valley floor. They passed by an ancient one, broken off at the base, whose skeletal ribs now lay rotting on the ground, providing a home for orange Mexican poppies.

They halted at the sound of grunting and snuffling in the brush just ahead. Paris's heart picked up speed until it matched the rhythm of a pounding locomotive before she recognized several adult peccaries foraging under some paloverdes. Like tame pigs they rooted with their pointed snouts, grunting as they moved. Occasionally, they released high-pitched yips and barks or growled at youngsters, no bigger than rabbits, following obediently behind their parents on thin, fragile-looking legs. Then, suddenly, one of them spotted the trespassers and released a shrill cry of alarm. In seconds the entire herd had thundered away to safety.

Overhead, a procession of white-throated swifts streamed into the canyon, swooping with amazing speed and accuracy into their nests hidden in the crevices of the cliffs. After their sudden appearance and disappearance, the canyon seemed more hauntingly quiet than it had before.

Nate and Paris continued to follow the stream for another thirty yards. Then, rounding a bend, they found themselves face to face with the bulk of Santa Isabel.

The empty openings of small windows resembled dark, shuttered eyes watching their approach. For a fleeting instant, Paris had the odd and disturbing sensation that real eyes were hidden in the shadows. But, as quickly as the thought came, she chastised herself for thinking it. The place was deserted, of course. Once the Yaquis must have filled the canyon with their presence, busily making adobe bricks from the earth and the spring water. Father Castañeda had wandered among them in his dark robe, giving instruction and prayer. He had stood here, possibly in the same spot as they, and watched his dream built brick by brick. Maybe he had been a man of great ambition and had helped in the bricklaying and in the spreading of the final layer of white clay plaster over it all. The plaster was peeling from Isabel's face, revealing the bricks beneath, but enough remained for her to still claim her beauty. It was obvious to even an untrained eye that the mission had been built to endure the weathering of time. Even the arched wooden doors leading into the nave hung tightly in place, still closed against the elements that would have long ago violated the sanctity of the room within.

Paris's feet took her toward the mission, while Nate veered toward the springs. "We'll need to set up camp," he said. "It'll be too dark to see pretty soon."

"I thought we could spend the night inside," she said.

A look of horror carved itself into his face. "If you're hankering for sleeping indoors, Paris, you'll have to go it alone. I prefer the stars."

"To what? To being indoors or just to being indoors in the mission? Honestly, Nate, how can you believe all the ghost stories? This is just an old building. Nothing more."

"I wasn't worried about ghosts. I was thinking more along the lines of being boxed in and attacked by Indians."

Paris didn't believe that excuse for a minute. "That's not likely. I suspect they're as afraid of this place as you are."

"I'm not afraid of it," he insisted. "I just don't like sleeping in old, dank buildings and on hard floors where the mice and rats are more likely to chew on your ears and your toes. Or having a hundred-and-twenty-year-old roof fall down on us. It may look strong but that doesn't mean it is. We'll go through the mission tomorrow, in daylight. That'll be soon enough. If that padre put a curse on his treasure, he might have also set some traps in there for people who were unlucky enough to find it."

Paris could see he was adamant, and she knew he wasn't going to be coaxed, shamed, or bulldozed into doing something he didn't want to do, but she balked at his unreasonable insistence to wait until morning. "Nate, we're here. I've finally found what I came here to find. At least humor me by taking a brief look inside. I want to know what's on the other side of those double doors."

Nate made no attempt to hide his irritation. "You can take one of the lanterns and go explore all you want," he said. "I'll set up camp while you're visiting with Father Castañeda—or maybe I should say his ghost."

Paris knew there was no point in arguing over that. "Very well. If I can't get you to go with me, then I have no choice but to go alone."

"It's not going anywhere," he said wryly. "Why not just wait until morning?"

"No," she replied stubbornly. "I'm here, and I'm going inside."

He finally shrugged. "All right, suit yourself. But don't wander too far away. You never know if there might be an old mine shaft around here, or even a rotted wine cellar."

She went with Nate to the springs first to help set up camp. The water, trickling through a crack in the canyon wall, was fresh and cold, and they drank their fill before doing anything else. The water was also abundant enough that it supported a few cottonwoods next to its edge, trees that normally didn't grow that far south.

By the time Nate had a fire going, darkness had snugly enclosed the valley. Paris eyed the back of the mission and wondered if it would be better to wait until morning when Nate would go with her.

She didn't understand it and didn't like to think about it, but a mysterious and frightening spell did indeed seem to be cast over the valley and the silent mission.

Questioning her own courage, she took care of her horse and helped unpack and stake the pack animals. She wasn't sure she was ready when Nate handed her the lantern, but she took it, not wanting to admit that all the talk of ghosts and curses was finally working on her imagination, too.

"Sure you won't come?" she asked in a bold tone that she hoped concealed her increasing apprehension.

He gave her a wry smile. "No. I'll just stay here and exercise my fine culinary skills." He waved a hand toward the mission. "Take your time and watch out for snakes and ghosts. I imagine they'd both like the coolness of the mission."

Tossing him a dirty look, Paris stepped into the wavering golden path opened by the lantern. The light was so close it nearly blinded her, forcing her to look away to the black perimeters and the objects that clung to the shadows like curious observers of her intentions. With each giant saguaro whose arms spread out in those dim reaches, she had to catch her breath and remind herself they were only plants, trees of the desert.

Fifty feet from Nate's fire, she debated whether to go back and say she had decided she was too tired after all for exploration. It had been more difficult to leave his company than she had imagined. But the mission was just up ahead and she didn't want to give him the satisfaction of knowing he had sufficiently put some frightening doubts in her mind.

She walked around to the front of the mission, realizing how tall the grass was surrounding it. Fed by the springs and seepage from the canyon walls, it grew past the tops of her riding boots.

Even though it was dark, Paris could see the two belfry portals on either side of the main entrance. Both bells were still in place. Each bell tower contained not only the bell tower windows but several smaller windows in either the front or the sides of the tower itself. The front entrance had been embellished with an extensive design of wood and clay around the door. The main entrance was graced by a false front that rose high above the doors, and between the two belfries the arched facade was richly ornamented with a Moorish star window. Perched on top of the facade, as well as on top of the bell towers, were wooden crosses, finely carved and standing silhouetted against the moon.

The front door beckoned Paris like a silent voice. A few feet from it, her light revealed its sun-faded, peeling surface. The exterior had been treated with a black substance that resembled creosote, and she was sure that could be credited for the lack of wood rot.

When she reached tentatively for the iron handle she felt a burst of anger at Nate for not coming with her. He was carrying this superstition thing entirely too far. Her anger ultimately gave her courage that she might not have otherwise had. She wouldn't allow his fear to deter her from getting what she wanted.

The hinges creaked, just as she had expected them to. After all, a hundred-plus years was a long time for a door to go without oiling. But, even without oil, the heavy doors swung easily aside on iron hinges that had successfully withstood time. The lantern light touched upon a ridge of sand that had blown beneath the door, piling up until no more could enter. She stepped over it, her boot heels resounding on the dark tile floor.

The lantern was too weak to give her a good view of the room, but she could see it was not extremely large as one would have thought gauging from the outer appearance of the building. And it was empty. In that moment she knew without a shadow of a doubt that this was Santa Isabel. The absence of pews was a stark reminder that the building hadn't been built to accommodate worshippers. It had been built only as the secret receptacle for riches.

Keeping her eyes trained to the floor for the snakes Nate had warned her about, she lifted her light only when she paused occasionally on sure footing. The golden light fell upon an arcaded corridor to the right and other closed doors that she assumed must lead to quarters and store-rooms.

Her footsteps echoed hollowly on the dark tiles. She paused in the center of the pewless chapel and saw that the walls were also void of decoration. No paintings of Christ or the Virgin Mary. No statues standing silently in the corners. Only adobe brick surrounded her, its plaster crumbling from time and lack of repair. Had everything been stolen, or had there never been anything here?

Her advancing footsteps frightened a mouse that in turn frightened her. She gasped, clutching her heart as the mouse scurried under a wooden door that was deeply hidden in the shadows beneath the massive wood and stone arcade.

At the front of the room, she saw a wooden pulpit, the only stick of furniture in the empty room. She wondered if the Yaqui Indians had settled, cross-legged on the tile floor, finding temporary respite from their work and from the intense heat of the sun, to listen to Father Castañeda tell them about God and how they must protect the treasures of God which were secreted here. But where?

Turning to the right, her light danced over the doors beneath the arcade. She took a step toward one of them when a noise behind her, like a soft footfall on the tile, brought her whirling around in a flash of alarm.

But there was nothing there. Only shadowed corners that the dim light of the lantern could not fully penetrate unless she drew closer. Yet there seemed to be a shadow within a shadow, a dark presence as tall as a man. As tall as a man in black robes. As tall as Father Castañeda . . .

Suddenly, she bolted for the door.

Blindly, she ran toward the safety beyond. She had barely cleared the sill when she ran headlong into a solid wall of towering flesh. She screamed. From sheer survival instinct she whirled on her attacker, kicking and clawing and swinging the lantern in her defense.

"My God, Paris! Stop it! What's wrong with you?"

The sound of Nate's voice brought such a surge of relief that she collapsed in his arms. But only for a second, then grabbing his hand, she hurried away from the doors once again. It wasn't until she had them both several yards from the church that she finally looked over her shoulder.

"Were you just inside?" she demanded in a voice that sounded tremulous, even to her.

"No." Nate was clearly confused and concerned.

A chill rippled down Paris's spine as she kept her eyes trained on that yawning black hole of the open doors, expecting something evil to emerge at any moment.

"Paris, are you all right? Did something happen in there?"

"No. . . . I just heard something, probably a mouse. Is supper ready?"

His arm slipped around her waist. The security of it made her fears melt away. He had his revolver. If anybody attacked them, he would protect her. But then she remembered uneasily what he had said about not being able to protect her from everything.

"No," he responded. "I just decided I'd better come

with you. I . . . don't like the feel of this place. And don't try to fool me. Something happened in there."

She tossed one final look over her shoulder at the mission's reticent face. "Like I said, it was just a mouse, or maybe a bat in the belfry. I think I've been listening to too many tall desert tales," she said, hoping to convince herself as much as him. "It's just an abandoned old church."

"You mean there weren't piles of spun gold in the corners?"

His sarcasm wasn't what she needed to hear at the moment. "No, the chapel was empty. But there are other rooms. The padre would have hidden it. Maybe even buried it."

"Then you plan to tear up the floors, walls, everything? It's a holy place, Paris. Have you forgotten that?"

"I'll determine what to do according to what I find. You never did say if you'd help me."

He paused on the path back to camp, turning her so that she faced him, so that she was held in the curve of his arm. With his lantern and hers, they were caught in a golden circle of light that anyone could see. Paris was uneasy about that and wondered if they should extinguish the lanterns. She couldn't tell her fears to Nate, however, without making his superstitions worse. He might just fork his horse and high-tail it. She wasn't so sure she wouldn't be right behind him. Was someone else here, too, looking for the treasure?

She lifted her eyes from the darkness to meet his. "Well? Do you intend to help me?"

Words seemed stuck in his throat, but he managed to give her a positive nod of his head.

She stepped away from him, anxious to put more distance between them and the mission. "We'll get at it first thing then. The sooner we find the treasure, the sooner we can leave."

"Amen to that."

The breeze riffled Paris's hair with invisible, inquisitive fingers. She shivered. "Yes, amen to that."

Paris remained close to the comforting heat and light of the fire, finding that the soothing blaze not only served to frighten away wild animals but gave the illusion of keeping away, too, the imaginary ghouls that had inserted themselves in her mind. She decided fear was a contagious disease. Alejandro had given it to Nate, and Nate had given it to her. Tomorrow, she was positive, she would find an explanation for the tall shadow that had so greatly resembled a priest in black robes. Her mind had played tricks on her, nothing more.

"Where's your appetite, Paris?"

Nate's question brought her mind back to her untouched plate of stew. She set to work feigning interest in it, knowing she should enjoy it since the supply of potatoes and onions they'd brought was nearly gone. At least they hadn't lost any of them in the flash flood.

"It's really good, Nate," she tried for enthusiasm. "I'm just tired and I can't believe I'm finally here. It's a funny thing about dreams." She glanced at the stars as if that was where dreams resided, then her gaze slid back to the graceful profile of the mission in the moonlight. "Somehow a person doesn't expect to ever really reach dreams, I suppose."

"You haven't yet, Paris," he quietly reminded her.

"Maybe the only thing Santa Isabel holds in her womb is hopes and memories . . . and dreams."

Paris met his sagacious blue eyes. She was unexpectedly bit by anger again, and she lashed out. "Why do you always want to make me face reality, Nate? Why can't you let me have my dreams, even for just a little while? Do you have to remind me that there might not be anything in the mission and that I might leave here facing an uncertain future?"

She tossed her plate down, spilling the majority of the stew onto the ground. She curled up on her bedroll with her back to him. Couldn't he see how the darkness inched closer to her blankets and, in that darkness, the shadows of things she didn't understand and didn't want to face?

She heard him break up more brush and add it to the fire. She heard the fire snap and pop and roar as it hastily consumed the finer branches and dead leaves. Then she felt him near, very near. Still feeling the fury, she turned her head to look over her shoulder at him. She was about to make a remark, but his face wasn't shadowed by the Stetson. In his features, she saw a pain that went deeper than words. She knew then that he understood everything she felt, for at some time in his life he had felt that way, too.

She also realized, in those seconds, that he meant more to her than any amount of buried treasure. If anything happened to him because he'd come here with her, she would never be able to forgive herself.

He lowered to his knees next to her. His whisper had the quality of the wind brushing gently over the sand. "I don't think we need the fire separating us tonight."

He stretched out next to her, conforming his body to hers. The arm he put over her effectively blocked out the fear of creeping shadows. The kiss placed on her ear made her close her eyes and wait for more to follow. But Nate Brannigan only held her.

After a while, the desert chill began to settle in and he pulled a wool blanket over them. Paris was not a woman to throw herself at a man, no matter the need she felt inside. When she realized he was not going to make love to her, she finally closed her eyes. She'd done a lot of foolish things lately, and perhaps the greatest was losing her heart to him. In the end, the treasure was all she would walk away with—if that. She could dream of love, but for Paris Frances McKenna love was as elusive as the ghosts of Santa Isabel.

The bloodcurdling scream brought Paris awake and upright.

"My God, Nate. What was that?" She looked into the darkness, her eyes huge with fear.

"Nothing but a wildcat. We're invading his territory, and he doesn't like it."

The spine-chilling cry of the puma suddenly echoed again through the narrow valley walls, making Paris press close to Nate's chest. The sound lifted their eyes to the towering cliffs and to the silhouette of the great beast sketched against the star-studded sky.

"Is he after our animals?" Paris queried nervously.

"It's possible, but they're close enough to us that I don't think he'll take the chance."

Minutes passed, Paris didn't know how many, but finally the mountain lion moved on. In the next second it was gone, dropping down out of sight over the backside of the mountains. As she relaxed and was finally able to take a breath, she became strongly aware of Nate's hand pressed against her lower back, holding her tightly against him. His hand seemed so finely imprinted on her flesh that she felt the pressure of each separate fingertip. The need she'd suppressed earlier began to rumble again, like an advancing fire storm gaining momentum with each additional yard it consumed.

To her disappointment, Nate must not have shared the feelings. He released her, came to his feet, added more fuel to the fire, then shouldered his Winchester.

"Go on back to sleep," he said without looking at her. "I'll keep watch for a while just to make sure he doesn't come back."

Paris watched him walk from camp in a stride that seemed more determined to put distance between him and her than to find a spot for a night watch. He finally stopped near a jumble of rocks next to one of the springs. She watched him remove one of the cigars from his pocket and touch a match flame to its tip. The flickering yellow-orange light drew a distinctive profile of his rugged face.

In minutes the pungent aroma tickled her nostrils, and she decided it wasn't such a bad smell after all. She supposed that for the rest of her life when she smelled it she would be reminded of Nathaniel Brannigan, the bounty hunter who had, once upon a time, stolen her heart.

He blew the match out. The profile of his face was plunged back into darkness. Because he sat with mesquite behind him, it was hard to make out the details of his form. Paris focused on the red tip of his cigar and drew upon her memory to see what her eyes could not.

He smoked the cigar until there was only a stub remaining. She watched him drop it and press it deep into the sandy soil with the toe of his boot. She wasn't sure her eyes were seeing things accurately in the next few minutes, but she couldn't pull her gaze away from him. She realized he was removing his clothes, tossing them onto the ground in the casual manner that she sensed was shared by most men. Nate Brannigan wasn't a man overly concerned with his clothing as long as it protected him from the sun and was rugged enough to stand up to the country he inhabited.

He must have thought she would be asleep because he stood naked at the edge of the water, never glancing her way. The moonlight shone on his narrow hips, strong thighs, and broad shoulders more brightly than it had on his dark clothes. He turned, and the faint, silvery light molded itself around the length of his extended manhood, making it clearly visible to her. Then he stepped into the pool, wincing a little at the coldness of the water before submerging himself.

Like a woman caught up in a magical spell, Paris left her blankets and walked to the rock-encircled spring. Nate saw her before she had gone but a few feet, and he watched her approach with eyes that held unfathomable thoughts.

He sat in the pool, the water lapping at his chest and caressing its mat of dark hair. Simultaneously the gentle movement of the water mesmerized Paris's senses, lifting her desires to dangerous levels. His gaze locked with hers and she couldn't look away.

"Do you mind if I join you?"

In slowly consuming contemplation, his eyes took in her every detail. "Is it a bath you want, Paris, or are you just too hot to sleep?"

Oh, yes, she was too hot to sleep. And she could tell by the smoldering glow in his eyes that he knew the heat was from a fire that burned within. She doubted even the cool water could quench that tumultuous internal blaze. Something in his eyes warned her that to step into the pond would be the equivalent of stepping into quicksand. Once she began to sink, she would be lost. All judgment, whether right or wrong, would perish. The other night, lost to the enchantment of his touch, she'd never doubted her course of action. But now she wasn't so sure. Nate Brannigan had made it more than clear that he wasn't a staying sort of man.

Caught in her earlier turmoil, she hadn't changed into her nightgown. Now, she reached for the hem of her shirt-waist and pulled it free of the trousers' waistband. His eyes strayed from hers to the fingers that slid the buttons through the buttonholes, releasing them and opening a view to her camisole. The shirtwaist fell away from her shoulders and hands, settling into a white patch on the dark ground. Soon the trousers and each piece of under-wear followed in the same manner until she stood self-consciously naked in front of him. She tried to discern if he thought she was pretty, but she could read nothing from his expression. Her only sure knowledge was that when she stepped into the water she would be in his arms again, and her heart began to thunder with anticipation.

The water twisted coldly around her ankles, then her calves. She went to her knees next to him and felt it ripple up around her thighs.

"You should have stayed on your blankets, Paris," he said in an impassioned whisper. "You'll only get into trouble fooling with a man like me."

She touched his cheek and he caught her hand in his, as if her touch had burned him and he wanted to prevent it from happening again.

"Maybe I have too much of my daddy's gambling streak," she whispered.

"I can't keep saving you from me, Paris. If you ante into this game, you play to the finish, no matter what hand will be the final one."

So he was telling her she was foolish to want him, to throw away her love on him? Maybe she was. All she knew for sure was that she'd never wanted a man the way she wanted Nate Brannigan. How could she explain or even understand that powerful and primitive physical desire? That awful and yet wonderful need that would make her gamble so recklessly?

He rolled her hand over in his and kissed her palm. His eyes waited, giving her that last chance to run, to save her virginity for a man who truly loved her and who would marry her. But she couldn't move; the fire was raging and it needed quenching.

His fingers curled around hers and he pulled her down into his embrace . . . and into the quicksand of her own desire.

Sixteen

Nate drew Paris down into the water, molding her naked body to the length of his. While his lips learned every intimate detail of hers, his hand memorized the contours of his back and the curve of her buttocks. His fingers pressed gently into her lower back, shifting her hips closer to the hardened length of his manhood. It strained against her, searching for ultimate satisfaction.

He rose to his knees and brought her with him into the same position. She sank an inch or two into the sandy bottom of the pool. The tiny pebbles bit into her knees, but any twinge of discomfort was readily consumed by the wondrous trail of fiery kisses he left burning along her neck, over her collarbone, and to the swell of her bosom. Feeling a powerful and swiftly growing ecstasy, she clung to his lean waist for support. At the heady touch of his mouth closing over first one nipple and then the other, broiling sensations shot to the core of her. An un-controllable moan of delight escaped her throat and she tilted her head back, losing herself to the rapture of his touch. She moved her hands from his waist to his narrow hips, and gripping his firm, flat buttocks, drew him closer. She heard his faint intake of air, felt the hesitation at her breast. She thrilled with the knowledge that he wanted her as badly as she wanted him. Even if it was only for the moment, only for their sojourn in the desert, he wanted her.

Then he was on his feet, bringing her with him. His lips ravaged her with more urgency, more possession. When he broke away from her, she heard his ragged breathing and felt her own heart thumping wildly. He lifted her into his arms as easily as if she were a child. With no difficulty he stepped from the pond and carried her to his blankets. In seconds they were once again entwined securely in each other's arms.

His blue eyes locked with hers, questioning her final decision as his words had earlier. He was giving her one last chance to change her mind, but she steadily met his gaze.

"Nate," she said huskily. "I've never done this before."

His lips slanted over hers in a slow kiss, his tongue twining with hers. She wondered how a kiss alone could so easily stoke the fires within her.

"There aren't any rules, Paris. Just go with what you feel."

Paris stroked his cheek and the high bones beneath that gave his face its rugged, masculine contours. Her fingertips slid over his mouth, along his jaw and neckline, and into the silky texture of his black hair. It had grown some in the weeks since she'd first met him and now it curled slightly over his ears.

Her fingers familiarized themselves with this man she had decided to make her own; her lips touched his throat with a shy kiss. His arms tightened around her, and she sensed that the kiss must have felt good for him, so she grew bolder and followed it with more.

Her hands explored his neck and fanned out over his shoulders and collarbone, followed by kisses. She marveled at the textures she felt: the smoothness of his muscular shoulders, the coarseness of the black hair on his chest, the rock-hard weight of his thighs pressing against hers, the calloused palms gliding up her arms, the tenderness of his fingers sinking beneath the mass of her loose hair.

He accepted her ministerings quietly for a few minutes, as if allowing the sensations to have their full impact on him. Then he rolled to his back, drawing her on top of him.

"I don't think you really understand what you're doing to me, do you, Paris?"

She gazed down at him through the heavy mass of her red hair that had all fallen forward. With the firelight flickering just a few feet away, it seemed as if it, too, was ablaze. He picked up one side of it and draped it back over her shoulder.

"Am I doing something you don't like?" she whispered, very much concerned. "Shall I stop?"

A chuckle rumbled deep in his throat. His hands glided up over her hips, along her slender rib cage and to her breasts flaunted enticingly just above his chest. He took them in his palms. "Would you dangle a canteen of water in front of a man dying of thirst?"

Wide-eyed, she shook her head. "No, of course not."

"Then there's your answer, my love."

His hands returned to her waist. Easily he lifted her, repositioning her above him so he could take the tender peaks of her breasts into his mouth and gently suckle. Paris, bracing herself with her hands on either side of his head, spontaneously responded to the stimulation by arching her back and pressing her loins against his taut stomach.

Wildfire raged within her and drove her instinctively,

just as he had said it would. She was no longer shy or remotely hesitant about enfolding him in her loving embrace and allowing her fingers to explore every inch of his sinewed body.

Santa Isabel had been her destiny, but now so was the superstitious bounty hunter with his noisome cigars, his gravelly whisper, his impatient pessimism, all things she had truly come to care for, to love, although she would never have admitted that until this moment.

Her kisses became fervent as the need inside drove her on. Then she was on her back with Nate over her, settling into position between her legs. He had somehow known that she had come to that point where kisses could no longer quench her unbearable thirst.

With exquisite skill, he played every part of her body with his lips and his hands. But when his fingertips caressed her most secret part and then slid inside her, she thought she would erupt into a million dazzling pieces. With primitive knowledge she knew she must have him now, and he her.

She wrapped her legs more fully around him and pressed against the silken wand that would bring her satisfaction. He hesitated, lowered his head, and kissed the corner of her lip, the soft skin next to her eye. He whispered. "Is this really your first time, Paris?"

She said nothing, just nodded and waited impatiently for him to give her what she wanted, what she needed.

"I'll be gentle."

She gripped his shoulders. "Just don't stop now."

Nate suddenly realized, with a sudden fear, that he had never made love to a virgin. But the lift of her hips toward him grew more urgent, as did her hands roaming his shoulders and back, her kisses falling on whatever part of his body they could reach.

He found her maidenhead pressed too deliciously against his throbbing need. The worry seemed to go out of him then and instinct took over. She was moist, eager, and one quick thrust opened her fully to him. He began moving inside her slowly, and she responded, gripping him tightly.

He needed her so badly, it took all his willpower to focus his mind elsewhere so he could satisfy her first before taking his own pleasure. This was her first time and he wanted very much for it to be something she would never regret with pain or disappointment.

He rolled to his back again and brought her into the dominant position.

"Ride the wind, love," he whispered.

Sensations tumbled over her in tumultuous waves, driving her higher and higher like a ship caught on a stormy sea, being tossed from one crest to the next. Instinct told her there was an ultimate crest that she must strive to reach. Occasionally she wondered if she would literally drown in the wonderment of it all.

And then she was there, bursting through the storm of pleasure to the glittering, blinding rays of fulfillment. Tremendous heat rushed over her and through every part of her. She felt Nate shudder, reaching that crest with her. Together they sank into a halcyon sea, breathing heavily and deeply, still clinging to each other in awe of the journey they had traveled together.

Paris held him tightly, wanting to never let him go. She scattered kisses over his neck and shoulder, his jaw, wherever her lips could reach. He buried his face in her hair, breathing deeply with satisfaction and peace.

They lay like that for a long time. Then ultimately they had to part again. Nate held her in his arms until she fell asleep. Carefully, so as not to wake her, he covered her up with the blanket. Then he left the camp, deciding he needed a cigar and some time alone to seriously think about what had just transpired between them.

Paris stirred, feeling the coolness. Realizing Nate was gone, she sat up. Before she could call out his name, she saw him leaving camp for the darkness beyond the fire. She watched him pick his way carefully around the cacti and brush and back to the pond. There he pulled on his pants and boots. He searched his vest for a cigar and matches. After lighting it and clamping the cigar between his teeth, he gathered the clothes in a bundle and rejoined her, dropping the load next to her bedroll. He was surprised to see her awake and said so.

"I got cold."

He stretched out by her side, flat on his back with an arm beneath his head, staring upward and blowing smoke to the star-studded sky.

A troubled, pensive look settled on his face, making her feel as if he had forgotten her presence or regretted what they'd done. She hadn't expected him to tell her he loved her, but she had expected something after what they'd just shared. Maybe to be held, to share a simple discussion, to be smiled at and caressed, just some little thing to keep the intimacy alive. The longer he stared at the stars the further away he seemed to drift. She sensed she had lost him to another time, another place, probably the memory of another woman. He didn't seem to be trying to be cruel, but he was succeeding just the same, succeeding in making her feel used and like a border town whore.

Angrily she sat up and started yanking her underwear back on, finding the camisole was wrong side out and having to take it off and try again.

"What's wrong?" he turned his head to watch her.

"Nothing. I just wish you would have told me right from the start that you had another woman. I wouldn't have. . . . Well, anyway, I just wish you would have let me know."

His expression changed from surprise to amusement. He watched her struggle with her clothes in the dark and finally snuffed out his cigar in the sand and reached for her, propelling her back down against him.

"You're my woman now, Paris," he said easily. "It's just you and me here on the Sonoran."

As if to prove his ownership, his lips seared hers again and his hands slid over her breasts cushioning their fullness in his palms. He rolled her back onto the blankets and secured her tightly in his embrace. Her heart and mind cried out for her not to be taken advantage of again, but her body succumbed much too easily to his fiery touch. Now that her body knew the way to heaven, it seemed to have a mind of its own in deciding to make the journey again, and again.

He held her in the crook of his arm afterward. She saw that distant look enter his eyes again and she knew, with a heart that was suddenly heavy, that she would never be more to him than his "woman." She didn't know what she had hoped for when she first made love to him, but what she wanted to hear now were words of love, of commitment, to know that he felt something for her the way she did him. But it didn't happen.

She should leave his side, tell him to go back to his bedroll, and yet she couldn't. Maybe she was just a glutton for punishment or a willing slave. All she knew for certain was that she had gambled and lost. But then hadn't he cheated? Hadn't he made her think he cared?

A cavernous hole opened up inside her and there was a force in the hole robbing her will, her ambition, her hope. She grabbed that last thing, hope, and held onto it fiercely. She gritted her teeth against the tears that would weaken the last of her resolve.

She'd taken a wrong step and stumbled, that was all. She would get back up. In the morning she would start looking for the hidden treasure. Then she would ride away from the Sonoran desert, from the bounty hunter, and never look back. She would merely write it all off as a poor decision. And if she happened to find herself pregnant, well . . .

She would cross that bridge if she came to it. With the treasure of Santa Isabel in hand she wouldn't have to worry about the future. She could start a new identity, a new life.

She closed her eyes. She needed to sleep. She had a big day ahead of her tomorrow, and she would find the treasure.

Sleep drifted over her surprisingly easily. But her pleasant dreams were soon transformed into a nightmare world of golden, dancing candlesticks . . . and the taunting kisses of a ghost whose face was Nate Brannigan's.

Nate was startled awake by Paris's outcry. He was surprised he had even gone to sleep, remembering that his last thoughts had been of Paloma. But the fear in Paris's eyes and her frantic attempts to get away from him shocked all other thoughts, as well as sleep, from his mind. He struggled with her, trying to hold her to him.

"Hey, Paris, what did I do?"

She was wild-eyed, desperate to be free of his restricting arms. "It was you . . . and yet it wasn't. Oh, it was just a bad dream. Let me go."

He held her tighter, ignoring her command. "I like to have women dream about me, honey, but I don't like to give them nightmares. What's this all about?"

The nightmare cleared from Paris's mind and slowly she relaxed in his embrace. Instead of trying to push him away, she clung to him. But fear still darted nervously in her eyes as she looked beyond him to the darkness.

"It was Father Castañeda and he was watching us. Sometimes his face would become yours." Her gray eyes, huge with fear, lifted to his. "This is going to sound crazy, but I feel as if he still is."

"Still is what?"

"Watching us."

Nate was more than a little disturbed, but he tried to maintain a clear head. For all its beauty, he didn't like this little valley. There was an eerie quality about it that made his hair prickle and his skin crawl. He'd tried to blame it on his imagination, his superstition, but maybe it went much deeper than that. He, too, felt the eyes.

"How about putting more wood on the fire," she suggested.

Nate finally released her, but reluctantly, wondering if it was just a ploy for her to leave his side and return to her own bedroll. But she remained where she was, drawing his blanket up around her. He sensed it wasn't so much to keep out the cold as it was to keep out prying eyes.

He did her bidding, dropping more brush and sticks on the fire. He watched it leap into high flames again, pushing back the darkness around their campsite. While Paris may have felt more comfortable with a large fire, he didn't. If he had his preference, he would slip into the darkness. There he would be on equal footing with whoever, or whatever, was watching them.

But who could it be? Was it merely a curious animal, a deer, a coyote, the mountain lion they'd seen earlier? Or was it a person? Was it the same thing, the same presence, that had frightened Paris so badly that she'd come running out of the church as if it was on fire?

He returned to her side and settled down next to her, pulling her into his arms. The urge to make love to her again was strong, but it was overshadowed by the unseen and unknown watcher somewhere out there in the dark.

"It's nothing," he heard himself say to her, trying to allay her fears . . . and maybe his own. "We're out here alone, Paris. Just you and me."

"And Father Castañeda," she added, giving him a humorless smile.

He chuckled. "So I have you believing in ghosts now, too?"

"I never believed he was a ghost, Nate. I don't believe he's a real padre either. What if he's really an impostor and plans to kill us to keep us from taking the treasure?"

Nate kissed her forehead, cradling her tightly in his arms.

"If this guy dressed as a monk had wanted to kill us, he could have done it long before now. He had the perfect opportunity earlier."

The memory of the intimacy they'd shared flashed across her face for him to see, and he was relieved that the fear in her eyes softened for just a moment. He pressed a kiss to her lips, feeling the swell of desire once again flood to his loins. He could make love to her all night, but right now she just needed to be held and comforted.

"Maybe he's just waiting to see if we find the treasure," Paris added. "Then he plans to kill us."

"If that's the case, then there's no reason for us to worry about it until we find the treasure . . . if we find the treasure."

She offered no more argument, nor did she offer to leave the security of his arms. He felt a calming sense of closeness to her as he held her, and shortly she fell back to sleep. It was only then that he allowed the dark feeling to descend upon him totally. It was not merely the dark fearing of a killer, or even a ghost named Castañeda and an ancient curse, it was a feeling that went beyond that and into his mind, into his past.

He knew Paris had not been completely satisfied that he didn't have another woman. But he honestly didn't. He had only the memory of another woman, a memory that would not die. He didn't understand it exactly, but since he'd met Paris, that memory was coming back to haunt him more frequently, plaguing him, tormenting him, making him feel as if he had to choose between it and . . . and what? Between the past and the future? Between it and Paris?

He had never told anyone about the woman he had loved. No one would have understood. Even she had not known. Beautiful Paloma had thought he was only a good friend, only the "nice" brother of Alejandro, her husband. Nate had never let her know otherwise. He had taken the role of brother-in-law and had loved her from afar.

He'd tried to forget her. He had even become engaged

to another woman, but at the last minute he had called the wedding off. There had been a tremendous scandal after that and he had gotten the reputation as being a blackguard among all the eligible young women of Santa Fe. But he simply hadn't been able to go through with that marriage. Only Alejandro and Paloma had not chastised him for leading his fiancée on a merry chase and then calling it off. They seemed to understand that one could never truly "learn to love."

Nate had lived solely on his dreams then. He had suffered Paloma's death in silence. When he had cried alone at night it had been for himself, not Alejandro. His loss was, in its way, even greater than Alejandro's. His brother had at least been able to love Paloma, and he had the memories of her returning his love. All Nate had ever had were dreams, and then suddenly even those were gone.

Don Diego had come to him once a few years before and said, "You should go and find yourself a good woman, Nathaniel. You should let yourself fall in love. Have children to enrich your life."

Nate had replied, "A man can stand to lose too much when he loves, my father. He stands to have his sanity decimated. He stands to end up a lonely man living out on the desert, tending to corn and chili peppers, with no future but remembering the past."

"But you're not Alejandro."

"No. But I'm very much like him. He hides in the desert. I hide in Nogales."

Nate thought that maybe Don Diego had guessed the truth of it then, or maybe he had always known. But he had had much sympathy for him. He hadn't pressed him any further. He had placed a hand on his shoulder and had given him a look of sad understanding. "Someday we will all come out of hiding, my son. But first our wounds must heal."

Nate had spent the years quietly searching for another Paloma, another dark-haired, sultry-eyed woman. He had never found her. Instead, he'd found a little redheaded keg of dynamite that resembled Paloma in absolutely no way whatsoever and yet who seemed to be crowding into his mind until thoughts of her were taking up the larger portion of his waking hours.

The love he'd had for Paloma had left him feeling desolate. The love he'd had for his fiancée had made him feel smothered. The feeling he had for Paris left him warm but confused, even a little tormented.

He glanced down at her, sleeping peacefully in his arms. Her small hand rested on his chest as if it was the most natural place in the world for it to be. And maybe it was, because he had no desire for her to remove it.

At that moment a whimper escaped her petal-soft lips and her brow puckered. Impulsively he placed a kiss on the top of her head and held her tighter, feeling an odd rush of protectiveness and possessiveness.

Paris made him feel young and crazy and carefree again, even wild and reckless, the way he'd felt before he'd lost his heart to Paloma when he'd been just a boy of eighteen. Oh, it seemed so long ago, so many miles ago. Sometimes he felt frustrated and ready to strangle Paris, but the next moment he wanted to feel her legs around him and her lips tracing sweet patterns across his cheek. Yes, she certainly left him tormented.

But he wouldn't tell her about Paloma. There was no need. Paloma had never been a part of his life, only his dreams. And some dreams were simply best kept secret.

A soft rustle in the grass drew Nate's head around. His

heart began to thump with increased wariness, but across the fire he saw nothing. He wondered if the puma had returned. Or perhaps it was only a night snake slithering through the tall grass looking for a mouse. Whatever it was, he had the inexplicable and disturbing feeling that they were being watched again. He glanced to where he had left his revolver and his Winchester, both too far away to reach without disturbing Paris.

Pedro appeared from wherever he'd been sleeping and came to curl up next to them, seeking their companionship. It was something he usually didn't do at night, preferring to dig himself a hole in the sand somewhere and curl up alone. It seemed the dog had finally, if not reluctantly, accepted Nate as someone who wasn't going to go away. Nate patted his head, wondering if the dog had made the noise he'd heard.

He waited. He didn't hear the sound again. The watching eyes apparently posed no immediate threat. Being watched for the sake of being watched was somehow more disturbing than knowing there was an enemy out there ready to ambush them. He could deal with a head-on confrontation. He couldn't deal with something he couldn't see.

He carefully slipped his arm from beneath Paris's head. She stirred a little, but settled back to sleep. He put another piece of brush on the fire, thinking that it must be the puma watching them. The fire would keep the animal away should it get ideas to take down one of the horses or mules.

But what if it wasn't the puma?

He watched the flames grow until they lifted the darkness from Paris's face, pointed out the freckles, and flickered over her hair making it appear to be a fire all its own.

After a time, he decided he had simply let his imagination run wild.

He sat down on his own bedroll, lit his cigar again, and stared at Paris from across the fire. With surprise, he realized that out of all the emotions she caused to churn inside him, one of the greatest that presented itself was fear. She frightened him, truly frightened him. She threatened the serenity of the way of life he'd fallen into and had come to accept, even to enjoy in a cynical sort of way. Her beauty and vivaciousness, even her stubborn determination, intruded on his complacency and insisted on calling for decisions, for action. The feel of her lips and her body made him question the direction he had chosen to take. Her hands and her gray, steady eyes nagged at his heart, calling for life and emotion that he was afraid to experience again. Her hope and optimism demanded change, and he was afraid of change. Her smile and her spark made the doors to the future swing wide and beckon him to step through, to taste of something new and exciting. Her quick, eager step begged him to follow her, even if he could not see what awaited him over distant horizons. Her laughter made him want to sing and to forget the painful things. It was a sound he knew he would never forget, nor want to forget, and he imagined the sound of it would lay in his memory to haunt him like all his other senseless dreams.

Even now he wanted to take her in his arms and kiss her, make love to her, cherish her. But would she want him to after she'd found her precious treasure? She was so single-minded. What guarantees did he have that she wouldn't take the padre's gold and say, *"Adios, amigo. We'll have to do it again sometime."*

She'd willingly given herself to him. He'd selfishly

taken her virginity. While he felt a special bond with her because he was the only man she'd ever had, he still lacked trust. How could a man blindly step forward and joyously gamble away his heart? His heart was tired of pain and loneliness.

All the things that had stopped him from taking her virginity before had vanished beneath his own lusty desire. Now he might very well pay the price for his inability to control his needs. What sweet wonder it had been to teach her about love, to be her first. She'd been such a willing subject. He felt a growing bond with her. But what did she feel for him? Had he merely been a teacher for her?

He knew from experience that answers were seldom found in the darkness, only more questions, more grief, more insecurities, more confusion. It seemed things could never find their rightful course until the light of day shone down. Maybe the morning would tell him what he needed to know about his heart, and about hers. Maybe they would have no decision whatsoever to make.

Maybe Isabel would make it for them.

Seventeen

In the gentle light of early morning, Santa Isabel
watched their approach with what appeared to be serene
patience. Paris wondered if the grand lady was merely
confident that her visitors would never depart from the
valley with the treasure that had been placed in her divine
custody.

In daylight, Paris saw that her path to the mission the
night before had skirted an old garden. The garden had
been fenced in by organ pipe cactus, obviously planted
by a persevering and loving hand. She sensed the hand
that had transplanted the cacti had been that of Father
Castañeda during the construction of the mission. And the
food grown in it had been used to feed the hungry Yaqui
laborers.

Inside the natural barrier of the organ pipe was a low
area where the water from the ponds had drained and
formed a *cienga,* and in the *cienga* grew a thick mass of
tules and tall arrowhead, the latter with its starchy, potato-
like tubers a staple in the diet of the desert Indians.

Before the sun set she might be a very rich woman.
While that had been a delicious prospect a few weeks ago,
the promise of it on this bright and beautiful morning was
overshadowed by matters of the heart. Beside her, walking
quietly, was Nate. She was his woman now, at least in his

opinion. She'd needed time away from him in the morning to consider their situation, and she had even suggested he go hunting. But he had said, "Maybe if I help you, we'll find the treasure quicker and then we can leave. Our food supplies are getting low."

Did he have other reasons for wanting to leave quickly? It was no secret that he didn't like the place. He didn't like the idea of digging up cursed treasure any more than he had before, and he didn't like the idea of Father Castañeda's ghost. Despite what he denied about another woman, Paris still felt there was one so deeply ingrained in his mind that she could never hope to take her place.

Paris forged her way through the tall grass surrounding the mission and past a mesquite that had taken root near the front door. She paused at the door, remembering the frightening shadow that had put her in flight the night before. To her surprise, Nate reached around her, lifted the iron latch, and gave the door a push. Squeaking again, it moved aside. The morning sunlight rushed in to warm the dark interior and to spread a bright beam across the tiled floor.

Paris knew the fear that threatened to smother her was silly. This was just an ancient church, nothing more. That it might contain cursed treasure was beside the point; she didn't believe in curses.

She stepped inside. Nate followed.

The sun filtered in through a window on the southern wall of the mission, casting diffused light into the nave's large-beamed, high ceiling. The light fell softly, encompassing them and lending a spiritual hush to the long rectangular room. It was in relatively good repair. The only real sign of age was the dust coating everything and the plaster peeling from the walls. Even the latter seemed minimal for a building as old as this one.

Paris moved into the center of the room. Nate stayed close beside her. She found herself relaxing in the tranquil atmosphere. How could she have allowed the darkness to distort the perfect sanctity of this extraordinary creation?

"There's nothing in here," Paris said. Her whispered words resounded loudly in the empty room. "Maybe we should try those doors under the arcade."

Nate balked. "I think you're wasting your time, Paris. If this mission had been built just as a receptacle for the priests' booty then why build all those rooms?"

"Religious services might never have been conducted here," Paris insisted, "but someone has stayed here, a long time ago. W.W. said Father Castañeda didn't take the ship the others did but returned here to live out his life, guard the church's precious inventory, and continue preaching to the Yaqui Indians. He must have built this mission for his own use. Perhaps he even had contact with someone from the outside world, and maybe he was waiting here, believing that the Jesuits would be reinstated in New Spain. When they weren't, he eventually died here, alone."

Uneasy with his surroundings, Nate left her side and moved to the doors in the shadow of the arcade. He opened the door to the first room. A storeroom, it contained only a few old barrels with their lids off. Their contents were now nothing more than tracings of grain, corn, rice, beans, and other unrecognizable seeds. The rooms that had been quarters still contained a few rustic, handmade bed frames. But the mattresses had fallen to the floors to rot or be largely consumed by mice. Other rooms mutely indicated what their purposes had once been: a kitchen, a refectory, a tiny office with a table and one broken chair, a room with a dirt floor where the smell of leather harnesses, horse brushes, and cotton ropes still lingered even after a century.

In the very back was a smithy, an exterior extension off the mission wall. It could be entered from the inside of the mission as well as from the outside. It had been made as a lean-to, and the overhanging roof had collapsed, filling the area with timbers and tiles. They were practically lost to the drifting of desert sands, but the air was so dry that rotting had been slow. The smithy's dirt floor was stained with dark splotches of lubricating oils and greases and piles of silver shavings where metals and horseshoes had been fired in the forge and hammered on the anvil. Even the anvil was in remarkable condition, protected from the rains by the majority of the fallen roof. Very little rust tarnished its black iron surface. It had probably seen a lot of use during the construction of the mission, less when the padre had lived there alone. One thing was certain, no one had lived here recently, which destroyed the theory that the padre they'd seen at Angel Springs, claiming to be Father Castañeda, was making it his home.

Nate made his way over the rubble and into the sunlight, his eyes locked with hers, hinting at sympathy. "We might as well go, Paris. If there was something here once, it's gone now."

"Father Castañeda wouldn't have left the treasure in plain sight," Paris replied stubbornly, refusing to give up. "There's probably a secret passage around here, a false door, maybe even a hidden wine cellar. Why, it might be buried beneath this fallen roof."

Nate removed his hat and ran a hand through his hair. Sympathy was gone, replaced by exasperation that he couldn't control. "Do you plan to tear up the entire floor, Paris, just because it might be there?"

She stiffened defiantly. "If I have to. I'm surely not going to give up after a cursory glance and head back to Tombstone, especially after all we've been through."

"All right," he responded belligerently. "Where do you want me to start?" He took a few steps and kicked at the loose edge of a tile. "How about here? Or maybe over there?" He stalked to another heap of rubble that was mostly a pile of sand where some cacti and grass had taken root.

Paris brushed past him. "We'll search the grounds first. Maybe it's not in the church."

"Then why build the church?"

"As a decoy, I suppose."

"A lot of effort for nothing. Why not just bury it in a hole in the ground, cover it up, and no one would be the wiser. I mean, nobody would ever be able to find it then."

Paris was having a difficult time dealing with his contrariness and her own lagging spirits. What if the treasure was only a myth? What if someone before her had already taken off with it? She turned on her heel and took off running through the tall grass. Tears blinded her. She stumbled once and fell, landing on a cholla. The plant's sharp spines brought blood to her hands, but she leaped up and kept running, hearing Nate's thundering steps behind her.

He caught her and whirled her around. She fought him, but he was too strong for her. "Stop it, Paris! What do you think you're doing? That could have been a rattler you landed on as easily as a cactus."

"What do you care? If I'd been snake-bit, you could bury me and get the hell out of here!"

She struggled to get away from him again, but he refused to let her go. "Damn it, Paris," he said in a gruff but amazingly tender voice. "Don't put yourself through any more of this hell. Come back with me to Nogales. I'll take care of you."

She drew back as if she had been slapped. "If I'd wanted a man to take care of me, I wouldn't be here! I'd be back in Tombstone bedding Tully Thatcher. Now let me go! I'm not going to give up. Do you hear me!"

He released her so suddenly she nearly fell again. Just as suddenly, her defiance vanished and she felt as if she would collapse. She felt so defeated and overwhelmed by an array of emotions that she couldn't sort out.

"Just give me a few more days, Nate," she whispered, staring off toward the calm white face of Isabel. "I'll search the grounds and then I'll go."

He said nothing. His eyes were hard, angry, and unyielding. But she didn't care anymore. Unexpectedly he shifted his attention to her hands. He took her by both wrists and turned her palms so he could clearly see them. "Come back to camp, Paris, and I'll get those thorns out for you. The spines of a cholla can turn into some nasty wounds."

"I'll do it myself."

"Don't be so stubborn for once in your life."

He gave her no opportunity to object further. Leading her by the wrist, he headed back to camp. She sat obediently on a rock while he carefully and patiently removed the thorns, disinfected the wounds with whiskey, then smeared them with salve and bandaged them.

Later, she pretended to take a siesta, but as soon as Nate left his bedroll and vanished into the mesquite looking for fresh meat for supper, she hurried back to the mission.

With a growing trepidation at being alone once again, she reentered the church. This time her feet gravitated across the dark tile floor toward the stairs that spiraled up into the bell tower on the southern side of the building. Even though the adobe mission was very effective at keeping out the desert heat, the temperature in the bell tower was cooler still than elsewhere in the church.

A hundred years of dust and sand had sifted in on the stairs through the bell tower windows. She made her way cautiously up their dizzying spiral, holding to the rough hand rail and putting her weight carefully on each step lest it give beneath her weight. About halfway up, she paused, glancing up to the huge bell hanging from the massive crossbeams. She glanced down the way she'd come, seeing an occasional boot print she'd left behind. She couldn't help but wonder if hers had been the only feet to touch those stairs in a hundred years.

The next step creaked beneath her weight, screeching loudly in the acute silence of the tower. She felt very much the trespasser. She paused again, debating whether she should go back. She could see now that the bell tower was not a likely place for anything of any size to be hidden, and yet the big iron bell hanging motionless overhead silently beckoned her up, up until she had reached the very top.

The upper landing had been built with durability in mind, as had the entire mission. Three thicknesses of two-inch lumber criss-crossed the area, making it strong enough to support great weight and to withstand time. The bell was still inaccessible, being too high to reach without a ladder or scaffolding. She moved to the window facing west. Directly below her was the roof of the mission, missing hundreds of the original clay tiles. In their place were the bare boards of the ceiling. In many places plants had sprouted up between the tiles where the wind had carried and deposited both dirt and seeds.

She leaned out the window. The thick adobe sill was warm on her hands, the late afternoon sun hot on her face. Across the backyard she saw the springs and the campsite with the horses and mules staked on long ropes, cropping the lush grass.

Looking back in the direction of the trail that had brought them, she caught sight of Nate moving on quiet hunter's feet through a tangle of large mesquite. Watching him brought a piercing pain to her heart. Why had she been so unfortunate to want what she couldn't have? Even the treasure of Santa Isabel seemed closer to her grasp than Nate Brannigan's love. It hurt even worse that he had so offhandedly offered to take care of her. It had been done to temporarily appease her and convince her to leave. She had thought he was better than Tully, but maybe she had been wrong.

A loud creak made her whirl to face the stairwell. It was the same stair that had creaked beneath her weight. Was someone coming?

Her heart began to pound furiously. She glanced over her shoulder at the long, slender window openings, but just as quickly dismissed them as a means of escape. It was too far to jump to the ground. If she chose to leap onto the chapel roof, she was sure it would collapse beneath her weight. Pressing herself into the corner, she hoped to vanish into the shadows, knowing even as she did it that the sunlight was too bright for her to be concealed. She listened intently for more footsteps, but the blood pulsed so fast and loud in her head that she could hear nothing else.

Who was there? Was it the same person she'd felt watching them? Was it someone impersonating Father Castañeda to frighten them away? Or was it actually the padre's ghost?

With her hands and back pressed against the cool adobe wall, her head began to spin until she feared she might faint. She waited. And waited. How long did it take someone to come up those steps? Nothing more happened. She heard no more noises. Unexpectedly a breeze brushed over her, much too cool to have come from outside. A second later the breeze touched the bell, stirring it slightly and causing it to creak on the massive crossbar overhead. In that second she felt as if she was not alone. There was a presence in the tower with her. She would swear it.

Just as quickly as the feeling had come, it was gone. The cool breeze winged through the belfry windows like a departing bat. Once again she felt the heat of the afternoon sun, this time on the back of her neck.

Forcing herself to a calmness she didn't feel, she descended the tower steps as carefully as she had climbed them. Once outside, however, she succumbed to the nervous tension and collapsed in the middle of the sunlit, grassy yard. Glancing back at the church, she wondered how she had allowed her imagination to run so wildly away from her. Or had she? Had there really been a presence in the bell tower?

She had to go back inside. There was the other bell tower that needed to be explored. It, too, would probably contain nothing, but she could let no stone go unturned. However, she would wait until later. She would explore the garden next, the garden that was outdoors and in full sunlight. There might be something there, like a burial site for the treasure.

She pushed herself to her feet and dusted off her pants. The blast of Nate's rifle jarred her for a moment, but she instantly relaxed, knowing he would be bringing in something to eat. On legs that still quivered, she started for the garden.

After a thirty minute search, the area offered very little that didn't have spines, thorns, claws, or poison. She disturbed one rattler, two scorpions, and three mice that managed to escape the snake, for now.

Feeling utterly discouraged and suffocatingly hot, she propped herself against the large rock on the perimeter of the garden and pushed her hat to the back of her head. Where was a breeze when she needed it? The valley was stagnant with heat. Not even a spear of grass moved.

Her gaze moved slowly over the high canyon walls that so effectively hid Santa Isabel from the prying eyes of strangers. She lifted the binoculars to her eyes and scanned them again, looking for something, possibly a place where Father Castañeda might have buried the treasure other than in the church, though she still thought it was foolish to build the church if he hadn't intended on—

She jerked the binoculars back. There was something there, in a crevice, something white. Whatever it was, it didn't seem to belong there. It didn't seem to be part of the landscape. Lowering the binoculars, she found the spot with her naked eye and headed toward it, winding her way carefully through cacti and mesquite, watching for more venomous creatures that were now seeking shade from the heat of the day.

At the site, Paris found she was too short to see inside the narrow crevice despite a rise of land beneath it. But she was tall enough to see that at one time the crevice had been much wider and longer. It had been mortared shut with stones and then covered over with mud. The mud had crumbled over the years and some of the stones were now falling out. She searched the ground for a large rock and, watching to make sure it wasn't harboring a snake or a family of scorpions beneath it, she pushed and rolled it to a position beneath the crevice. Climbing up on it and balancing precariously, she dug her fingers into the lip of the crevice to balance herself. She removed a few pieces of the loose rock and mortar to get a better look at the white thing. And then suddenly it was there, coming from the crevice and right for her face. Releasing a scream, she tumbled backward off the rock, scrambled to her feet, and ran without looking back.

Nate heard her frantically yelling his name long before she got to camp. Leaving the half-plucked quail, he headed out to meet her with Colt in hand. He caught her in flight, grabbing her by the shoulders and dragging her to the ground to take cover. He would have shot her pursuer but he saw nothing but saguaro standing their usual watch with untiring uplifted arms. Paris clung to him, her face buried in his chest. He cradled her protectively. "What's the matter, Paris? What's happened?"

"I . . . I thought it was the . . . treasure, but it . . . it was a . . . a *body!*"

His frown tightened, as did his grip on the Colt. "A body? Where?"

"Over there in the canyon wall. A crevice. Somebody shoved it in there."

"Did you see anything or anybody else?"

She shook her head against his chest. "No."

He came to his feet, bringing her with him. Keeping a cautious eye out, he said, "Take me there."

A few minutes later, at the base of the crevice, Nate Brannigan took one look at the dangling arm and put his Colt back in its holster. "For Pete's sake, Paris, you nearly scared ten years off my life. This isn't a body. It's a skeleton."

"What's the difference?"

"Several years, I'd say. Give or take five."

"Well, it doesn't matter. Whoever it was was probably murdered."

"Or tried to take the treasure and died."

Paris didn't want to hear about that. "If he had, how would he have gotten there?"

"How should I know? Maybe our wandering Father Castañeda put him there."

"After he killed him?"

"Maybe."

Paris stared at the dangling skeleton's arm. Suddenly her expression burst with excitement and she grabbed the bony hand, no longer afraid of it. "My God, Nate! Look at this. This is Four Finger Fred, Beacher Cogan's brother. It has to be. He only has three fingers and a thumb on his right hand! This means he did find the mission. But how would he have gotten buried in this crevice?"

"Somebody had to do it."

"But who?"

"The only one that knew he was here was his brother. And W.W."

"And Father Castañeda."

"Father Castañeda's ghost, you mean. Come on, Paris. Let's get the hell out of here. We'll never know who buried old Fred. But my guess is that he died because he found that treasure and the curse that old Castañeda put on it killed him just like it's killed everybody else who's gotten too close."

"Don't be ridiculous. My hunch is that Beacher killed his own brother and buried him here himself so he could have the treasure all to himself. Either that or Beacher, being afraid of the curse, was so worried that Fred would find the treasure, since he'd already found the mission, that the two of them fought about it and Fred accidentally got killed. Then Beacher, distressed at his brother's death, went to Tombstone, got drunk, and gambled the map off to my father."

"Nice theory, Paris, but everybody that could tell you anything is dead. And we're going to be, too, if we don't get out of here." Nate took her by the arm and started back to camp.

She allowed herself to be led but only because she was too deep in thought to rebel. Finally, one of her ideas came out. "But what if the treasure's in that crevice with the skeleton?"

"I'm not a grave robber, Paris. If you want to find that out, you'll have to dig the old boy out all by yourself."

Paris had to give that some consideration. Before she knew it she found herself back in camp. She settled on a rock and watched Nate finish cleaning the quail. With his sharp Bowie he easily sectioned the bird into pieces and set it in the pan for cooking. He then went about preparing a pot of coffee.

"Are you sure you won't help me?"

"Positive."

It was a difficult decision to make, and Paris thought about it while she made soda biscuits to go with the quail. They cooked the meal in relative silence. Her decision to disturb the skeleton's resting place worked alongside the uneasiness she always felt in Nate's presence. By the time the meal was cooked, eaten, and cleaned up the only decision she'd actually come to was that she couldn't remain in his company for very much longer. She needed to find the treasure, head back to Nogales, and from there get on with her life, whatever course it might take.

Tossing his hat aside, he settled back on his bedroll and lit a cigar. "I would imagine you'd need a pick and a chisel to get that mortar out of there. Maybe even some dynamite, and if it wasn't set just right, there wouldn't be anything left of the skeleton or the contents of the cave after it blew. Of course, if you had somebody like W.W. doing it for you, you might be able to salvage whatever might be in there."

Paris stood up, surprised that he'd actually been contemplating the problem. "I think I'll go look in the church some more. You go ahead and take your siesta."

"There's nothing in there, Paris. We've gone over it all."

"We may have missed something."

He came to his feet, reaching for his hat. "Well, if you're determined, I'd better come with you in case you unearth any more skeletons."

He was taking it all so lightly it was irritating. "You're just humoring me. You have been all along."

The steady probe of Nate's blue eyes was extremely unsettling. "Yes, I'll admit I humored you in the beginning, Paris," he said. "I thought coming along with you would be an easy way to make a couple of hundred bucks and ease the boredom back in Nogales. I was wrong. But if you're determined to go it alone in this world, then I'll do my best to help you get set up so you can. I'll even help you find that treasure, if that's what you really want. But you'd better seriously consider the ramifications. You've heard the stories, seen the proof in old Four Finger Fred out there and in Beacher Cogan . . . maybe even in your own father's death.

"Sometimes we can't explain the supernatural things that take place in this world. I don't want to believe there's an honest-to-god curse on this place, but I'm not convinced at all that there isn't. And I won't be until you have that treasure and we ride away from here still breathing." He took her by the arm. "Come on, let's get down to some serious searching."

"What do you think I've been doing?"

"Scratching an itch, honey. Just scratching an itch."

They went back inside the mission. Nate led the way into the section where the quarters had been. Once again they searched all the side doors and Nate pounded on any of the inner walls that were covered with rough wood boards to see if any were hollow. He examined all the walls and floors carefully to see if there might be any indication of something buried behind or beneath them. Paris wanted to know why he hadn't done that before, but his only answer was a shrug of his broad shoulders. She knew then that he hadn't really wanted her to find anything.

They proceeded in this fashion until they'd covered every room. The only place left before resorting to tearing things up was the second bell tower. Nate told her nothing could be hidden in the towers, but she wanted to climb to the top anyway to see if she might be able to spot a location outside the church where something might be hidden in the canyon walls.

She ascended the stairs of the second tower with Nate

right behind her. This time at the top, however, the binoculars revealed nothing, not even any more skeletons.

The hope Paris had clung to throughout the journey
and the search finally disintegrated, crumbling like old
adobe bricks that had seen too much sun and rain. The
hopelessness was made worse by the look of sympathy in
Nate's eyes. She had wanted his understanding, his sympathy, his compassion, but suddenly it was more than she
could bear. It was as if he was saying, "I told you so."

Instead, he said, "I guess there just isn't anything here.
I'm sorry, Paris. I really am."

The dam of restraint inside her broke. She was struck
with a lightning bolt of fury that rapidly accelerated into
tears. She straightened from the wall, lifting her shoulders
defiantly. "You're not sorry, Nate Brannigan! You're glad
because now you don't have to worry about that stupid
curse and you can get back to your cards and women and
whiskey in Nogales!"

She started down the old tower stairs as swiftly as she
could go, with Nate clamoring right behind her. Her temper tantrum had been matched by his own.

"That's about enough, Paris McKenna! If you would
just admit that coming out here was pretty senseless in
the first place, then you could quit blaming all your hard
luck on me. You just got struck with gold fever, like thousands of other people, but most of them don't ever find
gold. And people like W.W. spend their entire lives searching. You have to make your own fortune, Paris, and your
own luck. You can't expect to find it hidden in lost missions and lost mines."

He tried to grab her arm from behind but she eluded
him as she raced blindly on, her tears making everything
a blur before her. She didn't want him to see her cry, and

she didn't want him to even think about comforting her. Most of the tears were because of him anyway. How could he possibly heal a hurt he had inflicted?

In those agonizing moments she admitted that her pain was due in part to the fact that she hadn't found the treasure, but the deeper source seemed to be that she knew that when they left she would never see Nate Brannigan again. Why she would want to see him was ridiculous, and yet her heart cried out not to be separated from him. He'd made the offer to take care of her, but she wouldn't become a bought woman.

She was only eight steps from the bottom landing when she tripped. She reached out for a banister, only to be met with thin air and a rough adobe wall that scraped her hand as she tumbled headlong. She heard Nate yell her name, but he was too far behind to stop her fall.

When she hit the landing, the old wood gave way beneath her, splintering from the impact of her body. Then Nate was there, rolling her over onto her back. She could only stare into his worried face, feeling dazed.

"My God, Paris," he said in a tone both angry and concerned. "Are you all right?"

"I . . . don't know." She tried to get up and he pressed her back down.

"Lie still," he commanded. "Don't move until the feeling comes back and you can tell where you've been hurt. I need to be able to determine if you've been seriously hurt before I move you."

A sardonic smile lifted her lips. Already she felt a few places that were throbbing: her back, her hips, her right shoulder, her head. Was there any place left that didn't hurt?

"What do you care?" she managed in a half moan. "If

you're lucky, maybe I broke my neck and you can bury me with Fred out there."

She saw something in his eyes then. Something that read an awful lot like hurt. Seeing that hurt was like a knife stabbing into her own heart. She forgot her other aches and pains and felt like crying all over again.

"I care a lot, Paris," he whispered. "Don't you know that by now?"

Did he really? She probed deeply the pools of his blue eyes. At least for the moment she honestly did see true concern there. So maybe he cared. But did his caring go as deeply as loving? Or did he only care because he still hadn't received all his payment for the job?

She tried to rise again, but he told her a second time to remain still. He prodded and poked her arms and legs, her head, shoulders, and back to make sure nothing was broken.

"Can't you hurry?" she asked. "It's cold on this damn floor."

Finally satisfied, he helped her to her feet, steadying her with an arm around her waist. For a moment their eyes locked in wordless understanding, then Nate started to lead her from the bell tower.

She didn't know why she looked back at the last minute, but when she did, she saw the broken plank and remembered the cool breeze she'd felt in both towers. Driven by a hunch, or maybe just curiosity, she disengaged her arm from Nate's and started back to the broken planks.

Dropping to her knees, she shivered again. This time it wasn't from a cool breeze. It was from something eerie, a sixth sense crawling through her. She curled her hands around one of the planks and tried to pull it up. It held fast on the ends, but the rotten wood gave way in her hands.

Nate came back inside, towering over her. "What are you doing, Paris?"

"Help me. I don't know why, but I have a feeling something could be buried under this floor." She glanced up at his face, her tears completely gone now. She saw something in his eyes bordering on hope and excitement. She explained to him about the drafts of air she'd felt in both bell towers. "I'm beginning to think there might be a cellar under here."

Nate dropped to his knees next to her. "Let's just hope it isn't any more dead bodies."

Together they ripped up more of the floorboards, enough to see that there was a subfloor. Through the gaps in the subfloor they could feel cold air against their hands. They continued to remove as much of the top floor as they could, but the old nails on the ends of the boards held, finally halting further progress. Nate, alive with excitement—to Paris's amazement—volunteered to go into the smithy and try to find some old tools they could use to pry the boards off.

While he was gone, the stillness of the mission settled over Paris again. A draft came up through the subfloor, a welcome coolness to her overheated body. With it came the smell of dirt that hadn't seen light for a long time. All the while Nate was gone, her eyes kept darting to the door and up the bell tower stairs. It was quiet, too quiet. She listened to the sounds of the mission and found there were very few. There was not even a breeze to move the bell dangling so far above her.

She felt eyes watching her again. Unnerved, she turned to the door Nate had exited, hoping he had returned. She saw nothing, just the sunlight slanting into the cubicle that had been closed against it for over a century.

She breathed a sigh of relief when she heard Nate's familiar footsteps. This time there was an urgency to them. He was clearly as excited about finding out what was beneath the floor as she was. If he was afraid of a curse, his curiosity had overshadowed his fear and qualms. He went to one knee and began prying up the subfloor boards with a crowbar he'd found in the smithy. After removing five boards, he set the crowbar aside and peered down through the subfloor. Paris leaned over his shoulder.

"What do you see?"

He didn't reply but reached behind him for her hand, drawing her down next to him. She peered into the hole. At first she saw only darkness peering back. The sunlight filtering down from the bell tower windows didn't seem sufficient to illuminate the depths of the hole. Then she saw something bright, something golden in color.

"My God." She could scarcely breathe, let alone speak. Her heart was beating so wildly she suddenly felt faint. She gripped the boards at the edge of the hole to steady herself. "I think we've found it, Nate."

He nodded, his voice nearly as awestruck as hers. "Yes, I think we have."

"Well, well," came a deep male voice from behind them. "Tell us exactly what it is you've found, Paris, darling."

Paris whirled, jarred by the familiarity of the voice. Tully Thatcher's deviously handsome face stared back at her. He sauntered into the room, gun drawn. Behind him were two more men.

"It seems we got here just in time, boys," he said. "My little thief has led me right to the treasure."

Eighteen

Nate rose warily to his feet, drawing Paris next to him. "Who the hell are you?" he demanded of the black-haired intruder.

Tully's gaze slithered to Paris. His derisive smile became even more pronounced. "Ask the lady."

Paris shifted uneasily, not sure if she would be any safer in Nate's arms than Tully's once Nate learned the truth . . . the whole truth. Maybe she would be wise not to tell him everything just yet.

"This is Tully Thatcher," she said, watching Nate make a concentrated assessment of him. She saw a lot of questions in Nate's eyes, but he didn't voice them.

Tully saw them, too, and chuckled. "I guess the little lady already told you about me."

"She mentioned you."

"Good. Then I won't have to waste precious time explaining why I'm here."

"How did you know where I'd go?" Paris asked. "How did you find us?"

"I've got a good mind for detail, Paris, like memorizing things on old maps and knowing when those old maps are missing from my safe. When I realized it was you who had stolen it, I also knew you would come out here, looking for whatever that map promised. I just inquired along the way until I found Cerro Trueno. Then we picked up your tracks. A gunshot earlier brought us right to the valley. Of course we had to kill a stupid Mexican because he claimed he hadn't seen you, but an old prospector told us all we needed to know. A friendly old buzzard. At least he was smart enough to know we'd blow his head off if he didn't talk."

At the mention of the Mexican, Paris had felt Nate tense beside her. He spoke in a low, threatening voice, "What was the Mexican's name, Thatcher?"

Tully shrugged. "I don't know. But he had him a nice little place. He lived alone from the looks of it. Of course, there isn't much left to the place now. He really should have cooperated with us more than he did."

Nate lunged for Tully, knocking him up against the tower wall and sending his gun flying from his hand. Tully yelled for his men to shoot, but all Lennox and Smith could do was to look at each other, confused over what was taking place. Paris thrust herself into the middle of the fracas, trying to pull the two men apart. Neither of them paid her any more mind than if she had been a kangaroo rat hopping in and out between their feet. It wasn't until Lennox yanked Paris away, wrapped his arm around her throat, and put his revolver to her head that Nate finally listened.

"I'll kill the woman, Brannigan," Lennox warned in a not-too-confident voice. "You'd better back off. I mean it."

Nate reluctantly obeyed, not trusting the crazed, frightened look in Lennox's eyes. Immediately his gun was removed from his holster by a cautious Smith. Tully struggled to his feet, gingerly touching a cut over his eye and one at the corner of his mouth. Both were bleeding quite freely.

Glaring at Nate, he said, "Get the stuff out of the hole, boys. It's mine now."

"Damn you, Tully," Paris said. "I found it."

"Yes, with a map you stole from *my* safe." He reached down and retrieved his gun.

Paris felt Nate's eyes on her again. She couldn't bear the questioning look that shifted to disbelief and then disappointment. At the moment it was easier to face Tully.

"I only took it because it had my daddy's name on it," she said. "Somebody named Cogan had signed it over to him so I figured I had a right to it."

"Yes, all that's true, but the map was in my possession."

"Maybe so, but you probably cheated my daddy out of it."

"Nobody can cheat Blackjack McKenna, Paris. He was always too good for that. No, in order to get that map I had to kill him."

Paris's knees began to quiver, threatening to buckle. She reached for the wall behind her to steady herself. "You killed my father?"

Tully's eyes glinted with an evilness Paris had never seen before. "It was the only way to get it."

Paris could barely think straight. All she wanted to do was light into Tully with claws bared. She made a move toward him, but Nate caught her arm and held her back. He couldn't stop her mouth though.

"How could you, you slime?" she demanded of Tully. "How could you ask me to be your mistress when you'd killed my father?"

"Paris, you're not naive," Tully casually replied. "That map was only one of the reasons I killed him. I thought that someday I might go looking for this so-called treasure, but I knew that with your dad dead you would have no one to turn to. I thought I could put you in a position that you would be forced to turn to me." He shrugged. "I guess I underestimated your determination to support yourself. But maybe you're not supporting yourself. Maybe you just turned me down so you could go to Brannigan. Has he been your lover all along?"

Tully waited, but all he got was silence and a hateful glare from them both.

"I don't hear a denial, Paris," he prodded. "Is he your lover?"

Still she didn't respond.

"You know," he continued, "if I thought he wasn't, I would ask you to go with me, to share what we find in that floor. I would take care of you in finery. What will your answer be, sweetheart?"

Nate's arm tightened around Paris's waist. "Forget it, Thatcher," he answered for her. "She won't be going anywhere with you."

Tully's expression was one of feigned sorrow and regret. "It's really a shame you couldn't have been loyal to me, Paris. You could have lived in such luxury."

"Boss," said Lennox from the hole. "You ought to come and see this."

Tully moved cautiously past Nate and Paris and leaned over the gaping hole in the floor. He stared in silence for several moments then turned to his prisoners. His face was alight with satisfaction and the distinctive gleam of greed.

"It's too bad you didn't find this sooner, Paris. You certainly would have been rich. Boys," he turned to Lennox and Smith, "haul it out and load it on the packhorses."

Lennox gaped at the dark hole. "I don't think it's all gonna fit on our horses, boss."

"We'll take what we can. Use Brannigan's horses and mules, too. He and Paris won't be needing them. What we can't get out this trip, we'll come back for."

While Lennox went to get the horses and mules, Smith tied Nate's and Paris's hands behind their backs. They were ushered outside and held at Tully's gunpoint while Lennox and Smith proceeded to empty the bell tower of its treasure and deposit it in front of the mission.

The glittering pile increased rapidly before their disbelieving eyes. The afternoon sunlight fell upon the dazzling array, making it almost difficult to look at it for the intense brightness. It was everything the legend had promised. There were incredible amounts of old Spanish reales spilling from rotting leather bags, jeweled gold and silver icons, solid gold candlesticks, cups, bejeweled goblets, silver pots and bowls, gold altars, ornate necklaces and rings heavy with rubies, emeralds, and diamonds.

With a sick heart, Paris watched Tully's men load her treasure in packs and then evenly distribute it on the pack saddles. The items were heavy, and some of them should have been left behind. But Tully was too greedy to forfeit even one gilt-edged letter opener. The things too big and cumbersome to successfully pack were bundled into blankets and strapped to a quickly constructed travois made of mesquite trunks. Paris and Nate both wondered how they were going to get it up out of the valley floor on the treacherous, winding narrow trail, but neither said anything.

When they were ready to go, Tully sauntered over to where Paris and Nate sat in the shade of the mission. Squatting down on his haunches, he lifted Paris's chin.

His smile made her think of Satan. "Now see, if you would have chosen to be my woman, you could have gone with me. Brannigan says no, but what do you say?"

Hope surged through Paris. If Tully would let her go, she could then find a way to escape and get back to Nate. But the thoughts had barely cleared her head when Tully's strident laughter split the stillness. "Don't even think it, Paris. If I took you along, I'd just go ahead and put a bullet in Brannigan's head so you wouldn't be tempted to double-cross me and come back for him."

Her last flame of hope guttered out. "You'd better get moving, Tully," she snapped. "You'll be hard-pressed to get to the next group of springs before dark with the load you've got on those animals."

Tully didn't seem to think it was something to be worried about. "You know," he continued. "I'm glad you are as independent as you are, Paris. I'm glad you decided you didn't want me. If you hadn't, I might never have found the incentive to go looking for this treasure. But the simple fact that you stole my map, drugged me, and left me looking like a fool in front of the whole town of Tombstone was what made me do it. And now I'm a very rich man."

He tossed his head back and laughed again, an ugly gloating sort of cackle that made Paris shiver.

"There's a rumor that it's cursed, Tully," she said. "A lot of people have died trying to take it out of here. I just thought you ought to know."

The words struck fear on the faces of Lennox and Smith, but Tully found the comment extremely amusing. "Don't think you can scare me, Paris. I'm not going to fall for such nonsense. Besides, if you believed it, you certainly weren't letting it stop you."

"No, but I thought you should know that you could be taking a chance with your life. I was willing to take it because I didn't have anything to lose. Are you?"

Tully accepted the comment as inconsequential. He turned to his men, seemingly unaware that the whites of their eyes were as big as saguaro blossoms in full bloom. "Well, boys, the time has come for us to leave."

"What you gonna do with them, boss?" Lennox asked, eyeing Paris. "Want me to shoot 'em?"

Tully studied Paris, too, deciding her fate. "No," he finally said. "That's too quick and easy. I want this red-headed two-timer to suffer. She deserves to die a slow, miserable death after what she put me through. We'll leave them tied up in the chapel. They can scream for help for days, but nobody is going to find them in this valley . . . at least not in this century."

Lennox and Smith nudged Nate and Paris back into the mission at gunpoint, shoving them against the wall beneath the arcade. Lennox tied their feet. Paris saw a deep, simmering rage in Nate's eyes, but there was nothing he could do trussed up like a Sunday goose.

Tully squatted down on his haunches next to Paris. "Ah, little Paris," he said in a regretful tone. "We could have had such a lovely life together."

"I doubt that, Tully. You may be able to force a woman to your bed but you can't make her like it."

He shrugged. "Maybe." Then he gave her a kiss which made her want to retch. As soon as he'd finished she tried to wipe it off with her shoulder. Tully just laughed and turned to Nate.

"Well, Brannigan. It looks like you got yourself involved with the wrong woman. You have to watch women, they can surely lead a man down the jolly path to hell." He shifted positions and picked up one of Nate's boots. "Fine boots, Brannigan. A little worn but fine just the same. You won't be needing them anymore, so I think I'll have them."

Nate tried kicking him in the face but succeeded only in setting him off balance and toppling him over on his backside. Lennox and Smith rushed forward and put their guns to Nate's temples. Tully got up, dusted himself off, and proceeded to remove the boots. When Nate was down to his socks, Tully tucked the boots under his arm and plucked Nate's hat from his head.

"Fine hat, too."

He led the way from the mission, getting a profane blessing from Nate. Lennox and Smith dutifully followed, glancing back only once as if they weren't sure they agreed with Tully's choice of a death sentence.

Paris and Nate listened to the sounds of the heavily laden horses and mules moving away from the mission. They heard occasional shouts and curses as the three men tried to get the animals up the narrow, precipitous trail that led out of the canyon. After a time the valley returned to silence. Nature resumed its activities. Small animals scurried outside, and occasionally inside the mission door in their constant quest for food. Birds squawked and flew past the door Tully had left open, the shadows of their flights cutting through the last of the day's light streaming across the tile floor. Shadows lengthened.

Pedro wandered in, looking dazed with blood on his head from a cut. Whimpering, he came and curled up on Paris's lap.

"What's happened to him?" she cried out in dismay.

"From the looks of him, I'd say one of Tully's men must have coldcocked him to keep him from barking. That was the only way they could have sneaked up on us the way they did. He's probably been unconscious all this time."

"My word, Nate. They could have killed him."

"Yes, he's lucky they didn't."

"I guess they wouldn't have left anything of value in the camp, like a knife to cut these ropes with."

"No, I'm sure they didn't."

Paris felt numb. "How long does it take to die of thirst, Nate?" she whispered, her words echoing beneath the arcade and into the high ceiling of the chapel.

"We're not going to die," he replied stubbornly, almost angrily. "But Tully Thatcher is. When I get my hands on him, he'll wish he'd never laid eyes on those boots . . . or me."

Paris gave him a sidelong look, then asked incredulously, "You're mad because he took your boots?"

"Damn right. Those were hand-crafted by an old cobbler down in Mexico, a friend of mine for years. Don't tell me you wouldn't be furious if they'd left you in your stocking feet? I'm going to have to walk across this desert without my boots, Paris. That's the worst thing one man can do to another, short of stealing his horse."

"Well, I suppose it is . . . but it really doesn't look as if we're going to be going anywhere."

"Paris, turn around so your back is facing mine. I'll try to get your ropes undone so we can get out of here."

His positive attitude was uplifting. Paris did as she was told. Nate worked on the ropes until darkness filled the chapel and the ends of his fingers were raw and bleeding. Still he couldn't loosen the knots. Paris, in turn, tried but to no avail.

Finally, they slumped, back to back. "We'll just take a rest," Nate said. "Then we'll try again."

Paris didn't want to tell him that she was beginning to think it was hopeless. Tully tied knots like a sailor. As each minute, each hour, slipped past her spirits lagged more. She began to think of the moments in Nate's arms when they'd made love. She couldn't possibly regret it now, now that she was facing death. At least she had experienced the wonder of it and wouldn't go to her grave not knowing the joy that a man and woman could give to each other. But there were other things she regretted, things she needed to tell Nate.

"Nathaniel," she said, realizing it was probably the first time she'd called him that. He must have noticed it, too, because his head turned sharply toward her. She couldn't see him clearly, but, she felt the coil of awareness in him.

"What is it, Paris?"

"Well, it's just that in lieu of all that's happened, I feel . . . I feel as if I need to apologize to you. I want you to know I'm sorry for dragging you into this. I'm sorry you're going to die because of me."

His lengthy hesitation made Paris wonder what thoughts he harbored. He shifted positions, leaning close to her so that his breath brushed her cheek, then his lips in a brief but tender kiss. His blue eyes probed hers deeply. When he finally spoke, it was in a coarse, rough whisper. "I'm not sorry, Paris honey. We've had a pretty good time out here on the old Sonoran, don't you think? Besides, I wouldn't have come if I hadn't wanted to."

She thought she might lose her way in the depths of those eyes of his. They were fathomless, like a dark forest whose interior lays hidden but whose depth one can sense nonetheless. His eyes had gone very serious, despite the flippant tone of his words. Suddenly, she wanted to cry for the both of them, rotting there in the old lost mission because of no one's foolishness but her own. But she didn't cry. She tried to make him think she hadn't given up yet, that this interlude was just another part of the adventure.

"Nobody makes you do anything you don't want to, do they, Nate?"

He smiled. "No, I guess not."

"Unless it's at gunpoint?"

"Well, yes. That's always a deciding factor." He paused and his tone shifted to one of seriousness. "Paris?"

Her heartbeat quickened, thinking he might be making a confession, too. A confession of his love for her. "Yes, Nate?"

"I'm real sorry I couldn't get the jump on Thatcher," he said. "Maybe I should have tried harder."

Paris's heartbeat returned to normal. How could she expect Brannigan to confess something he wasn't guilty of? Namely love. "We were outnumbered, Nate," she replied.

"I've been outnumbered before."

"It's all right. I don't hold it against you."

Silence slid between them and Paris thought he'd said all he was going to. But then he spoke again; this time his tone was self-reprimanding. "I should have told you to go with him."

"But if you had, he would have killed you."

"Better one of us than both."

"Why did you want me to stay?" That peculiar beat of hope began in her heart again.

He shifted, placing his back fully against hers again. His hands groped until they found hers and his fingers twined with hers. He laid his head so that it rested against hers. "Because I was selfish, Paris. I didn't want to lose you to another man. All I could think of was keeping you for myself."

Her fingers tightened on his. "I wouldn't have gone anyway. Death is preferable to life with Tully. You could have only made me go at gunpoint. And you didn't have a gun."

She wanted to say so much more. She wanted to profess her love. Several times the words were on the tip of her tongue, but each time something stopped them from coming. Did it really matter now anyway? Or did it matter now more than ever?

Silence and reality, heavy and tangible, flowed between them in the darkness. With nothing more to say, Paris closed her eyes, as if by doing so she might be able to shut off the entrance of more fear to her mind, or at least keep what was there from growing to insane proportions.

She didn't know when she fell asleep. She remembered only Nate's strong shoulder beneath her cheek, serving as a pillow. When she awoke to the darkness once again, it was also to the murmur of movement, the soft brush of footsteps across the tile floor. The haze of sleep clung heavily to her. Through the gauze of it, she saw a tall man dressed in a long bulky and shapeless garment, moving silently toward the open door. For a moment he stood motionlessly silhouetted against the light of the stars and the quarter moon. She tried to blink the sleepy blur away, to blink the darkness away. Then, as if it had all been truly a dream, he was gone, vanishing before her eyes.

She glanced over her shoulder at Nate. He had slid sideways, the wall holding him upright by one shoulder. His other shoulder held her up. Pedro still lay curled in her lap. Both man and dog were sound asleep. The dog had, once again, not noticed the presence of the padre. And it had to be the padre. Father Castañeda.

She looked back to the silver stream of light coming from outside into the dark chapel. She saw the object then, just outside the chapel door, silhouetted as the man had been. She couldn't tell for certain what it was, except that it greatly resembled a hunting knife with its blade plunged several inches into the soil. If she wasn't dreaming, the gleam she saw down one side of it was the moonlight reflecting off a very sharp edge.

She tried to convince herself that what she saw was an illusion caused by the moonlight and the night, that it was probably just a rodent standing on its hind legs, looking into the mission. She waited, and waited. It did not move.

She stuck an elbow into Nate's ribs. He jerked and came awake, mumbling, "What? What is it?"

"Look over there," she whispered. "What's that object in the doorway?"

It took Nate a minute to clear his head of sleep. When he did, he sought out the object but was as perplexed as she was. "It looks a lot like a . . . knife."

"That's what I thought."

"How did it get there?"

"I don't know. I woke up hearing footsteps. I saw . . . a man . . . in a black robe. He disappeared . . . right before my eyes."

She couldn't see Nate's expression. She could see only his silhouette, but the set to his jaw told her he was unsettled too, and he had no explanation for it.

"Who in the hell is here besides us?"

"Father Castañeda?"

He was silent for a long time, so long in fact that Paris knew he wasn't going to comment.

"You know I've felt a presence ever since we've been here, Nate," she continued. "I've felt as if we were being watched. I didn't want to make something out of it because I was afraid you'd want to leave. You don't think Tully and his men were here all along, do you?"

He immediately dismissed it as a possibility. "No. They haven't been here. And I know what you mean about the . . . presence. I've felt it, too. But whoever it is, he apparently doesn't mean us any harm. If he'd wanted to kill us, he wouldn't have given us a knife."

With no more conjecturing they struggled to their knees and then to their feet. Hopping like kids running a sack race, they made their way to the entrance of the mission, where they both went back down to their knees next to the object. It was indeed a knife, a very old hunting knife. Someone had stabbed its gleaming steel blade into the soil just outside the door, the perfect enticement for escape.

Nate glanced nervously about. "How in the hell did it get here?"

"Do you think one of Tully's men felt sorry for us and came back and left it?"

"No. Look at it, Paris. I don't think it came from that pile of treasure. There's nothing fancy about it. The handle has been hand-carved from wood. And it's old. My God, it looks like it came from the Spanish Inquisition."

"But it's still sharp."

"Yes, it's that. So sharp it looks like it was just taken off a grinding stone."

"Somebody put it there for us, Nate." There was ex-

citement in her voice. "I know it was Father Castañeda.
But why would he try to save our lives?"

"Why did he spare Tully and his men and allow them
to take the treasure?"

"Because there's no curse, of course. I've said it all
along. All we have to do is catch up to Tully and take
back the treasure."

"If there's no curse, then who's the guy in the robes?"

"Who knows? But I'll have to thank him sometime.
Now, let's get the knife."

"I'm not convinced there's no curse. What if the knife
is cursed, too?"

She flashed him an annoyed look. "Tully and his men
hauled all that treasure out of here and none of them
keeled over dead. Nothing's going to happen if we take
that knife and free ourselves. Besides, we're going to die
anyway in our present situation, unless you think we can
hop our way back to W.W.'s."

She turned around, backed up to the knife and curled
her fingers around the handle. With a little tug she pulled
it from the ground. Nothing happened. The earth didn't
quake. The stars didn't fall. Lightning didn't strike. They
didn't die.

Nate took the knife in hand, maneuvered it around, and
soon had sawed through her ropes. In another minute,
Paris had freed Nate and found herself being hauled into
his arms. Before she knew what had happened, he had
kissed her thoroughly, leaving her breathless.

She lifted inquiring eyes, but all he said in explanation
was, "I never knew how good it could feel to be alive."

"Me neither."

"We're heading after them," Nate said with a determined note in his voice as he released her and set off,

mincing his way in his stocking feet toward camp. "The moon's high enough that we'll be able to follow them. That travois is cutting deep gouges in the dirt that will be easy to follow. They won't get too far ahead of us."

Before Paris followed, she turned back to the chapel and stared silently into the darkness. "Well, Father Castañeda," she whispered, "if you're within earshot, thank you."

Almost immediately she felt the unearthly presence again and the cold brush of a breeze across her face.

They will die, Sister Frances. But return my treasure and you will be spared.

She heard the deep, gruff voice with the heavy Spanish accent as clearly as if the words had been spoken out loud, which they hadn't.

A chill ran through her. She eased back from the door. Then she turned on her heel and ran. The treasure of Santa Isabel might not be cursed, but the mission was definitely haunted.

Following the moonlit trail, with an unwilling and sad Pedro tagging along behind, they left the valley carrying what they could of their remaining possessions in their saddlebags and two rolled up blankets. Tully had never anticipated that they would get loose, so he had taken only those things he wanted for himself: their weapons and their canteens. But they had the knife. And they had Nate's whiskey flask, which Tully's men had drained and then cast aside. It was the only thing they had to carry water. The amount it would hold wouldn't last long, but their only alternative was some old clay pitchers they'd found in the refectory that were too big and clumsy to take along.

Nate's hat problem was solved easily. Paris dug her smashed flat-brimmed hat from her carpetbag and gave Nate the sombrero. The biggest problem was Nate's lack of boots. But Paris, feeling responsible for the situation, bravely offered the uppers of her soft riding boots in any way Nate could use them. So, using the knife once again, Nate sliced through the fine leather uppers. From them he was able to make soles that came up over his feet. He then tied the soles in place with strips of cloth from Paris's nun's habit. The "boots" didn't want to stay together, though, and Nate found himself constantly tying them back together. The cloth wore out rapidly from the burning desert soil, and more strips of cloth were constantly needed to replace the shredded ones.

By late afternoon of the second day they had long since left the springs of Cerro Trueno behind and were still on Tully's trail. But with horses and water he was covering the terrain much swifter than they could. The heat was beginning to take its toll. They had drunk the last of the water with no sign of a spring in sight. Nate stopped for the hundredth time and impatiently retied his boots.

"I can abide a lot of things, even an ancient curse," he said, "but I can't abide a man who will leave another man without a canteen, boots, a hat, or a horse in the middle of the Sonoran desert."

Paris dropped to the ground next to him, convinced that even though they were free of the ropes, they were still going to die from dehydration. The desert was a long place to get across on foot. Now she fully understood why people were hanged for horse stealing.

"Do you feel all right, Nate?" she asked.

He looked up at her sharply, his eyebrows knitting together suspiciously beneath the brim of the sombrero. "Yes, aren't you?"

"I'm fine, but you keep saying the same thing over and over again, so I thought maybe the heat had done something to your brain."

Relieved that she wasn't dying of the curse, he went back to fixing his footgear. "Your *friend* Tully is lower than a horned sidewinder in a dry riverbed, and I'm going to kill him. If I keep repeating it, it'll give me the strength to keep going."

"Tully isn't my friend."

Nate stripped a fresh piece of cloth from the habit. "And that's another thing, Paris. I hadn't mentioned it before, but you should have told me you stole that map from Tully. You shouldn't keep secrets from your guide. If I'd thought there was someone on our back trail, we wouldn't have been caught flat-footed."

She glanced at his feet. "Or barefooted."

The lines between his eyes deepened until they looked like runnels in a canyon after a flash flood. He set out again, leaving her to struggle to her feet by herself.

"My, aren't we a gentleman," she mumbled. "Nate, wait up. I know this is my fault and I'm sorry. But I was desperate. Can't you understand that?"

"Yes, I can understand it. And in case you hadn't noticed, you're always desperate."

"Where's all that understanding you showed earlier?"

"Back in the shade of Santa Isabel. You ought to know by now that I'm not a walking sort of man."

"This isn't entirely my fault."

"It isn't?"

"No!" She felt bad enough without him rubbing it in.

"So I made a mistake," she said belligerently. "I'm sorry for that, too. But it was either you or Tully."

He stopped so suddenly she collided with his hot, sweaty back. "It's nice to be put in the same category as that skunk, Paris honey. But I suppose I should be happy that you consider me the lesser of two evils."

She lifted her hat, thankful Tully hadn't had the foresight to consider it worth taking, and wiped the sweat off her face. She was so hot and tired and thirsty and angry and sorry that she'd ever laid eyes on that map that she wanted to cry. But she didn't.

"Yes!" she blurted. "Or at least I thought so at the time. But maybe I was wrong about that, too!"

With a surge of motivation she moved on ahead of him, leaving him in the wake of her fury. She didn't even look back to see if he was following. She didn't give a damn. How could she have ever thought she loved him? It must have just been a moment of sentiment clouding her judgment. She was glad now she hadn't made some stupid confession.

She had gone two or three hundred feet when she heard a distant voice calling her name. It sounded like Nate's, but it was so far away she began to think there was something wrong with him. Finally, she gave in to her curiosity and turned around. First she saw Pedro, midway between the two of them, looking confused as to which one he should follow. Then she saw Nate. He was about five hundred feet away and had to shout for her to hear him, but his voice traveled clearly through the calm desert day.

"You're going the wrong way!" he yelled.

"Oh?" She yelled back, putting her hands on her hips in a defiant stance. "And how would you know? If I recall you're not exactly immune from getting lost, Mr. Bounty

Hunter! Besides, I'm just following Tully, which is what I thought you wanted to do. He's got your boots, remember? And your horse and your hat and my treasure! Don't you still want to kill him?"

"More than ever, honey, but not so bad that I feel like following him all the way to the Gulf of California with nothing but a whiskey flask to carry water in and a pair of boots made out of a nun's habit. I'm headed to W.W's to reoutfit. Then I'll come back and find him."

"What are you talking about? The Gulf of California?"

"Your friend Tully is headed in the wrong direction, Paris. In short, I daresay the fool is lost." Even from the distance she saw him shrug. "But if you want to follow him suit yourself, Miss Dance Hall Girl-who-just-lost-all-her-treasure!" He turned and headed off . . . in the wrong direction.

Or was it the wrong direction?

Paris glanced around at the nearby hills and at the distant peaks skimming the horizons. Damn this country for never looking on the straight and level. Well, if she was going to be lost, she'd rather be lost with him. After all, he had the knife, the matches, and the whiskey flask.

Nineteen

Paris was beginning to think death wouldn't be so bad. It would be better than having to place one blistered, aching foot in front of the other, better than the pounding in her brain that blurred her vision, better than the blinding sun burning her skin and sapping her body of its strength and its moisture. It would be better than feeling like she was going to choke on her own tongue. How many times in the last twenty-four hours had she wished for the extra water she'd consumed those first few days out of Nogales when Nate had told her to take just a sip and she'd taken a gulp? If she had all that water now, she would not be thirsty. She would not be dying this slow and miserable death.

Nate had told her to stay in the shade of the mesquite until he got back, but he hadn't said where he was going and he'd been gone a long time. Or it seemed a long time. But every second now without water seemed a decade.

Maybe he'd given up on her and decided to save himself. That would explain why he had been gone so long.

She struggled to her hands and knees. She would follow his tracks. And she did, on her hands and knees, wondering all the while that it hadn't seemed to be a great distance from W.W.'s to Cerro Trueno. But then they had been on horses and they had had full canteens of cool, fresh water. Well, maybe the water had been warm and tepid, but at least it had been wet. They probably wouldn't be in this fix if they hadn't found that last spring dry, the one that had contained water only a couple of weeks ago. Nate had said it wasn't unusual in the desert for that to happen. She could only hope they wouldn't find the next one dry as well.

Stickers and thorns jabbed into her palms and knees, and she sat back on her fanny, remembering that she didn't have her gloves on. She pulled them from her belt and put them on. She tried to stand but her head began to spin. She reached for a large jumble of rocks and leaned back against them. Even the plant life drooped in the oppressive heat. The only things moving were the three buzzards circling slowly overhead. They'd been following them now for miles. Occasionally they had touched ground, each time moving in closer and closer on their awkward feet. Paris wanted to believe they were just giving their heavy wings a rest, but Nate expended precious energy throwing stones at them and yelling that they'd have a while longer before they'd have his hide.

Beneath the portable shade of her hat she saw Nate sitting down some distance away doing something with the knife. The flashing of the blade in the sun drew her attention and curiosity, enough to give her the strength to stumble the fifty yards to his side.

"What're you doing?" She fell down next to him.

"I told you to stay in the shade," he said without looking up.

"I thought you'd left me."

For a second or two his gaze locked with hers. She wasn't sure, but beyond the trace of desperation, and the dullness of pain and thirst, she thought she detected something else, an emotion that ran deeper. It was an emotion she wasn't sure how to name, but it made her want to touch his face, gently and lovingly. And, with death hovering over them, why should it matter to hold her feelings inside?

His face was hot and prickly against her palm. His beard's stubble was several days long, but the strength still present in his hard jaw was a welcome force that emanated into her. He took her hand in his, removed the glove, and placed a kiss in the center of her palm. If anything could have given Paris the strength to go on, it was that kiss. Words of love rose in her throat but caught on her tongue. Maybe she was just feeling sentimental again, and like before, it would pass.

"Are you still mad at me, Nate?" she whispered instead.

He went back to whatever he was doing with the knife. "No."

She had wanted him to say more, to tell her he couldn't possibly be mad at her because he loved her. But no such consolation was forthcoming.

Even if she felt like giving up on everything, even love, she made herself sit up and focus on what he was doing. He had a small barrel cactus anchored between his makeshift boots and was trying to cut through the tough, curved spines to the center of it. It appeared to be a difficult task.

She'd heard about people getting water from cactus and she wished he would have resorted to it sooner. But then, maybe it was indeed a last resort.

In anticipation of moisture, any kind of moisture, she temporarily forgot her misery and watched as he worked for what seemed futile hours cutting the top off then using the handle of the knife to pound juice from the inner pulp. At last he told her to hold out her hands—the only cup available—and he poured a few precious drops into them. Gratefully she drank, only to gag on the less than pleasant taste of the pulp. Yet it was moisture, life.

He pounded at the pulp again and this time Paris declined. "You take it. Hold out your hands and I'll pour you some." She had to put her gloves back on to protect her hands from the cactus spines. Tenderness washed over her at the sight of his cracked lips, and after he'd drunk she leaned forward and kissed him gently. She removed the small tin of ointment from her trouser pocket and smoothed some of it over his lips. She decided his lips were the best a man could have—strong, masculine, but perhaps too grim. It saddened her that he hadn't smiled much in the weeks she had known him. Before they died, she would like to see him laugh.

She sat back on her heels. "I've said this before, Nate, but I want you to believe me when I say that I'm truly sorry for dragging you into this. I was wrong to lie, to not tell you the truth about taking the map from Tully. My foolishness is going to kill us, isn't it?"

He was slow to respond. Maybe he was so weary and weak, as she was, that it was difficult for his mind to function. That frightened her because not only couldn't she imagine herself without him but she knew she would probably never make it out of here without him.

"It isn't far to W.W.'s now," he finally said. "Maybe fifteen miles."

She looked at the distant horizon. "Fifteen miles without water in this heat. It might as well be a thousand. Where's the monsoon when you need it?"

Nate squinted into the brightness of the August sky. Gauzy strips of cloud floated to the east and south. Darker clouds touched the northern and western horizons, suggesting rain in those areas.

"It's skirting around us. Probably getting Tully and his men. But it'll be dusk soon. We'll rest and travel then."

"I'm afraid if I don't keep going, I might not be able to later," she admitted.

The dullness was becoming more pronounced in Nate's eyes, and she wondered if he could see her dying right before his eyes as she could see him. And if he could, did he care? Was it hurting him the way it was hurting her?

"It's too hot right now, Paris. It must be a hundred and twenty degrees in the shade. It'll sap our last reserves. We'll wait until dark."

He proceeded to pound as much juice from the cactus as he could. This time he gave some to Pedro who looked as if he could not go another step. Exhausted from the effort, the heat, and the miles, Nate stretched out beneath the shade of some creosote bushes and instantly fell asleep.

Paris studied him, feeling love tighten around her heart and remorse rise to choke her. If he died, she'd have only herself to blame. If either of them made it out of there, it should be him. This wasn't his doing. He was just an innocent bystander, a man who had been willing to help. A man to whom she had lost her heart.

She knew it was going to be hot, but she scooted down under the bushes with him and lengthened her short frame next to his tall one. Carefully she placed her hand on his chest and a light kiss to his cheek. He didn't stir.

Pedro curled up next to her, placing his nose on her knee. He whined once, probably from thirst, and then fell asleep. It took Paris considerably longer to drift away from her guilty conscience.

* * *

It always amazed Nate how destinations on the desert had a way of getting more distant even when a man had a good horse and a full canteen of water. But without them, it was as if death played a game of continually inserting two miles for each one walked. They had covered quite a bit of territory by moonlight, but now the mid-day sun was again scorching the life blood from them.

Swaying on his feet, he finally halted. The strips of cloth holding his makeshift boots together were falling apart again from the constant gouging of rocks and thorns. Even the leather Paris had donated from her boots for soles was beginning to show tremendous wear. The fine leather had simply never been intended to take the place of sturdy soles. He tried to lick his lips but his tongue was too swollen to move. It felt as if it was getting so big it would choke him long before he actually died of thirst.

Paris staggered to a stop next to him. She didn't look as if she could hold on much longer, and he was worried about her.

"How much farther is the next spring?" she asked.

"It should be on the other side of that hook-nosed outcropping on those mountains . . . if I've got my directions straight."

She started toward it, weaving one way and then the other. "Then let's go," she managed to say from over her shoulder. "We'll rest when we get there."

He watched her take a few steps. Then in slow motion, she wilted like the fragile Angel's Trumpet that lasts but a single night; it gives of its nectar to the night moths, and then collapses in a heap by dawn.

He hurried to her side but was not quick enough to

catch her fall. Gently, he turned her over and into his arms. He had to shake her and tap her face lightly to make her open her eyes. "Wake up, Paris," he urged. "You have to."

"I can't go on," she muttered. "You go without me."

"Don't quit now, honey. We're almost there."

But she didn't hear him. She'd lost consciousness again.

"You're going to keep going, Paris Frances McKenna," he said with a set to his jaw. "I'm not going on without you. For one thing I don't have the strength to come back for you. For another, I love you too much to leave you out here alone. I won't let you die."

He lifted her into his arms and struggled to his feet. He took only a few steps and shifted her to his shoulder, draping her over it like a sack of barley. But she was decidedly easier to carry that way. Pinning his sights on the distant mountain, and his hand on her rump to steady her, he placed one foot in front of the other by sheer determination alone.

"That damn Tully Thatcher isn't going to beat us, Paris. He'll pay for putting you in such a situation in the first place as to have to come out here looking for some damn, cursed treasure. But then . . . I guess if he hadn't, I never would have met you . . ." *God, Paris, don't die. Please, don't die. I love you more than you can ever know.*

It was an utter eternity before he lowered her onto the grass next to the spring and collapsed beside her, his lungs burning and his throat so dry and constricted he was beginning to taste blood.

He didn't know how long he laid there before he was able to find the strength to force himself back up and to his knees. Clutching Paris under the arms, he dragged her to the water's edge. Without much finesse he cupped the water in his hands and splashed her face with it. She didn't stir. He placed his head over her heart and barely heard a beat. Feeling frantic, afraid she was too far gone to revive, he hauled her up into his lap and scooped more water onto her, splashing it all over her face, her neck, her bosom. Slowly she opened her eyes and pulled herself groggily back from the world she'd nearly sank into for eternity.

"Where . . ."

He drew her up into his arms, close to his heart and his lips. "At the springs, Paris," he said, kissing her forehead, her cheek, her hair. "We're at the springs. Everything will be all right now."

Nate's foot was itching and he was dreaming that Alejandro was tickling it with a long piece of grass like he used to do when they were kids and Alejandro wanted Nate to wake up. But he always wanted Nate to wake up even before the roosters crowed and it always put Nate in a cranky mood.

Nate needed to scratch his foot but he couldn't wake up. He didn't want to wake up. He tried to turn over and found he was all tangled up with another body, a woman's body.

That brought him from the deep throes of sleep and he opened his eyes to the lovely, gentle sleeping face of Paris. He lifted a fallen strand of red hair from her cheek and gently kissed her nose. The heat of passion began to rise in his loins, but his damn foot was still itching. And one of the horses was stamping impatiently a few feet away, as if its foot was itching too.

One of the horses!

Nate bolted upright, releasing Paris. He reached for the knife by his side just as his eyes fell on the smiling man holding the long blade of grass.

"So, *mi hermano,*" Alejandro said, grinning, "You are alive after all."

Nate couldn't believe his eyes. He flung himself at Alejandro and gave him a bear hug, not seeing the pain streaking across the mestizo's face. "Damn it, brother. They said they'd killed you."

Alejandro patted Nate on the back then pushed him away, smiling widely. "They tried, Nathaniel, but Nogales has a very good doctor who has much experience in removing bullets. I will admit, I am still in pain and not very strong, but I am here."

Nate laughed. "You always were in the wrong place at the wrong time, Alejandro. Where were you yesterday when I really needed you?"

Alejandro knew he was only joking, and his perfect white teeth gleamed in an even broader smile. "I was listening to the rantings of an old prospector named W.W." He glanced at Paris. "So, you say I came at a bad time? Would you like me to leave and come back later?"

Nate finally allowed himself a grin just as Paris came awake, looking around with confusion etched on her face. "No, you can stay if you've got something besides rattler meat in that pack."

Alejandro turned his smile to Paris. "Good morning, *Señorita* McKenna. How does bacon and fresh biscuits sound for breakfast?"

Paris didn't question Alejandro's appearance at that moment. That he was there was enough. She didn't even care if he, too, was a ghost. "It sounds like heaven."

Nate and Paris wanted to know exactly what had happened after they had left Alejandro's home, so while he cooked, he told them. He concluded his story by saying, "So you see, I would have been here much sooner, but the doctor said I had lost too much blood to be going anywhere. I didn't go anywhere for a few days, but then I told him I did not understand his English, and I put on my clothes and I left. He was not happy with me, but I have a settlement to make with a certain man named Tully Thatcher, who seems to also have a settlement to make with the lovely *señorita,* who has apparently decided to no longer be a nun." He glanced pointedly at Paris, who looked away guiltily. He turned to Nate. "Tell me, Nathaniel, what brought you to such a sad state of affairs that you are left with no horse, no boots, and no hat of your own?"

Between Nate and Paris they explained their adventures and misadventures to Alejandro and watched the smile fade from his face when they said they had actually found the mission and the treasure, although neither told him where, and that they intended to go after Tully, who had stolen it from them.

Looking worried and pensive, Alejandro absently prodded the bacon with a fork. "You should let them go. It is too dangerous to pursue this treasure."

Nate was the one to argue. "I don't want the treasure, Alejandro. But no man leaves me for dead in the middle of the Sonoran desert. He's going to pay for that."

Alejandro stared into the morning fire. Pedro came to sit next to him. The little dog had been very happy and relieved to see him. No doubt he wished now that he had not been lured away from safety and comfort and water by the sweet voice of a redheaded woman in black skirts.

Alejandro absently scratched the dog's ear. "Thatcher

has probably already paid, *mi hermano,"* he said softly. "I suspect the buzzards are at this very minute having a feast on him and his friends."

"I want to make sure. I want my horse back—and my boots."

Paris said nothing through it all. Nor did she voice her desires on the ride back to W.W.'s, where she was given the privilege of riding the horse while the men walked. She offered to take turns but they both refused.

Little did they know that she wanted to go out after Tully, too. Not for her horse, not to get even, not even to make sure he was dead. She still wanted the treasure of Santa Isabel. Because as long as she was alive, nothing had changed for her.

W.W. didn't own a horse. The closest thing he had was old Frank and a couple of sturdy little burros. But he was more than willing to loan the bunch of them to Nate and Alejandro so they could go after Tully Thatcher and his men. He also loaned Nate his "town" boots, which were two sizes too big but decidedly better than nothing. It seemed the old man was feeling guilty for giving Tully their whereabouts. Nate and Paris didn't blame him. If he hadn't, they would have killed him. Neither of them wanted his death on their conscience.

After a day of rest, Nate saddled Frank, Alejandro saddled his horse, and they packed what they would need for a two-week search. That is, until Paris marched from the house, looking refreshed and beautiful and determined to join them.

When she openly stated her intentions, Nate scowled at her. "You can't be serious, Paris. This is men's work going after outlaws. It's no place for a woman. Besides, you nearly died day before yesterday. How could you even think of going out there and maybe risking it all again?"

Paris tightened the string on her hat. "I came out here to get a treasure, Nate Brannigan," she announced, "and I'm still empty-handed. I thought I could ride behind you on Frank. W.W. says I don't weigh enough to slow him down. And the burros can carry the packs."

Nate was about to set into another argument when Alejandro sauntered forth and took Paris's hand. In his most courtly manner he lifted her hand to his lips. "Your presence will be like a bouquet of spring wildflowers brightening the morning table, *Señorita* Paris," he said. "You will be most welcome to ride behind me on my horse. He is big and strong, he will not mind your presence there at all. Nor will I. But I will continue to dissuade you from taking the treasure, should we find it." His brow wrinkled. "I would hate to see a woman of your exquisite beauty become a victim of the curse. It would be too great of a loss to mankind."

Paris was flattered, but she couldn't help feeling that Alejandro was being much too agreeable. She wondered if he thought he could convince her to stay behind by using his aristocratic charm. Well, it wouldn't work. Besides, she hated to see Nate ride away. What would she do if he didn't return?

"You've been so very kind, Alejandro," she said with a sincere smile, "but I still don't believe in the curse."

"Ah, but I believe you do, *señorita*. I noticed that neither you nor Nate told W.W. you had found the mission and the treasure. You merely told him that Thatcher had left Nathaniel to die for stealing his woman, and he left you to die for running away from him. He believes Nate and I are going out to get your horses back, and to make him pay for what he did to you. You did not even tell me where you found the mission, not that I would ever want to know."

"Well, it never hurts to play things safe, now does it?"

"No, *señorita*. But you are not one to play things safe. If you were, you would never have come out here with my brother."

At the mention of Nate, they both lifted their gazes to him.

They didn't know he'd been listening to their conversation with growing irritation and downright jealousy, but he had. He'd lost one woman he loved to the suave Alejandro, and he wasn't about to let it happen again.

He plucked Paris's hand neatly from Alejandro's and headed toward Frank with a stride that Paris could barely match. "You won't convince her to change her mind, Alejandro," he said. "Believe me. I know her. If we don't take her, she'll probably follow us. As long as she's so damn determined to get herself killed or get that treasure, she'll ride with me. That way I can keep an eye on her."

He heard Alejandro's chuckle but found he had to focus on the woman who had suddenly turned into a hellcat in his hand. "Let me go, Nathaniel Brannigan! I can ride with Alejandro. At least he's a gentleman. Why couldn't you have learned some manners from him? Don't you know you can't just drag women around, positioning them where you want them like so much baggage!"

Ignoring her question, Nate circled her waist with both hands and hoisted her into the saddle, then swung up behind her before she could even think about going anywhere else. "Because you wouldn't like me if I had manners," he whispered in her ear.

"Just what makes you think I wouldn't like you if you had manners?"

He leaned around her, touching her ear with his lips. "I remember the way you made love to me," he whispered so only she could hear. "And I don't believe you feigned the response. Besides, Paris honey, if I had manners, then you would probably feel obliged to have some, too, and I wouldn't want to cramp your style."

"Let's just be on our way," she finally said, evading his eyes.

But Nate noticed the way her pale skin had turned scarlet. He knew perfectly well that this time her color wasn't caused by the heat, and he was immensely pleased. He was also immensely pleased that she had wanted to come along. It was dangerous, true, but he was beginning to feel not completely whole without her by his side.

He glanced at Alejandro astride his horse. "Are you ready?"

Alejandro nodded, amusement dancing in his dark eyes as he watched Nate and Paris. *"Sí, mi amigos.* It is time to pay our debts. And time for *Señor* Thatcher to pay his, too."

They moved out. W.W. came from his mine and wished them well. Pedro ran and hid in the shade, having had enough adventure in the Sonoran sun to last him a lifetime.

Twenty

By the second day out, Paris ended up riding behind Alejandro on his big black gelding. Old Frank tried to keep pace with the long-legged horse, but it seemed the only way he could do so was to trot. For some reason the mule had never learned to lope and didn't even seem to know that particular gait existed. He simply couldn't accomplish it. Trotting was tolerable to Nate because he could stand up in the stirrups, but for Paris, who had been relegated to the rear after the first day, the trotting had become a constant bone-jarring annoyance until Alejandro had come to her rescue.

Frank's trotting wasn't even the jackass's worst fault. It was his keen ability to tell time that caused the most frustration. When six o'clock rolled around every night he stopped and absolutely refused to budge another foot. The first night they'd had to use Alejandro's horse to drag Frank to the campsite, a spring that was only a quarter of a mile away from where Frank had belligerently halted. Since then they'd been lucky enough to time their travels so that they reached water holes or springs before Frank's quitting time.

Now Nate brought up the rear as usual; his legs were too tired from constantly nudging the mule on, so he remained a good ten yards behind, watching Alejandro and

Paris talking and laughing, exchanging pleasantries as if they were on a Sunday afternoon ride instead of a serious manhunt. He felt foolish enough riding the long-eared jackass, but he was beginning to feel like a little kid tagging along behind the adults. He was boiling inside and it wasn't all due to the heat either. Nor was it due to the fact that a rain storm had gone through some days before and washed out Tully's tracks. No, he was boiling mad because he couldn't stand the torment of seeing Paris's hands occasionally gripping Alejandro's slender waist to steady herself. Nor could he cope with knowing that her breasts were brushing the Spaniard's back the way they had his. He loved his brother dearly, but this was one time he wished he would have stayed at his desert retreat tending his corn and goats . . . or at least cleaning up the mess Tully and his men had left.

Nate had never thought he would actually welcome the sight of buzzards, but such was the case when on the fifth day he say them circling low in the sky above a distant promontory. Of course, Alejandro and Paris didn't see them. They were too busy discussing the timid nature of chuckwallas, one of which they'd seen just minutes before.

Alejandro's deep voice drifted back to Nate. "Did you know, Paris, that when chuckwallas are frightened they will hide in a rock crevice and inflate their bodies to the size of the crevice, wedging themselves in place?"

"But why?" she responded, genuinely interested. By then Nate had determined she was extremely interested in everything Alejandro said and did, and he surely had a way to bring out her smile.

Alejandro shrugged. "I don't know unless it is to conceal themselves and to keep a predator from being able to drag them out."

"How interesting."

Nate trotted up next to them, standing in the stirrups to keep Frank from jarring his teeth out. "And so are those buzzards up ahead," he inserted.

Alejandro easily cast aside all trivialities. His gaze sharpened on the distant birds. He said to Paris, "Can you believe Nate has such good eyesight? He has always been able to see great distances, just like an eagle." Then to Nate, "They are in the direction our *Señor* Thatcher was taking before the rain washed away his tracks. Maybe we will find something, no?"

"It's possible. Or it could just be a dead deer they killed for meat. But we'd better approach with caution."

Conversation did not resume between Alejandro and Paris, something for which Nate was grateful. He caught her glance several times, but whatever was in her thoughts behind those lucid gray eyes he couldn't discern. Was she falling for Alejandro? Would the two of them ride away together in the end? Would he head back to Nogales alone?

With the pain of that possibility piercing his heart, he led the way to the rocky hill and around its base. Before them spread a broad valley covered with scrub mesquite, creosote bush, and a line of saguaro cacti bordering a narrow arroyo in the middle of the valley. The pungent aroma of the creosote and the steamy quality of the air indicated that a lot of rain had dropped there not long before. As a matter of fact, a flash flood appeared to have coursed through the valley, leaving rocks and brush and dead animals in its wake. But the rain had also brought new life. Plants everywhere blooming again—ocotillo, to-matillo, and the fairy duster. Vines with fresh tendrils of growth were creeping up and around the trunks of the saguaro, and sand verbenas showed brilliant new pink blossoms.

The buzzards' carrion was still close to a mile distant, but by using W.W.'s binoculars Nate was able to tell what it was.

"Well?" Alejandro and Paris asked simultaneously as he lowered the glasses from his eyes.

Nate put the binoculars in his saddlebags. "They didn't get far from Trueno. Looks like we've got us a burying job."

"Are you sure it's Tully?" Paris prodded.

"It's him all right. I can't see much of the bodies from this distance, but I recognize the horses. It looks like they got caught in the flash flood. The pack animals have lost some of their packs, but they seem contented to stay where there's grass and water . . . for now. They're shaded up in a thicket of mesquite."

"Then you think Tully and his men were killed by the flash flood and not Indians?"

Nate grimly scanned the terrain with his keen eyes. "Yes, I would say so. The signs indicate a huge torrent of water came through here. I'm surprised the horses survived. If Apaches had done this handiwork, the horses would have been gone."

"Unless the Apaches have just done this thing recently and are still close by," Alejandro inserted, searching the horizon of the broad valley for any sign of mounted renegades.

"Tully and his men would have been all the way to the Gulf of California by now," Nate replied. "No, I believe they were victims of the flash flood within the first twenty-four hours of leaving the mission. This is not far from where Paris and I decided to head to W.W.'s to reoutfit. They've been dead at least a week."

Nate nudged old Frank and led the way to the bodies.

The buzzards were reluctant to leave, and Nate and Alejandro didn't want to shoot at them. Not only was it a waste of ammunition, but it might alert attention to them if there were Indians or bandits around. As they rode through the flock of ugly birds, some of them managed to lift their heavy, awkward bodies into the air and fly away a few feet, but most didn't even try. They just hobbled awkwardly out of the way, then circled back to their meal plate.

Nate, wanting to spare Paris the unpleasant sight, quickly alighted and covered the men's faces and torsos with brush that had been uprooted and washed up around the bodies by the flood. "Since we don't have a shovel, we'll have to pile rocks over them, I guess."

"I will help," Alejandro stepped to the ground.

"No. You're in no shape to pack rocks," Nate said.

Alejandro, knowing Nate was more than right about his condition, took the reins of his horse and the mule and found the uprooted stump of a paloverde and perched himself on it to better watch his brother labor. "It is as I have said all along, Nathaniel. These men are dead because of the curse of Santa Isabel. I know you do not want to believe me, but I am sure of it now. The flash flood makes it look like an accident, but it was the curse."

One large bird flew up on Tully's bloated chest and sat there, as if guarding the body. Nate tried to shoo him off but he wouldn't budge. Finally, Nate gave him a good swift kick with his foot and the hideous creature flew away squawking.

Paris started gathering rocks. The quicker they could

get the men buried, the quicker they could get out of there. Bile kept rising in her throat from the stench of the bodies, and she was sure she was going to vomit any second. She didn't want to do that in front of the men, but she wasn't sure how long she would be able to hold it back.

Nate agreed wholeheartedly with Alejandro about the curse. "What I don't get is why they were allowed to get this far. No one else has ever found the treasure, let alone gotten it out of the valley."

"There is no point in questioning what is," Alejandro said. "Who is to say that this entire scenario wasn't done for some reason that we are not yet aware of. For a reason we may never be aware of. God moves in mysterious ways . . . or so it is said."

Paris, normally ready to dispute anything pertaining to the curse, found herself speechless. She could not even blame her lack of words on the bile that kept rising in her throat, blocking the exit of whatever she might have been inclined to say. Her silence could be blamed on something else entirely. It had to do with the chill that brushed over her skin from nowhere in a way that was now very familiar. She shivered, despite the heat. Those eyes were watching her again, and Castañeda's voice was saying, *How can one so beautiful and so brave have no integrity? If you want to live, and if you want Nathaniel Brannigan to live, then you must return the treasure. It does not have to be your destiny to die.*

Paris remembered all too well the creaking stairs, the tall shadow in the chapel, the man silhouetted in the moonlight, the knife that had appeared from nowhere. It had been his mission, Father Castañeda's, and they had been intruders. The treasure was his, too. She didn't understand why he had allowed Tully and his men to leave the valley with it. Questioning his reasoning for wishing to spare her and Nate was beyond her understanding of the situation, too. But if it was not her destiny to die, then she would accept that and thank God for his divine intervention.

"Would you mind if I don't help you bury them?" she asked, suddenly feeling faint. "I . . ."

Nate reached for her arm. "Are you all right, Paris? Maybe you should sit down."

"I'll be fine." She met his concerned eyes, wanting nothing more than to go into his arms. And suddenly she did. She threw herself into those strong arms and began to sob. She wasn't weeping for Tully. She was weeping for herself and her bad fortune. "Isn't it just my luck to find a treasure worth thousands and then have it be cursed!"

Nate held her tightly until the tears had run their course. Despite his condition, Alejandro left his perch and stacked a few small rocks on the bodies. The buzzards weren't happy about it.

"I've got to take it back," she announced.

Nate tensed. "Let's just leave it here, Paris. Bury it."

She looked up at him through her tears. "If I don't return it, we'll die."

He shifted uneasily. "How can you be so sure?"

She looked past his shoulder to the distant horizon, to where Cerro Trueno and Cerro Risa rose above the other mountains in the cordillera. "I can't explain it. I just keep hearing Father Castañeda's voice inside my head telling me that I must bring it back if I want us to live. He has said he will spare us if I do this."

Nate glanced uncertainly at Alejandro, who didn't seem surprised at all by Paris's words. He said, "She may be right, Nathaniel. If she is feeling this way, then it must be done. But, if you will pardon me, I would prefer not to go with you. I don't know where the treasure came from and I do not want to know. We cannot tell secrets we do not know."

"I don't understand how he could be telling her this," Nate said, totally dismayed.

"It is something we must accept. I have told you all along, *mi hermano,* we cannot explain or understand what comes from beyond this world. It is something we must believe, something you must believe, if you want to live."

Nate and Paris exchanged a resigned look. They finished covering the bodies with rocks. Nate gathered the animals, then he and Paris reloaded their packs, making them more secure and comfortable. Alejandro refused to touch any of the articles that had come from the mission. Paris and Nate didn't press for his assistance.

They led the horses from the valley and found a place to camp for the night. No one felt like cooking, so they made a meal of jerky and coffee. Each rolled out a bedroll near the fire and no one spoke of what had transpired. Paris longed to be in Nate's arms, but Alejandro's presence prevented such intimacy.

The next day Nate loaded up the animals again. Alejandro helped Paris fix a breakfast of bacon, coffee, and fried soda biscuits. Afterward, the men stood by the mules while Paris finished packing her saddlebags for the journey back to Santa Isabel.

"I hope you will understand the way I feel about this," Alejandro said confidentially but with some worry in his voice. "Do not be angry with me, Nathaniel."

Nate couldn't muster a smile. He hadn't felt like eating but had forced himself to. He didn't want to draw attention to the fact that he wasn't feeling well. He had been watching Paris and wondering if she was feeling ill, too. But she'd said nothing and gave no indication that anything was out of the ordinary with her. Had the curse begun to work on him? Or was it just suggestion that was making him queasy and light-headed?

"Don't worry, Alejandro. I don't blame you a bit. If I wasn't in this up to my neck already, I'd be backing out, too. But, if we don't come back, you'll guess what happened to us."

"I will wait for you at my place. When you return then we will leave the desert together."

Nate was surprised. "You're going to leave?"

Alejandro glanced at Paris. After a contemplative moment, he said, "There has been some good that has come out of this adventure after all. You see, Nathaniel, I have decided it is time for me to face the world. I must go back to our father's hacienda before it is too late. He is getting old. He has needed me these years and I have thought only of my own grief. I have not thought of his.

"When you and Paris return, I hope you will come to the hacienda and we will have a big fandango. Or maybe a wedding celebration."

Again Alejandro glanced at Paris in a knowing way.

Nate's heart began to pump so furiously it made him feel even more light-headed than before. Anger and frustration surged through him. He wouldn't stand by and lose another woman to his brother, especially this woman, who meant more to him than Paloma ever had. He had only been infatuated with Paloma, he knew that now. With Paris he felt right, as if she were his soul mate.

But how did Paris feel? What if she had fallen in love with Alejandro? Had they made plans, or even insinuated a future together, while he had been tagging along behind them on W.W.'s mule?

Nate lowered his voice, increasing the sharp edge of stubborn determination. "If we come back, Alejandro, you need to know that I intend on asking Paris to be my wife."

Alejandro grinned and slapped him on the back. "But of course, *mi hermano!* I knew this. Why do you think I suggested a wedding celebration?"

The force went out of Nate's words. "You knew?"

"Of course. I know you well, Nathaniel, and I recognized the love in your eyes . . . and in hers. I want to thank you for letting her ride with me. It gave me the opportunity to get to know her. Now I am sure you have not fallen in love with the wrong woman. But may I make a suggestion?"

Nate was dismayed by his brother's keen perception. He was more dismayed at himself for just committing himself to love and marriage. But as the sinking feeling went through him—that flash of doubt—it was replaced by a feeling of great relief, as if a burden had been lifted from his shoulders and the door to the past had finally been closed. He had willingly chosen the course for his future, and he did not regret it. He truly wanted to remain with Paris forever. He only hoped she felt the same way. With no treasure to lure her away, could she be tempted to answer the call of love?

Alejandro continued. "Do not wait too long to ask her to marry you, Nathaniel. I do not think that she knows you love her. Sometimes women must be told."

"Thanks for the advice. I'll keep it in mind."

"What are big brothers for if not advice? Now, I must go. Take care of her. She is worth more than all the treasure on those horses."

Nate watched as Alejandro rode up alongside Paris, took her chin in his hand, and kissed her forehead. "Take care of *mi hermano,* Paris. And do not be tempted by the treasure. Remember the padre's words. There are greater treasures in the world than gold. Remember."

Waving, Alejandro rode away, leaving them to face the journey back to Santa Isabel. Paris had enjoyed his pleasant conversation, but she was glad to be alone with Nate again, and to have her buckskin back.

She met Nate's waiting gaze. "Are you ready?"

He nodded. "Let's return it to Father Castañeda."

She began to cry again, the tears welling suddenly and unexpectedly. She tried to wipe them away as quickly as they came, but the effort was useless. She felt Nate's hand in hers, warm and comforting. It took all her strength to keep from hiding in the protection of his arms again, hiding away from the world and all its misfortune that had lately seemed aimed at her.

"It's the only way, Paris," he said softly, lifting her chin and wiping at her tears with his thumbs. "There are some things we simply have to accept."

Her lips trembled beneath his in an unexpected but much needed kiss. "I hope we're not too late."

Worry furrowed his brow. His gaze sharpened on every detail of her face. "Why, Paris? Is something wrong?"

She looked into the blue eyes she had come to know and love, eyes that, for just a moment, seemed to reflect some of the love she felt. They had been through so much together. "I don't know, Nate. Maybe it's just my imagination. Maybe it's just the trauma of everything finally catching up to me . . . seeing Tully dead. I didn't wish that on him."

"What do you mean?" he prodded, feeling the pain increase in his stomach.

"I've just had this pain in my stomach," she said, gathering the buckskin's reins. "It was probably something we ate, or maybe too much sun. Damn it, I'm not going to let this curse thing get to me!"

Hollowness seemed to expand inside him. "I hate to say it, Paris, but we may not have any more choice than Tully did."

"But Castañeda told me he'd spare us if we returned the treasure," she insisted defiantly. "We're doing as he asked, so it can't be the curse!"

Nate swung into the saddle and looked toward Cerro Trueno. "Maybe he just wants to make sure we don't change our minds."

They remembered quite well the way to Santa Isabel, or maybe they were being led by a supernatural power. Whichever, the return trip went smoothly, directly, and without a problem. They wound the two strings of animals down into the green valley once again. It was almost like coming home, except there was no joy associated with it.

They did not discuss how poorly they felt, not wanting to alarm each other, but they saw the illness reflected in each other's eyes. They were sure now that it was caused by the curse. They had returned the treasure, but they had touched it, and they knew the secret of its location. They would die, too, right there at Santa Isabel.

With hardly a word exchanged, they unloaded the treasure at the door of the bell tower and systematically carried it all back inside, returning it to the hole in the floor. Paris even stuffed the map and the copy from her journal inside one of the goblets. Never again would it tempt someone the way it had her.

They found old planks from the collapsed smithy roof and from other rooms in the mission. They had even been fortunate enough to find old nails that had been protected from the weather and weren't rusted. They rebuilt the sub-floor and the main floor despite the fierce pain that now pervaded every limb and muscle in their bodies. They completed the task like zombies, working on into the night by lantern light.

When they were finished, they collapsed on their bedrolls beneath the arcade, staring at the circle of light the lanterns cast on the ancient columns and ceiling. They were too weak to attempt a departure from the valley.

"Well, there you go, Father Castañeda," Paris whispered to the darkness. "It's all back, safe and sound. Now I expect you to live up to your promise."

She curled up in a ball, but the pain throbbed with renewed intensity. Nate stretched out next to her, his thigh touching her leg.

After a while, Paris said, "I thought that if I brought it back, he would spare us. He seemed to be telling me that. I guess I was wrong."

"Either that or Castañeda lied in order to get the treasure back. Perhaps he had no intention of sparing us. Maybe he feels he can't risk having us leave this place, knowing what we know."

"But why would he allow Tully to take it in the first place?"

"Who knows? Maybe he didn't believe we would ever find it, so he went off haunting Angel Springs and wasn't around when Tully stepped into the picture."

Paris chuckled. "You're making him less omniscient."

Nate attempted a chuckle. "Who can understand a ghost, or a priest so devoted to his church that he places a curse on a hoard of gold trinkets? He was dedicated in life, and apparently that dedication carried over in death."

"He said he thought I was beautiful and brave, and that it was not my destiny to die."

Nate considered that, not questioning the things she had heard in her head. He would have believed just about anything at this point. "Alejandro made the comment that at least one thing good had come out of this. He said this adventure had made him see that it was time for him to return home. All things happen for a reason. Maybe that was the reason for this."

Paris put a hand on his cheek. "I'll bet you wish you were back in Nogales drinking whiskey and losing at solitaire."

"Losing?" he said indignantly. "What do you mean losing?"

Did she detect some fire in him? Good, maybe he wasn't as close to death as she was. If they had to die, she would rather be the first. "Yes. You're not a very good player. You could have won that hand you were playing the day I met you."

"Why didn't you tell me?"

"I wanted you to go with me. I figured if you lost, then maybe you'd be discouraged enough to try something new. If I'd ever thought it would come to this, I would never have . . ."

He shifted to his elbow and placed a finger over her lips. "There's no point in looking back and wishing we'd done things differently, Paris. It all turned out fine. If you hadn't come into the cantina that day, I never would have met you. I never would have been able to put the past behind me. And I never would have known the difference between infatuation and love."

Her fevered eyes searched the depths of his. Impending death gave her the courage to ask the question that had been on her mind for a long time. "Who was the woman who captured your heart and whose death has been on your conscience?"

Nate hesitated, but only a moment. He was no longer troubled about the past, and he wanted no secrets between them. "I had two women's deaths on my conscience. Doña LaReina, my mother, and Alejandro's wife, Paloma. I was in love with Paloma, but she never knew. I grieved when she died as much as Alejandro did. But he never knew either. I loved her, yes, but it was not a complete, true love. True love is when the person you love loves you back. True love is when you bond in a physical and emotional way with that special person."

"It was not your fault, nor Alejandro's, that they were killed."

"I know, but I doubt either of us will ever truly forgive ourselves for not being there. We tarried, as young men will do, when haste would have been in order.

"I see our lives taking peculiar courses, Paris. Courses we cannot see until they are behind us. I am beginning to understand possibly why God spared you and me from the curse of Santa Isabel."

"Why is that, Nate?"

"To make us both open our eyes to reality. Sometimes we have to suffer adversity, and we have to lose something very important to us before we can fully count our blessings. You lost your parents. I lost my mother and a woman who was very dear. Long ago a dedicated priest placed a curse on a mission and on some golden trinkets. Whether the curse is real or in our minds does not matter. What does matter is that those events brought you and me together. Without those things happening, you never would have dressed up like a nun and walked into the Nogales cantina. And I never would have been there, waiting for you. Perhaps God had it planned all along."

He lifted a weak hand and slid his fingers through her hair. "It feels like fire. Alejandro was right."

Confusion flickered across her expression. "What?"

"Your hair. It is the color of fire . . . as hot as fire. And it is love I feel for you. All my life there has been something missing inside me, although I didn't realize what it was. I had come to accept that particular piece of emptiness as part of my existence. But when you're by my side, and in my arms, I feel like a whole man. I understand you. And I think you understand me. You're the missing piece of my life, Paris. The missing part of me."

Paris could hardly believe what she was hearing and wondered if delirium had taken over his mind, or hers. "Oh, Nate," she whispered. Then she was in his arms with his lips on hers, her body snug and safe and warm and alive against his. "I love you, too," she murmured. "I could only hope that you might feel the same about me. I thought you would never be able to see anything in a woman with a penchant for getting you into trouble."

"Trouble? I'd call it adventure. You've brought the adventure back to my life."

His kiss, long and drugging, stirred desires in her that chased away all the pain and all the thoughts of dying, of curses, of lost treasure, of ghosts.

"I should have told you sooner," he said, "but I thought you would leave me when you had your treasure, and I didn't have anything to offer you except my love, and some hopes and dreams for the future. A man should have more than that to offer a woman."

"I can think of nothing better than hopes and dreams shared with a person who loves you. We could have made them come true together."

"Then you would have married me . . . if this hadn't happened?"

Her eyes memorized in full detail every angle and nuance of the handsome face she had come to love so dearly. She traced his lips with her fingertips, and he responded with a tender kiss. "Yes. I would have married you."

He pulled her into his arms again with a strength that surprised her. His kisses found her lips, her hair. In the light of the lanterns, he removed her clothing and she his. They were too ill to make love but not to hold each other tightly. That closeness, and the confession of their love, was a powerful antidote to the pain that pierced their bodies with gnawing death claws. Each bore it in silence, singularly focusing on the last moments they would share.

Paris felt the feverish quality of Nate's forehead and body. She was sure hers felt the same to him. She supposed a woman couldn't ask for a better way to die than in the arms of the man she loved. She vaguely wondered what some explorer a hundred years in the future would think if he stumbled onto Santa Isabel and found the skeletons of her and Nate in the corner beneath the arcade, entwined, and buried beneath the rubble of another century.

"You are my treasure, Paris," Nate murmured against her ear, his lips hot with fever. "The only treasure I'll ever need."

They were the last words Paris remembered before unconsciousness mercifully eased her away from the pain and the fever, into a world of light and joy.

Paris walked slowly, almost blindly, through a gray haze up a winding staircase where, overhead, bells were ringing out a resonant announcement of a new and glorious day. It wasn't until she neared the top of the bell tower that the haze vanished and was replaced by brilliant shafts of light that finally enabled her to see clearly.

She had expected to look out over the luscious green valleys of heaven but was surprised to see instead the interior of the mission. She was surprised to smell not the clean scents of clouds and to hear not the lovely chords of harps but the earthy scent of clay tiles tickling her nostrils and the buzzing of flies landing on the blanket that covered her bare shoulder.

But the bells were still ringing.

She felt Nate lying next to her. He was so still that a sudden and deep fear struck her as memories from the night before tumbled back into her mind. She placed a hand on his arm and shook him. To her relief he came awake immediately, seemingly as surprised as she was to be alive, to be free of the pain.

"Who's ringing the bells?" he asked.

"I don't know."

"Then let's go see."

Like children on a quest, they each grabbed a blanket, hurried to the bell tower and up the stairs. They didn't have to go all the way, though, to see that no one was in the tower and that there was still no rope attached to the bells. As they watched, the bells slowed and finally stopped, the last sound being one final, dull note.

Paris glanced at Nate, who stood on the stair just below her. "It must have just been the wind."

They left the bell tower and wandered outside into the bright sunlight of the new day. The wind wasn't blowing.

Nate glanced at the bells again, hanging motionless as they usually did. "Maybe it was just a gust."

"Yes . . . or a ghost."

He pulled her into his arms, a smile lurking beneath his moustache. "You don't really believe that stuff, do you? I never would have thought you were a superstitious woman."

"Of course I don't believe in it!" She lifted her chin to an indignant angle. "How silly do you think I am?"

Nate glanced at the open doorway of the mission. He wondered about the strange illness, as he was sure Paris did, too. They might blame it on some bad meat or maybe some bad water, but somehow he didn't believe it. And he knew she didn't either.

He put his arms around her, pulling her hips closely to his rigid manhood. His blanket fell to the ground. "But do you still believe I love you?"

Her blanket joined his at their feet as she lifted her arms around his neck. "Unless you only said that last night under duress."

"I meant it, honey. Every word. Now, can I prove it to you?"

She stroked his neck with her fingers, lifted on her tiptoes to follow the caress with a kiss. "I'd like nothing better," she murmured against his skin. "But not in the mission."

He scooped up the blankets and then her. On bare feet, and buck naked, he carried her over and around brush and cacti toward their former campsite by the springs. Paris laughed at his mincing steps and sympathized when he yowled from a rock or a thorn in the tender pads of his feet.

"You should have feet as tough as leather after our stroll through the desert," she gibed.

"Whose idea was this anyway?" He continued to pick his way with a great deal of concentration. "God, what a man won't do for the woman he loves."

"Yes, but this woman appreciates it a great deal."

He paused just a moment to sink into her loving eyes. Knowing that the love he saw shining brightly there was for him. It made his desire for her leap in bounds. The fire in him raged as hot as the Sonoran sun. His lips took hers in a brief moment of hot possession that promised more to come. "I really don't mind at all," he whispered huskily.

At the campsite, he lowered her to her feet and they spread out the blankets in the shade of some paloverdes and cottonwoods. Paris gathered his feet in her lap and lovingly removed the few stickers he'd collected. When she announced that there didn't seem to be any more, he drew her into his arms and down onto the sun-heated blankets. Sunlight filtered through the cottonwoods and lacy paloverdes, dappling their naked bodies.

"I can't remember a time in my life, Paris, when my heart felt this light, this good."

She tilted her head back to better meet his love-filled blue eyes. "Neither can I. I didn't know what joy truly meant until this moment. What more could a person ask for? We're alive, and we're in love."

Nate's gaze boldly absorbed the beautiful curves of this woman he would have by his side forevermore. His hands sank into the wavy cascades of fiery, erotic hair falling over her shoulders. But merely looking at her was not enough. Soon his kisses and caresses touched every curve, committing her lovely body to a memory that went beyond sight, encompassing also the senses of taste and touch and smell.

Paris rolled him to his back and straddled him. He took her breasts in his hands, gently kneading, gently rolling the pert nipples beneath his thumbs. She closed her eyes and sank into the feelings he incited inside her. She leaned forward and, where his thumbs had been, his mouth took over, easily drawing from her the ultimate sexual pleasure. A few minutes later she shifted positions again and took him into her fully.

"Where do you want to go from here, Paris," he asked in that gravelly voice she had come to love so much, that voice that sent an exciting shiver down her spine by the sheer sound of it. "Just name the destination, honey, and I'll take you there."

Her eyes came open slowly as she forced herself momentarily away from the sensations controlling her mind and body. Nate saw the flame of passion burning in the gray, satisfied depths. Her hands stroked his thighs and she leaned forward, opening her lips over his. Her tongue did a brief but wanton dance with his before she sat up again. Closing her eyes again, she tilted her head back and slowly began moving in that ancient rhythmic dance of desire.

"Take me to heaven," she whispered breathlessly. "Take me there . . . now."

Her words ended in an escalating moan of pleasure and passion. He rolled her to her back. She lifted her legs to his hips, pulling him deeper inside her while eagerly encouraging and meeting his lusty thrusts. Their joining was more than physical. Their love drew them together in a solid emotional bonding that would remain forever.

When at last they lay fulfilled in each other's arms, Paris tightly held this man she loved to her bosom, finding it a miracle that fate had brought them together and that love would keep them there.

"Now you can take me home, Nathaniel," she said, stroking the hard masculine contours of his face. "To your home in New Mexico. I'd like nothing more than to meet Don Diego."

"Yes, it's time to go back," he replied. "Alejandro told me even he has decided to go home, so he will ride with us, if you don't mind."

"Of course not. I like your brother very much." She gave him a sly, coquettish smile and lowered her tone to a sensual stroke as soft as velvet. "But not as much as I like you."

He smiled, relieved to hear that. Then he continued. "You'll love my father, Paris. I'm looking forward to seeing his eyes light up when we tell him we want him to host our wedding."

"He won't mind?"

"He'll be delighted."

"Then we should go. Immediately."

The prospect of their wedding and their future together encouraged them to make haste in leaving the valley. They knew they would have the rest of their lives together to make love, wherever and whenever, but all they could think about was grasping their dreams and setting them into motion, making them come true right now.

They loaded their few belongings on their horses and, without even a cup of morning coffee, started out of the valley. Nate took the front, leading the string of horses and mules. Paris followed, in charge of W.W.'s two little burros.

She turned around once and thought she saw a dark-robed man standing in the bell tower window. "Thank you for sparing our lives, Father Castañeda," she whispered. "Your secret is safe with the Brannigans."

She thought she saw him lift a hand in farewell just before he vanished.

"I wonder, Nate," Paris called from behind him. "Do you think there was treasure in the other bell tower, too?"

His head snapped around; a scowl drew his brows together beneath the brim of his hat. "Don't even think it, Paris McKenna."

She laughed delightedly. Seeing she was only teasing, his face settled into a youthful smile.

Paris never looked back, and neither did Nate. Once away from the narrow trail, she rode next to him. He lifted her hand to his lips for a brief kiss, then they rode side by side with their fingers entwined.

"Do you think anyone will ever go looking for it again?" he asked after a time.

Paris looked to the far horizon, toward the new adventure of their future together. "I don't know, darling, but if anyone does, it won't be me. I may have lost one treasure, but I've gained another worth so much more." She leaned across the short distance between them and kissed his lips.

And Nathaniel Brannigan knew she meant every word of it.

Author's Note

In the region of the Sonora desert, the legend of the lost mission of Santa Isabel has been passed down for generations and is a common tale around campfires. Numerous stories are told of people who have mysteriously died while searching for her treasure. Several of the incidents mentioned in this book have become part of the legend.

Every story concerning the lost mission seems to place it in an entirely different location, ranging from California to Arizona to Mexico, but always it is hidden deep in a mountain canyon. The Pajaro Mountains in this book do not, to my knowledge, exist.

Father Castañeda is a fictional character, and I have altered the legend by allowing Paris and Nate to return the treasure and thus be spared from death. However, as far as the legend goes, no one who has actually found the lost mission of Santa Isabel has ever lived long enough to pocket her treasure, or to tell the tale twice.

If you enjoyed *Desire's Treasure* and would like to know about my previous or upcoming releases, please send your letters to me, along with a legal-sized, self-addressed, stamped envelope, to:

P. O. Box 293
Iona, ID 83427

Best Wishes,
Linda Sandifer

JANELLE TAYLOR

ZEBRA'S BEST-SELLING AUTHOR

DON'T MISS ANY OF HER
EXCEPTIONAL, EXHILARATING, EXCITING

ECSTASY SERIES

SAVAGE ECSTASY	(3496-2, $4.95/$5.95)
DEFIANT ECSTASY	(3497-0, $4.95/$5.95)
FORBIDDEN ECSTASY	(3498-9, $4.95/$5.95)
BRAZEN ECSTASY	(3499-7, $4.99/$5.99)
TENDER ECSTASY	(3500-4, $4.99/$5.99)
STOLEN ECSTASY	(3501-2, $4.99/$5.99)